THE TRACER OF LOST PERSONS

◆ ◆ ◆

THE TREE OF HEAVEN

ROBERT W. CHAMBERS

INTRODUCTION BY
MIKE ASHLEY

Stark House Press • Eureka California

THE TRACER OF LOST PERSONS / THE TREE OF HEAVEN

Published by Stark House Press
1315 H Street
Eureka, CA 95501, USA
griffinskye3@sbcglobal.net
www.starkhousepress.com

THE TRACER OF LOST PERSONS
Originally published by D. Appleton and Company, New York, 1906,
and copyright © 1906 by Robert W. Chambers

THE TREE OF HEAVEN
Originally published by D. Appleton and Company, New York & London,
1907, and copyright © 1907 by Robert W. Chambers

"Soul Mates" copyright © 2017 by Mike Ashley

ISBN-13: 978-1-944520-39-7

Book design by Mark Shepard, SHEPGRAPHICS.COM
Cover art by Edmund Frederick

First Stark House Press Edition: December 2017

FIRST EDITION

THE TRACER OF LOST PERSONS

"Keen & Co. are prepared to locate the whereabouts of anybody on earth. No charges will be made unless the person searched for is found…"

But what if you are looking for someone who doesn't exist? Say, the perfect woman of your dreams. Or what if you are looking for someone who has been dead for centuries?… an Egyptian princess who lies in suspended animation. Or perhaps you are a famous artist who has been rendering the "ideal" woman for so long that you have now fallen in love with your own epitome of beauty. Can Westrel Keen, the Tracer of Lost Persons, find that ideal…?

THE TREE OF HEAVEN

"There was nothing particularly remarkable about the dinner; it was the usual excellent affair one might expect; the wines perfect, the service flawless…"

The host has studied in the ways of the Eastern adept. Now, with his friends about him, he begins to predict their futures. One man will "uproot a Tree of Dreams but not the dream," and one has a good-natured ghost following him about. One of them, a doctor, is about to learn a stranger truth than is locked up among the molecules in his laboratory, while the young officer is destined to anchor "in the Port of the Golden Pool." They may not understand these predictions, but each of their fates await them…

Table of Contents

Soul Mates
Introduction by Mike Ashley

Devotees of old-time radio may well remember the long-running series *Mr. Keen, Tracer of Lost Persons* which ran for over 1600 episodes from 1937 to 1955. It was based, very loosely, on Chambers's series "The Tracer of Lost Persons" which ran irregularly in the *Saturday Evening Post* from June 1905 to May 1906 before being "novelized" in 1906.

The radio series developed the character of Westrel Keen into a standard detective, but Chambers's original character was more of a match-maker. At the start of this book you might be excused into thinking it is simply another of Chambers's romantic novels, admittedly with an unusual twist. Keen agrees to help his client find his ideal woman—not a genuine lost person, but to see if such an ideal person does exist. It's an intriguing premise and Chambers warmed to it as the series progressed and included several episodes which are mystical and even supernatural.

At the same time Chambers was writing the Westrel Keen series, he was also writing the stories later collected as *The Tree of Heaven* in 1907. In fact, most of these were written before he began "The Tracer of Lost Persons", the earliest being "The Bridal Pair" (*Saturday Evening Post*, December 1902). Their provenance shows that Chambers did not start out to write a cohesive series, but found, when he came to write the short story "The Tree of Heaven" (collected as "The Carpet of Belshazzar"), in 1904, that he could unite the stories within the frame of a mystic who is able to predict for a group of friends how their lives will develop and the stories follow that fulfilment. Chambers clearly had fun with this series and it allowed some of his old vision to return so that the mystical and uncanny develop unhindered, producing moments equal to his work of a decade earlier.

Many critics have dismissed Chambers's later works. Even during his lifetime, he was hailed chiefly as the writer of *The King in Yellow*, certainly one of the basic texts of weird fiction, rather than his later works. It was as if Chambers's star shone brightly in the mid-1890s and then steadily faded.

But that's not quite true. At times Chambers could return to the magic of *The King in Yellow*, certainly in the title story of *The Maker of Moons*, which I believe is his single most wondrous story, and in the other-worldly settings of the stories in *The Mystery of Choice*. He produced the highly entertaining series of cryptozoological adventures in *In Search of the Unknown* and *Police!!!*, whilst the stories contained here in *The Tracer of Lost Persons* and *The Tree of Heaven* show a more esoteric and at times arcane side to his imagination.

Yet these are only seven titles out of over eighty books that Chambers wrote. Do we search in vain for anything else their equal.

The real point is that we should be grateful he wrote these seven books because although *The King in Yellow* made his reputation, it was his historical novels and social romances that created his popularity and made him a wealthy man—or rather, even wealthier than he was already.

His first book, *In the Quarter* (1894), drew upon his bohemian artistic life in Paris, much of which continued over into *The King in Yellow*. Chambers's mother was French, which already gave him a knowledge of the country's history and culture. His experiences in France and his interest in its recent history, notably the Franco-Prussian War, drew him to write several novels, starting with *The Red Republic* (1895) and including *Lorraine* (1898), *Ashes of Empire* (1898) and *The Maids of Paradise* (1903). These were all well received. Critics saw him as a rising star, an effulgence helped by the Ruritanian romance *A King and a Few Dukes* (1896) and the first of a series of novels about the American Revolutionary War, *Cardigan* (1901). Chambers's paternal great (and great-great) grandparents fought in the Revolutionary War and he was able to use stories (and characters) passed down through the family.

The only blot in his copy-book during the 1890s was *Outsiders* (1899) which many regarded as his worst novel, though seen from the vantage point of a century later, it may well be his most distinctive. It was written from the heart. Chambers was a private person—he dismissed reporters and anyone preying upon his time and did not like the growing commercialism of the United States. He assailed American culture and status in *Outsiders* and the establishment did not like it.

After his Revolutionary War sequence he wrote another satire about American society, *Iole* (1905), exploring the views of eight country girls when confronted with New York Society. This time it was written tongue-in-cheek and the critics accepted it. He now entered upon his most financially rewarding period with his society romances at least two of which, *The Fighting Chance* (1906) and *The Younger Set* (1907) were official bestsellers of over 200,000 copies and two others, *The Firing Line* (1908) and

The Danger Mark (1909) saw him writing at his best, using his powers of artistic observation, and his ability to monitor society from the outside, producing works of wry perception, with a powerful message.

But by now Chambers was writing to a formula. He had discovered what the public liked and he knew he could produce it easily. He would often work on two or three books at once, allowing him to return to a half-finished text, edit and polish it and bring it to a conclusion without a demanding pace. Although he was prolific, he was not as prodigious as some believed. It was only that this process meant he would finish two or three books in quick succession, even though they may have been in production for over a year. Nevertheless, although Chambers believed he was good at editing his works, most critics thought he over wrote. They became tired of his formulaic prolixity.

Critics differ on what they regard as his last good work. *Ailsa Paige* (1910), set during the American Civil War, although running to 500 pages, was nevertheless praised for its historical detail and the fact that Chambers pulled no punches in portraying the horrors of combat. They believed *The Streets of Ascalon* (1912) showed more care and self-control, but it was still a formulaic society novel that said nothing new. *Who Goes There!* (1915), the first of his novels set during World War One, was seen as original and daring. Some go as far as to say *The Flaming Jewel* (1922), an action-packed adventure set in the jungles of South America just after the First World War or *The Mystery Lady* (1925), a thriller where victims try to outwit villains in a race to find pirate gold off the coast of California, marked a revival of his flair and verve. Maybe his last novel of any merit was *The Man They Hanged* (1926) in which he showed how Captain Kidd was not a pirate but a scapegoat for the British government.

This list shows that Chambers could ring the changes and amidst these novels are a few where he returned to the supernatural and fantastic which are often overlooked. The one later title most remember is *The Slayer of Souls* (1920), a Rohmeresque occult adventure which tries to explain the cause of the horrors of the Great War by revealing an evil strain of Chinese, the Yezidees, who are able to broadcast psychic emanations which corrupt humanity. Though it has some moments of the old magic few treat it with much regard. This novel has a counterpart in *The Talkers* (1923), a variant blend of *Svengali* and *Dr. Jekyll and Mr. Hyde*. A Svengali-like psychic uses his abilities to implant a rival and more evil soul in the body of another. There are also experiments that succeed in reviving the dead. Chambers handles this novel rather too clumsily, despite the abundance of ideas.

There are two books of rather more merit that explore the psychic and clairvoyant. *The Green Mouse* (1910), written as a series of humorous stories for the *Saturday Evening Post* during 1908 and 1909, shares a common theme with *The Tracer of Lost Persons*, that everyone has their psychic partner or soul-mate. An electrical engineer, Destyn (the play on "destiny" is too obvious) invents a radio-style machine which can track psychic waves in the ether and allows him to pair those with a mutual affinity. It shares the same mischievous fun as both *Tracer* and *The Tree of Heaven*. *Athalie* (1915) is an overlooked novel about a girl who is clairvoyant, though she only fully develops these skills in her young adulthood when she takes over an apartment where a medium once lived. At one point she uses her talent to help an explorer find a lost city in the South American jungle. Although rather saccharine in its romance it does treat the clairvoyant theme in a more sympathetic and less sensational way than many other novels of the period.

Two other novels are worth mentioning. *The Gay Rebellion* (1913) is a fix-up from a series of stories run in *Hampton's Magazine* during 1911 and considers how women, in the form of highly militant suffragettes, might use their power to manipulate men and find their best partner. The book was inspired in part by the concept of eugenics, but is treated here too flippantly. *The Hidden Children* (1914) is an historical novel of some power. Set during the early colonial days of the 1770s, it follows a township of colonists in their battle against the Iroquois Native Americans who use their own native sorcery against the townsfolk.

These examples show that there is more to the work of Robert W. Chambers than a simple summation of historical novels and society romances suggests. He knew how to write to a formula, but he also knew when to experiment with that formula and to produce works of a more unusual nature. The two books included here, *The Tracer of Lost Souls* and *The Tree of Heaven* show how well he could blend the romantic novel with his fascination for the unusual and psychic, seasoned with both humour and a sense of the strange. We should certainly not dismiss Chambers's other works out of hand. He was an experienced writer who knew what he was doing and there is much that is worth revisiting.

—Chatham, UK
October 2017

The Tracer of Lost Persons
By Robert W. Chambers

To Mr. and Mrs. William A. Hall

For the harmony of the world, like that of a harp, is made up of discords.

—*HERACLITUS.*

CHAPTER I

He was thirty-three, agreeable to look at, equipped with as much culture and intelligence as is tolerated east of Fifth Avenue and west of Madison. He had a couple of elaborate rooms at the Lenox Club, a larger income than seemed to be good for him, and no profession. It follows that he was a pessimist before breakfast. Besides, it's a bad thing for a man at thirty-three to come to the conclusion that he has seen all the most attractive girls in the world and that they have been vastly overrated. So, when a club servant with gilt buttons on his coat tails knocked at the door, the invitation to enter was not very cordial. He of the buttons knocked again to take the edge off before he entered; then opened the door and unburdened himself as follows:

"Mr. Gatewood, sir, Mr. Kerns's compliments, and wishes to know if 'e may 'ave 'is coffee served at your tyble, sir."

Gatewood, before the mirror, gave a vicious twist to his tie, inserted a pearl scarf pin, and regarded the effect with gloomy approval.

"Say to Mr. Kerns that I am—flattered," he replied morosely; "and tell Henry I want him."

"'Enry, sir? Yes, sir."

The servant left; one of the sleek club valets came in, softly sidling.

"Henry!"

"Sir?"

"I'll wear a white waistcoat, if you don't object."

The valet laid out half a dozen.

"Which one do you usually wear when I'm away, Henry? Which is *your* favorite?"

"Sir?"

"Pick it out and don't look injured, and *don't* roll up your eyes. I merely desire to borrow it for one day."

"Very good, sir."

"And, Henry, hereafter always help yourself to my *best* cigars. Those I smoke may injure you. I've attempted to conceal the keys, but you will, of course, eventually discover them under that loose tile on the hearth."

"Yes, sir; thanky', sir," returned the valet gravely.

"And—Henry!"

"Sir?" with martyred dignity.

"When you are tired of searching for my olivine and opal pin, just find it, for a change. I'd like to wear that pin for a day or two if it would not inconvenience you."

"Very good, sir; I will 'unt it hup, sir."

Gatewood put on his coat, took hat and gloves from the unabashed valet, and sauntered down to the sunny breakfast room, where he found Kerns inspecting a morning paper and leisurely consuming grapefruit with a cocktail on the side.

"Hullo," observed Kerns briefly.

"I'm not on the telephone," snapped Gatewood.

"I beg your pardon; how are you, dear friend?"

"*I* don't know how I am," retorted Gatewood irritably; "how the devil should a man know how he is?"

"Everything going to the bowwows, as usual, dear friend?"

"*As* usual. Oh, read your paper, Tommy! You know well enough I'm not one of those tail-wagging imbeciles who wakes up in the morning singing like a half-witted lark. Why should I, with this taste in my mouth, and the laundress using vitriol, and Henry sneering at my cigars?" He yawned and cast his eyes toward the ceiling. "Besides, there's too much gilt all over this club! There's too much everywhere. Half the world is stucco, the rest rococo. Where's that Martini I bid for?"

Kerns, undisturbed, applied himself to cocoa and toasted muffins. Grapefruit and an amber-tinted accessory were brought for the other and sampled without mirth. However, a little later Gatewood said: "Well, are you going to read your paper all day?"

"What you need," said Kerns, laying the paper aside, "is a job—any old kind would do, dear friend."

"I don't want to make any more money."

"I don't want you to. I mean a job where you'd lose a lot and be scared into thanking Heaven for carfare. *You're* a nice object for the breakfast table!"

"Bridge. I will be amiable enough by noon time."

"Yes, you're endurable by noon time, as a rule. When you're forty you may be tolerated after five o'clock; when you're fifty your wife and children might even venture to emerge from the cellar after dinner—"

"Wife!"

"I said wife," replied Kerns, as he calmly watched his man.

He had managed it well, so far, and he was wise enough not to overdo it. An interval of silence was what the situation required.

"I wish I *had* a wife," muttered Gatewood after a long pause.

"Oh, haven't you said that every day for five years? Wife! Look at the willing assortment of dreams playing Sally Waters around town. Isn't this borough a bower of beauty—a flowery thicket where the prettiest kind in all the world grow under glass or outdoors? And what do you do? You used to pretend to prowl about inspecting the yearly crop of posies, growling, cynical, dissatisfied; but you've even given that up. Now you only point your nose skyward and squall for a mate, and yowl mournfully that you never have seen your ideal. *I* know *you*."

"I never have seen my ideal," retorted Gatewood sulkily, "but I know she exists—somewhere between heaven and Hoboken."

"You're sure, are you?"

"Oh, *I'm* sure. And, rich or poor, good or bad, she was fashioned for me alone. That's a theory of mine; *you* needn't accept it; in fact, it's none of your business, Tommy."

"All the same," insisted Kerns, "did you ever consider that if your ideal does exist somewhere, it is morally up to you to find her?"

"Haven't I inspected every debutante for ten years? You don't expect me to advertise for an ideal, do you—object, matrimony?"

Kerns regarded him intently. "Now, I'm going to make a vivid suggestion, Jack. In fact, that's why I subjected myself to the ordeal of breakfasting with you. It's none of my business, as you so kindly put it, but—*shall* I suggest something?"

"Go ahead," replied Gatewood, tranquilly lighting a cigarette. "I know what you'll say."

"No, you don't. Firstly, you are having such a good time in this world that you don't really enjoy yourself—isn't that so?"

"I—well, let it go at that."

"Secondly, with all your crimes and felonies, you have one decent trait left: you really would like to fall in love. And I suspect you'd even marry."

"There are grounds," said Gatewood guardedly, "for your suspicions. *Et après?*"

"Good. Then there's a way! I know—"

"Oh, don't tell me you 'know a girl,' or anything like that!" began Gatewood sullenly. "I've heard that before, and I won't meet her."

"I don't want you to; I don't know anybody. All I desire to say is this: I do know a way. The other day I noticed a sign on Fifth Avenue:

KEEN & CO.
TRACERS OF LOST PERSONS

It was a most extraordinary sign; and having a little unemployed imagination I began to speculate on how Keen & Co. might operate, and I wondered a little, too, that the conditions of life in this city could enable a firm to make a living by devoting itself exclusively to the business of hunting up missing people."

Kerns paused, partly to light a cigarette, partly for diplomatic reasons.

"What has all this to do with me?" inquired Gatewood curiously; and diplomacy scored one.

"Why not try Keen & Co.?"

"Try them? Why? I haven't lost anybody, have I?"

"You haven't precisely *lost anybody*, but the fact remains that you can't *find somebody*," returned Kerns coolly. "Why not employ Keen & Co. to look for her?"

"Look for whom, in Heaven's name?"

"Your ideal."

"Look for—for my ideal! Kerns, you're crazy. How the mischief can anybody hunt for somebody who doesn't exist?"

"You *say* that she *does* exist."

"But I can't prove it, man."

"You don't have to; it's up to Keen & Co. to prove it. That's why you employ them."

"What wild nonsense you talk! Keen & Co. might, perhaps, be able to trace the concrete, but how are they going to trace and find the abstract?"

"She isn't abstract; she is a lovely, healthy, and youthful concrete object—if, as you say, she *does* exist."

"How can I *prove* she exists?"

"You don't have to; they do that."

"Look here," said Gatewood almost angrily, "do you suppose that if I were ass enough to go to these people and tell them that I wanted to find my ideal—"

"*Don't* tell them *that!*"

"But how—"

"There is no necessity for going into such trivial details. All you need say is: 'I am very anxious to find a young lady'—and then describe her as minutely as you please. Then, when they locate a girl of that description they'll notify you; you will go, judge for yourself whether she is the one woman on earth—and, if disappointed, you need only shake your head and murmur: 'Not *the* same!' And it's for them to find another."

"I won't do it!" said Gatewood hotly.

"Why not? At least, it would be amusing. You haven't many mental resources, and it might occupy you for a week or two."

Gatewood glared.

"You have a pleasant way of putting things this morning, haven't you?"

"I don't want to be pleasant: I want to jar you. Don't I care enough about you to breakfast with you? Then I've a right to be pleasantly unpleasant.

I can't bear to watch your mental and spiritual dissolution—a man like you, with all your latent ability and capacity for being nobody in particular—which is the sort of man this nation needs. Do you want to turn into a club-window gazer like Van Bronk? Do you want to become another Courtlandt Allerton and go rocking down the avenue—a grimacing, tailor-made sepulcher?—the pompous obsequies of a dead intellect?—a funeral on two wavering legs, carrying the corpse of all that should be deathless in a man? Why, Jack, I'd rather see you in bankruptcy—I'd rather see you trying to lead a double life in a single flat on seven dollars and a half a week—I'd almost rather see you every day at breakfast than have it come to that!

"Wake up and get jocund with life! Why, you could have all good citizens stung to death if you chose. It isn't that I want you to make money; but I want you to worry over somebody besides yourself—not in Wall Street—a pool and its money are soon parted. But in your own home, where a beautiful wife and seven angel children have you dippy and close to the ropes; where the housekeeper gets a rake off, and the cook is red-headed and comes from Sligo, and the butler's cousin will bear watching, and the chauffeur is a Frenchman, and the coachman's uncle is a Harlem vet, and every scullion in the establishment lies, drinks, steals, and supports twenty satiated relatives at your expense. That would mean the making of you; for, after all, Jack, you are no genius—you're a plain, non-partisan, uninspired, clean-built, wholesome citizen, thank God!—the sort whose unimaginative mission is to pitch in with eighty-odd millions of us and, like the busy coral creatures, multiply with all your might, and make this little old Republic the greatest, biggest, finest article that an overworked world has ever yet put up! ... Now you can call for help if you choose."

Gatewood's breath returned slowly. In an intimacy of many years he had never suspected that sort of thing from Kerns. That is why, no doubt, the opinions expressed by Kerns stirred him to an astonishment too innocent to harbor anger or chagrin.

And when Kerns stood up with an unembarrassed laugh, saying, "I'm going to the office; see you this evening?" Gatewood replied rather vacantly: "Oh, yes; I'm dining here. Good-by, Tommy."

Kerns glanced at his watch, lingering. "Was there anything you wished to ask me, Jack?" he inquired guilelessly.

"Ask you? No, I don't think so."

"Oh; I had an idea you might care to know where Keen & Co. were to be found."

"*That*," said Gatewood firmly, "is foolish."

"I'll write the address for you, anyway," rejoined Kerns, scribbling it and handing the card to his friend.

Then he went down the stairs, several at a time, eased in conscience, satisfied that he had done his duty by a friend he cared enough for to breakfast with.

"Of course," he ruminated as he crawled into a hansom and lay back buried in meditation—"of course there may be nothing in this Keen & Co. business. But it will stir him up and set him thinking; and the longer Keen & Co. take to hunt up an imaginary lady that doesn't exist, the more anxious and impatient poor old Jack Gatewood will become, until he'll catch the fever and go cantering about with that one fixed idea in his head. And," added Kerns softly, "no New Yorker in his right mind can go galloping through these five boroughs very long before he's roped, tied, and marked by the 'only girl in the world'—the *only* girl—if you don't care to turn around and look at another million girls precisely like her. O Lord!—precisely like her!"

Here was a nice exhorter to incite others to matrimony.

CHAPTER II

Meanwhile, Gatewood was walking along Fifth Avenue, more or less soothed by the May sunshine. First, he went to his hatters, looked at straw hats, didn't like them, protested, and bought one, wishing he had strength of mind enough to wear it home. But he hadn't. Then he entered the huge white marble palace of his jeweler, left his watch to be regulated, caught a glimpse of a girl whose hair and neck resembled the hair and neck of his ideal, sidled around until he discovered that she was chewing gum, and backed off, with a bitter smile, into the avenue once more.

Every day for years he had had glimpses of girls whose hair, hands, figures, eyes, hats, carriage, resembled the features required by his ideal; there always was something wrong somewhere. And, as he strolled moodily, a curious feeling of despair seized him—something that, even in his most sentimental moments, even amid the most unexpected disappointment, he had never before experienced.

"I do want to love *somebody!*" he found himself saying half aloud; "I want to marry; I—" He turned to look after three pretty children with their maids—"I want several like those—several!—seven—ten—I don't care how many! I want a house to worry me, just as Tommy described it; I want to see the same girl across the breakfast table—or she can sip her cocoa in bed if she desires—" A slow, modest blush stole over his features; it was one of the nicest things he ever did. Glancing up, he beheld across the way a white sign, ornamented with strenuous crimson lettering:

KEEN & CO.
TRACERS OF LOST PERSONS

The moment he discovered it, he realized he had been covertly hunting for it; he also realized that he was going to climb the stairs. He hadn't quite decided what he meant to do after that; nor was his mind clear on the matter when he found himself opening a door of opaque glass on which was printed in red:

KEEN & CO.

He was neither embarrassed nor nervous when he found himself in a big carpeted anteroom where a negro attendant bowed him to a seat and took his card; and he looked calmly around to see what was to be seen.

Several people occupied easy chairs in various parts of the room—an old woman very neatly dressed, clutching in her withered hand a photograph which she studied and studied with tear-dimmed eyes; a young man wearing last year's most fashionable styles in everything except his features: and soap could have aided him there; two policemen, helmets resting on their knees; and, last of all, a rather thin child of twelve, staring open-mouthed at everybody, a bundle of soiled clothing under one arm. Through an open door he saw a dozen young women garbed in black, with white cuffs and collars, all rattling away steadily at typewriters. Every now and then, from some hidden office, a bell rang decisively, and one of the girls would rise from her machine and pass noiselessly out of sight to obey the summons. From time to time, too, the darky servant with marvelous manners would usher somebody through the room where the typewriters were rattling, into the unseen office. First the old woman went—shakily, clutching her photograph; then the thin child with the bundle, staring at everything; then the two fat policemen, in portentous single file, helmets in their white-gloved hands, oiled hair glistening.

Gatewood's turn was approaching; he waited without any definite emotion, watching newcomers enter to take the places of those who had been summoned. He hadn't the slightest idea of what he was to say; nor did it worry him. A curious sense of impending good fortune left him pleasantly tranquil; he picked up, from the silver tray on the table at his elbow, one of the firm's business cards, and scanned it with interest:

KEEN & CO.
TRACERS OF LOST PERSONS

> *Keen & Co. are prepared to locate the whereabouts of anybody on earth. No charges will be made unless the person searched for is found.*
> *Blanks on application.*
>
> WESTREL KEEN, *Manager.*

"Mistuh Keen will see you, suh," came a persuasive voice at his elbow; and he rose and followed the softly moving colored servant out of the room, through a labyrinth of demure young women at their typewriters, then sharply to the right and into a big, handsomely furnished office, where a sleepy-looking elderly gentleman rose from an armchair and bowed. There could not be the slightest doubt that he was a gentleman; every movement, every sound he uttered, settled the fact.

"Mr. Keen?"

"Mr. Gatewood?"—with a quiet certainty which had its charm. "This is very good of you."

Gatewood sat down and looked at his host. Then he said: "I'm searching for somebody, Mr. Keen, whom you are not likely to find."

"I doubt it," said Keen pleasantly.

Gatewood smiled. "If," he said, "you will undertake to find the person *I* cannot find, I must ask you to accept a retainer."

"We don't require retainers," replied Keen. "Unless we find the person sought for, we make no charges, Mr. Gatewood."

"I must ask you to do so in my case. It is not fair that you should undertake it on other terms. I desire to make a special arrangement with you. Do you mind?"

"What arrangement had you contemplated?" inquired Keen, amused.

"Only this: charge me in advance exactly what you would charge if successful. And, on the other hand, do not ask me for detailed information— I mean, do not insist on any information that I decline to give. Do you mind taking up such an extraordinary and unbusinesslike proposition, Mr. Keen?"

The Tracer of Lost Persons looked up sharply:

"About how much information *do* you decline to give, Mr. Gatewood?"

"About enough to incriminate and degrade," replied the young man, laughing.

The elderly gentleman sat silent, apparently buried in meditation. Once or twice his pleasant steel-gray eyes wandered over Gatewood as an expert, a connoisseur, glances at a picture and assimilates its history, its value, its artistic merit, its every detail in one practiced glance.

"I think we may take up this matter for you, Mr. Gatewood," he said, smiling his singularly agreeable smile.

"But—but you would first desire to know something about me—would you not?"

Keen looked at him: "You will not mistake me—you will consider it entirely inoffensive—if I say that I know something about you, Mr. Gatewood?"

"About *me?* How can you? Of course, there is the social register and the club lists and all that—"

"And many, many sources of information which are necessary in such a business as this, Mr. Gatewood. It is a necessity for us to be almost as well informed as our clients' own lawyers. I could pay you no sincerer compliment than to undertake your case. I am half inclined to do so even *without* a retainer. Mind, I haven't yet said that I *will* take it."

"I prefer to regulate any possible indebtedness in advance," said Gatewood.

"As you wish," replied the older man, smiling. "In that case, suppose you draw your check" (he handed Gatewood a fountain pen as the young man fished a check-book from his pocket)—"your check for—well, say for $5,000, to the order of Keen & Co."

Gatewood met his eye without wincing; he was in for it now; and he was always perfectly game. He had brought it upon himself; it was his own proposition. Not that he would have for a moment considered the sum as high—or any sum exorbitant—if there had been a chance of success; one cannot compare and weigh such matters. But how could there be any chance for success?

As he slowly smoothed out the check and stub, pen poised, Keen was saying: "Of course, we should succeed sooner or later—if we took up your case. We might succeed to-morrow—to-day. That would mean a large profit for us. But we might not succeed to-day, or next month, or even next year. That would leave us little or no profit; and, as it is our custom to go on until we do succeed, no matter how long it may require, you see, Mr. Gatewood, I should be taking all sorts of chances. It might even cost us double your retainer before we found her—"

"Her? How did—*why* do you say '*her*'?"

"Am I wrong?" asked Keen, smiling.

"No—you are right."

The Tracer of Lost Persons sank into abstraction again. Gatewood waited, hoping that his case might be declined, yet ready to face any music started at his own request.

"She is young," mused Keen aloud, "very beautiful and accomplished.

Is she wealthy?" He looked up mildly.

Gatewood said: "I don't know—the truth is I don't care—" And stopped.

"O-ho!" mused Keen slowly. "I—think—I understand. Am I wrong, Mr. Gatewood, in surmising that this young lady whom you seek is, in your eyes, very—I may say ideally gifted?"

"She is my ideal," replied the young man, coloring.

"*Exactly*. And—her general allure?"

"Charming!"

"*Exactly*; but to be a trifle more precise—if you could give me a sketch, an idea, a mere outline delicately tinted, now. *Is* she more blond than brunette?"

"Yes—but her eyes are brown. I—I insist on that."

"Why should you not? *You* know her; I don't," said Keen, laughing. "I merely wished to form a mental picture.... You say her hair is—"

"It's full of sunny color; that's all I can say."

"*Exactly*—I see. A rare and lovely combination with brown eyes and creamy skin, Mr. Gatewood. I fancy she might be, perhaps, an inch or two under your height?"

"Just about that. Her hands should be—*are* beautiful—"

"*Exactly*. The ensemble is most vividly portrayed, Mr. Gatewood; and—you have intimated that her lack of fortune—er—we might almost say her pecuniary distress—is more than compensated for by her accomplishments, character, and very unusual beauty.... *Did* I so understand you, Mr. Gatewood?"

"That's what I meant, anyhow," he said, flushing up.

"You *did* mean it?"

"I did: I do."

"Then we take your case, Mr. Gatewood.... No haste about the check, my dear sir—pray consider us at your service."

But Gatewood doggedly filled in the check and handed it to the Tracer of Lost Persons.

"I wish you happiness," said the older man in a low voice. "The lady you describe exists; it is for us to discover her."

"Thank you," stammered Gatewood, astounded.

Keen touched an electric button; a moment later a young girl entered the room.

"Miss Southerland, Mr. Gatewood. Will you be kind enough to take Mr. Gatewood's dictation in Room 19?"

For a second Gatewood stared—as though in the young girl before him the ghost of his ideal had risen to confront him—only for a second; then he bowed, matching her perfect acknowledgment of his presence by a bearing and courtesy which must have been inbred to be so faultless.

And he followed her to Room 19.

What had Keen meant by saying, "The lady you describe exists!" Did this remarkable elderly gentleman suspect that it was to be a hunt for an ideal? Had he deliberately entered into such a bargain? Impossible!

His disturbed thoughts reverted to the terms of the bargain, the entire enterprise, the figures on his check. His own amazing imbecility appalled him. What idiocy! What sudden madness had seized him to entangle himself in such unheard-of negotiations! True, he had played bridge until dawn the night before, but, on awaking, he had discovered no perceptible hold-over. It must have been sheer weakness of intellect that permitted him to be dominated by the suggestions of Kerns. And now the game was on: the jack declared, cards dealt, and his ante was up. Had he openers?

Room 19, duly labeled with its number on the opaque glass door, contained a desk, a table and typewriter, several comfortable chairs, and a window opening on Fifth Avenue, through which the eastern sun poured a stream of glory, washing curtain, walls, and ceiling with palest gold.

And all this time, preoccupied with new impressions and his own growing chagrin, he watched the girl who conducted him with all the unconscious assurance and grace of a young chatelaine passing through her own domain under escort of a distinguished guest.

When they had entered Room 19, she half turned, but he forestalled her and closed the door, and she passed before him with a perceptible inclination of her finely modeled head, seating herself at the desk by the open window. He took an armchair at her elbow and removed his gloves, looking at her expectantly.

CHAPTER III

"This is a list of particular and general questions for you to answer, Mr. Gatewood," she said, handing him a long slip of printed matter. "The replies to such questions as you are able or willing to answer you may dictate to me." The beauty of her modulated voice was scarcely a surprise— no woman who moved and carried herself as did this tall young girl in black and white could reasonably be expected to speak with less distinction—yet the charm of her voice, from the moment her lips unclosed, so engrossed him that the purport of her speech escaped him.

"Would you mind saying it once more?" he asked.

She did so; he attempted to concentrate his attention, and succeeded sufficiently to look as though some vestige of intellect remained in him. He saw her pick up a pad and pencil; the contour and grace of two deliciously fashioned hands arrested his mental process once more.

"I *beg* your pardon," he said hastily; "what were you saying, Miss Southerland?"

"Nothing, Mr. Gatewood. I did not speak."

And he realized, hazily, that she had not spoken—that it was the subtle eloquence of her youth and loveliness that had appealed like a sudden voice—a sound faintly exquisite echoing his own thought of her.

Troubled, he looked at the slip of paper in his hand; it was headed:

SPECIAL DESCRIPTION BLANK
(Form K)

And he read it as carefully as he was able to—the curious little clamor of his pulses, the dazed sense of elation, almost of expectation, distracting his attention all the time.

"I wish you would read it to me," he said; "that would give me time to think up answers."

"If you wish," she assented pleasantly, swinging around toward him in her desk chair. Then she crossed one knee over the other to support the pad, and, bending above it, lifted her brown eyes. She could have done nothing in the world more distracting at that moment.

"What is the sex of the person you desire to find, Mr. Gatewood?"

"Her sex? I—well, I fancy it is feminine."

She wrote after "Sex" the words "She is probably feminine"; looked at him absently, glanced at what she had written, flushed a little, rubbed out the "she is probably," wondering why a moment's mental wandering should have committed her to absurdity.

"Married?" she asked with emphasis.

"No," he replied, startled; then, vexed, "I beg your pardon—you mean to ask if *she* is married!"

"Oh, I didn't mean *you*, Mr. Gatewood; it's the next question, you see"— she held out the blank toward him. "Is the person you are looking for married?"

"Oh, no; she isn't married, either—at least—I trust—not—because if she *is* I don't want to find her!" he ended, entangled in an explanation which threatened to involve him deeper than he desired. And, looking up, he saw the beautiful brown eyes regarding him steadily. They reverted to the paper at once, and the white fingers sent the pencil flying.

"He trusts that she is unmarried, but if she *is* (underlined) married he doesn't want to find her," she wrote.

"That," she explained, "goes under the head of 'General Remarks' at the bottom of the page"—she held it out, pointing with her pencil. He nodded, staring at her slender hand.

"Age?" she continued, setting the pad firmly on her rounded, yielding knee and looking up at him.

"Age? Well, I—as a matter of fact, I could only venture a surmise. You know," he said earnestly, "how difficult it is to guess ages, don't you, Miss Southerland?"

"How old do you *think* she is? Could you not hazard a guess—judging, say, from her appearance?"

"I have no data—no experience to guide me." He was becoming involved again. "Would you, for practice, permit me first to guess your age, Miss Southerland?"

"Why—yes—if you think that might help you to guess hers."

So he leaned back in his armchair and considered her a very long time—having a respectable excuse to do so. Twenty times he forgot he was looking at her for any purpose except that of disinterested delight, and twenty times he remembered with a guilty wince that it was a matter of business.

"Perhaps I had better tell you," she suggested, her color rising a little under his scrutiny.

"Is it eighteen? Just *her* age!"

"Twenty-one, Mr. Gatewood—and you said you didn't know her age."

"I have just remembered that I *thought* it might be eighteen; but I dare say I was shy three years in her case, too. You may put it down at twenty-one."

For the slightest fraction of a second the brown eyes rested on his, the pencil hovered in hesitation. Then the eyes fell, and the moving fingers wrote.

"Did you write 'twenty-one'?" he inquired carelessly.

"I did not, Mr. Gatewood."

"What did you write?"

"I wrote: 'He doesn't appear to know much about her age.'"

"But I *do* know—"

"You said—" They looked at one another earnestly.

"The next question," she continued with composure, "is: 'Date and place of birth?' Can you answer any part of *that* question?"

"I trust I may be able to—some day.... What *are* you writing?"

"I'm writing: 'He trusts he may be able to, some day.' Wasn't that what you said?"

"Yes, I did say that. I—I'm not perfectly sure what I meant by it."

She passed to the next question:

"Height?"

"About five feet six," he said, fascinated gaze on her.

"Hair?"

"More gold than brown—full of—er—gleams—" She looked up quickly; his eyes reverted to the window rather suddenly. He had been looking at her hair.

"Complexion?" she continued after a shade of hesitation.

"It's a sort of delicious mixture—bisque, tinted with a pinkish bloom—ivory and rose—" He was explaining volubly, when she began to shake her head, timing each shake to his words.

"Really, Mr. Gatewood, I think you are hopelessly vague on that point—unless you desire to convey the impression that she is speckled."

"Speckled!" he repeated, horrified. "Why, I am describing a woman who is my ideal of beauty—"

But she had already gone to the next question: "Teeth?"

"P-p-perfect p-p-pearls!" he stammered. The laughing red mouth closed like a flower at dusk, veiling the sparkle of her teeth.

Was he trying to be impertinent? Was he deliberately describing her? He did not look like that sort of man; yet *why* was he watching her so closely, so curiously at every question? Why did he look at her teeth when she laughed?

"Eyes?" Her own dared him to continue what, coincidence or not, was plainly a description of herself.

"B-b-b—" He grew suddenly timorous, hesitating, pretending to a perplexity which was really a healthy scare. For she was frowning.

"Curious I can't think of the color of her eyes," he said; "is—isn't it?"

She coldly inspected her pad and made a correction; but all she did was to rub out a comma and put another in its place. Meanwhile, Gatewood, chin in his hand, sat buried in profound thought. "*Were* they blue?" he murmured to himself aloud, "or *were* they brown? Blue begins with a *b* and brown begins with a *b*. I'm convinced that her eyes began with a *b*. They were not, therefore, gray or green, because," he added in a burst of confidence, "it is utterly impossible to spell gray or green with a *b!*"

Miss Southerland looked slightly astonished.

"All you can recollect, then, is that the color of her eyes began with the letter *b?*"

"That is absolutely all I can remember; but I *think* they *were*—brown."

"If they *were* brown they must be brown now," she observed, looking out of the window.

"That's true! Isn't it curious I never thought of that? What are you writing?"

"Brown," she said, so briefly that it sounded something like a snub.

"Mouth?" inquired the girl, turning a new leaf on her pad.

"Perfect. Write it: there is no other term fit to describe its color, shape, its sensitive beauty, its— *What* did you write just then?"

"I wrote, 'Mouth, ordinary.'"

"I don't want you to! I want—"

"Really, Mr. Gatewood, a rhapsody on a girl's mouth is proper in poetry, but scarcely germane to the record of a purely business transaction. Please answer the next question tersely, if you don't mind: 'Figure?'"

"Oh, I *do* mind! I can't! Any poem is much too brief to describe her figure—"

"Shall we say 'Perfect'?" asked the girl, raising her brown eyes in a glimmering transition from vexation to amusement. For, after all, it could be *only* a coincidence that this young man should be describing features peculiar to herself.

"Couldn't you write, 'Venus-of-Milo-like'?" he inquired. "That is laconic."

"I could—if it's true. But if you mean it for praise—I—don't think any modern woman would be flattered."

"I always supposed that she of Milo had an ideal figure," he said, perplexed.

She wrote, "A good figure." Then, propping her rounded chin on one lovely white hand, she glanced at the next question:

"Hands?"

"White, beautiful, rose-tipped, slender yet softly and firmly rounded—"

"How *can* they be soft and firm, too, Mr. Gatewood?" she protested; then, surprising his guilty eyes fixed on her hands, hastily dropped them and sat up straight, level-browed, cold as marble. *Was* he deliberately being rude to her?

CHAPTER IV

As a matter of fact, he was not. Too poor in imagination to invent, on the spur of the moment, charms and qualities suited to his ideal, he had, at first unconsciously, taken as a model the girl before him; quite unconsciously and innocently at first—then furtively, and with a dawning perception of the almost flawless beauty he was secretly plagiarizing. Aware, now, that something had annoyed her; aware, too, at the same moment that there appeared to be nothing lacking in her to satisfy his imagination of the ideal, he began to turn redder than he had ever turned in all his life.

Several minutes of sixty seconds each ensued before he ventured to stir a finger. And it was only when she bent again very gravely over her pad that he cautiously eased a cramped muscle or two, and drew a breath—a long, noiseless, deep and timid respiration. He realized the enormity of what he had been doing—how close he had come to giving unpardonable offense by drawing a perfect portrait of her as the person he desired to find through the good offices of Keen & Co.

But there was no such person—unless she had a double: for what more could a man desire than the ideal traits he had been able to describe only by using her as his inspiration.

When he ventured to look at her, one glance was enough to convince him that she, too, had noticed the parallel—had been forced to recognize her own features in the portrait he had constructed of an ideal. And she had caught him in absent-minded contemplation of the hands he had been describing. He knew that his face was the face of a guilty man.

"What is the next question?" he stammered, eager to answer it in a manner calculated to allay her suspicions.

"The next question?" She glanced at the list, then with a voice of velvet which belied the eyes, clear as frosty brown pools in November: "The next question requires a description of her feet."

"Feet! Oh—they—they're rather large—why, her feet are enormous, I believe—"

She looked at him as though stunned; suddenly a flood of pink spread, wave on wave, from the white nape of her neck to her hair; she bent low over her pad and wrote something, remaining in that attitude until her face cooled.

"Somehow or other I've done it again!" he thought, horrified. "The best thing I can do is to end it and go home."

In his distress he began to hedge, saying: "Of course, she is rather tall and her feet are in some sort of proportion—in fact, they are perfectly symmetrical feet—"

Never in his life had he encountered a pair of such angrily beautiful eyes. Speech stopped with a dry gulp.

"We now come to 'General Remarks,'" she said in a voice made absolutely steady and emotionless. "Have you any remarks of that description to offer, Mr. Gatewood?"

"I'm willing to make remarks," he said, "if I only knew what you wished me to say."

She mused, eyes on the sunny window, then looked up. "Where did you last see her?"

"Near Fifth Avenue."

"And what street?"

He named the street.

"Near *here?*"

"Rather," he said timidly.

She ruffled the edges of her pad, wrote something and erased it, bit her scarlet upper lip, and frowned.

"Out of doors, of course?"

"No; indoors," he admitted furtively.

She looked up with a movement almost nervous. "Do you dare—I mean, care—to be more concise?"

"I would rather not," he replied in a voice from which he hoped he had expelled the tremors of alarm.

"As you please, Mr. Gatewood. And would you care to answer any of these other questions: Who and what are or were her parents? Give all particulars concerning all her relatives. Is she employed or not? What are her social, financial, and general circumstances? Her character, personal traits, aims, interests, desires? Has she any vices? Any virtues? Talents? Ambitions? Caprices? Fads? Are you in love with her? Is—"

"Yes," he said, "I am."

"Is she in love with you?"

"No; she hates me—I'm afraid."

"Is she in love with anybody?"

"That is a very difficult—"

The girl wrote: "He doesn't know," with a satisfaction apparently causeless.

"Is she a relative of yours, Mr. Gatewood?" very sweetly.

"No, Miss Southerland," very positively.

"You—you desire to marry her—you say?"

"I do. But I didn't say it."

She was silent; then:

"What is her name?" in a low voice which started several agreeable thrills chasing one another over him.

"I—I decline to answer," he stammered.

"On what grounds, Mr. Gatewood?"

He looked her full in the eyes; suddenly he bent forward and gazed at the printed paper from which she had been apparently reading.

"Why, all those questions you are scaring me with are not there!" he exclaimed indignantly. "You are making them up?"

"I—I know, but"—she was flushing furiously—"but they are on the other forms—some of them. Can't you see you are answering 'Form K'? That is a special form—"

"But why do you ask me questions that are not on Form K?"

"Because it is my duty to do all I can to secure evidence which may lead to the discovery of the person you desire to find. I—I assure you, Mr. Gatewood, this duty is not—not always agreeable—and some people make it harder still."

Gatewood looked out of the window. Various emotions—among them shame, mortification, chagrin—pervaded him, and chased each other along his nervous system, coloring his neck and ears a fiery red for the enlightenment of any observer.

"I—I did not mean to offend you," said the girl in a low voice—such a gently regretful voice that Gatewood swung around in his chair.

"There is nothing I would not be glad to tell you about the woman I have fallen in love with," he said. "She is overwhelmingly lovely; and—when I dare—I will tell you her name and where I first saw her—and where I saw her last—if you desire. Shall I?"

"It would be advisable. When will you do this?"

"When I dare."

"You—you don't dare—now?"

"No ... not now."

She absently wrote on her pad: "He doesn't dare tell me now." Then, with head still bent, she lifted her mischief-making, trouble-breeding brown eyes to his once more.

"I am to come here, of course, to consult you?" he asked dizzily.

"Mr. Keen will receive you—"

"He may be busy."

"He may be," she repeated dreamily.

"So—I'll ask for you."

"We *could* write you, Mr. Gatewood."

He said hastily: "It's no trouble for me to come; I walk every morning."

"But there would be no use, I think, in your coming very soon. All I— all Mr. Keen could do for a while would be to report progress—"

"That is all I dare look for: progress—for the present."

During the time that he remained—which was not very long—neither of them spoke until he arose to take his departure.

"Good-by, Miss Southerland. I hope you may find the person I have been searching for."

"Good-by, Mr. Gatewood.... I hope we shall; ... but I—don't—know."

And, as a matter of fact, she did not know; she was rather excited over nothing, apparently; and also somewhat preoccupied with several rather disturbing emotions the species of which she was interested in determining. But to label and catalogue each of these emotions separately required privacy and leisure to think—and she also wished to look very earnestly at the reflection of her own face in the mirror of her own chamber. For it is a trifle exciting—though but an innocent coincidence—to be compared, feature by feature, to a young man's ideal. As far as that went, she excelled it, too; and, as she stood by the desk, alone, gathering up her notes, she suddenly bent over and lifted the hem of her gown a trifle—sufficient to reassure herself that the dainty pair of shoes she wore, would have baffled the efforts of any Venus ever sculptured. And she was perfectly right.

"Of course," she thought to herself, "his ideal runaway hasn't enormous feet. He, too, must have been struck with the similarity between me and his ideal, and when he realized that I also noticed it, he was frightened by my frown into saying that her feet were enormous. How silly! ... For I didn't *mean* to frighten him.... He frightened me—once or twice—I mean he irritated me—no, interested me, is what I *do* mean.... Heigho! I wonder why she ran away? I wonder why he can't find her? ... It's—it's silly to run away from a man like that.... Heigho! ... She doesn't deserve to be found. There is nothing to be afraid of—nothing to alarm anybody in a man like that."

So she gathered up her notes and walked slowly out and across to the private office of the Tracer of Lost Persons.

"Come in," said the Tracer when she knocked. He was using the telephone; she seated herself rather listlessly beside the window, where spring sunshine lay in gilded patches on the rug and spring breezes stirred the curtains. She was a little tired, but there seemed to be no good reason why. Yet, with the soft wind blowing on her cheek, the languor grew; she rested her face on one closed hand, shutting her eyes.

When they opened again it was to meet the fixed gaze of Mr. Keen.

"Oh—I beg your pardon!"

"There is no need of it, child. Be seated. Never mind that report just now." He paced the length of the room once or twice, hands clasped behind him; then, halting to confront her:

"What sort of a man is this young Gatewood?"

"What *sort*, Mr. Keen? Why—I think he is the—the sort—that—"

"I see that you don't think much of him," said Keen, laughing.

"Oh, indeed I did not mean that at all; I mean that he appeared to be—to be—"

"Rather a cad?"

"Why, *no!*" she said, flushing up. "He is absolutely well-bred, Mr. Keen."

"You received no unpleasant impression of him?"

"On the contrary!" she said rather warmly—for it hurt her sense of justice that Keen should so misjudge even a stranger in whom she had no personal interest.

"You think he looks like an honest man?"

"Honest?" She was rosy with annoyance. "Have you any idea that he is dishonest?"

"Have you?"

"Not the slightest," she said with emphasis.

"Suppose a man should set us hunting for a person who does not exist—on our terms, which are no payment unless successful? Would that be honest?" asked Keen gravely.

"Did—did *he* do that?"

"No, child."

"I knew he *couldn't* do such a thing!"

"No, he—er—couldn't, because I wouldn't allow it—not that he tried to!" added Keen hastily as the indignant brown eyes sparkled ominously. "Really, Miss Southerland, he must be all you say he is, for he has a stanch champion to vouch for him."

"All I *say* he is? I haven't said anything about him!"

Mr. Keen nodded. "*Ex*actly. Let us drop him for a moment.... Are you perfectly well, Miss Southerland?"

"Why, yes."

"I'm glad of it. You are a trifle pale; you seem to be a little languid.... When do you take your vacation?"

"You suggested May, I believe," she said wistfully.

The Tracer leaned back in his chair, joining the tips of his fingers reflectively.

"Miss Southerland," he said, "you have been with us a year. I thought it might interest you to know that I am exceedingly pleased with you."

She colored charmingly.

"But," he added, "I'm terribly afraid we're going to lose you."

"Why?" she asked, startled.

"However," he continued, ignoring her half-frightened question with a smile, "I am going to promote you—for faithful and efficient service."

"O-h!"

"With an agreeable increase of salary, and new duties which will take you into the open air. You ride?"

"I—I used to before—"

"*Ex*actly; before you were obliged to earn your living. Please have yourself measured for habit and boots this afternoon. I shall arrange for horse, saddle, and groom. You will spend most of your time riding in the Park—for the present."

"But—Mr. Keen—am I to be one of your agents—a sort of detective?"

Keen regarded her absently, then crossed one leg over the other.

"Read me your notes," he said with a smile.

She read them, folded them, and he took them from her, thoughtfully regarding her.

"Did you know that your mother and I were children together?" he asked.

"No!" She stared. "Is *that* why you sent for me that day at the school of stenography?"

"That is why.... When I learned that my playmate—your mother—was dead, is it not reasonable to suppose that I should wish her daughter to have a chance?"

Miss Southerland looked at him steadily.

"She was like you—when she married.... I never married.... Do you wonder that I sent for you, child?"

Nothing but the clock ticking there in the sunny room, and an old man staring into two dimmed brown eyes, and the little breezes at the open window whispering of summers past.

"This young man, Gatewood," said the Tracer, clearing his voice of its hoarseness—"this young man ought to be all right, if I did not misjudge his father—years ago, child, years ago. And he is all right—" He half turned toward a big letter-file; "his record is clean, so far. The trouble with him is idleness. He ought to marry."

"Isn't he trying to?" she asked.

"It looks like it. Miss Southerland, we *must* find this woman!"

"Yes, but I don't see how you are going to—on such slight information—"

"Information! Child, I have all I want—all I could desire." He laughed, passing his hands over his gray hair. "We are going to find the girl he is in love with before the week ends!"

"Do you really think so?" she exclaimed.

"Yes. But you must do a great deal in this case."

"I?"

"*Exactly.*"

"And—and what am I to do?"

"Ride in the Park, child! And if you see Mr. Gatewood, don't you dare take your eyes off him for one moment. Watch him; observe everything he does. If he should recognize you and speak to you, be as amiable to him as though it were not by my orders."

"Then—then I *am* to be a detective!" she faltered.

The Tracer did not appear to hear her. He took up the notes, turned to the telephone, and began to send out a general alarm, reading the description of the person whom Gatewood had described. The vast, intricate and delicate machinery under his control was being set in motion all over the Union.

"Not that I expect to find her outside the borough of Manhattan," he said, smiling, as he hung up the receiver and turned to her; "but it's as well to know how many types of that species exist in this Republic, and who they are—in case any other young man comes here raving of brown eyes and 'gleams' in the hair."

Miss Southerland, to her own intense consternation, blushed.

"I think you had better order that habit at once," said the Tracer carelessly.

"Tell me, Mr. Keen," she asked tremulously, "am I to spy upon Mr. Gatewood? And report to you? ... For I simply cannot bear to do it—"

"Child, you need report nothing unless you desire to. And when there is something to report, it will be about the woman I am searching for. Don't you understand? I have already located her. You will find her in the Park. And when you are *sure* she is the right one—and if you care to report it to me—I shall be ready to listen.... I am always ready to listen to you."

"But—I warn you, Mr. Keen, that I have perfect faith in the honor of Mr. Gatewood. I *know* that I could have nothing unworthy to report."

"I am sure of it," said the Tracer of Lost Persons, studying her with eyes that were not quite clear. "Now, I think you had better order that habit.... Your mother sat her saddle perfectly.... We rode very often—my lost playmate and I."

He turned, hands clasped behind his back, absently pacing the room, backward, forward, there in the spring sunshine. Nor did he notice her lingering, nor mark her as she stole from the room, brown eyes saddened and thoughtful, wondering, too, that there should be in the world so much room for sorrow.

CHAPTER V

Gatewood, burdened with restlessness and gnawed by curiosity, consumed a week in prowling about the edifice where Keen & Co. carried on an interesting profession.

His first visit resulted merely in a brief interview with Mr. Keen, who smilingly reported progress and suavely bowed him out. He looked about for Miss Southerland as he was leaving, but did not see her.

On his second visit he mustered the adequate courage to ask for her, and experienced a curiously sickly sensation when informed that Miss Southerland was no longer employed in the bureau of statistics, having been promoted to an outside position of great responsibility. His third visit proved anything but satisfactory. He sidled and side-stepped for ten minutes before he dared ask Mr. Keen *where* Miss Southerland had gone. And when the Tracer replied that, considering the business he had undertaken for Mr. Gatewood, he really could not see why Mr. Gatewood should interest himself concerning the whereabouts of Miss Southerland, the young man had nothing to say, and escaped as soon as possible, enraged at himself, at Mr. Keen, and vaguely holding the entire world guilty of conspiracy.

He had no definite idea of what he wanted, except that his desire to see Miss Southerland again seemed out of all proportion to any reasonable motive for seeing her. Occasional fits of disgust with himself for what he had done were varied with moody hours of speculation. Suppose Mr. Keen did find his ideal? What of it? He no longer wanted to see her. He had no use for her. The savor of the enterprise had gone stale in his mouth; he was by turns worried, restless, melancholy, sulky, uneasy. A vast emptiness pervaded his life. He smoked more and more and ate less and less. He even disliked to see others eat, particularly Kerns.

And one exquisite May morning he came down to breakfast and found the unspeakable Kerns immersed in grapefruit, calm, well balanced, and bland.

"How-de-dee, dear friend?" said that gentleman affably. "Any news from Cupid this beautiful May morning?"

"No; and I don't want any," returned Gatewood, sorting his mail with a scowl and waving away his fruit.

"Tut, tut! Lovers must be patient. Dearie will be found some day—"

"Some day," snarled Gatewood, "I shall destroy you, Tommy."

"Naughty! Naughty!" reflected Kerns, pensively assaulting the breakfast food. "Lovey must *not* worry; Dovey shall be found, and all will be joy and gingerbread.... If you throw that orange I'll run screaming to the governors. Aren't you ashamed—just because you're in a love tantrum!"

"One more word and you get it!"

"May I sing as I trifle with this frugal fare, dear friend? My heart is *so* happy that I should love to warble a few wild notes—"

He paused to watch his badgered victim dispose of a Martini.

"I wonder," he mused, "if you'd like me to tell you what a cocktail before breakfast does to the lining of your stomach? Would you?"

"No. I suppose it's what the laundress does to my linen. What do I care?"

"*Don't* be a short sport, Jack."

"Well, I don't care for the game you put me up against. Do you know what has happened?"

"I really don't, dear friend. The Tracer of Lost Persons has not found her—*has* he?"

"He says he has," retorted Gatewood sullenly, pulling a crumpled telegram from his pocket and casting it upon the table. "I don't want to see her; I'm not interested. I never saw but one girl in my life who interested me in the slightest; and she's employed to help in this ridiculous search."

Kerns, meanwhile, had smoothed out the telegram and was intently perusing it:

"*John Gatewood, Lenox Club, Fifth Avenue:*
"Person probably discovered. Call here as soon as possible.

W. KEEN."

"*What* do you make of that?" demanded Gatewood hoarsely.

"Make of it? Why, it's true enough, I fancy. Go and see, and if it's she, be hers!"

"I won't! I don't want to see any ideal! I don't want to marry. Why do you try to make me marry somebody?"

"Because it's good for you, dear friend. Otherwise you'll go to the doggy-dogs. You don't realize how much worry you are to me."

"Confound it! Why don't *you* marry? Why didn't I ask you that when you put me up to all this foolishness? What right have you to—"

"Tut, friend! *I* know there's no woman alive fit to wed me and spend her life in stealing kisses from me. *I* have no ideal. *You* have an ideal."

"I haven't!"

"Oh, yes, dear friend, there's a stub in your check book to prove it. You simply bet \$5,000 that your ideal existed. You've won. Go and be her joy and sunshine."

"I'll put an end to this whole business," said Gatewood wrathfully, "and I'll do it now!"

"Bet you that you're engaged within the week!" said Kerns with a placid smile.

The other swung around savagely: "What will you bet, Tommy? You may have what odds you please. I'll make you sit up for this."

"I'll bet you," answered Kerns, deliberately, "an entire silver dinner service against a saddle horse for the bride."

"That's a fool bet!" snapped Gatewood. "What do you mean?"

"Oh, if you don't care to—"

"What do I want of a silver service? But, all right; I'll bet you anything."

"*She'll* want it," replied Kerns significantly, booking the bet. "I may as well canter out to Tiffany's this morning, I fancy.... Where are you going, Jack?"

"To see Keen and confess what an ass I've been!" returned Gatewood sullenly, striding across the breakfast room to take his hat and gloves from the rack. And out he went, mad all over.

On his way up the avenue he attempted to formulate the humiliating confession which already he shrank from. But it had to be done. He simply could not stand the prospect of being notified month after month that a lady would be on view somewhere. It was like going for a fitting; it was horrible. Besides, what use was it? Within a week or two an enormous and utterly inexplicable emptiness had yawned before him, revealing life as a hollow delusion. He no longer cared.

Immersed in bitter reflection, he climbed the familiar stairway and sent his card to Mr. Keen, and in due time he was ushered into the presence of the Tracer of Lost Persons.

"Mr. Keen," he began, with a headlong desire to get it over and be done with it, "I may as well tell you how impossible it is for you, or anybody, to find that person I described—"

Mr. Keen raised an expostulatory hand, smiling indulgence.

"It is more than possible, Mr. Gatewood, more than probable; it is almost an accomplished fact. In other words, I think I may venture to congratulate you and say that she is found."

"Now, *how* can she be found, when there isn't—"

"Mr. Gatewood, the magician will always wave his magic wand for you and show you his miracles for the price of admission. But for that price he does not show you how he works his miracles," said Keen, laughing.

"But I ought to tell you," persisted Gatewood, "that it is utterly impossible you should find the person I wished to discover, because she—"

"I can only prove that you are wrong," smiled Keen, rising from his easy chair.

"Mr. Keen," said the young man earnestly, "I have been more or less of a chump at times. One of those times was when I came here on this errand. All I desire, now, is to let the matter rest as it is. I am satisfied, and you have lost nothing. Nor have you found anything or anybody. You think you have, but you haven't. I do not wish you to continue the search, or to send me any further reports. I want to forget the whole miserable matter—to be free—to feel myself freed from any obligations to that irritating person I asked you to find."

The Tracer regarded him very gravely.

"Is that your wish, Mr. Gatewood? I can scarcely credit it."

"It is. I've been a fool; I simply want to stop being one if anybody will permit it."

"And you decline to attempt to identify the very beautiful person we have discovered to be the individual for whom you asked us to search?"

"I do. She may be beautiful; but I know well enough she can't compare with—some one."

"I am sorry," said Keen thoughtfully. "We take so much pride in these matters. When one of my agents discovered where this person was, I was rather—happy; for I have taken a peculiar personal interest in your case. However—"

"Mr. Keen," said Gatewood, "if you could understand how ashamed and mortified I am at my own conduct."

Keen gazed pensively out of the window. "I also am sorry; Miss Southerland was to have received a handsome bonus for her discovery—"

"Miss S-S-S-S-outherland!"

"*Exactly*; without quite so many *S's*," said Keen, smiling.

"Did *she* discover that—that person?" exclaimed the young man, startled.

"She thinks she has. I am not sure she is correct; but I am absolutely certain that Miss Southerland could eventually discover the person you were in search of. It seems a little hard on her—just on the eve of success—to lose. But that can't be helped now."

Gatewood, more excited and uncomfortable than he had ever been in all his life, watched Keen intently.

"Too bad, too bad," muttered the Tracer to himself. "The child needs the encouragement. It meant a thousand dollars to her—" He shrugged his shoulders, looked up, and, as though rather surprised to see Gatewood still there, smiled an impersonal smile and offered his hand in adieu. Gatewood winced.

"Could I—I see Miss Southerland?" he asked.

"I am afraid not. She is at this moment following my instructions to— but that cannot interest you now—"

"Yes, it does!—if you don't mind. Where is she? I—I'll take a look at the person she discovered; I will, really."

"Why, it's only this: I suspected that you might identify a person whom I had reason to believe was to be found every morning riding in the Park. So Miss Southerland has been riding there every day. Yesterday she came here, greatly excited—"

"Yes—yes—go on!"

Keen gazed dreamily at the sunny window. "She thought she had found your—er—the person. So I said you would meet her on the bridle path, near—but that's of no interest now—"

"Near where?" demanded Gatewood, suppressing inexplicable excitement. And as Keen said nothing: "I'll go; I want to go, I really do! Can't—can't a fellow change his mind? Oh, I know you think I'm a lunatic, and there's plenty of reason, too!"

Keen studied him calmly. "Yes, plenty of reason, plenty of reason, Mr. Gatewood. But do you suppose you are the only one? I know another who was perfectly sane two weeks ago."

The young man waited impatiently; the Tracer paced the room, gray head bent, delicate, wrinkled hands clasped loosely behind his bent back.

"You have horses at the Whip and Spur Club," he said abruptly. "Suppose you ride out and see how close Miss Southerland has come to solving our problem."

Gatewood seized the offered hand and wrung it with a fervor out of all reason; and it is curious that the Tracer of Lost Persons did not appear to be astonished.

"You're rather impetuous—like your father," he said slowly. "I knew him; so I've ventured to trust his son—even when I heard how aimlessly he was living his life. Mr. Gatewood! May I ask you something—as an old friend of your father?"

The young man nodded, subdued, perplexed, scarcely understanding.

"It's only this: If you *do* find the woman you could love—in the Park—to-day—come back to me some day and let me tell you all those foolish, trite, tiresome things that I should have told a son of mine. I am so old that you will not take offense—you will not mind listening to me, or forgetting the dull, prosy things I say about the curse of idleness, and the habits of cynical thinking, and the perils of vacant-minded indulgence. You will forgive me—and you will forget me. That will be as it should be. Good-by."

Gatewood, sobered, surprised, descended the stairs and hailed a hansom.

CHAPTER VI

All the way to the Whip and Spur Club he sat buried in a reverie from which, at intervals, he started, aroused by the heavy, expectant beating of his own pulses. But what did he expect, in Heaven's name? Not the discovery of a woman who had never existed. Yet his excitement and impatience grew as he watched the saddling of his horse; and when at length he rode out into the sunshine and cantered through the Park entrance, his sense of impending events and his expectancy amounted to a fever which colored his face attractively.

He saw her almost immediately. Her horse was walking slowly in the dappled shadows of the new foliage; she, listless in her saddle, sometimes watching the throngs of riders passing, at moments turning to gaze into the woodland vistas where, over the thickets of flowering shrubbery, orioles and robins sped flashing on tinted wings from shadow to sun, from sun to shadow. But she looked up as he drew bridle and wheeled his mount beside her; and, "Oh!" she said, flushing in recognition.

"I have missed you terribly," he said quietly.

It was dreamy weather, even for late spring: the scent of lilacs and mock-orange hung heavy as incense along the woods. Their voices unconsciously found the key to harmonize with it all.

She said: "Well, I think I have succeeded. In a few moments she will be passing. I do not know her name; she rides a big roan. She is very beautiful, Mr. Gatewood."

He said: "I am perfectly certain we shall find her. I doubted it until now. But now I know."

"Oh-h, but I *may* be wrong," she protested.

"No; you cannot be."

She looked up at him.

"You can have no idea how happy you make me," he said unsteadily.

"But—I—but I may be all wrong—dreadfully wrong!"

"Y-es; you may be, but I shall not be. For do you know that I have already seen her in the Park?"

"When?" she demanded incredulously, then turned in the saddle, repeating: "Where? Did she pass? How perfectly stupid of me! And *was* she the—the right one?"

"She *is* the right one.... Don't turn: I have seen her. Ride on: I want to say something—if I can."

"No, no," she insisted. "I must know whether I was right—"

"You *are* right—but you don't know it yet.... Oh, very well, then; we'll turn if you insist." And he wheeled his mount as she did, riding at her bridle again.

"How can you take it so coolly—so indifferently?" she said. "Where has that woman—where has she gone? ... Never mind; she must turn and pass us sooner or later, for she lives uptown. *What* are you laughing at, Mr. Gatewood?"—in annoyed surprise.

"I am laughing at myself. Oh, I'm so many kinds of a fool—you can't think how many, and it's no use!"

She stared, astonished; he shook his head.

"No, you don't understand yet. But you will. Listen to me: this very beautiful lady you have discovered is nothing to me!"

"Nothing—to you!" she faltered. Two pink spots of indignation burned in her cheeks. "How—how dare you say that!—after all that has been done—all that you have said. You said you loved her; you *did* say so—to *me!*"

"I don't love her now."

"But you did!" Tears of pure vexation started; she faced him, eye to eye, thoroughly incensed.

"What sort of man are you?" she said under her breath. "Your friend Mr. Kerns is wrong. You are not worth saving from yourself."

"Kerns!" he repeated, angry and amazed. "What the deuce has Kerns to do with this affair?"

She stared, then, realizing her indiscretion, bit her lip, and spurred forward. But he put his horse to a gallop, and they pounded along in silence. In a little while she drew bridle and looked around coldly, grave with displeasure.

"Mr. Kerns came to us before you did. He said you would probably come, and he begged us to strain every effort in your behalf, because, he said, your happiness absolutely depended upon our finding for you the woman you were seeking.... And I tried—very hard—and now she's found. You admit that—and *now* you say—"

"I say that one of these balmy summer days I'll assassinate Tommy Kerns!" broke in Gatewood. "What on earth possessed that prince of butters-in to go to Mr. Keen?"

"To save you from yourself!" retorted the girl in a low, exasperated voice. "He did not say what threatened you; he is a good friend for a man to have. But we soon found out what you were—a man well born, well bred, full of brilliant possibility, who was slowly becoming an idle, cynical, self-centered egoist—a man who, lacking the lash of need or the spur of ambition, was degenerating through the sheer uselessness and inanity of his life. And, oh, the pity of it! For Mr. Keen and I have taken a—a curiously personal interest in you—in your case. I say, the pity of it!"

Astounded, dumb under her stinging words, he rode beside her through the brilliant sunshine, wheeled mechanically as she turned her horse, and rode north again.

"And now—*now!*" she said passionately, "you turn on the woman you loved! Oh, you are not worth it!"

"You are quite right," he said, turning very white under her scorn. "Almost all you have said is true enough, I fancy. I amount to nothing; I am idle, cynical, selfish. The emptiness of such a life requires a stimulant; even a fool abhors a vacuum. So I drink—not so very much yet—but more than I realize. And it is close enough to a habit to worry me.... Yes, almost all you say is true; Kerns knows it; I know it—now that you have told me.

You see, he couldn't tell me, because I should not have believed him. But I believe you—all you say, except one thing. And that is only a glimmer of decency left in me—not that I make any merit of it. No, it is merely instinctive. For I have *not* turned on the woman I loved."

Her face was pale as her level eyes met him:

"You said she was nothing to you.... Look there! Do you see her? Do you see?"

Her voice broke nervously as he swung around to stare at a rider bearing down at a gallop—a woman on a big roan, tearing along through the spring sunshine, passing them with wind-flushed cheeks and dark, incurious eyes, while her powerful horse carried her on, away through the quivering light and shadow of the woodland vista.

"Is *that* the person?"

"Y-es," she faltered. "Was I wrong?"

"Quite wrong, Miss Southerland."

"But—but you said you had seen her here this morning!"

"Yes, I have."

"Did you speak to her before you met me?"

"No—not before I met you."

"Then you have not spoken to her. Is she still here in the Park?"

"Yes, she is still here."

The girl turned on him excitedly: "Do you mean to say that you will not speak to her?"

"I had rather not—"

"And your happiness depends on your speaking?"

"Yes."

"Then it is cowardly not to speak."

"Oh, yes, it is cowardly.... If you wish me to speak to her I will. Shall I?"

"Yes.... Show her to me."

"And you think that such a man as I am has a right to speak of love to her?"

"I—we believe it will be your salvation. Mr. Kerns says you must marry her to be happy. Mr. Keen told me yesterday that it only needed a word from the right woman to put you on your mettle.... And—and that is my opinion."

"Then in charity say that word!" he breathed, bending toward her. "Can't you see? Can't you understand? Don't you know that from the moment I looked into your eyes I loved you?"

"How—how dare you!" she stammered, crimsoning.

"God knows," he said wistfully. "I am a coward. I don't know how I dared. Good-by...."

He walked his horse a little way, then launched him into a gallop, tearing on and on, sun, wind, trees swimming, whirling like a vision, hearing nothing, feeling nothing, save the leaden pounding of his pulse and the breathless, terrible tightening in his throat.

When he cleared his eyes and looked around he was quite alone, his horse walking under the trees and breathing heavily.

At first he laughed, and the laugh was not pleasant. Then he said aloud: "It is worth having lived for, after all!"—and was silent. And again: "I could expect nothing; she was perfectly right to side-step a fool.... And *such* a fool!"

The distant gallop of a horse, dulled on the soft soil, but coming nearer, could not arouse him from the bitter depths he had sunk in; not even when the sound ceased beside him, and horse snorted recognition to horse. It was only when a light touch rested on his arm that he looked up heavily, caught his breath.

"Where is the other—woman?" she gasped.

"There never was any other."

"You said—"

"I said I loved my ideal. I did not know she existed—until I saw you."

"Then—then we were searching for—"

"A vision. But it was your face that haunted me.... And I am not worth it, as you say. And I know it ... for you have opened my eyes."

He drew bridle, forcing a laugh. "I cut a sorry figure in your life; be patient; I am going out of it now." And he swung his horse. At the same moment she did the same, making a demitour and meeting him halfway, confronting him.

"Do you—you mean to ride out of my life without a word?" she asked unsteadily.

"Good-by." He offered his hand, stirring his horse forward; she leaned lightly over and laid both hands in his. Then, her face surging in color, she lifted her beautiful dark eyes to his as the horses approached, nearer, nearer, until, as they passed, flank brushing flank, her eyes fell, then closed as she swayed toward him, and clung, her young lips crushed to his.

There was nobody to witness it except the birds and squirrels—nobody but a distant mounted policeman, who almost fainted away in his saddle.

Oh, it was awful, awful! Apparently she had been kissed speechless, for she said nothing. The man fool did all the talking, incoherently enough, but evidently satisfactory to her, judging from the way she looked at him, and blushed and blushed, and touched her eyes with a bit of cambric at intervals.

All the policeman heard as they passed him was: "I'm going to give you this horse, and Kerns is to give us our silver; and what do you think, my darling?"

"W-what?"

But they had already passed out of earshot; and in a few moments the shady, sun-flecked bridle path was deserted again save for the birds and squirrels, and a single mounted policeman, rigid, wild eyed, twisting his mustache and breathing hard.

CHAPTER VII

The news of Gatewood's fate filled Kerns with a pleasure bordering upon melancholy. It was his work; he had done it; it was good for Gatewood too—time for him to stop his irresponsible cruise through life, lower sail, heave to, set his signals, and turn over matters to this charming pilot.

And now they would come into port together and anchor somewhere east of Fifth Avenue—which, Kerns reflected, was far more proper a place for Gatewood than somewhere east of Suez, where young men so often sail.

And yet, and yet there was something melancholy in the pleasure he experienced. Gatewood was practically lost to him. He knew what might be expected from engaged men and newly married men. Gatewood's club life was ended—for a while; and there was no other man with whom he cared to embark for those brightly lighted harbors twinkling east of Suez across the metropolitan wastes.

"It's very generous of me to get him married," he said frequently to himself, rather sadly. "I did it pretty well, too. It only shows that women have no particular monopoly in the realms of diplomacy and finesse; in fact, if a man really chooses to put his mind to such matters, he can make it no trumps and win out behind a bum ace and a guarded knave."

He was pleased with himself. He followed Gatewood about explaining how good he had been to him. An enthusiasm for marrying off his friends began to germinate within him; he tried it on Darrell, on Barnes, on Yates, but was turned down and severely stung.

Then one day Harren of the Philippine Scouts turned up at the club, and they held a determined reunion until daylight, and they told each other all about it all and what upper-cuts life had handed out to them since the troopship sailed.

And after the rosy glow had deepened to a more gorgeous hue in the room, and the electric lights had turned into silver pinwheels; and after they had told each other the story of their lives, and the last siphon fizzed impotently when urged beyond its capacity, Kerns arose and extended his hand, and Harren took it. And they executed a song resembling "Auld Lang Syne."

"Ole man," said Kerns reproachfully, "there's one thing you have been deuced careful not to mention, and that is about what happened to you three years ago—"

"Steady!" said Harren; "there is nothing to tell, Tommy."

"Nothing?"

"Nothing. I never saw her again. I never shall."

Kerns looked long and unsteadily upon his friend; then very gravely fumbled in his pocket and drew forth the business card of Westrel Keen, Tracer of Lost Persons.

"That," he said, "will be about all." And he bestowed the card upon Harren with magnificent condescension.

And about five o'clock the following afternoon Harren found the card among various effects of his, scattered over his dresser.

It took him several days to make up his mind to pay any attention to the card or the suggestion it contained. He scarcely considered it seriously even when, passing along Fifth Avenue one sunny afternoon, he chanced to glance up and see the sign

KEEN & CO.
TRACERS OF LOST PERSONS

staring him in the face.

He continued his stroll, but that evening, upon mere impulse, he sat down and wrote a letter to Mr. Keen.

The next morning's mail brought a reply and an appointment for an interview on Wednesday week. Harren tossed the letter aside, satisfied to let the matter go, because his leave expired on Tuesday, and the appointment was impossible.

On Sunday, however, the melancholy of the deserted club affected his spirits. A curious desire to see this Tracer of Lost Persons seized him with a persistence unaccountable. He slept poorly, haunted with visions.

On Monday he went to see Mr. Keen. It could do no harm; it was too late to do either harm or good, for his leave expired the next day at noon.

The business of Keen & Co., Tracers of Lost Persons, had grown to enormous proportions; appointments for a personal interview with Mr. Keen were now made a week in advance, so when young Harren sent in his card, the gayly liveried negro servant came back presently, threading his way through the waiting throng with pomp and circumstance, and returned the card to Harren with the date of appointment rewritten in ink across the top. The day named was Wednesday. On Tuesday Harren's leave expired.

"That won't do," said the young man brusquely; "I must see Mr. Keen to-day. I wrote last week for an appointment."

The liveried darky was polite but obdurate.

"Dis here am de 'pintment, suh," he explained persuasively.

"But I want to see Mr. Keen at once," insisted Harren.

"Hit ain't no use, suh," said the darky respectfully; "dey's mi'ions an' mi'ions ob gemmen jess a-settin' roun' an' waitin' foh Mistuh Keen. In dis here perfeshion, suh, de fustest gemman dat has a 'pintment is de fustest gemman dat kin see Mistuh Keen. You is a military gemman yohse'f, Cap'm Harren, an' you is aware dat precedence am de rigger."

The bronzed young man smiled, glanced at the date of appointment written on his card, which also bore his own name followed by the letters U. S. A., then his amused gray eyes darkened and he glanced leisurely around the room, where a dozen or more assorted people sat waiting their turns to interview Mr. Keen: all sorts and conditions of people—smartly gowned women, an anxious-browed business man or two, a fat German truck driver, his greasy cap on his knees, a surly policeman, and an old Irishwoman, wearing a shawl and an ancient straw bonnet. Harren's eyes reverted to the darky.

"You will explain to Mr. Keen," he said, "that I am an army officer on leave, and that I am obliged to start for Manila to-morrow. This is my excuse for asking an immediate interview; and if it's not a good enough excuse I must cancel this appointment, that is all."

The darky stood, irresolute, inclined to argue, but something in the steel-gray eyes of the man set him in involuntary motion, and he went away once more with the young man's message. Harren turned and walked back to his seat. The old woman with the faded shawl was explaining volubly to a handsomely gowned woman beside her that she was looking for her boy, Danny; that her name was Mrs. Regan, and that she washed for the aristocracy of Hunter's Point at a liberal price per dozen, using no deleterious substances in the suds as Heaven was her witness.

The German truck driver, moved by this confidence, was stirred to begin an endless account of his domestic misfortunes, and old Mrs. Regan, becoming impatient, had already begun to interrupt with an account of Regan's recent hoisting on the wings of a premature petard, when the dark servant reappeared.

"Mistuh Keen will receive you, suh," he whispered, leading the way into a large room where dozens of attractive young girls sat very busily engaged at typewriting machines. Door after door they passed, all numbered on the ground-glass panes, then swung to the right, where the darky bowed him into a big, handsomely furnished room flooded with the morning sun. A tall, gray man, faultlessly dressed in a gray frock suit and wearing white spats, turned from the breezy, open window to inspect him; the lean, well groomed, rather lank type of gentleman suggesting a retired colonel of cavalry; unmistakably well bred from the ends of his drooping gray mustache to the last button on his immaculate spats.

"Captain Harren?" he said pleasantly.

"Mr. Keen?"

They bowed. Young Harren drew from his pocket a card. It was the business card of Keen & Co., and, glancing up at Mr. Keen, he read it aloud, carefully:

KEEN & CO.

TRACERS OF LOST PERSONS

Keen & Co. are prepared to locate the

whereabouts of anybody on earth.

No charges will be made unless

the person searched for

is found.

Blanks on Application.

WESTREL KEEN, Manager.

Harren raised his clear, gray eyes. "I assume this statement to be correct, Mr. Keen?"

"You may safely assume so," said Mr. Keen, smiling.

"Does this statement include *all* that you are prepared to undertake?"

The Tracer of Lost Persons inspected him coolly. "What more is there, Captain Harren? I undertake to find lost people. I even undertake to find the undiscovered ideals of young people who have failed to meet them. What further field would you suggest?" Harren glanced at the card which he held in his gloved hand; then, very slowly, he re-read, "the whereabouts of anybody *on earth*," accenting the last two words deliberately as he encountered Keen's piercing gaze again.

"Well?" asked Mr. Keen laughingly, "is not that sufficient? Our clients could scarcely expect us to invade heaven in our search for the vanished."

"There are other regions," said Harren.

"*Exactly.* Sit down, sir. There is a row of bookcases for your amusement. Please help yourself while I clear decks for action."

Harren stood fingering the card, his gray eyes lost in retrospection; then he sauntered over to the bookcases, scanning the titles. The Searcher for Lost Persons studied him for a moment or two, turned, and began to pace the room. After a moment or two he touched a bell. A sweet-faced young girl entered; she was gowned in black and wore a white collar, and cuffs turned back over her hands.

"Take this memorandum," he said. The girl picked up a pencil and pad, and Mr. Keen, still pacing the room, dictated in a quiet voice as he walked to and fro:

"Mrs. Regan's Danny is doing six months in Butte, Montana. Break it to her as mercifully as possible. He is a bad one. We make no charge. The truck driver, Becker, can find his wife at her mother's house, Leonia, New Jersey. Tell him to be less pig-headed or she'll go for good some day. Ten dollars. Mrs. M., No. 36001, can find her missing butler in service at 79 Vine Street, Hartford, Connecticut. She may notify the police whenever she wishes. His portrait is No. 170529, Rogues' Gallery. Five hundred dollars. Miss K. (No. 3679) may send her letter, care of Cisneros & Co., Rio, where the person she is seeking has gone into the coffee business. If she decides that she really does love him, he'll come back fast enough. Two hundred and fifty dollars. Mr. W. (No. 3620) must go to the morgue for further information. His repentance is too late; but he can see that there is a decent burial. The charge: one thousand dollars to the Florence Mission. You may add that we possess his full record."

The Tracer paused and waited for the stenographer to finish. When she looked up: "Who else is waiting?" he asked.

The girl read over the initials and numbers.

"Tell that policeman that Kid Conroy sails on the *Carania* to-morrow. Fifty dollars. There is nothing definite in the other cases. Report progress and send out a general alarm for the cashier inquired for by No. 3608. You will find details in vol. xxxix under B."

"Is that all, Mr. Keen?"

"Yes. I'm going to be very busy with"—turning slowly toward Harren—"with Captain Harren, of the Philippine Scouts, until to-morrow—a very complicated case, Miss Borrow, involving cipher codes and photography—"

CHAPTER VIII

Harren started, then walked slowly to the center of the room as the pretty stenographer passed out with a curious level glance at him.

"Why do you say that photography plays a part in my case?" he asked.

"Doesn't it?"

"Yes. But how—"

"Oh, I only guessed it," said Keen with a smile. "I made another guess that your case involved a cipher code. Does it?"

"Y-es," said the young man, astonished, "but I don't see—"

"It also involves the occult," observed Keen calmly. "We may need Miss Borrow to help us."

Almost staggered, Harren stared at the Tracer out of his astonished gray eyes until that gentleman laughed outright and seated himself, motioning Harren to do likewise.

"Don't be surprised, Captain Harren," he said. "I suppose you have no conception of our business, no realization of its scope—its network of information bureaus all over the civilized world, its myriad sources of information, the immensity of its delicate machinery, the endless data and the infinitesimal details we have at our command. You, of course, have no idea of the number of people of every sort and condition who are in our employ, of the ceaseless yet inoffensive surveillance we maintain. For example, when your letter came last week I called up the person who has charge of the army list. There you were, Kenneth Harren, Captain Philippine Scouts, with the date of your graduation from West Point. Then I called up a certain department devoted to personal detail, and in five minutes I knew your entire history. I then touched another electric button, and in a minute I had before me the date of your arrival in New York, your present address, and"—he looked up quizzically at Harren—"and several items of general information, such as your peculiar use of your camera, and the list of books on Psychical Phenomena and Cryptograms which you have been buying—"

Harren flushed up. "Do you mean to say that I have been spied upon, Mr. Keen?"

"No more than anybody else who comes to us as a client. There was nothing offensive in the surveillance." He shrugged his shoulders and made a deprecating gesture. "Ours is a business, my dear sir, like any other. We, of course, are obliged to know about people who call on us. Last week you wrote me, and I immediately set every wheel in motion; in other words, I had you under observation from the day I received your letter to this very moment."

"You learned much concerning me?" asked Harren quietly.

"*Exactly*, my dear sir."

"But," continued Harren with a touch of malice, "you didn't learn that my leave is up tomorrow, did you?"

"Yes, I learned that, too."

"Then why did you give me an appointment for the day after to-morrow?" demanded the young man bluntly.

The Tracer looked him squarely in the eye. "Your leave is to be extended," he said.

"What?"

"*Exactly.* It has been extended one week."

"How do you know that?"

"You applied for extension, did you not?"

"Yes," said Harren, turning red, "but I don't see how you knew that I—"

"By cable?"

"Y-yes."

"There's a cablegram in your rooms at this very moment," said the Tracer carelessly. "You have the extension you desired. And now, Captain Harren," with a singularly pleasant smile, "what can I do to help you to a pursuit of that true happiness which is guaranteed for all good citizens under our Constitution?"

Captain Harren crossed his long legs, dropping one knee over the other, and deliberately surveyed his interrogator.

"I really have no right to come to you," he said slowly. "Your prospectus distinctly states that Keen & Co. undertake to find *live* people, and I don't know whether the person I am seeking is alive or or—"

His steady voice faltered; the Tracer watched him curiously.

"Of course, that is important," he said. "If she is dead—"

"*She!*"

"Didn't you say 'she,' Captain?"

"No, I did not."

"I beg your pardon, then, for anticipating you," said the Tracer carelessly.

"Anticipating? *How* do you know it is not a man I am in search of?" demanded Harren.

"Captain Harren, you are unmarried and have no son; you have no father, no brother, no sister. Therefore I infer—several things—for example, that you are in love."

"I? In love?"

"Desperately, Captain."

"Your inferences seem to satisfy you, at least," said Harren almost sullenly, "but they don't satisfy me—clever as they appear to be."

"*Exactly.* Then you are *not* in love?"

"I don't know whether I am or not."

"I do," said the Tracer of Lost Persons.

"Then you know more than I," retorted Harren sharply.

"But that is my business—to know more than you do," returned Mr. Keen patiently. "Else why are you here to consult me?" And as Harren made no reply: "I have seen thousands and thousands of people in love. I have reduced the superficial muscular phenomena and facial symptomatic aspect of such people to an exact science founded upon a schedule approximating the Bertillon system of records. And," he added, smiling, "out of the twenty-seven known vocal variations your voice betrays twenty-five unmistakable symptoms; and out of the sixteen reflex muscular symptoms your face has furnished six, your hands three, your limbs and feet six. Then there are other superficial symptoms—"

"Good heavens!" broke in Harren; "how can you prove a man to be in love when he himself doesn't know whether he is or not? If a man isn't in love no Bertillon system can make him so; and if a man doesn't know whether or not he is in love, who can tell him the truth?"

"I can," said the Tracer calmly.

"What! When I tell you I myself don't know?"

"*That*," said the Tracer, smiling, "is the final and convincing symptom. *You* don't know. *I* know because you *don't* know. That is the easiest way to be sure that you are in love, Captain Harren, because you always are when you are not sure. You'd know if you were *not* in love. Now, my dear sir, you may lay your case confidently before me."

Harren, unconvinced, sat frowning and biting his lip and twisting his short, crisp mustache which the tropical sun had turned straw color and curly.

"I feel like a fool to tell you," he said. "I'm not an imaginative man, Mr. Keen; I'm not fanciful, not sentimental. I'm perfectly healthy, perfectly normal—a very busy man in my profession, with no time and no inclination to fall in love."

"Just the sort of man who does it," commented Keen. "Continue."

Harren fidgeted about in his chair, looked out of the window, squinted at the ceiling, then straightened up, folding his arms with sudden determination.

"I'd rather be boloed than tell you," he said. "Perhaps, after all, I *am* a lunatic; perhaps I've had a touch of the Luzon sun and don't know it."

"I'll be the judge," said the Tracer, smiling.

"Very well, sir. Then I'll begin by telling you that I've seen a ghost."

"There are such things," observed Keen quietly.

"Oh, I don't mean one of those fabled sheeted creatures that float about at night; I mean a phantom—a real phantom—in the sunlight—standing before my very eyes in broad day! ... Now do you feel inclined to go on with my case, Mr. Keen?"

"Certainly," replied the Tracer gravely. "Please continue, Captain Harren."

"All right, then. Here's the beginning of it: Three years ago, here in New

York, drifting along Fifth Avenue with the crowd, I looked up to encounter the most wonderful pair of eyes that I ever beheld—that any living man ever beheld! The most—wonderfully—beautiful—"

He sat so long immersed in retrospection that the Tracer said: "I am listening, Captain," and the Captain woke up with a start.

"What was I saying? How far had I proceeded?"

"Only to the eyes."

"Oh, I see! The eyes were dark, sir, dark and lovely beyond any power of description. The hair was also dark—very soft and thick and—er—wavy and dark. The face was extremely youthful, and ornamental to the uttermost verges of a beauty so exquisite that, were I to attempt to formulate for you its individual attractions, I should, I fear, transgress the strictly rigid bounds of that reticence which becomes a gentleman in complete possession of his senses."

"*Exactly*," mused the Tracer.

"Also," continued Captain Harren, with growing animation, "to attempt to describe her figure would be utterly useless, because I am a practical man and not a poet, nor do I read poetry or indulge in futile novels or romances of any description. Therefore I can only add that it was a figure, a poise, absolutely faultless, youthful, beautiful, erect, wholesome, gracious, graceful, charmingly buoyant and—well, I cannot describe her figure, and I shall not try."

"*Exactly*; don't try."

"No," said Harren mournfully, "it is useless"; and he relapsed into enchanted retrospection.

"Who was she?" asked Mr. Keen softly.

"I don't know."

"You never again saw her?"

"Mr. Keen, I—I am not ill-bred, but I simply could not help following her. She was so b-b-beautiful that it hurt; and I only wanted to look at her; I didn't mind being hurt. So I walked on and on, and sometimes I'd pass her and sometimes I'd let her pass me, and when she wasn't looking I'd look—not offensively, but just because I couldn't help it. And all the time my senses were humming like a top and my heart kept jumping to get into my throat, and I hadn't a notion where I was going or what time it was or what day of the week. She didn't see me; she didn't dream that I was looking at her; she didn't know me from any of the thousand silk-hatted, frock-coated men who passed and repassed her on Fifth Avenue. And when she went into St. Berold's Church, I went, too, and I stood where I could see her and where she couldn't see me. It was like a touch of the Luzon sun, Mr. Keen. And then she came out and got into a Fifth Avenue stage, and

I got in, too. And whenever she looked away I looked at her—without the slightest offense, Mr. Keen, until, once, she caught my eye—"

He passed an unsteady hand over his forehead.

"For a moment we looked full at one another," he continued. "I got red, sir; I felt it, and I couldn't look away. And when I turned color like a blooming beet, she began to turn pink like a rosebud, and she looked full into my eyes with such a wonderful purity, such exquisite innocence, that I— I never felt so near—er—heaven in my life! No, sir, not even when they ambushed us at Manoa Wells—but that's another thing—only it is part of this business."

He tightened his clasped hands over his knee until the knuckles whitened.

"*That's* my story, Mr. Keen," he said crisply.

"All of it?"

Harren looked at the floor, then at Keen: "No, not all. You'll think me a lunatic if I tell you all."

"Oh, you saw her again?"

"N-never! That is—"

"Never?"

"Not in—in the flesh."

"Oh, in dreams?"

Harren stirred uneasily. "I don't know what you call them. I have seen her since—in the sunlight, in the open, in my quarters in Manila, standing there perfectly distinct, looking at me with such strange, beautiful eyes—"

"Go on," said the Tracer, nodding.

"What else is there to say?" muttered Harren.

"You saw her—or a phantom which resembled her. Did she speak?"

"No."

"Did you speak to her?"

"N-no. Once I held out my—my arms."

"What happened?"

"She wasn't there," said Harren simply.

"She vanished?"

"No—I don't know. I—I didn't see her any more."

"Didn't she fade?"

"No. I can't explain. She—there was only myself in the room."

"How many times has she appeared to you?"

"A great many times."

"In your room?"

"Yes. And in the road under a vertical sun; in the forest, in the paddy fields. I have seen her passing through the hallway of a friend's house—

turning on the stair to look back at me! I saw her standing just back of the firing-line at Manoa Wells when we were preparing to rush the forts, and it scared me so that I jumped forward to draw her back. But—she wasn't there, Mr. Keen....

"On the transport she stood facing me on deck one moonlit evening for five minutes. I saw her in 'Frisco; she sat in the Pullman twice between Denver and this city. Twice in my room at the Vice-Regent she has sat opposite me at midday, so clear, so beautiful, so real that—that I could scarcely believe she was only a—a—" He hesitated.

"The apparition of her own subconscious self," said the Tracer quietly. "Science has been forced to admit such things, and, as you know, we are on the verge of understanding the alphabet of some of the unknown forces which we must some day reckon with."

Harren, tense, a trifle pale, gazed at him earnestly.

"Do *you* believe in such things?"

"How can I avoid believing?" said the Tracer. "Every day, in my profession, we have proof of the existence of forces for which we have as yet no explanation—or, at best, a very crude one. I have had case after case of premonition; case after case of dual and even multiple personality; case after case where apparitions played a vital part in the plot which was brought to me to investigate. I'll tell you this, Captain: I, personally, never saw an apparition, never was obsessed by premonitions, never received any communications from the outer void. But I have had to do with those who undoubtedly did. Therefore I listen with all seriousness and respect to what you tell me."

"Suppose," said Harren, growing suddenly red, "that I should tell you I have succeeded in photographing this phantom."

The Tracer sat silent. He was astounded, but he did not betray it.

"You have that photograph, Captain Harren?"

"Yes."

"Where is it?"

"In my rooms."

"You wish me to see it?"

Harren hesitated. "I—there is—seems to be—something almost sacred to me in that photograph.... You understand me, do you not? Yet, if it will help you in finding her—"

"Oh," said the Tracer in guileless astonishment, "you desire to find this young lady. Why?"

Harren stared. "Why? Why do I want to find her? Man, I—I can't live without her!"

"I thought you were not certain whether you really could be in love."

The hot color in the Captain's bronzed cheeks mounted to his hair.

"*Exactly*," purred the Tracer, looking out of the window. "Suppose we walk around to your rooms after luncheon. Shall we?"

Harren picked up his hat and gloves, hesitating, lingering on the threshold. "You *don't* think she is—a—dead?" he asked unsteadily.

"No," said Mr. Keen, "I don't."

"Because," said Harren wistfully, "her apparition is so superbly healthy and—and glowing with youth and life—"

"That is probably what sent it half the world over to confront you," said the Tracer gravely; "youth and life aglow with spiritual health. I think, Captain, that she has been seeing you, too, during these three years, but probably only in her dreams—memories of your encounters with her subconscious self floating over continents and oceans in a quest of which her waking intelligence is innocently unaware."

The Captain colored like a schoolboy, lingering at the door, hat in hand. Then he straightened up to the full height of his slim but powerful figure.

"At three?" he inquired bluntly.

"At three o'clock in your room, Hotel Vice-Regent. Good morning, Captain."

"Good morning," said Harren dreamily, and walked away, head bent, gray eyes lost in retrospection, and on his lean, bronzed, attractive face an afterglow of color wholly becoming.

CHAPTER IX

When the Tracer of Lost Persons entered Captain Harren's room at the Hotel Vice-Regent that afternoon he found the young man standing at a center table, pencil in hand, studying a sheet of paper which was covered with letters and figures.

The two men eyed one another in silence for a moment, then Harren pointed grimly to the confusion of letters and figures covering dozens of scattered sheets lying on the table.

"That's part of my madness," he said with a short laugh. "Can you make anything of such lunatic work?"

The Tracer picked up a sheet of paper covered with letters of the alphabet and Roman and Arabic numerals. He dropped it presently and picked up another comparatively blank sheet, on which were the following figures:

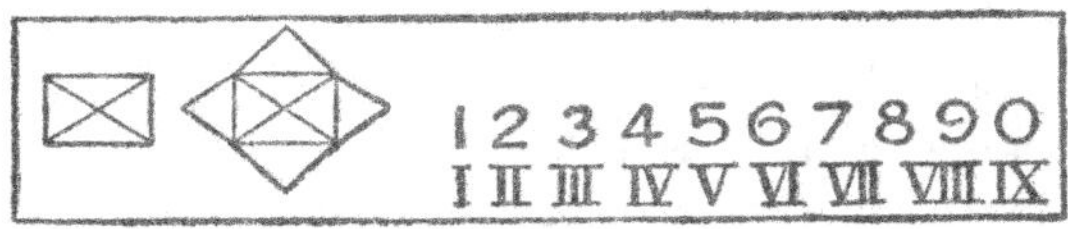

He studied it for a while, then glanced interrogatively at Harren.

"It's nothing," said Harren. "I've been groping for three years—but it's no use. That's lunatics' work." He wheeled squarely on his heels, looking straight at the Tracer. "*Do* you think I've had a touch of the sun?"

"No," said Mr. Keen, drawing a chair to the table. "Saner men than you or I have spent a lifetime over this so-called Seal of Solomon." He laid his finger on the two symbols—

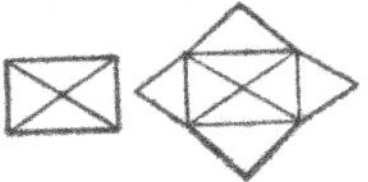

Then, looking across the table at Harren: "What," he asked, "has the Seal of Solomon to do with your case?"

"*She*—" muttered Harren, and fell silent.

The Tracer waited; Harren said nothing.

"Where is the photograph?"

Harren unlocked a drawer in the table, hesitated, looked strangely at the Tracer.

"Mr. Keen," he said, "there is nothing on earth I hold more sacred than this. There is only one thing in the world that could justify me in showing it to a living soul—my—my desire to find—her—"

"No," said Keen coolly, "that is not enough to justify you—the mere desire to find the living original of this apparition. Nothing could justify your showing it unless you love her."

Harren held the picture tightly, staring full at the Tracer. A dull flush mounted to his forehead, and very slowly he laid the picture before the Tracer of Lost Persons.

Minute after minute sped while the Tracer bent above the photograph, his finely modeled features absolutely devoid of expression. Harren had drawn his chair beside him, and now sat leaning forward, bronzed cheek resting in his hand, staring fixedly at the picture.

"When was this—this photograph taken?" asked the Tracer quietly.

"The day after I arrived in New York. I was here, alone, smoking my pipe and glancing over the evening paper just before dressing for dinner. It was growing rather dark in the room; I had not turned on the electric light. My camera lay on the table—there it is!—that kodak. I had taken a few snapshots on shipboard; there was one film left."

He leaned more heavily on his elbow, eyes fixed upon the picture.

"It was almost dark," he repeated. "I laid aside the evening paper and stood up, thinking about dressing for dinner, when my eyes happened to fall on the camera. It occurred to me that I might as well unload it, let the unused film go, and send the roll to be developed and printed; and I picked up the camera—"

"Yes," said the Tracer softly.

"I picked it up and was starting toward the window where there remained enough daylight to see by—"

The Tracer nodded gently.

"Then I saw *her!*" said Harren under his breath.

"Where?"

"There—standing by that window. You can see the window and curtain in the photograph."

The Tracer gazed intently at the picture.

"She looked at me," said Harren, steadying his voice. "She was as real as you are, and she stood there, smiling faintly, her dark, lovely eyes meeting mine."

"Did you speak?"

"No."

"How long did she remain there?"

"I don't know—time seemed to stop—the world—everything grew still.... Then, little by little, something began to stir under my stunned senses—that germ of misgiving, that dreadful doubt of my own sanity.... I scarcely knew what I was doing when I took the photograph; besides, it had grown quite dark, and I could scarcely see her." He drew himself erect with a nervous movement. "How on earth could I have obtained that photograph of her in the darkness?" he demanded.

"N-rays," said the Tracer coolly. "It has been done in France."

"Yes, from living people, but—"

"What the N-ray is in living organisms, we must call, for lack of a better term, the subaura in the phantom."

They bent over the photograph together. Presently the Tracer said: "She is very, very beautiful?"

Harren's dry lips unclosed, but he uttered no sound.

"She is beautiful, is she not?" repeated the Tracer, turning to look at the young man.

"Can you not see she is?" he asked impatiently.

"No," said the. Tracer.

Harren stared at him.

"Captain Harren," continued the Tracer, "I can see nothing upon this bit of paper that resembles in the remotest degree a human face or figure."

Harren turned white.

"Not that I doubt that *you* can see it," pursued the Tracer calmly. "I simply repeat that I see absolutely nothing on this paper except a part of a curtain, a window pane, and—and—"

"What! for God's sake!" cried Harren hoarsely.

"I don't know yet. Wait; let me study it."

"Can you not see her face, her eyes? *Don't* you see that exquisite slim figure standing there by the curtain?" demanded Harren, laying his shaking finger on the photograph. "Why, man, it is as clear, as clean cut, as distinct as though the picture had been taken in sunlight! Do you mean to say that there is nothing there—that I am crazy?"

"No. Wait."

"Wait! How can I wait when you sit staring at her picture and telling me that you can't see it, but that it is doubtless there? Are you deceiving me, Mr. Keen? Are you trying to humor me, trying to be kind to me, knowing all the while that I'm crazy—"

"Wait, man! You are no more crazy than I am. I tell you that I can see something on the window pane—"

He suddenly sprang up and walked to the window, leaning close and examining the glass. Harren followed and laid his hand lightly over the pane.

"Do you see any marks on the glass?" demanded Keen.

Harren shook his head.

"Have you a magnifying glass?" asked the Tracer.

Harren pointed back to the table, and they returned to the photograph, the Tracer bending over it and examining it through the glass.

"All I see," he said, still studying the photograph, "is a corner of a curtain and a window on which certain figures seem to have been cut.... Look, Captain Harren, can you see them?"

"I see some marks—some squares."

"You can't see anything written on that pane—as though cut by a diamond?"

"Nothing distinct."

"But you see *her?*"

"Perfectly."

"In minute detail?"

"Yes."

The Tracer thought a moment: "Does she wear a ring?"

"Yes; can't you see?"

"Draw it for me."

They seated themselves side by side, and Harren drew a rough sketch of the ring which he insisted was so plainly visible on her hand:

"Oh," observed the Tracer, "she wears the Seal of Solomon on her ring."

Harren looked up at him. "That symbol has haunted me persistently for three years," he said. "I have found it everywhere—on articles that I buy, on house furniture, on the belts of dead ladrones, on the hilts of creeses, on the funnels of steamers, on the headstalls of horses. If they put a laundry mark on my linen it's certain to be this!

If I buy a box of matches the sign is on it. Why, I've even seen it on the brilliant wings of tropical insects. It's got on my nerves. I dream about it."

"And you buy books about it and try to work out its mystical meaning?" suggested the Tracer, smiling.

But Harren's gray eyes were serious. He said: "*She* never comes to me without that symbol somewhere about her.... I told you she never spoke to me. That is true; yet once, in a vivid dream of her, she did speak. I—I was almost ashamed to tell you of that."

"Tell me."

"A—a dream? Do you wish to know what I dreamed?"

"Yes—if it was a dream."

"It was. I was asleep on the deck of the *Mindinao*, dead tired after a fruitless hike. I dreamed she came toward me through a young woodland all lighted by the sun, and in her hands she held masses of that wild flower we call Solomon's Seal. And she said—in the voice I know must be like hers: 'If you could only read! If you would only understand the message I send you! It is everywhere on earth for you to read, if you only would!'

"I said: 'Is the message in the seal? Is that the key to it?'

"She nodded, laughing, burying her face in the flowers, and said:

"'Perhaps I can write it more plainly for you some day; I will try very, very hard.'

"And after that she went away—not swiftly—for I saw her at moments far away in the woods; but I must have confused her with the glimmering shafts of sunlight, and in a little while the woodland grew dark and I woke with the racket of a Colt's automatic in my ears."

He passed his sun-bronzed hand over his face, hesitated, then leaned over the photograph once more, which the Tracer was studying intently through the magnifying glass.

"There is something on that window in the photograph which I'm going to copy," he said. "Please shove a pad and pencil toward me."

Still examining the photograph through the glass which he held in his right hand, Mr. Keen picked up the pencil and, feeling for the pad, began very slowly to form the following series of symbols:

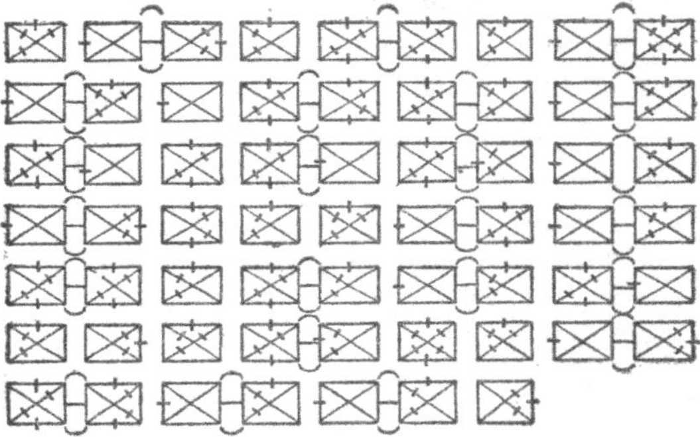

"What on earth are you doing?" muttered Captain Harren, twisting his short mustache in perplexity.

"I am copying what I see through this magnifying glass written on the window pane in the photograph," said the Tracer calmly. "Can't you see those marks?"

"I—I do now; I never noticed them before particularly—only that there were scratches there."

When at length the Tracer had finished his work he sat, chin on hand, examining it in silence. Presently he turned toward Harren, smiling.

"Well?" inquired the younger man impatiently; "do those scratches representing Solomon's Seal mean anything?"

"It's the strangest cipher I ever encountered," said Mr. Keen—"the strangest I ever heard of. I have seen hundreds of ciphers—hundreds—secret codes of the State Department, secret military codes, elaborate Oriental ciphers, symbols used in commercial transactions, symbols used by criminals and every species of malefactor. And every one of them can be solved with time and patience and a little knowledge of the subject. But this"—he sat looking at it with eyes half closed—"this is *too* simple."

"Simple!"

"Very. It's so simple that it's baffling."

"Do you mean to say you are going to be able to find a meaning in squares and crosses?"

"I—I don't believe it is going to be so very difficult to translate them."

"Great guns!" said the Captain. "Do you mean to say that you can ultimately translate that cipher?"

The Tracer smiled. "Let's examine it for repetitions first. Here we have

this symbol

repeated five times. It's likely to be the letter E. I think—" His voice ceased; for a quarter of an hour he pored over the symbols, pencil in hand, checking off some, substituting a letter here and there.

"No," he said; "the usual doesn't work in this case. It's an absurdly simple cipher. I have a notion that numbers play a part in it—you see where these crossed squares are bracketed—those must be numbers requiring two figures—"

He fell silent again, and for another quarter of an hour he remained motionless, immersed in the problem before him, Harren frowning at the paper over his shoulder.

CHAPTER X

"Come!" said the Tracer suddenly; "this won't do. There are too few symbols to give us a key; too few repetitions to furnish us with any key basis. Come, Captain, let us use our intellects; let us talk it over with that paper lying there between us. It's a simple cipher—a childishly simple one if we use our wits. Now, sir, what I see repeated before us on this sheet of paper is merely one of the forms of a symbol known as Solomon's Seal. The symbol is, as we see, repeated a great many times. Every seal

has been dotted or crossed on some one of the lines composing it; some seals are coupled with brackets and armatures."

"What of it?" inquired Harren vacantly.

"Well, sir, in the first place, that symbol

is supposed to represent the spiritual and material, as you know. What else do you know about it?"

"Nothing. I bought a book about it, but made nothing of it."

"Isn't it supposed," asked Mr. Keen, "to contain within itself the nine numerals, 1, 2, 3, 4, 5, 6, 7, 8, 9, and even the zero symbol?"

"I believe so."

"*Ex*actly. Here's the seal

Now I'll mark the one, two, and three by crossing the lines, like this:

one, ⊠ two, ⊠ three, ⊠

Now, eliminating all lines not crossed there remains

the one, 1 the two, Z the three, 3

And here is the entire series:

1 Z 3 4 5 6 7 8 9

and the zero— ▷ "

A sudden excitement stirred Harren; he leaned over the paper, gazing earnestly at the cipher; the Tracer rose and glanced around the room as though in search of something.

"Is there a telephone here?" he asked.

"For Heaven's sake, don't give this up just yet," exclaimed Harren. "These things mean numbers; don't you see? Look at that!" pointing to a linked pair of seals,

"That means the number nineteen! You can form it by using only the crossed lines of the seal

Don't you see, Mr. Keen?"

"Yes, Captain Harren, the cipher is, as you say, very plain; quite as easy to read as so much handwriting. That is why I wish to use your telephone— at once, if you please."

"It's in my bedroom; you don't mind if I go on working out this cipher while you're telephoning?"

"Not in the least," said the Tracer blandly. He walked into the Captain's bedroom, closing the door behind him; then he stepped over to the telephone, unhooked the receiver, and called up his own headquarters.

"Hello. This is Mr. Keen. I want to speak to Miss Borrow."

In a few moments Miss Borrow answered: "I am here, Mr. Keen."

"Good. Look up the name Inwood. Try New York first—Edith Inwood is the name. Look sharp, please; I am holding the wire."

He held it for ten full minutes; then Miss Borrow's low voice called him over the wire.

"Go ahead," said the Tracer quietly.

"There is only one Edith Inwood in New York, Mr. Keen—Miss Edith Inwood, graduate of Barnard, 1902—left an orphan 1903 and obliged to support herself—became an assistant to Professor Boggs of the Museum of Inscriptions. Is considered an authority upon Arabian cryptograms. Has written a monograph on the Herati symbol—a short treatise on the Swastika. She is twenty-four years of age. Do you require further details?"

"No," said the Tracer; "please ring off."

Then he called up General Information. "I want the Museum of Inscriptions. Get me their number, please." After a moment: "Is this the Museum of Inscriptions?"

"Is Professor Boggs there?"

"Is this Professor Boggs?"

"Could you find time to decipher an inscription for me at once?"

"Of course I know you are extremely busy, but have you no assistant who could do it?"

"What did you say her name is? Miss Inwood?"

"Oh! And will the young lady translate the inscription at once if I send a copy of it to her by messenger?"

"Thank you very much, Professor. I will send a messenger to Miss Inwood with a copy of the inscription. Good-by."

He hung up the receiver, turned thoughtfully, opened the door again, and walked into the sunlit living room.

"Look here!" cried the Captain in a high state of excitement. "I've got a lot of numbers out of it already."

"Wonderful!" murmured the Tracer, looking over the young man's broad shoulders at a sheet of paper bearing these numbers:

9—14—5—22—5—18—19—1—23—25—15—21—2—21—20—
15—14—3—5— 9—12—15—22—5—25—15—21—5—4—9—20 —
8—14—23—15—15—4.

"Marvelous!" repeated the Tracer, smiling. "Now what *do* you suppose those numbers can stand for?"

"Letters!" announced the Captain triumphantly. "Take the number nine, for example. The ninth letter in the alphabet is I! Mr. Keen, suppose we try writing down the letters according to that system!"

"Suppose we do," agreed the Tracer gravely.

So, counting under his breath, the young man set down the letters in the following order, not attempting to group them into words:

INEVERSAWYOUBUTONCEILOVEYOUEDITHINWOOD.

Then he leaned back, excited, triumphant.

"There you are!" he said; "only, of course, it makes no sense." He examined it in silence, and gradually a hopeless expression effaced the animation. "How the deuce am I going to separate that mass of letters into words?" he muttered.

"This way," said the Tracer, smilingly, taking the pencil from his fingers, and he wrote: I — NEVER — SAW — YOU — BUT — ONCE. I — LOVE — YOU. EDITH INWOOD.

Then he laid the pencil on the table and walked to the window.

Once or twice he fancied that he heard incoherent sounds behind him. And after a while he turned, retracing his steps leisurely. Captain Harren, extremely pink, stood tugging at his short mustache and studying the papers on the desk.

"Well?" inquired the Tracer, amused.

The young man pointed to the translation with unsteady finger. "W-what on earth does that mean?" he demanded shakily. "Who is Edith Inwood? W-what on earth does that cryptogram mean on the window pane in the photograph? How did it come there? It isn't on my window pane, you see!"

The Tracer said quietly: "That is not a photograph of your window."

"What!"

"No, Captain. Here! Look at it closely through this glass. There are sixteen small panes in that sash; now count the panes in your window—eight! Besides, look at that curtain. It is made of some figured stuff like chintz. Now, look at your own curtain yonder! It is of plain velour."

"But—but I took that photograph! She stood there—there by that very window!"

The Tracer leaned over the photograph, examining it through the glass. And, studying it, he said: "Do you still see *her* in this photograph, Captain Harren?"

"Certainly. Can you not see her?"

"No," murmured the Tracer, "but I see the window which she really stood by when her phantom came here seeking you. And that is sufficient.

Come, Captain Harren, we are going out together."

The Captain looked at him earnestly; something in Mr. Keen's eyes seemed to fascinate him.

"You think that—that it's likely we are g-going to see—*her!*" he faltered.

"If I were you," mused the Tracer of Lost Persons, joining the tips of his lean fingers meditatively—"If I were you I should wear a silk hat and a frock coat. It's—it's afternoon, anyhow," he added deprecatingly, "and we are liable to make a call."

Captain Harren turned like a man in a dream and entered his bedroom. And when he emerged he was dressed and groomed with pathetic precision.

"Mr. Keen," he said, "I—I don't know why I am d-daring to hope for all s-sorts of things. Nothing you have said really warrants it. But somehow I'm venturing to cherish an absurd notion that I may s-see her."

"Perhaps," said the Tracer, smiling.

"Mr. Keen! You wouldn't say that if—if there was no chance, would you? You wouldn't dash a fellow's hopes—"

"No, I wouldn't," said Mr. Keen. "I tell you frankly that I expect to find her."

"To-day?"

"We'll see," said Mr. Keen guardedly. "Come, Captain, don't look that way! Courage, sir! We are about to execute a turning movement; but you look like a Russian general on his way to the south front."

Harren managed to laugh; they went out, side by side, descended the elevator, and found a cab at the *porte-cochère*. Mr. Keen gave the directions and followed the Captain into the cab.

"Now," he said, as they wheeled south, "we are first going to visit the Museum of Inscriptions and have this cipher translation verified. Here is the cipher as I copied it. Hold it tightly, Captain; we've only a few blocks to drive."

Indeed they were already nearly there. The hansom drew up in front of a plain granite building wedged in between some rather elaborate private dwelling-houses. Over the door were letters of dull bronze:

AMERICAN MUSEUM OF INSCRIPTIONS

and the two men descended and entered a wide marble hall lined with glass-covered cabinets containing plaster casts of various ancient inscriptions and a few bronze and marble originals. Several female frumps were nosing the exhibits.

An attendant in livery stood in the middle distance. The Tracer walked over to him. "I have an appointment to consult Miss Inwood," he whispered.

"This way, sir," nodded the attendant, and the Tracer signaled the Captain to follow.

They climbed several marble stairways, crossed a rotunda, and entered a room—a sort of library. Beyond was a door which bore the inscription:

ASSISTANT CURATOR

"Now," said the Tracer of Lost Persons in a low voice to Captain Harren, "I am going to ask you to sit here for a few minutes while I interview the assistant curator. You don't mind, do you?"

"No, I don't mind," said Harren wearily, "only, when are we going to begin to search for—*her?*"

"Very soon—I may say extremely soon," said Mr. Keen gravely. "By the way, I think I'll take that sheet of paper on which I copied the cipher. Thank you. I won't be long."

The attendant had vanished. Captain Harren sat down by a window and gazed out into the late afternoon sunshine. The Tracer of Lost Persons, treading softly across the carpeted floor, approached the sanctuary, turned the handle, and walked in, carefully closing the door behind him.

There was a young girl seated at a desk by an open window; she looked up quietly as he entered, then rose leisurely.

"Miss Inwood?"

"Yes."

She was slender, dark-eyed, dark-haired—a lovely, wholesome young creature, gracious and graceful. And that was all—for the Tracer of Lost Persons could not see through the eyes of Captain Harren, and perhaps that is why he was not able to discern a miracle of beauty in the pretty girl who confronted him—no magic and matchless marvel of transcendent loveliness—only a quiet, sweet-faced, dark-eyed young girl whose features and figure were attractive in the manner that youth is always attractive. But then it is a gift of the gods to see through eyes anointed by the gods.

The Tracer touched his gray mustache and bowed; the girl bowed very sweetly.

"You are Mr. Keen," she said; "you have an inscription for me to translate."

"A mystery for young eyes to interpret," he said, smiling. "May I sit here—and tell my story before I show you my inscription?"

"Please do," she said, seating herself at her desk and facing him, one slender white hand supporting the oval of her face.

The Tracer drew his chair a little forward. "It is a curious matter," he said. "May I give you a brief outline of the details?"

"By all means, Mr. Keen."

"Then let me begin by saying that the inscription of which I have a copy was probably scratched upon a window pane by means of a diamond."

"Oh! Then—then it is not an ancient inscription, Mr. Keen."

"The theme is ancient—the oldest theme in the world—love! The cipher is old—as old as King Solomon." She looked up quickly. The Tracer, apparently engrossed in his own story, went on with it. "Three years ago the young girl who wrote this inscription upon the window pane of her—her bedroom, I think it was—fell in love. Do you follow me, Miss Inwood?"

Miss Inwood sat very still—wide, dark eyes fixed on him.

"Fell in love," repeated the Tracer musingly, "not in the ordinary way. That is the point, you see. No, she fell in love at first sight; fell in love with a young man whom she never before had seen, never again beheld—and never forgot. Do you still follow me, Miss Inwood?"

She made the slightest motion with her lips.

"No," mused the Tracer of Lost Persons, "she never forgot him. I am not sure, but I think she sometimes dreamed of him. She dreamed of him awake, too. Once she inscribed a message to him, cutting it with the diamond in her ring on the window pane—"

A slight sound escaped from Miss Inwood's lips. "I beg your pardon," said the Tracer, "did you say something?"

The girl had risen, pale, astounded, incredulous. "Who are you?" she faltered. "What has this—this story to do with me?"

"Child," said the Tracer of Lost Persons, "the Seal of Solomon is a splendid mystery. All of heaven and earth are included within its symbol. And more, more than you dream of, more than I dare fathom; and I am an old man, my child—old, alone, with nobody to fear for, nothing to dread, not even the end of all—because I am ready for that, too. Yet I, having nothing on earth to dread, dare not fathom what that symbol may mean, nor what vast powers it may exert on life. God knows. It may be the very signet of Fate itself; the sign manual of Destiny."

He drew the paper from his pocket, unrolled it, and spread it out under her frightened eyes.

"*That!*" she whispered, steadying herself blindly against the arm he offered. She stood a moment so, then, shuddering, covered her eyes with both hands. The Tracer of Lost Persons looked at her, turned and opened the door.

"Captain Harren!" he called quietly. Harren, pacing the anteroom, turned and came forward. As he entered the door he caught sight of the girl crouching by the window, her face hidden in her hands, and at the same moment she dropped her hands and looked straight at him.

"*You!*" she gasped.

The Tracer of Lost Persons stepped out, closing the door. For a moment he stood there, tall, gaunt, gray, staring vacantly into space.

"She *was* beautiful—when she looked at him," he muttered.

For another minute he stood there, hesitating, glancing backward at the closed door. Then he went away, stooping slightly, his top hat held close against the breast of his tightly buttoned frock coat.

CHAPTER XI

During his first year of wedded bliss, Gatewood cut the club. When Kerns wanted to see him he had to call like other people or, like other people, accept young Mrs. Gatewood's invitations.

"Why," said Gatewood scornfully, "should I, thirty-four years of age and safely married, go to a club? Why should I, at my age, idle with a lot of idlers and listen to stuffy stories from stuffier individuals? Do you think that stale tobacco smoke, and the idiotically reiterated click of billiard balls, and the vacant stare of the fashionably brainless, and the meaningless exchange of banalities with the intellectually aimless have any attractions for me?"

Mrs. Gatewood raised her pretty eyes in silence; Kerns returned her amused gaze rather blankly.

"Clubs!" sniffed Gatewood. "What are clubs but pretexts for wasting time? What mental, what spiritual stimulus can a man expect to find in a club? Why, Kerns, when I look back a year and think what I was, and when I look at you and think what you still are—"

"John," said Mrs. Gatewood softly.

"Oh, he knows it!" insisted her husband, "don't you, Tommy? You know the sort of life you're leading, don't you? You know what a miserable, aimless, selfish, unambitious, pitiable existence an unmarried man leads who lives at his club; don't you?"

"Certainly," said Kerns, blinking into the smiling gaze of Mrs. Gatewood.

"Then why don't you marry?"

But Kerns had risen and was making his adieus with cheerful decision; and Mrs. Gatewood was laughing as she gave him her slender hand.

"Now I know a girl—" began Gatewood; but his wife was still speaking to Kerns, so he circled around them, politely suppressing the excitement of a sudden idea struggling for utterance.

Mrs. Gatewood was saying: "I do wish John would go to his clubs occasionally. Because a man is married is no reason for his losing touch with his clubs—"

"I know a girl," broke in Gatewood excitedly, laying his arm on Kerns's to detain him; but Kerns slid sideways through the door with a smile so noncommittal that Mrs. Gatewood laughed again and, linking her arm in her husband's, faced partly toward him. This maneuver, and the slightest pressure of her shoulder, obliged her husband to begin a turning movement, so that Kerns might reasonably make his escape in the middle of Gatewood's sentence; which he did with nimble and circumspect agility.

"I—I know a—" began Gatewood desperately, twisting his head over his shoulder, only to hear the deadened patter of his friend's feet over the velvet stair carpet and the subdued clang of the front door.

"Isn't it extraordinary?" he said to his wife. "I've been trying to tell Tommy, every time he comes here, about a girl I know—just the very girl he ought to marry; and something prevents him from listening every time."

The attractive young matron beside him turned her face so that her eyes were directly in line with his.

"Did you ever know any people named Manners?" she asked.

"No. Why?"

"You never knew a girl named Marjorie Manners, did you, John?"

"No. What about her?"

"You never heard Mr. Kerns speak of her, did you, dear?"

"No, never. Tommy doesn't talk about girls."

"You never heard him speak of a Mrs. Stanley?"

"Never. Who are these two women?"

"One and the same, dear. Marjorie Manners married an Englishman named Stanley six years ago. Do you happen to recollect that Mr. Kerns took his vacation in England six years ago?"

"Yes. What of it?"

"He crossed to Southampton with Marjorie and her mother. He didn't know she was going over to be married, and she didn't tell him. She wrote to me about it, though. I was in school at Farmington; she left school to marry—a mere child of eighteen, undeveloped for her age, thin, almost scrawny, with pipe-stem arms and neck, red hair, a very sweet, full-lipped mouth, and gray eyes that were too big for her face."

"Well," said Gatewood with a short laugh, "what about it? You don't think Kerns fell in love with an insect of that genus, do you?"

"Yes, I do," smiled Mrs. Gatewood.

"Nonsense. Besides, what of it? She's married, you say."

"Her husband died of enteric at Ladysmith. She wrote me. She has never remarried. Think of it, John—in all these years she has never remarried!"

"Oh!" said Gatewood pityingly; "do you really suppose that Tommy Kerns has been nursing a blighted affection all these years without ever giving *me* an inkling? Besides, men don't do that; men don't curl up and blight. Besides, men don't take any stock in big-eyed, flat-chested, redheaded pipe stems. Why do you think that Kerns ever cared for her?"

"I know he did."

"How do you know it?"

"From Marjorie's letters."

"The conceited kid! Well, of all insufferable nerve! A man like Kerns— a man—one of the finest, noblest characters—spiritually, intellectually, physically—a practically faultless specimen of manhood! And a red-headed, spindle-legged—Oh, my! Oh, fizz! Dearest, men don't worship a cage of bones with an eighteen-year-old soul—like a nervous canary pecking out at the world!"

"She created a furor in England," observed his wife, smiling.

"Oh, I dare say she might over there. Besides, she's doubtless fattened up since then. But if you suppose for one moment that Tommy could even remember a girl like that—"

Mrs. Gatewood smiled again—the wise, sweet smile of a young matron in whom her husband's closest friend had confided. And after a moment or two the wise smile became more thoughtful and less assured; for that very day the Tracer of Lost Persons had called on her to inquire about a Mrs. Stanley—a new client of his who had recently bought a town house in East Eighty-third Street and a country house on Long Island; and who had applied to him to find her fugitive butler and a pint or two of family jewels. And, after her talk with the Tracer of Lost Persons, Mrs. Gatewood knew that her favorite among all her husband's friends, Mr. Kerns, would never of his own volition go near that same Marjorie Manners who had flirted with him to the very perilous verge before she told him why she was going to England—and who, now a widow, had returned with her five-year-old daughter to dwell once more in the city of her ancestors.

Kerns had said very simply: "She has spoiled women for me—all except you, Mrs. Gatewood. And if Jack hadn't married you—"

"I understand, Mr. Kerns. I'm awfully sorry."

"Don't feel sorry; only, if you can, call Jack off. He's been perfectly possessed to marry me to somebody ever since he married you. And if I told him why I don't care to consider the matter he wouldn't believe me—he'd spend his life in trying to bring me around. Besides, I couldn't ever tell him about—Marjorie Manners. Anyhow, nothing on earth could ever induce me to look at her again.... You say she is now a widow?"

"Yes, Mr. Kerns, and very beautiful."

"Never again," muttered Kerns. "Never! She was homely enough when I asked her to marry me. I don't want to see her; I don't want to know what she looks like. I'm glad she has changed so I wouldn't recognize her, for that means the end of it all—the final elimination of the girl I remember on the ship.... It was probably a sort of diseased infatuation, wasn't it, Mrs. Gatewood? Think of it! A few days on shipboard and—and I asked her to marry me! ... I don't blame her, after all, for letting me dangle. It was an excellent opportunity for her to study a rare species of idiot. She was justified and I am satisfied. Only, do call Jack off with a hint or two."

"I shall try," said young Mrs. Gatewood thoughtfully—very thoughtfully, for already every atom and fiber of her femininity was aroused in behalf of these two estranged young people whom Providence certainly had not meant to put asunder.

CHAPTER XII

"Nothing," said Gatewood firmly, "can make me believe that Kerns ought not to marry somebody; and I'm never going to let up on him until he does. I'll bet I could fix him for life if I called in the Tracer to help me. Isn't it extraordinary how Kerns has kept out of it all these years?"

The attractive girl beside him turned her face once more so that her clear, sweet eyes were directly in line with his.

"It *is* extraordinary," she said seriously. "I think you ought to drop in at the club some day when you can corner him and bully him."

"I don't want to go to the club," said the infatuated man.

"Why, dear?"

He looked straight at her and she flushed prettily, while a tint of color touched his own face. Which was very nice of him. So she didn't say what she was going to say—that it would be perhaps better for them both if he practiced on her an artistic absence now and then. Younger in years, she was more mature than he. She knew. But she was too much in love with him to salt their ambrosia with common sense or suggest economy in their use of the nectar bottle.

However, the gods attend to that, and she knew they would, and she let them. So one balmy evening late in May, when the new moon's ghost floated through the upper haze, and the golden Diana above Manhattan turned flame color, and the electric lights began to glimmer along Fifth Avenue, and the first faint scent of the young summer freshened the foliage in square and park, Kerns, stopping at the club for a moment, found Gatewood seated at the same window they both were wont to haunt in earlier and more flippant days.

"Are you dining *here?*" inquired Kerns, pushing the electric button with enthusiasm. "Well, that's the first glimmer of common sense you've betrayed since you've been married!"

"Dining here!" repeated Gatewood. "I should hope not! I am just going home—"

"He's thoroughly cowed," commented Kerns; "every married man you meet at the club is just going home." But he continued to push the button, nevertheless.

Gatewood leaned back in his chair and gazed about him, nose in the air. "What a life!" he observed virtuously. "It's all I can do to stand it for ten minutes. You're here for the evening, I suppose?" he added pityingly.

"No," said Kerns; "I'm going uptown to Billy Lee's house to get my suit case. His family are out of town, and he is at Seabright, so he let me camp there until the workmen finish papering my rooms upstairs. I'm to lock up the house and send the key to the Burglar Alarm Company to-night. Then I go to Boston on the 12.10. Want to come? There'll be a few doing."

"To Boston! What for?"

"Contracts! We can go out to Cambridge when I've finished my business. There'll be *etwas* doing."

"*Can't* you ever recover from being an undergraduate?" asked Gatewood, disgusted.

"Well—is there anything the matter with a man getting next to a little amusement in life?" asked Kerns. "Do you object to my being happy?"

"Amusement? You don't know how to amuse yourself. You don't know how to be happy. Here you sit, day after day, swallowing Martinis—" He paused to finish his own, then resumed: "Here you sit, day after day, intellectually stultified, unemotionally ignorant of the higher and better life—"

"No, I don't. I've a book upstairs that tells all about that. I read it when I have holdovers—"

"Kerns, I wish to speak seriously. I've had it on my mind ever since I married. May I speak frankly?"

"Well, when I come back from Boston—"

"Because I know a girl," interrupted Gatewood—"wait a moment, Tommy!"—as Kerns rose and sauntered toward the door—"you've plenty of time to catch your train and be civil, too! I mean to tell you about that girl, if you'll listen."

Kerns halted and turned upon his friend a pair of eyes, unwinking in their placid intelligence.

"I was going to say that I know a girl," continued Gatewood, "who is just the sort of a girl you—"

"No, she isn't!" said Kerns, wheeling to resume his progress toward the cloakroom.

"Tom!"

Kerns halted.

"*You're* a fine specimen!" commented Gatewood scornfully. "You spent the best years of your life in persuading me to get married, and the first time I try to do the same for you, you make for the tall timber!"

"I know it," admitted Kerns, unashamed; "I'm bashful. I'm a chipmunk for shyness, so I'll say good night—"

"Come back," said Gatewood coldly.

"But my suit case—"

"You left it at the Lee's, didn't you? Well, you've time enough to go there, get it, make your train, and listen to me, too. Look here, Kerns, have you any of the elements of decency about you?"

"No," said Kerns, "not a single element." He seated himself defiantly in the club window facing Gatewood and began to button his gloves. When he had finished he settled his new straw hat more comfortably on his head, and, leaning forward and balancing his malacca walking stick across his knees, gazed at Gatewood with composure.

"Crank up!" he said pleasantly; "I'm going in less than three minutes." He pushed the electric knob as an afterthought, and when the gilt buttons of the club servant glimmered through the dusk, "Two more," he explained briskly. After a few moments' silence, broken by the tinkle of ice in thin glassware, Gatewood leaned forward, menacing his friend with an impressive forefinger:

"Did you or didn't you once tell me that a decent citizen ought to marry?"

"I did, dear friend."

"Did I or didn't I do it?"

"In the words of the classic, you *done* it," admitted Kerns.

"Was I or wasn't I going to the devil before I had the sense to marry?" persisted Gatewood.

"You was! You *was*, dear friend!" said Kerns with enthusiasm. "You had almost went there ere I appeared and saved you."

"Then why shouldn't you marry and let me save you?"

"But I'm not going to the bowwows. *I'm* all right. I'm a decent citizen. I awake in the rosy dawn with a song on my lips; I softly whistle rag time as I button my collar; I warble a few delicious vagrant notes as I part my sparse hair; I'm not murderous before breakfast; I go down town, singing, to my daily toil; I fish for fat contracts in Georgia marble; I return uptown immersed in a holy calm and the evening paper. I offer myself a cocktail; I bow and accept; I dress for dinner with the aid of a rascally valet, but— *do* I swear at him? No, dear friend; I say, 'Henry, I have known far, far worse scoundrels than you. Thank you for filling up my bay rum with water. Bless you for wearing my imported hosiery! I deeply regret that my new shirts do not fit you, Henry!' And my smile is a benediction upon that wayward scullion. Then, dear friend, why, why do you desire to offer me up upon the altar of unrest? What is a little wifey to me or I to any wifey?"

"Because," said Gatewood irritated, "you offered me up. I'm happy and I want you to be—you great, hulking, self-satisfied symbol of supreme self-centered selfishness—"

"Oh, splash!" said Kerns feebly.

"Yes, you are. What do you do all day? Grub for money and study how to make life agreeable to yourself! Every minute of the day you are occupied in having a good time! You've admitted it! You wake up singing like a fool canary; you wear imported hosiery; you've made a soft, warm wallow for yourself at this club, and here you bask your life away, waddling downtown to nail contracts and cut coupons, and uptown to dinners and theaters, only to return and sprawl here in luxury without one single thought for posterity. *Your* crime is race suicide!"

"I—my—*what!*"

"Certainly. Some shirk taxes, some jury duty. *You* shirk fatherhood, and all its happy and sacred obligations! You deny posterity! You strike a blow at it! You flout it! You menace the future of this Republic! Your inertia is a crime against the people! Instead of *pro bono publico* your motto is *pro bono tempo*—for a good time! And, dog Latin or not, it's the truth, and our great President—"

"Splash!" said Kerns, rising.

"I've a good mind," said Gatewood indignantly, "to put the Tracer of Lost Persons on your trail. He'd rope you and tie you in record time!"

Kerns's smile was a provocation.

"I'll do it, too!" added Gatewood, losing his temper, "if you dare give me the chance."

"Seriously," inquired Kerns, delighted, "*do* you think your friend, Mr. Keen, could encompass my matrimony against my better sense and the full enjoyment of my unimpaired mental faculties?"

"Didn't he—fortunately for me—force me into matrimony when I had never seen a woman I would look at twice? Didn't you put him up to it? Very well, why can't I put him on your trail then? Why can't *he* do the same for you?"

"Try it, dear friend," retorted Kerns courteously.

"Do you mean that you are not afraid? Do you mean you give me full liberty to set him on you? And do you realize what that means? No, you don't; for you haven't a notion of what that man, Westrel Keen, can accomplish. You haven't the slightest idea of the machinery which he controls with a delicacy absolutely faultless; with a perfectly terrifying precision. Why, man, the Pinkerton system itself has become merely a detail in the immense complexity of the system of control which the Tracer of Lost Persons exercises over this entire continent. The urban police, the State constabulary of Pennsylvania, the rural systems of surveillance, the Secret Service, all municipal, provincial, State, and national organizations form but a few strands in the universal web he has woven. Custom officials, revenue officers, the militia of the States, the army, the navy, the personnel of every city, State, and national legislative bodies form interdependent threads in the mesh he is master of; and, like a big beneficent spider, he sits in the center of his web, able to tell by the slightest tremor of any thread exactly where to begin investigations!"

Flushed, earnest, a trifle out of breath with his own eloquence, Gatewood waved his hand to indicate a Ciceronian period, adding, as Kerns's incredulous smile broadened: "Say splash again, and I'll put you at his mercy!"

"Ker-splash! dear friend," observed Kerns pleasantly. "If a man doesn't want to marry, the army, the navy, the Senate, the white wings, and the great White Father at Washington can't make him."

"I tell you I want to see you happy!" said Gatewood angrily.

"Then gaze upon me. I'm it!"

"You're not! You don't know what happiness is."

"Don't I? Well, I don't miss it, dear friend—"

"But if you've never had it, and therefore don't miss it, it's time somebody found some real happiness for you. Kerns, I simply can't bear to see you missing so much happiness—"

"Why grieve?"

"Yes, I will! I do grieve—in spite of your grinning skepticism and your bantering attitude. See here, Tom; I've started about a thousand times to say that I knew a girl—"

"Do you want to hear that splash again?"

Gatewood grew madder. He said: "I could easily lay your case before Mr. Keen and have you in love and married and happy whether you like it or not!"

"If I were not going to Boston, my son, I should enjoy your misguided efforts," returned Kerns blandly.

"Your going to Boston makes no difference. The Tracer of Lost Persons doesn't care where you go or what you do. If he starts in on your case, Tommy, you can't escape."

"You mean he can catch me now? Here? At my own club? Or on the public highway? Or on the classic Boston train?"

"He *could*. Yes, I firmly believe he could land you before you ever saw the Boston State House. I tell you he can work like lightning, Kerns. I know it; I am so absolutely convinced of it that I—I almost hesitate—"

"Don't feel delicate, about it," laughed Kerns; "you may call him on the telephone while I go uptown and get my suit case. Perhaps I'll come back a blushing bridegroom; who knows?"

"If you'll wait here I'll call him up now," said Gatewood grimly.

"Oh, very well. Only I left my suit case in Billy's room, and it's full of samples of Georgia marble, and I've got to get it to the train."

"You've plenty of time. If you'll wait until I talk to Mr. Keen I'll dine with you here. Will you?"

"What? Dine in this abandoned joint with an outcast like me? Dear friend, are you dippy this lovely May evening?"

"I'll do it if you'll wait. Will you? And I'll bet you now that I'll have you in love and sprinting toward the altar before we meet again at this club. Do you dare bet?"

"The terms of the wager, kind friend?" drawled Kerns, delighted; and he fished out a notebook kept for such transactions.

"Let me see," reflected Gatewood; "you'll need a silver service when you're married.... Well, say, forks and spoons and things against an imported trap gun—twelve-gauge, you know."

"Done. Go and telephone to your friend, Mr. Keen." And Kerns pushed the electric button with a jeering laugh, and asked the servant for a dinner card.

CHAPTER XIII

Gatewood, in the telephone booth, waited impatiently for Mr. Keen; and after a few moments the Tracer of Lost Persons' agreeable voice sounded in the receiver.

"It's about Mr. Kerns," began Gatewood; "I want to see him happy, and the idiot won't be. Now, Mr. Keen, you know what happiness you and he brought to me! You know what sort of an idle, selfish, aimless, meaningless life you saved me from? I want you to do the same for Mr. Kerns. I want to ask you to take up his case at once. Besides, I've a bet on it. Could you attend to it at once?"

"To-night?" asked the Tracer, laughing.

"Why—ah—well, of course, that would be impossible. I suppose—"

"My profession is to overcome the impossible, Mr. Gatewood. Where is Mr. Kerns?"

"Here, in this club, defying me and drinking cocktails. He won't get married, and I want you to make him do it."

"Where is he spending the evening?" asked the Tracer, laughing again.

"Why, he's been stopping at the Danforth Lees' in Eighty-third Street until the workmen at the club here finish putting new paper on his walls. The Lees are out of town. He left his suit case at their house and he's going up to get it and catch the 12.10 train for Boston."

"He goes from the Lenox Club to the residence of Mr. W. Danforth Lee, East Eighty-third Street, to get a suit case," repeated the Tracer. "Is that correct?"

"Yes."

"What is in the suit case?"

"Samples of that new marble he's quarrying in Georgia."

"Is it an old suit case? Has it Mr. Kerns's initials on it?"

"Hold the wire; I'll find out."

And Gatewood left the telephone and walked into the great lounging room, where Kerns sat twirling his stick and smiling to himself.

"All over, dear friend?" inquired Kerns, starting to rise. "I've ordered a corking dinner."

"Wait!" returned Gatewood ominously. "What sort of a suit case is that one you're going after?"

"What sort? Oh, just an ordinary—"

"Is it old or new?"

"Brand new. Why?"

"Is your name on it?"

"No; why? Would that thicken the plot, dear friend? Or is the Tracer foiled, ha! ha!"

Gatewood turned on his heel, went back to the telephone, and, carefully shutting the door of the booth, took up the receiver.

"It's a new suit case, Mr. Keen," he said; "no initials on it—just an ordinary case."

"Mr. Lee's residence is 38 East Eighty-third Street, between Madison and Fifth, I believe."

"Yes," replied Gatewood.

"And the family are out of town?"

"Yes."

"Is there a caretaker there?"

"No; Mr. Kerns camped there. When he leaves to-night he will send the key to the Burglar Alarm Company."

"Very well. Please hold the wire for a while."

For ten full minutes Gatewood sat gleefully cuddling the receiver against his ear. His faith in Mr. Keen was naturally boundless; he believed that whatever the Tracer attempted could not result in failure. He desired nothing in the world so ardently as to see Kerns safely married. His own happiness may have been the motive power which had set him in action in behalf of his friend—that and a certain indefinable desire to practice a species of heavenly revenge, of grateful retaliation upon the prime mover and *collaborateur*, if not the sole author, of his own wedded bliss. Kerns had made him happy.

"And I'm hanged if I don't pay him off and make him happy, too!" muttered Gatewood. "Does he think I'm going to sit still and see him go tearing and gyrating about town with no responsibility, no moral check to his evolutions, no wholesome home duties to limit his acrobatics, no wife to clip his wings? It's time he had somebody to report to; time he assumed moral burdens and spiritual responsibilities. A man is just as happy when he is certain where he is going to sleep. A man can find just as much enjoyment in life when he feels it his duty to account for his movements. I don't care whether Kerns is comparatively happy or not—there's nothing either sacred or holy in that kind of happiness, and I'm not going to endure the sort of life he likes any longer!"

Immersed in moral reflections, inspired by affectionate obligations to violently inflict happiness upon Kerns, the minutes passed very agreeably until the amused voice of the Tracer of Lost Persons sounded again in the receiver.

"Mr. Gatewood?"

"Yes, I am here, Mr. Keen."

"Do you really think it best for Mr. Kerns to fall in love?"

"I do, certainly!" replied Gatewood with emphasis.

"Because," continued the Tracer of Lost Persons, "I see little chance for him to do otherwise if I take up this case. Fate itself, in the shape of a young lady, is already on the way here in a railroad train."

"Good! Good!" exclaimed Gatewood. "Don't let him escape, Mr. Keen! I beg of you to take up his case! I urge you most seriously to do so. Mr. Kerns is now exactly what I was a year ago—an utterly useless member of the community—a typical bachelor who lives at his clubs, shirking the duties of a decent citizen."

"*Exactly*," said the Tracer. "Do you insist that I take this case? That I attempt to trace and find for Mr. Kerns a sort of happiness he himself has never found?"

"I implore you to do so, Mr. Keen."

"*Exactly*. If I do—if I carry it out as it has been arranged—or rather as the case seems to have already arranged itself, for it is rather a simple matter, I fancy—I do not exactly see how Mr. Kerns can avoid experiencing a—ahem—a tender sentiment for the very charming young lady whom I— and chance—have designed for him as a partner through life."

"Excellent! Splendid!" shouted Gatewood through the telephone. "Can I do anything to aid you in this?"

"Yes," replied the Tracer, laughing. "If you can keep him amused for an hour or two before he goes after his suit case it might make it easier for me. This young lady is due to arrive in New York at eight o'clock—a client of mine—coming to consult me. Her presence plays an important part in Mr. Kerns's future. I wish you to detain Mr. Kerns until she is ready to receive him. But of this he must know nothing. Good-by, Mr. Gatewood, and would you be kind enough to present my compliments to Mrs. Gatewood?"

"Indeed I will! We never can forget what you have done for us. Good-by."

"Good-by, Mr. Gatewood. Try to keep Mr. Kerns amused for two or three hours. Of course, if you can't do this, there are other methods I may employ—a dozen other plans already partly outlined in my mind; but the present plan, which accident and coincidence make so easy, is likely to work itself out to your entire satisfaction within a few hours. We are already weaving a web around Mr. Kerns; we already have taken exclusive charge of his future movements after he leaves the Lenox Club. I do not believe he can escape us, or his charming destiny. Good night!"

Gatewood, enchanted, hung up the receiver. Song broke softly from his lips as he started in search of Kerns; his step was springy, buoyant—a sort of subdued and modest prance.

"Now," he said to himself, "Tommy must take out his papers. The time is ended when he can issue letters of marque to himself, hoist sail, square away, and go cruising all over this metropolis at his own sweet will."

CHAPTER XIV

In the meanwhile, at the other end of the wire, Mr. Keen, the Tracer of Lost Persons, was preparing to trace for Mr. Kerns, against that gentleman's will, the true happiness which Mr. Kerns had never been able to find for himself.

He sat in his easy chair within the four walls of his own office, inspecting a line of people who stood before him on the carpet forming a single and attentive rank. In this rank were five men: a policeman, a cab driver, an agent of the telephone company, an agent of the electric company, and a reformed burglar carrying a kit of his trade tools.

The Tracer of Lost Persons gazed at them, meditatively joining the tips of his thin fingers.

"I want the number on 36 East Eighty-third Street changed to No. 38, and the number 38 replaced by No. 36," he said to the policeman. "I want it done at once. Get a glazier and go up there and have it finished in an hour. Mrs. Kenna, caretaker at No. 36, is in my pay; she will not interfere. There is nobody in No. 38: Mr. Kerns leaves there to-night and the Burglar Alarm Company takes charge to-morrow."

And, turning to the others: "You," nodding at the reformed burglar, "know your duty. Mike!" to the cab driver, "don't miss Mr. Kerns at the Lenox Club. If he calls you before eleven, drive into the park and have an accident. And you," to the agent of the telephone company, "will sever all telephone connection in Mrs. Stanley's house; and you," to the official of the electric company, "will see that the circuit in Mrs. Stanley's house is cut so that no electric light may be lighted and no electric bell sound."

The Tracer of Lost Persons stroked his gray mustache thoughtfully. "And that," he ended, "will do, I think. Good night."

He rose and stood by the door as the policeman headed the solemn file which marched out to their duty; then he looked at his watch, and, as it was already a few minutes' after eight, he called up No. 36 East Eighty-third Street, and in a moment more had Mrs. Stanley on the wire.

"Good evening," he said pleasantly. "I suppose you have just arrived from Rosylyn. I may be a little late—I may be very late, in fact, so I called you up to say so. And I wished to say another thing; to ask you whether your servants could recollect ever having seen a young man about the place, a rather attractive young man with excellent address and manners, five feet eleven inches, slim but well built, dark hair, dark eyes, and dark mustache, offering samples of Georgia marble for sale."

"Really, Mr. Keen," replied a silvery voice, "I have heard them say nothing about such an individual. If you will hold the wire I will ask my maid." And, after a pause: "No, Mr. Keen, my maid cannot remember any such person. Do you think he was a confederate of that wretched butler of mine?"

"I am scarcely prepared to say that; in fact," added Mr. Keen, "I haven't the slightest idea that this young man could have been concerned in anything of that sort. Only, if you should ever by any chance see such a man, detain him if possible until you can communicate with me; detain him by any pretext, by ruse, by force if you can, only detain him until I can get there. Will you do this?"

"Certainly, Mr. Keen, if I can. Please describe him again?"

Mr. Keen did so minutely.

"You say he sells Georgia marble by samples, which he carries in a suit case?"

"He says that he has samples of Georgia marble in his suit case," replied the Tracer cautiously. "It might be well, if possible, to see what he has in his suit case."

"I will warn the servants as soon as I return to Rosylyn. When may I expect you this evening, Mr. Keen?"

"It is impossible to say, Mrs. Stanley. If I am not there by midnight I shall try to call next morning."

So they exchanged civil adieus; the Tracer hung up his receiver and leaned back in his chair, smiling to himself.

"Curious," he said, "that chance should have sent that pretty woman to me at such a time.... Kerns is a fine fellow, every inch of him. It hit him hard when he crossed with her to Southampton six years ago; it hit him harder when she married that Englishman. I don't wonder he never cared to marry after that brief week of her society; for she is just about the most charming woman I have ever met—red hair and all.... And if quick action is what is required, it's well to break the ice between them at once with a dreadful misunderstanding."

CHAPTER XV

The dinner that Kerns had planned for himself and Gatewood was an ingenious one, cunningly contrived to discontent Gatewood with home fare and lure him by its seductive quality into frequent revisits to the club which was responsible for such delectable wines and viands.

A genial glow already enveloped Gatewood and pleasantly suffused Kerns. From time to time they held some rare vintage aloft, squinting through the crystal-imprisoned crimson with deep content.

"Not that *my* word is necessarily the last word concerning Burgundy," said Gatewood modestly; "but I venture to doubt that any club in America can match this bottle, Kerns."

"Now, Jack," wheedled Kerns, "isn't it pleasant to dine here once in a while? Be frank, man! Look about at the other tables—at all the pleasant, familiar faces—the same fine fellows, bless 'em—the same smoky old ceiling, the same bum portraits of dead governors, the same old stag heads on the wall. Now, Jack, isn't it mighty pleasant, after all? Be a gentleman and admit it!"

"Y-yes," confessed Gatewood, "it's all right for me once in a while, because I know that I am presently going back to my own home—a jolly lamplit room and the prettiest girl in Manhattan curled up in an armchair—"

"You're fortunate," said Kerns shortly. And for the first time there remained no lurking mockery in his voice; for the first time his retort was tinged with bitterness. But the next instant his eyes glimmered with the same gay malice, and the unbelieving smile twitched at his clean-cut lips, and he raised his hand, touching the short ends of his mustache with that careless, amused cynicism which rather became him.

"All that you picture so entrancingly is forbidden the true believer," he said; and began to repeat:

> "'O weaver! weave the flowers of Feraghan
> Into the fabric that thy birth began;
> Iris, narcissus, tulips cloud-band tied,
> These thou shalt picture for the eye of Man;
> Henna, Herati, and the Jhelums tide
> In Sarraband and Saruk be thy guide,
> And the red dye of Ispahan beside
> The checkered Chinese fret of ancient gold;
> —So heed the ban, old as the law is old,

Nor weave into thy warp the laughing face,
Nor limb, nor body, nor one line of grace,
Nor hint, nor tint, nor any veiled device
Of Woman who is barred from Paradise!'"

"A nice sentiment!" said Gatewood hotly.

"Can't help it; you see I'm forbidden to monkey with the eternal looms or weave the forbidden into the pattern of my life."

Gatewood sat silent for a moment, then looked up at Kerns with something so closely akin to a grin that his friend became interested in its scarcely veiled significance, and grinned in reply.

"So you really expect that your friend, Mr. Keen, is going to marry me to somebody, *nolens volens?*" asked Kerns.

"I do. That's what I dream of, Tommy."

"My poor friend, dream on!"

"I am. Tommy, you're lost! I mean you're as good as married now!"

"You think so?"

"I *know* it! There you sit, savoring your Burgundy, idling over a cigar, happy, care free, fancy free, at liberty, as you believe, to roam off anywhere at any time and continue the eternal hunt for pleasure! That's what you *think!* Ha! Tommy, I know better! That's not the sort of man *I* see sitting on the same chair where you are now sprawling in such content! I see a doomed man, already in the shadow of the altar, wasting his time unsuspiciously while Chance comes whirling into the city behind a Long Island locomotive, and Fate, the footman, sits outside ready to follow him, and Destiny awaits him no matter what he does, what he desires, where he goes, wherever he turns to-night! Destiny awaits him at his journey's end!"

"Very fine," said Kerns admiringly. "Too bad it's due to the Burgundy."

"Never mind what my eloquence is due to," retorted Gatewood, "the fact remains that this is probably your last bachelor dinner. Kerns, old fellow! Here's to her! Bless her! I—I wish sincerely that we knew who she is and where to send those roses. Anyway, here's to the bride!"

He stood up very gravely and drank the toast, then, reseating himself, tapped the empty glass gently against the table's edge until it broke.

"You are certainly doing your part well," said Kerns admiringly. Then he swallowed the remainder of his Burgundy and looked up at the club clock.

"Eleven," he said with regret. "I've about time to go to Eighty-third Street, get my suit case, and catch my train at 125th Street." To a servant he said, "Call a hansom," then rose and sauntered downstairs to the cloakroom, where presently both men stood, hatted and gloved, swinging their sticks.

"That was a fool bet you made," began Kerns; "I'll release you, Jack."

"Sorry, but I must insist on holding you," replied Gatewood, laughing. "You're going to your doom. Come on! I'll see you as far as the cab door."

They walked out, and Kerns gave the cabby the street and number and entered the hansom.

"Now," said Gatewood, "you're in for it! You're done for! You can't help yourself! I've won my twelve-gauge trap gun already, and I'll have to set you up in table silver, anyway, so it's an even break. You're all in, Tommy! The Tracer is on your trail!"

In the beginning of a flippant retort Kerns experienced a curious sensation of hesitation. Something in Gatewood's earnestness, in his jeering assurance and delighted certainty, made him, for one moment, feel doubtful, even uncomfortable.

"What nonsense you talk," he said, recovering his equanimity. "Nothing on earth can prevent me driving to 38 East Eighty-third Street, getting my luggage, and taking the Boston express. Your Tracer doesn't intend to stop my hansom and drag me into a cave, does he? You haven't put knockouts into that Burgundy, have you? Then what in the dickens are you laughing at?"

But Gatewood, on the sidewalk under the lamplight, was still laughing as Kerns drove away, for he had recognized in the cab driver a man he had seen in Mr. Kern's office, and he knew that the Tracer of Lost Persons had Kerns already well in hand.

The hansom drove on through the summer darkness between rows of electric globes drooping like huge white moon flowers from their foliated bronze stalks, on up the splendid avenue, past the great brilliantly illuminated hotels, past the white cathedral, past clubs and churches and the palaces of the wealthy; on, on along the park wall edged by its double rows of elms under which shadowy forms moved—lovers strolling in couples.

"Pooh," sniffed Kerns, "the whole world has gone love mad, and I'm the only sane man left."

But he leaned back in his cab and fell a-thinking of a thin girl with red hair and great gray eyes—a thin, frail creature, scarcely more than a child, who had held him for a week in a strange sorcery only to release him with a frightened smile, leaving her indelible impression upon his life forever.

And, thinking, he looked up, realizing that the cab had stopped in East Eighty-third Street before one of a line of brownstone houses, all externally alike.

Then he leaned out and saw that the house number was thirty-eight. That was the number of the Lees' house; he descended, bade the cabman await him, and, producing his latch key, started up the steps, whistling gayly.

But he didn't require his key, for, as he reached the front door, he found, to his surprise and concern, that it swung partly open—just a mere crack.

"The mischief!" he muttered; "could I have failed to close it? Could anybody have seen it and crept in?"

He entered the hallway hastily and pressed the electric knob. No light appeared in the sconces.

"What the deuce!" he murmured; "something wrong with the switch!" And he hurriedly lighted a match and peered into the darkness. By the vague glimmer of the burning match he could distinguish nothing. He listened intently, tried the electric switch again without success. The match burned his fingers and he dropped it, watching the last red spark die out in the darkness.

Something about the shadowy hallway seemed unfamiliar; he went to the door, stepped out on the stoop, and looked up at the number on the transom. It was thirty-eight; no doubt about the house. Hesitating, he glanced around to see that his hansom was still there. It had disappeared.

"What an idiot that cabman is!" he exclaimed, intensely annoyed at the prospect of lugging his heavy suit case to a Madison Avenue car and traveling with it to Harlem.

He looked up and down the dimly lighted street; east, an electric car glided down Madison Avenue; west, the lights of Fifth Avenue glimmered against the dark foliage of the Park. He stood a moment, angry at the desertion of his cabman, then turned and reentered the dark hall, closing the door behind him.

Up the staircase he felt his way to the first landing, and, lighting a match, looked for the electric button.

"Am I crazy, or was there no electric button in this hall?" he thought. The match burned low; he had to drop it. Perplexed, he struck another match and opened the door leading into the front room, and stood on the threshold a moment, looking about him at the linen-shrouded furniture and pictures. This front room, closed for the summer, he had not before entered, but he stepped in now, poking about for any possible intruder, lighting match after match.

"I suppose I ought to go over this confounded house inch by inch," he murmured. "What could have possessed me to leave the front door ajar this morning?"

For an instant he thought that perhaps Mrs. Nolan, the woman who came in the morning to make his bed, might have left the door open, but he knew that couldn't be so, because he always waited for her to finish her work and leave before he went out. So either he must have left the door open, or some marauder had visited the house—was perhaps at that moment in the house! And it was his duty to find out.

"I'd better be about it, too," he thought savagely, "or I'll never make my train."

He struck his last match, looked around, and, seeing gas jets among the clustered electric bulbs of the sconces, tried to light one and succeeded.

He had left his suit case in the passageway between the front and rear rooms, and now, cautiously, stick in hand, he turned toward the dim corridor leading to the bedroom. There was his suit case, anyway! He picked it up and started to push open the door of the rear room; but at the same time, and before he could lay his hand on the knob, the door before him opened suddenly in a flood of light, and a woman stood there, dark against the gas-lit glare, a pistol waveringly extended in the general direction of his head.

CHAPTER XVI

"Good heavens!" he said, appalled, and dropped his suit case with a crash.

"W-what are you d-doing—" She controlled her voice and the wavering weapon with an effort. "What are you doing in this house?"

"Doing? In *this* house?" he repeated, his eyes protruding in the direction of the unsteady pistol muzzle. "What are *you* doing in this house—if you don't mind saying!"

"I—I m-must ask you to put up your hands," she said. "If you move I shall certainly s-shoot off this pistol."

"It will go off, anyway, if you handle it like that!" he said, exasperated. "What do you mean by pointing it at me?"

"I mean to fire it off in a few moments if you don't raise your hands above your head!"

He looked at the pistol; it was new and shiny; he looked at the athletic young figure silhouetted against the brilliant light.

"Well, if you make a point of it, of course." He slowly held up both hands, higher, then higher still. "Upon my word!" he breathed. "Held up by a woman!" And he said aloud, bitterly! "No doubt you have assistance close at hand."

"No doubt," she said coolly. "What have you been packing into that valise?"

"P-packing into *what?* Oh, into that suit case? That is my suit case."

"Of course it is," she said quietly, "but what have you inside it?"

"Nothing *you* or your friends would care for," he said meaningly.

"I must be the judge of that," she retorted. "Please open that suit case."

"How can I if my hands are in the air?" he expostulated, now intensely interested in the novelty of being held up by this graceful and vaguely pretty silhouette.

"You may lower your arms to unpack the suit case," she said.

"I—I had rather not if you are going to keep me covered with your pistol."

"Of course I shall keep you covered. Unpack your booty at once!"

"My—*what?*"

"Booty."

"Madam, do you take *me* for a thief? Have you, by chance, entered the wrong house? I—I cannot reconcile your voice with what I am forced to consider you—a housebreaker—"

"We will discuss that later. Unpack that bag!" she insisted.

"But—but there is nothing in it except samples of marble—"

"What!" she exclaimed nervously. "*What* did you say? Samples of *marble?*"

"Marble, madam! Georgia marble!"

"Oh! So *you* are the young man who goes about pretending to peddle Georgia marble from samples! Are you? The famous marble man I have heard of."

"I? Madam, I don't know what you mean!"

"Come! she said scornfully; "let me see the contents of that suit case. I—I am not afraid of you; I am not a bit afraid of you. And I shall catch your accomplice, too."

"Madam, you speak like an honest woman! You *must* have managed to enter the wrong house. This is number thirty-eight, where I live."

"It is number thirty-six; my house!"

"But I *know* it is number thirty-eight; Mr. Lee's house," he protested hopefully. "This is some dreadful mistake."

"Mr. Lee's house is next door," she said. "Do you not suppose I know my own house? Besides, I have been warned against a plausible young man who pretends he has Georgia marble to sell—"

"There is a dreadful mistake somewhere," he insisted. "Please p-p-put up your p-pistol and aid me to solve it. I am no robber, madam. I thought at first that you were. I'm living in Mr. Lee's house, No. 38 East Eighty-third Street, and I've looked carefully at the number over the door of this house and the number is thirty-eight, and the street is East Eighty-third. So I naturally conclude that I am in Mr. Lee's house."

"Your arguments and your conclusions are very plausible," she said, "but, fortunately for me, I have been expressly warned against a young man of your description. *You* are the marble man!"

"It's a mistake! A very dreadful one."

"Then how did you enter this house?"

"I have a key—I mean I found the front door unlatched. Please don't misunderstand me; I know it sounds unconvincing, but I really have a key to number thirty-eight."

He attempted to reach for his pocket and the pistol glittered in his face.

"Won't you let me prove my innocence?" he asked.

"You can't prove it by showing me a key. Besides, it's probably a weapon. Anyhow, if, as you pretend, you have managed to get into the wrong house, why did you bring that suit case up here?"

"It was here. It's mine. I left it here in this passageway."

"In *my* house?" she asked incredulously.

"In number thirty-eight; that is all I know. I'll open the suit case if you will let me. I have already described its contents. If it has samples of marble in it you *must* be convinced!"

"It will convince me that it is your valise. But what of that? I know it is yours already," she said defiantly. "I know, at least, that you are the marble man—if nothing worse!"

"But malefactors don't go about carrying samples of Georgia marble," he protested, dropping on one knee under the muzzle of her revolver and tugging at the straps and buckles. In a second or two he threw open the case—and the sight of the contents staggered him. For there, thrown in pellmell among small square blocks of polished marble was a complete kit of burglar's tools, including also a mask, a dark lantern, and a blackjack.

"What-w-w-what on earth is this?" he stammered. "These things don't belong to me. I won't have them! I don't want them. Who put them into my suit case? How the deuce—"

"You *are* the marble man!" she said with a shudder. "Your crimes are known! Your wretched accomplice will be caught! You are the marble man—or something worse!"

Kneeling there, aghast, bewildered, he passed his hand across his eyes as though to clear them from some terrible vision. But the suit case was still there with its incriminating contents when he looked again.

"I am sorry for you," she said tremulously. "I—if it were not for the marble—I would let you go. But you are the marble man!"

"Yes, and I'm probably a madman, too. I don't know what I am! I don't know what is happening to me. I ought to be going, that is all I know—"

"I cannot let you go."

"But I must! I've got to catch a train."

The feebleness of his excuse chilled her pity.

"I shall not let you go," she said, resting the hand which held the pistol on her hip, but keeping him covered. "I know you came to rob my house; I know you are a thoroughly bad and depraved young man, but for all that I could find it in my heart to let you go if you were not also the *marble man!*"

"What on earth is the marble man?" he asked, exasperated.

"I don't know. I have been earnestly warned against him. Probably he is a relative of my butler—"

"I'm not a relative of anybody's butler!"

"You *say* you are not. How do I know? I will make you an offer. I will give you one last chance. If you will return to me the jewels that my butler took—"

"Good heavens, madam! Do you really take me for a professional burglar?"

"How can I help it?" she said indignantly. "Look at your suit case full of lanterns and masks—full of *marble,* too!"

Speechless, he stared at the burglar's kit.

"I am sorry—" Her voice had altered again to a tremulous sweetness. "I can't help feeling sorry for you. You do not seem to be hardened; your voice and manner are not characteristically criminal. I—I can't see your face very clearly, but it does not seem to be a brutally inhuman face—"

An awful desire to laugh seized Kerns; he struggled against it; hysteria lay that way; and he covered his face with both hands and pinched himself.

She probably mistook the action for the emotion of shame and despair born of bitter grief; perhaps of terror of the law. It frightened her a little, but pity dominated. She could scarcely endure to do what she must do.

"This is dreadful, dreadful!" she faltered. "If you only would give me back my jewels—"

Sounds, hastily smothered, escaped him. She believed them to be groans, and it made her slightly faint.

"I—I've simply got to telephone for the police," she said pityingly. "I must ask you to sit down there and wait—there is a chair. Sit there—and please don't move, for I—this has unnerved me—I am not accustomed to doing cruel things; and if you should move too quickly or attempt to run away I feel certain that this pistol would explode."

"Are you going to telephone?" he asked.

"Yes, I am."

She backed away, cautiously, pistol menacing him, reached for the receiver, and waited for Central. She waited a long time before she realized that the telephone as well as the electric light was out of commission.

"Did *you* cut all these wires?" she demanded angrily.

"I? What wires?"

She reached out and pressed the electric button which should have rung a bell in her maid's bedroom on the top floor. She kept her finger on the button for ten minutes. It was useless.

"You laid deliberate plans to rob this house," she said, her cheeks pink with indignation. "I am not a bit sorry for you. I shall *not* let you go! I shall sit here until somebody comes to my assistance, if I have to sit here for weeks and weeks!"

"If you'd let me telephone to my club—" he began.

"Your club! You are very plausible. You didn't offer to call up any club until you found that the telephone was not working!"

He thought a moment. "I don't suppose you would trust me to go out and get a policeman?"

"Certainly not."

"Or go into the front room and open a window and summon some passer-by?"

"How do I know you haven't confederates waiting outside?"

"That's true," he said seriously.

There was a silence. Her nerves seemed to trouble her, for she began to pace to and fro in front of the passageway where he sat comfortably on his chair, arms folded, one knee dropped over the other.

The light being behind her he could not as yet distinguish her features very clearly. Her figure was youthful, slender, yet beautifully rounded; her head charming in contour. He watched her restlessly walking on the floor, small hand clutching the pistol resting on her hip.

The ruddy burnished glimmer on the edges of her hair he supposed, at first, was caused by the strong light behind her.

"This is atrocious!" she murmured, halting to confront him. "How dared you sever every electric connection in my house?"

As she spoke she stepped backward a pace or two, resting herself for a moment against the footboard of the bed—full in the gaslight. And he saw her face.

For a moment he studied her; an immense wave of incredulity swept over him—of wild unbelief, slowly changing to the astonishment of dawning conviction. Astounded, silent, he stared at her from his shadowy corner; and after a while his pulses began to throb and throb and hammer, and the clamoring confusion of his senses seemed to deafen him.

She rested a moment or two against the footboard of the bed, her big gray eyes fixed on his vague and shadowy form.

"This won't do," she said.

"No," he said, "it won't do."

He spoke very quietly, very gently. She detected the alteration in his voice and started slightly, as though the distant echo of a familiar voice had sounded.

"What did you say?" she asked, coming nearer, pistol glittering in advance.

"I said 'It won't do.' I don't know what I meant by it. If I meant anything I was wrong. It *will* do. The situation is perfectly agreeable to me."

"Insolence will not help you," she said sharply. And under the sharpness he detected the slightest quaver of a new alarm.

"I am going to free myself," he said coolly.

"If you move I shall certainly shoot!" she retorted.

"I am going to move—but only my lips. I have only to move my lips to free myself."

"I should scarcely advise you to trust to your eloquence. I have been duly warned, you see."

"Who warned you?" he asked curiously. And, as she disdained to reply: "Never mind. We can clear that up later. Now let me ask you something."

"You are scarcely in a position to ask questions," she said.

"May I not speak to you?"

"Is it necessary?"

He thought a moment. "No, not necessary. Nothing is in this life, you know. I thought differently once. Once—when I was younger—six years younger—I thought happiness was necessary. I found that a man might live without it."

She stood gazing at him through the shadows, pistol on hip.

"What do you mean?" she asked.

"I mean that happiness is not necessary to life. Life goes on all the same. My life has continued for six years without that happiness which some believe to be essential."

After a silence she said: "I can tell by the way you speak that you are well born. I—I dread to do what I simply must do."

He, too, sat silent a long time—long enough for an utterly perverse and whimsical humor to take complete possession of him.

"*Won't* you let me go—*this* time?" he pleaded.

"I cannot."

"You had better let me go while you can," he said, "because, perhaps, you may find it difficult to get rid of me later."

Affronted, she shrank back from the doorway and stood in the center of her room, angry, disdainful, beautiful, under the ruddy glory of her lustrous hair.

His perverse mood changed, too; he leaned forward, studying her minutely—the splendid gray eyes, the delicate mouth and nose, the full, sweet lips, the witchery of wrist and hand, and the flowing, rounded outline of limb and body under the pretty gown. Could this be *she?* This lovely, mature woman, wearing scarcely a trace of the young girl he had never forgotten—scarcely a trace save in the beauty of her eyes and hair—save in the full, red mouth, sweet and sensitive even in its sudden sullenness?

"Once," he said, and his voice sounded to him like voices heard in dreams—"once, years and years ago, there was a steamer, and a man and a young girl on board. Do you mind my telling you about it?"

She stood leaning against the footboard of the bed, not even deigning to raise her eyes in reply. So he made the slightest stir in his chair; and then she looked up quickly enough, pistol poised.

"The steamer," said Kerns slowly, "was coming into Southampton—six years ago. On deck these two people stood—a man of twenty-eight, a girl of eighteen—six years ago. The name of the steamer was the *Carnatic.* Did you ever hear of that ship?"

She was looking at him attentively. He waited for her reply; she made none; and he went on.

"The man had asked the girl something—I don't know what—I don't know why her gray eyes filled with tears. Perhaps it was because she could not do what the man asked her to do. It may have been to love him; it may have been that he was asking her to marry him and that she couldn't. Perhaps that is why there were tears in her eyes—because she may have been sorry to cause him the pain of refusal—sorry, perhaps, perhaps a little guilty. Because she must have seen that he was falling in love with her, and she— she let him—knowing all the time that she was to marry another man. Did you ever hear of that man before?"

She had straightened up, quivering, wide eyed, lips parted. He rose and walked slowly into her room, confronting her under the full glare of light.

Her pistol fell clattering to the floor. It did not explode because it was not loaded.

"Now," he said unsteadily, "will you give me my freedom? I have waited for it—not minutes—but years—six years. I ask it now—the freedom I enjoyed before I ever saw you. Can you give it back to me? Can you restore to me a capacity for happiness? Can you give me a heart to love with—love some woman, as other men love? Is it very much I ask of you— to give me a chance in life—the chance I had before I ever saw you?"

Her big gray eyes seemed fascinated; he looked deep into them, smiling;

and she turned white.

"Will you give me what I ask?" he said, still smiling.

She strove to speak; she could not, but her eyes never faltered. Suddenly the color flooded her neck and cheeks to the hair, and the quick tears glimmered.

"I—I did not understand; I was too young to be cruel," she faltered. "How could I know what I was doing? Or what—what you did?"

"I? To *you?*"

"Y-yes. Did you think that I escaped heart free? Do you realize what *my* punishment was—to—to marry—and *remember!* If I was too young, too inexperienced to know what I was doing, I was not too young to suffer for it!"

"You mean—" He strove to control his voice, but the sweet, fearless gray eyes met his; the old flame leaped in his veins. He reached out to steady himself and his hand touched hers—that soft, white hand that had held him all these years in the hollow of its palm.

"Did you *ever* love me?" he demanded.

Her eyes, wet with tears, met his straight as the starry gaze of a child.

"Yes," she said.

His hand tightened over hers; she swayed a moment, quivering from head to foot; then drawing a quick, sobbing breath, closed her eyes, imprisoned in his arms; and, after a long while, aroused, she looked up at him, her divine eyes unclosing dreamily.

"Somebody is hammering at the front door," he breathed. "Listen!"

"I hear. I believe it must be the Tracer of Lost Persons."

"What?"

"Only a Mr. Keen."

"O Lord!" said Kerns faintly, and covered his face with her fragrant hands.

Very tenderly, very gravely, she drew her hands away, and, laying them on his shoulders, looked up at him.

"You—you know what there is in your suit case," she faltered; "*are* you a burglar, dear?"

"Ask the Tracer of Lost Persons," said Kerns gently, "what sort of a criminal I am!"

They stood together for one blissful moment listening to the loud knocking below, then, hand in hand, they descended the dark stairway to admit the Tracer of Lost Persons.

CHAPTER XVII

On the thirteenth day of March, 1906, Kerns received the following cable from an old friend:

"Is there anybody in New York who can find two criminals for me? I don't want to call in the police.

"J. T. BURKE."

To which Kerns replied promptly:

"Wire Keen, Tracer of Lost Persons, N. Y."

And a day or two later, being on his honeymoon, he forgot all about his old friend Jack Burke.

On the fifteenth day of March, 1906, Mr. Keen, Tracer of Lost Persons, received the following cablegram from Alexandria, Egypt:

"*Keen, Tracer, New York:*—Locate Joram Smiles, forty, stout, lame, red hair, ragged red mustache, cast in left eye, pallid skin; carries one crutch; supposed to have arrived in America per S. S. *Scythian Queen*, with man known as Emanuel Gandon, swarthy, short, fat, light bluish eyes, Eurasian type.

"I will call on you at your office as soon as my steamer, *Empress of Babylon*, arrives. If you discover my men, keep them under surveillance, but on no account call in police. Spare no expense. Dundas, Gray & Co. are my bankers and reference.

"JOHN TEMPLETON BURKE."

On Monday, April 2d, a few minutes after eight o'clock in the morning, the card of Mr. John Templeton Burke was brought to Mr. Keen, Tracer of Lost Persons, and a moment later a well-built, wiry, sun-scorched young man was ushered into Mr. Keen's private office by a stenographer prepared to take minutes of the interview.

The first thing that the Tracer of Lost Persons noted in his visitor was his mouth; the next his eyes. Both were unmistakably good—the eyes which his Creator had given him looked people squarely in the face at every word; the mouth, which a man's own character fashions agreeably or mars, was pleasant, but firm when the trace of the smile lurking in the corners died out.

There were dozens of other external characteristics which Mr. Keen always looked for in his clients; and now the rapid exchange of preliminary glances appeared to satisfy both men, for they advanced toward each other and exchanged a formal hand clasp.

"Have you any news for me?" asked Burke.

"I have," said the Tracer. "There are cigars on the table beside you—matches in that silver case. No, I never smoke; but I like the aroma—and I like to watch men smoke. Do you know, Mr. Burke, that no two men smoke in the same fashion? There is as much character in the manner of holding a cigar as there is difference in the technic of artists."

Burke nodded, amused, but, catching sight of the busy stenographer, his bronzed features became serious, and he looked at Mr. Keen inquiringly.

"It is my custom," said the Tracer. "Do you object to my stenographer?"

Burke looked at the slim young girl in her black gown and white collar and cuffs. Then, very simply, he asked her pardon for objecting to her presence, but said that he could not discuss his case if she remained. So she rose, with a humorous glance at Mr. Keen; and the two men stood up until she had vanished, then reseated themselves *vis-a-vis*. Mr. Keen calmly dropped his elbow on the concealed button which prepared a hidden phonograph for the reception of every word that passed between them.

"What news have you for me, Mr. Keen?" asked the younger man with that same directness which the Tracer had already been prepared for, and which only corroborated the frankness of eyes and voice.

"My news is brief," he said. "I have both your men under observation."

"Already?" exclaimed Burke, plainly unprepared. "Do you actually mean that I can see these men whenever I desire to do so? Are these scoundrels in this town—within pistol shot?"

His youthful face hardened as he snapped out his last word, like the crack of a whip.

"I don't know how far your pistol carries," said Mr. Keen. "Do you wish to swear out a warrant?"

"No, I do not. I merely wish their addresses. You have not used the police in this matter, have you, Mr. Keen?"

"No. Your cable was explicit," said the Tracer. "Had you permitted me to use the police it would have been much less expensive for you."

"I can't help that," said the young man. "Besides, in a matter of this sort, a man cannot decently consider expense."

"A matter of what sort?" asked the Tracer blandly.

"Of *this* sort."

"Oh! Yet even now I do not understand. You must remember, Mr. Burke, that you have not told me anything concerning the reasons for your quest of these two men, Joram Smiles and Emanuel Gandon. Besides, this is the first time you have mentioned pistol range."

Burke, smoking steadily, looked at the Tracer through the blue fog of his cigar.

"No," he said, "I have not told you anything about them."

Mr. Keen waited a moment; then, smiling quietly to himself, he wrote down the present addresses of Joram Smiles and Emanuel Gandon, and, tearing off the leaf, handed it to the younger man, saying: "I omit the pistol range, Mr. Burke."

"I am very grateful to you," said Burke. "The efficiency of your system is too famous for me to venture to praise it. All I can say is 'Thank you'; all I can do in gratitude is to write my check—if you will be kind enough to suggest the figures."

"Are you sure that my services are ended?"

"Thank you, quite sure."

So the Tracer of Lost Persons named the figures, and his client produced a check book and filled in a check for the amount. This was presented and received with pleasant formality. Burke rose, prepared to take his leave, but the Tracer was apparently busy with the combination lock of a safe, and the young man lingered a moment to make his adieus.

As he stood waiting for the Tracer to turn around he studied the writing on the sheet of paper which he held toward the light:

> Joram Smiles, no profession, 613 West 24th Street.
> Emanuel Gandon, no profession, same address.
> Very dangerous men.

It occurred to him that these three lines of pencil-writing had cost him a thousand dollars—and at the same instant he flushed with shame at the idea of measuring the money value of anything in such a quest as this.

And yet—and yet he had already spent a great deal of money in his brief quest, and—was he any nearer the goal—even with the penciled addresses of these two men in his possession? Even with these men almost within pistol shot!

Pondering there, immersed in frowning retrospection, the room, the Tracer, the city seemed to fade from his view. He saw the red sand blowing in the desert; he heard the sickly squealing of camels at the El Teb Wells; he saw the sun strike fire from the rippling waters of Saïs; he saw the plain, and the ruins high above it; and the odor of the Long Bazaar smote him like a blow, and he heard the far call to prayer from the minarets of Sa-el-

Hagar, once Saïs, the mysterious—Saïs of the million lanterns, Saïs of that splendid festival where the Great Triad's worship swayed dynasty after dynasty, and where, through the hot centuries, Isis, veiled, impassive, looked out upon the hundredth king of kings, Meris, the Builder of Gardens, dragged dead at the chariot of Upper and Lower Egypt.

Slowly the visions faded; into his remote eyes crept the consciousness of the twentieth century again; he heard the river whistles blowing, and the far dissonance of the streets—that iron undertone vibrating through the metropolis of the West from river to river and from the Palisades to the sea.

His gaze wandered about the room, from telephone desk to bookcase, from the table to the huge steel safe, door ajar, swung outward like the polished breech of a twelve-inch gun.

Then his vacant eyes met the eyes of the Tracer of Lost Persons, almost helplessly. And for the first time the full significance of this quest he had undertaken came over him like despair—this strange, hopeless, fantastic quest, blindly, savagely pursued from the sand wastes of Saïs to the wastes of this vast arid city of iron and masonry, ringing to the sky with the menacing clamor of its five monstrous boroughs.

Curiously weary of a sudden, he sat down, resting his head on one hand. The Tracer watched him, bent partly over his desk. From moment to moment he tore minute pieces from the blotter, or drew imaginary circles and arabesques on his pad with an inkless pen.

"Perhaps I could help you, after all—if you'd let me try," he said quietly.

"Do you mean—*me?*" asked Burke, without raising his head.

"If you like—yes, you—or any man in trouble—in perplexity—in the uncertain deductions which arise from an attempt at self-analysis."

"It is true; I am trying to analyze myself. I believe that I don't know how. All has been mere impulse—so far. No, I don't know how to analyze it all."

"I do," said the Tracer.

Burke raised his level, unbelieving eyes.

"You are in love," said the Tracer.

After a long time Burke looked up again. "Do you think so?"

"Yes. Can I help you?" asked the Tracer pleasantly.

The young man sat silent, frowning into space; then:

"I tell you plainly enough that I have come here to argue with two men at the end of a pistol; and—you tell me I'm in love. By what logic—"

"It is written in your face, Mr. Burke—in your eyes, in every feature, every muscle's contraction, every modulation of your voice. My tables, containing six hundred classified superficial phenomena peculiar to all human emotions, have been compiled and scientifically arranged according to Bertillon's system. It is an absolutely accurate key to every phase of human emotion, from hate, through all its amazingly paradoxical phenomena, to love, with all its genera under the suborder—all its species, subspecies, and varieties."

He leaned back, surveying the young man with kindly amusement.

"You talk of pistol range, but you are thinking of something more fatal than bullets, Mr. Burke. You are thinking of love—of the first, great, absorbing, unreasoning passion that has ever shaken you, blinded you, seized you and dragged you out of the ordered path of life, to push you violently into the strange and unexplored! That is what stares out on the world through those haunted eyes of yours, when the smile dies out and you are off your guard; that is what is hardening those flat, clean bands of muscle in jaw and cheek; that is what those hints of shadow mean beneath the eye, that new and delicate pinch to the nostril, that refining, almost to sharpness, of the nose, that sensitive edging to the lips, and the lean delicacy of the chin."

He bent slightly forward in his chair.

"There is all that there, Mr. Burke, and something else—the glimmering dawn of desperation."

"Yes," said the other, "that is there. I am desperate."

"*Exactly.* Also you wear two revolvers in a light, leather harness strapped up under your armpits," said the Tracer, laughing. "Take them off, Mr. Burke. There is nothing to be gained in shooting up Mr. Smiles or converting Mr. Gandon into nitrates."

"If it is a matter where one man can help another," the Tracer added simply, "it would give me pleasure to place my resources at your command—without recompense—"

"Mr. Keen!" said Burke, astonished.

"Yes?"

"You are very amiable; I had not wished—had not expected anything except professional interest from you."

"Why not? I like you, Mr. Burke."

The utter disarming candor of this quiet, elderly gentleman silenced the younger man with a suddenness born of emotions long crushed, long relentlessly mastered, and which now, in revolt, shook him fiercely in every fiber. All at once he felt very young, very helpless in the world—that same world through which, until within a few weeks, he had roved so confidently, so arrogantly, challenging man and the gods themselves in the pride of his strength and youth.

But now, halting, bewildered, lost amid the strange maze of byways whither impulse had lured and abandoned him, he looked out into a world of wilderness and unfamiliar stars and shadow shapes undreamed of, and he knew not which way to turn—not even how to return along the ways his impetuous feet had trodden in this strange and hopeless quest of his.

"How can you help me?" he said bluntly, while the quivering undertone rang in spite of him. "Yes, I am in love; but how can any living man help me?"

"Are you in love with the dead?" asked the Tracer gravely. "For that only is hopeless. Are you in love with one who is not living?"

"Yes."

"You love one whom you know to be dead?"

"Yes; dead."

"How do you know that she is dead?"

"That is not the question. I knew that when I fell in love with her. It is not that which appals me; I ask nothing more than to live my life out loving the dead. I—I ask very little."

He passed his unsteady hand across his dry lips, across his eyes and forehead, then laid his clinched fist on the table.

"Some men remain constant to a memory; some to a picture—sane, wholesome, normal men. Some men, with a fixed ideal, never encounter its facsimile, and so never love. There is nothing strange, after all, in this; nothing abnormal, nothing unwholesome. Grunwald loved the marble head and shoulders of the lovely Amazon in the Munich Museum; he died unmarried, leaving the charities and good deeds of a blameless life to justify him. Sir Henry Guest, the great surgeon who worked among the poor without recompense, loved Gainsborough's 'Lady Wilton.' The portrait hangs above his tomb in St. Clement's Hundreds. D'Epernay loved Mlle. Jeanne Vacaresco, who died before he was born. And I—I love in my own fashion."

His low voice rang with the repressed undertone of excitement; he opened and closed his clinched hand as though controlling the lever of his emotions.

"What can you do for a man who loves the shadow of Life?" he asked.

"If you love the shadow because the substance has passed away—if you love the soul because the dust has returned to the earth as it was—"

"It has *not!*" said the younger man.

The Tracer said very gravely: "It is written that whenever 'the Silver Cord' is loosed, 'then shall the dust return unto the earth as it was, and the spirit shall return unto Him who gave it.'"

"The spirit—yes; *that* has taken its splendid flight—"

His voice choked up, died out; he strove to speak again, but could not. The Tracer let him alone, and bent again over his desk, drawing imaginary circles on the stained blotter, while moment after moment passed under the tension of that fiercest of all struggles, when a man sits throttling his own soul into silence.

And, after a long time, Burke lifted a haggard face from the cradle of his crossed arms and shook his shoulders, drawing a deep, steady breath.

"Listen to *me!*" he said in an altered voice.

And the Tracer of Lost Persons nodded.

CHAPTER XVIII

"When I left the Point I was assigned to the colored cavalry. They are good men; we went up Kettle Hill together. Then came the Philippine troubles, then that Chinese affair. Then I did staff duty, and could not stand the inactivity and resigned. They had no use for me in Manchuria; I tired of waiting, and went to Venezuela. The prospects for service there were absurd; I heard of the Moorish troubles and went to Morocco. Others of my sort swarmed there; matters dragged and dragged, and the Kaiser never meant business, anyway.

"Being independent, and my means permitting me, I got some shooting in the back country. This all degenerated into the merest nomadic wandering—nothing but sand, camels, ruins, tents, white walls, and blue skies. And at last I came to the town of Sa-el-Hagar."

His voice died out; his restless, haunted eyes became fixed.

"Sa-el-Hagar, once ancient Saïs," repeated the Tracer quietly; and the young man looked at him.

"You know *that?*"

"Yes," said the Tracer.

For a while Burke remained silent, preoccupied, then, resting his chin on his hand and speaking in a curiously monotonous voice, as though repeating to himself by rote, he went on:

"The town is on the heights—have you a pencil? Thank you. Here is the town of Sa-el-Hagar, here are the ruins, here is the wall, and somewhere hereabouts should be the buried temple of Neith, which nobody has found." He shifted his pencil. "Here is the lake of Saïs; here, standing all alone on the plain, are those great monolithic pillars stretching away into perspective—four hundred of them in all—a hundred and nine still upright. There were one hundred and ten when I arrived at El Teb Wells."

He looked across at the Tracer, repeating: "One hundred and ten—when I arrived. One fell the first night—a distant pillar far away on the horizon. Four thousand years had it stood there. And it fell—the first night of my arrival. I heard it; the nights are cold at El Teb Wells, and I was lying awake, all a-shiver, counting the stars to make me sleep. And very, very far away in the desert I heard and felt the shock of its fall—the fall of forty centuries under the Egyptian stars."

His eyes grew dreamy; a slight glow had stained his face.

"Did you ever halt suddenly in the Northern forests, listening, as though a distant voice had hailed you? Then you understand why that far, dull sound from the dark horizon brought me to my feet, bewildered, listening, as though my own name had been spoken.

"I heard the wind in the tents and the stir of camels; I heard the reeds whispering on Saïs Lake and the yap-yap of a shivering jackal; and always, always, the hushed echo in my ears of my own name called across the star-lit waste.

"At dawn I had forgotten. An Arab told me that a pillar had fallen; it was all the same to me, to him, to the others, too. The sun came out hot. I like heat. My men sprawled in the tents; some watered, some went up to the town to gossip in the bazaar. I mounted and cast bridle on neck—you see how much I cared where I went! In two hours we had completed a circle—like a ruddy hawk above El Teb. And my horse halted beside the fallen pillar."

As he spoke his language had become very simple, very direct, almost without accent, and he spoke slowly, picking his way with that lack of inflection, of emotion characteristic of a child reading a new reader.

"The column had fallen from its base, eastward, and with its base it had upheaved another buried base, laying bare a sort of cellar and a flight of stone steps descending into darkness.

"Into this excavation the sand was still running in tiny rivulets. Listening, I could hear it pattering far, far down into the shadows.

"Sitting there in the saddle, the thing explained itself as I looked. The fallen pillar had been built upon older ruins; all Egypt is that way, ruin founded on the ruin of ruins—like human hopes.

"The stone steps, descending into the shadow of remote ages, invited me. I dismounted, walked to the edge of the excavation, and, kneeling, peered downward. And I saw a wall and the lotus-carved rim of a vast stone-framed pool; and as I looked I heard the tinkle of water. For the pillar, falling, had unbottled the ancient spring, and now the stone-framed lagoon was slowly filling after its drought of centuries.

"There was light enough to see by, but, not knowing how far I might penetrate, I returned to my horse, pocketed matches and candles from the saddlebags, and, returning, started straight down the steps of stone.

"Fountain, wall, lagoon, steps, terraces half buried—all showed what the place had been: a water garden of ancient Egypt—probably royal—because, although I am not able to decipher hieroglyphics, I have heard some-where that these picture inscriptions, when inclosed in a cartouch like this"—he drew rapidly—

"or this

indicate that the subject of the inscription was once a king.

"And on every wall, every column, I saw the insignia of ancient royalty, and I saw strange hawk-headed figures bearing symbols engraved on stone—beasts, birds, fishes, unknown signs and symbols; and everywhere the lotus carved in stone—the bud, the blossom half-inclosed, the perfect flower."

His dreamy eyes met the gaze of the Tracer, unseeing; he rested his sun-burned face between both palms, speaking in the same vague monotone:

"Everywhere dust, ashes, decay, the death of life, the utter annihilation of the living—save only the sparkle of reborn waters slowly covering the baked bed of the stone-edged pool—strange, luminous water, lacking the vital sky tint, enameled with a film of dust, yet, for all that, quickening with imprisoned brilliancy like an opal.

"The slow filling of the pool fascinated me; I stood I know not how long watching the thin film of water spreading away into the dimness beyond. At last I turned and passed curiously along the wall where, at its base, mounds of dust marked what may have been trees. Into these I probed with my riding crop, but discovered nothing except the depths of the dust.

"When I had penetrated the ghost of this ancient garden for a thousand yards the light from the opening was no longer of any service. I lighted a candle; and its yellow rays fell upon a square portal into which led another flight of steps. And I went down.

"There were eighteen steps descending into a square stone room. Strange gleams and glimmers from wall and ceiling flashed dimly in my eyes un-der the wavering flame of the candle. Then the flame grew still—still as death—and Death lay at my feet—there on the stone floor—a man, square shouldered, hairless, the cobwebs of his tunic mantling him, lying face downward, arms outflung.

"After a moment I stooped and touched him, and the entire prostrate fig-ure dissolved into dust where it lay, leaving at my feet a shadow shape in thin silhouette against the pavement—merely a gray layer of finest dust shaped like a man, a tracery of impalpable powder on the stones.

"Upward and around me I passed the burning candle; vast figures in blue and red and gold grew out of the darkness; the painted walls sparkled; the shadows that had slept through all those centuries trembled and shrank away into distant corners.

"And then—and then I saw the gold edges of her sandals sparkle in the darkness, and the clasped girdle of virgin gold around her slender waist glimmered like purest flame!"

Burke, leaning far across the table, interlocked hands tightening, stared and stared into space. A smile edged his mouth; his voice grew wonderfully gentle:

"Why, she was scarcely eighteen—this child—lying there so motionless, so lifelike, with the sandals edging her little upturned feet, and the small hands of her folded between the breasts. It was as though she had just stretched herself out there—scarcely sound asleep as yet, and her thick, silky hair—cut as they cut children's hair in these days, you know—cradled her head and cheeks.

"So marvelous the mimicry of life, so absolute the deception of breathing sleep, that I scarce dared move, fearing to awaken her.

"When I did move I forgot the dusty shape of the dead at my feet, and left, full across his neck, the imprint of a spurred riding boot. It gave me my first shudder; I turned, feeling beneath my foot the soft, yielding powder, and stood aghast. Then—it is absurd!—but I felt as a man feels who has trodden inadvertently upon another's foot—and in an impulse of reparation I stooped hastily and attempted to smooth out the mortal dust which bore the imprint of my heel. But the fine powder flaked my glove, and, looking about for something to compose the ashes with, I picked up a papyrus scroll. Perhaps he himself had written on it; nobody can ever know, and I used it as a sort of hoe to scrape him together and smooth him out on the stones."

The young man drew a yellowish roll of paper-like substance from his pocket and laid it on the table.

"This is the same papyrus," he said. "I had forgotten that I carried it away with me until I found it in my shooting coat while packing to sail for New York."

The Tracer of Lost Persons reached over and picked up the scroll. It was flexible still, but brittle; he opened it with great care, considered the strange figures upon it for a while, then turned almost sharply on his visitor.

"Go on," he said.

And Burke went on:

"The candle was burning low; I lighted two more, placing them at her head and feet on the edges of the stone couch. Then, lighting a third candle, I stood beside the couch and looked down at the dead girl under her veil-like robe, set with golden stars."

He passed his hand wearily over his hair and forehead.

"I do not know what the accepted meaning of beauty may be if it was not there under my eyes. Flawless as palest amber ivory and rose, the smooth-flowing contours melted into exquisite symmetry; lashes like darkest velvet rested on the pure curve of the cheeks; the closed lids, the mouth still faintly stained with color, the delicate nose, the full, childish lips, sensitive, sweet, resting softly upon each other—if these were not all parts of but one lovely miracle, then there is no beauty save in a dream of Paradise....

"A gold band of linked scarabs bound her short, thick hair straight across the forehead; thin scales of gold fell from a necklace, clothing her breasts in brilliant discolored metal, through which ivory-tinted skin showed. A belt of pure, soft gold clasped her body at the waist; gold-edged sandals clung to her little feet.

"At first, when the stunned surprise had subsided, I thought that I was looking upon some miracle of ancient embalming, hitherto unknown. Yet, in the smooth skin there was no slit to prove it, no opening in any vein or artery, no mutilation of this sculptured masterpiece of the Most High, no cerements, no bandages, no gilded carven case with painted face to stare open eyed through the waiting cycles.

"This was the image of sleep—of life unconscious—not of death. Yet it was death—death that had come upon her centuries and centuries ago; for the gold had turned iridescent and magnificently discolored; the sandal straps fell into dust as I bent above them, leaving the sandals clinging to her feet only by the wired silver core of the thongs. And, as I touched it fearfully, the veil-like garment covering her, vanished into thin air, its metal stars twinkling in a shower around her on the stone floor."

The Tracer, motionless, intent, scarcely breathed; the younger man moved restlessly in his chair, the dazed light in his eyes clearing to sullen consciousness.

"What more is there to tell?" he said. "And to what purpose? All this is time wasted. I have my work cut out for me. What more is there to tell?"

"What you have left untold," said the Tracer, with the slightest ring of authority in his quiet voice.

And, as though he had added "Obey!" the younger man sank back in his chair, his hands contracting nervously.

"I went back to El Teb," he said; "I walked like a dreaming man. My sleep was haunted by her beauty; night after night, when at last I fell asleep, instantly I saw her face, and her dark eyes opening into mine in childish bewilderment; day after day I rode out to the fallen pillar and descended to that dark chamber where she lay alone. Then there came a time when I could not endure the thought of her lying there alone. I had never dared to touch her. Horror of what might happen had held me aloof lest she crumble at my touch to that awful powder which I had trodden on.

"I did not know what to do; my Arabs had begun to whisper among themselves, suspicious of my absences, impatient to break camp, perhaps, and roam on once more. Perhaps they believed I had discovered treasure somewhere; I am not sure. At any rate, dread of their following me, determination to take my dead away with me, drove me into action; and that day when I reached her silent chamber I lighted my candle, and, leaning above her for one last look, I touched her shoulder with my finger tip.

"It was a strange sensation. Prepared for a dreadful dissolution, utterly unprepared for cool, yielding flesh, I almost dropped where I stood. For her body was neither cold nor warm, neither dust-dry nor moist; neither the skin of the living nor the dead. It was firm, almost stiff, yet not absolutely without a certain hint of flexibility.

"The appalling wonder of it consumed me; fear, incredulity, terror, apathy succeeded each other; then slowly a fierce shrinking happiness swept me in every fiber.

"This marvelous death, this triumph of beauty over death, was mine. Never again should she lie here alone through the solitudes of night and day; never again should the dignity of Death lack the tribute demanded of Life. Here was the appointed watcher—I, who had found her alone in the wastes of the world—all alone on the outermost edges of the world—a child, dead and unguarded. And standing there beside her I knew that I should never love again."

He straightened up, stretching out his arm: "I did not intend to carry her away to what is known as Christian burial. How could I consign her to darkness again, with all its dreadful mockery of marble, all its awful emblems?

"This lovely stranger was to be my guest forever. The living should be near her while she slept so sweetly her slumber through the centuries; she should have warmth, and soft hangings and sunlight and flowers; and her unconscious ears should be filled with the pleasant stir of living things.... I have a house in the country, a very old house among meadows and young woodlands. And I—I had dreamed of giving this child a home—"

His voice broke; he buried his head in his hands a moment; but when he lifted it again his features were hard as steel.

"There was already talk in the bazaar about me. I was probably followed, but I did not know it. Then one of my men disappeared. For a week I hesitated to trust my Arabs; but there was no other way. I told them there was a mummy which I desired to carry to some port and smuggle out of the country without consulting the Government. I knew perfectly well that the Government would never forego its claim to such a relic of Egyptian antiquity. I offered my men too much, perhaps. I don't know. They hesitated for a week, trying by every artifice to see the treasure, but I never let them out of my sight.

"Then one day two white men came into camp; and with them came a government escort to arrest me for looting an Egyptian tomb. The white men were Joram Smiles and that Eurasian, Emanuel Gandon, who was partly white, I suppose. I didn't comprehend what they were up to at first. They escorted me forty miles to confront the official at Shen-Bak. When, after a stormy week, I was permitted to return to Saïs, my Arabs and the white men were gone. And the stone chamber under the water garden wall was empty as the hand I hold out to you!"

He opened his palm and rose, his narrowing eyes clear and dangerous.

"At the bazaar I learned enough to know what had been done. I traced the white men to the coast. They sailed on the *Scythian Queen*, taking with them all that I care for on earth or in heaven! And you ask me why I measure their distance from me by a bullet's flight!"

The Tracer also rose, pale and grave.

"Wait!" he said. "There are other things to be done before you prepare to face a jury for double murder."

"It is for them to choose," said Burke. "They shall have the choice of returning to me my dead, or of going to hell full of lead."

"*Exactly*, my dear sir. That part is not difficult," said the Tracer quietly. "There will be no occasion for violence, I assure you. Kindly leave such details to me. I know what is to be done. You are outwardly very calm, Mr. Burke—even dangerously placid; but though you maintain an admirable command over yourself superficially, you are laboring under terrible excitement. Therefore it is my duty to say to you at once that there is no cause for your excitement, no cause for your apprehension as to results. I feel exceedingly confident that you will, in due time, regain possession of all that you care for most—quietly, quietly, my dear sir! You are not yet ready to meet these men, nor am I ready to go with you. I beg you to continue your habit of self-command for a little while. There is no haste—that is to say, there is every reason to make haste slowly. And the quickest method is to seat yourself. Thank you. And I shall sit here beside you and spread out this papyrus scroll for your inspection."

Burke stared at the Tracer, then at the scroll. "What has that inscription to do with the matter in hand?" he demanded impatiently.

"I leave you to judge," said the Tracer. A dull tint of excitement flushed his lean cheeks; he twisted his gray mustache and bent over the unrolled scroll which was now held flat by weights at the four corners.

"Can you understand any of these symbols, Mr. Burke?" he asked.

"No."

"Curious," mused the Tracer. "Do you know it was fortunate that you put this bit of papyrus in the pocket of your shooting coat—so fortunate that, in a way, it approaches the miraculous?"

"What do you mean? Is there anything in that scroll bearing on this matter?"

"Yes."

"And you can read it? Are you versed in such learning, Mr. Keen?"

"I am an Egyptologist—among other details," said the Tracer calmly.

The young man gazed at him, astonished. The Tracer of Lost Persons picked up a pencil, laid a sheet of paper on the table beside the papyrus, and slowly began to copy the first symbol:

CHAPTER XIX

"The ancient Egyptian word for the personal pronoun 'I' was nuk," said the Tracer placidly. "The phonetic for à was the hieroglyph

a reed; for *n* the water symbol

for *u* the symbols

for *k*

Therefore this hieroglyphic inscription begins with the personal pronoun

or *I*. That is very easy, of course.

"Now, the most ancient of Egyptian inscriptions read vertically in columns; there are only two columns in this papyrus, so we'll try it vertically and pass downward to the next symbol, which is inclosed in a sort of frame or cartouch. That immediately signifies that royalty is mentioned; therefore, we have already translated as much as 'I, the king (or queen).' Do you see?"

"Yes," said Burke, staring.

"Very well. Now this symbol, number two,

spells out the word '*Meris*,' in this way: M (pronounced *me*) is phonetically symbolized by the characters

r by

(a mouth) and the comma

and the hieroglyph

i by two reeds

and two oblique strokes,

and *s* by

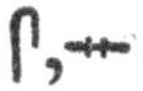

This gives us Meris, the name of that deposed and fugitive king of Egypt who, after a last raid on the summer palace of Mer-Shen, usurping ruler of Egypt, was followed and tracked to Saïs, where, with an arrow through his back, he crawled to El Teb and finally died there of his wound. All this Egyptologists are perfectly familiar with in the translations of the boastful tablets and inscriptions erected near Saïs by Mer-Shen, the three hundred and twelfth sovereign after Queen Nitocris."

He looked up at Burke, smiling. "Therefore," he said, "this papyrus scroll was written by Meris, ex-king, a speculative thousands of years before Christ. And it begins: 'I, Meris the King.'"

"How does all this bear upon what concerns me?" demanded Burke.

"Wait!"

Something in the quiet significance of the Tracer's brief command sent a curious thrill through the younger man. He leaned stiffly forward, studying the scroll, every faculty concentrated on the symbol which the Tracer had now touched with the carefully sharpened point of his pencil:

"That," said Mr. Keen, "is the ancient Egyptian word for 'little,'" '*Ket.*' The next, below, written in two lines, is 'Samaris,' a proper name—the name of a woman. Under that, again, is the symbol for the number 18; the decimal sign,

and eight vertical strokes,

Under that, again, is a hieroglyph of another sort, an ideograph representing a girl with a harp; and, beneath that, the symbol which always represented a dancing girl

and also the royal symbol inclosed in a cartouch,

which means literally 'the Ruler of Upper and Lower Egypt.' Under that is the significant symbol

representing an arm and a hand holding a stick. This always means *force*—to take forcibly or to use violence. Therefore, so far, we have the following literal translation: 'I, Meris the King, little Samaris, eighteen, a harpist, dancing girl, the Ruler of Upper and Lower Egypt, to take by violence—'"

"What does that make?" broke in Burke impatiently.

"*Wait!* Wait until we have translated everything literally. And, Mr. Burke, it might make it easier for us both if you would remember that I have had the pleasure of deciphering many hundreds of papyri before you had ever heard that there were such things."

"I beg your pardon," said the young man in a low voice.

"I beg yours for my impatience," said the Tracer pleasantly. "This deciphering always did affect my nerves and shorten my temper. And, no doubt, it is quite as hard on you. Shall we go on, Mr. Burke?"

"If you please, Mr. Keen."

So the Tracer laid his pencil point on the next symbol

"That is the symbol for night," he said; "and that

is the water symbol again, as you know; and that

is the ideograph, meaning a ship. The five reversed crescents

record the number of days voyage; the sign

means a house, and is also the letter H in the Egyptian alphabet.

"Under it, again, we have a repetition of the first symbol meaning *I*, and a repetition of the second symbol, meaning 'Meris, the King.' Then, below that cartouch, comes a new symbol,

which is the feminine personal pronoun, *sentus*, meaning '*she*'; and the first column is completed with the symbol for the ancient Egyptian verb, *nehes*, 'to awake,'

"And now we take the second column, which begins with the jackal ideograph expressing slyness or cleverness. Under it is the hieroglyph meaning 'to run away,' 'to escape.' And under that, Mr. Burke, is one of the rarest of all Egyptian symbols; a symbol seldom seen on stone or papyrus,

except in rare references to the mysteries of Isis. The meaning of it, so long in dispute, has finally been practically determined through a new discovery in the cuneiform inscriptions. It is the symbol of two hands holding two *closed* eyes; and it signifies power."

"You mean that those ancients understood hypnotism?" asked Burke, astonished.

"Evidently their priests did; evidently hypnotism was understood and employed in certain mysteries. And there is the symbol of it; and under it the hieroglyphs

meaning 'a day and a night,' with the symbol

as usual present to signify force or strength employed. Under that, again, is a human figure stretched upon a typical Egyptian couch. And now, Mr. Burke, *note carefully* three modifying signs: first, that it is a *couch* or *bed* on which the figure is stretched, not the funeral couch, not the embalming slab; second, there is no mummy mask covering the face, and no mummy case covering the body; third, that under the recumbent figure is pictured an *open* mouth, not a *closed* one.

"All these modify the ideograph, apparently representing death. But the sleep symbol is not present. Therefore it is a sound inference that all this simply confirms the symbol of hypnotism."

Burke, intensely absorbed, stared steadily at the scroll.

"Now," continued Mr. Keen, "we note the symbol of force again, always present; and, continuing horizontally, a cartouch quite empty except for the midday sun. That is simply translated; the midday sun illuminates nothing. Meris, deposed, is king only in name; and the sun no longer shines on him as 'Ruler of Upper and Lower Egypt.' Under that despairing symbol, 'King of Nothing,' we have

the phonetics which spell *sha*, the word for garden. And, just beyond this, horizontally, the modifying ideograph meaning 'a *water* garden';

a design of lotus and tree alternating on a terrace. Under that is the symbol for the word *'aneb,'*

a 'wall.' Beyond that, horizontally, is the symbol for 'house.' It should be placed under the wall symbol, but the Egyptians were very apt to fill up spaces instead of continuing their vertical columns. Now, beneath, we find

the imperative command

'arise!' And the Egyptian personal pronoun '*entuten*,'

which means 'you' or 'thou.'

"Under that is the symbol

which means 'priest,' or, literally, 'priest man.' Then comes the imperative 'awake to life!'

After that, our first symbol again, meaning '*I*,' followed horizontally by the symbol

signifying 'to go.'

"Then comes a very important drawing—you see?—the picture of a man with a jackal's head, not a dog's head. It is not accompanied by the phonetic in a cartouch, as it should be. Probably the writer was in desperate haste at the end. But, nevertheless, it is easy to translate that symbol of the man with a jackal's head. It is a picture of the Egyptian god, Anubis, who was supposed to linger at the side of the dying to conduct their souls. Anubis, the jackal-headed, is the courier, the personal escort of departing souls. And this is he.

"And now the screed ends with the cry 'Pray for me!'

the last symbol on this strange scroll—this missive written by a deposed, wounded, and dying king to an unnamed priest. Here is the literal translation in columns:

<table>
<tr><td>I</td><td>cunning</td></tr>
<tr><td>Meris the King</td><td>escape</td></tr>
<tr><td>little</td><td>hypnotize</td></tr>
<tr><td>Samaris</td><td>King of Nothing ⎫</td></tr>
<tr><td>eighteen</td><td>place forcibly ⎭</td></tr>
<tr><td>a harpist</td><td>garden ⎫</td></tr>
<tr><td>a dancing girl—Ruler of</td><td>water garden ⎭</td></tr>
<tr><td> Upper and Lower</td><td>wall</td></tr>
<tr><td> Egypt</td><td>house</td></tr>
<tr><td>took forcibly—night</td><td>Arise. Do</td></tr>
<tr><td>by water</td><td>Thou</td></tr>
<tr><td>five days</td><td>Priest Man</td></tr>
<tr><td>ship</td><td>Awake ⎫</td></tr>
<tr><td>house</td><td>To life ⎭</td></tr>
<tr><td>I</td><td>I go</td></tr>
<tr><td>Meris the King</td><td>Anubis</td></tr>
<tr><td>she</td><td>Pray</td></tr>
<tr><td>awake</td><td></td></tr>
</table>

"And this is what that letter, thousands of years old, means in this language of ours, hundreds of years young: 'I, Meris the King, seized little Samaris, a harpist and a dancing girl, eighteen years of age, belonging to the King of Upper and Lower Egypt, and carried her away at night on shipboard—a voyage of five days—to my house. I, Meris the King, lest she lie awake watching cunningly for a chance to escape, hypnotized her (or had her hypnotized) so that she lay like one dead or asleep, but breathing, and I, King no longer of Upper and Lower Egypt, took her and placed her in my house under the wall of the water garden. Arise! therefore, O thou priest; (go) and awaken her to life. I am dying (I go with Anubis!). Pray for me!'"

CHAPTER XX

For a full minute the two men sat there without moving or speaking. Then the Tracer laid aside his pencil.

"To sum up," he said, opening the palm of his left hand and placing the forefinger of his right across it, "the excavation made by the falling pillar raised in triumph above the water garden of the deposed king, Meris, by his rival, was the subterranean house of Meris. The prostrate figure which crumbled to powder at your touch may have been the very priest to whom this letter or papyrus was written. Perhaps the bearer of the scroll was a traitor and stabbed the priest as he was reading the missive. Who can tell how that priest died? He either died or betrayed his trust, for he never aroused the little Samaris from her suspended animation. And the water garden fell into ruins and she slept; and the Ruler of Upper and Lower Egypt raised his columns, lotus crowned, above the ruins; and she slept on. Then—you came."

Burke stared like one stupefied.

"I do not know," said the Tracer gravely, "what balm there may be in a suspension of sensation, perhaps of vitality, to protect the human body from corruption after death. I do not know how soon suspended animation or the state of hypnotic coma, undisturbed, changes into death— whether it comes gradually, imperceptibly freeing the soul; whether the soul hides there, asleep, until suddenly the flame of vitality is extinguished. I do not know how long she lay there with life in her."

He leaned back and touched an electric bell, then, turning to Burke:

"Speaking of pistol range," he said, "unstrap those weapons and pass them over, if you please."

And the young man obeyed as in a trance.

"Thank you. There are four men coming into this room. You will keep your seat, if you please, Mr. Burke."

After a moment the door opened noiselessly. Two men handcuffed together entered the room; two men, hands in their pockets, sauntered carelessly behind the prisoners and leaned back against the closed door.

"That short, red-haired, lame man with the cast in his eye—do you recognize him?" asked the Tracer quietly.

Burke, grasping the arms of his chair, had started to rise, fury fairly blazing from his eyes; but, at the sound of the Tracer's calm, even voice, he sank back into his chair.

"That is Joram Smiles? You recognize him?" continued Mr. Keen.

Burke nodded.

"*Exactly*—alias Limpy, alias Red Jo, alias Big Stick Joram, alias Pinky; swindler, international confidence man, fence, burglar, gambler; convicted in 1887, and sent to Sing Sing for forgery; convicted in 1898, and sent to Auburn for swindling; arrested by my men on board the S.S. *Scythian Queen*, at the cabled request of John T. Burke, Esquire, and held to explain the nature of his luggage, which consisted of the contents of an Egyptian vault or underground ruin, declared at the customhouse as a mummy, and passed as such."

The quiet, monotonous voice of the Tracer halted, then, as he glanced at the second prisoner, grew harder:

"Emanuel Gandon, general international criminal, with over half a hundred aliases, arrested in company with Smiles and held until Mr. Burke's arrival."

Turning to Burke, the Tracer continued: "Fortunately, the *Scythian Queen* broke down off Brindisi. It gave us time to act on your cable; we found these men aboard when she was signaled off the Hook. I went out with the pilot myself, Mr. Burke."

Smiles shot a wicked look at Burke; Gandon scowled at the floor.

"Now," said the Tracer pleasantly, meeting the venomous glare of Smiles, "I'll get you that warrant you have been demanding to have exhibited to you. Here it is—charging you and your amiable friend Gandon with breaking into and robbing the Metropolitan Museum of ancient Egyptian gold ornaments, in March, 1903, and taking them to France, where they were sold to collectors. It seems that you found the business good enough to go prowling about Egypt on a hunt for something to sell here. A great mistake, my friends—a very great mistake, because, after the Museum has finished with you, the Egyptian Government desires to extradite you. And I rather suspect you'll have to go."

He nodded to the two quiet men leaning against the door.

"Come, Joram," said one of them pleasantly.

But Smiles turned furiously on the Tracer. "You lie, you old gray rat!" he cried. "That ain't no mummy; that's a plain dead girl! And there ain't no extrydition for body snatchin', so I guess them niggers at Cairo won't get us, after all!"

"Perhaps," said the Tracer, looking at Burke, who had risen, pale and astounded. "Sit down, Mr. Burke! There is no need to question these men; no need to demand what they robbed you of. For," he added slowly, "what they took from the garden grotto of Saïs, and from you, I have under my own protection."

The Tracer rose, locked the door through which the prisoners and their escorts had departed; then, turning gravely on Burke, he continued:

"That panel, there, is a door. There is a room beyond—a room facing to the south, bright with sunshine, flowers, soft rugs, and draperies of the East. *She* is there—like a child asleep!"

Burke reeled, steadying himself against the wall; the Tracer stared at space, speaking very slowly:

"Such death I have never before heard of. From the moment she came under my protection I have dared to doubt—many things. And an hour ago you brought me a papyrus scroll confirming my doubts. I doubt still—Heaven knows what! Who can say how long the flame of life may flicker within suspended animation? A week? A month? A year? Longer than that?

Yes; the Hindoos have proved it. How long? The span of a normal life? Or longer? Can the life flame burn indefinitely when the functions are absolutely suspended—generation after generation, century after century—"

Burke, ghastly white, straightened up, quivering in every limb; the Tracer, as pale as he, laid his hand on the secret panel.

"If—if you dare say it—the phrase is this: '*O Ket Samaris, Nehes!*' 'O Little Samaris, awake!'"

"I—dare. In Heaven's name, open that door!"

Then, averting his head, the Tracer of Lost Persons swung open the panel.

A flood of sunshine flashed on Burke's face; he entered; and the paneled door closed behind him without a sound.

Minute after minute passed; the Tracer stood as though turned to stone, gray head bent.

Then he heard Burke's voice ring out unsteadily:

"O Ket Samaris—Samaris! O Ket Samaris—*Nehes!*"

And again: "Samaris! Samaris! O beloved, awake!"

And once more: "*Nehes!* O Samaris!"

Silence, broken by a strange, sweet, drowsy plaint—like a child awakened at midnight by a dazzling light.

"Samaris!"

Then, through the stillness, a little laugh, and a softly tremulous voice: "*Ari un āhā, O Entuk sen!*"

CHAPTER XXI

"What we want to do," said Gatewood over the telephone, "is to give you a corking little dinner at the Santa Regina. There'll be Mr. and Mrs. Tommy Kerns, Captain and Mrs. Harren, Mr. and Mrs. Jack Burke, Mrs. Gatewood, and myself. We want you to set the date for it, Mr. Keen, and we also wish you to suggest one more deliriously happy couple whom you have dragged out of misery and flung head-first into terrestrial paradise."

"Do you young people really care to do this for me?" asked the Tracer, laughing.

"Of course we do. We're crazy about it. We want one more couple, and you to set the date." There was the slightest pause; then the Tracer's voice, with the same undertone of amusement ringing through it:

"How would your cousin, Victor Carden, do?"

"He's all right, only he isn't married. We want two people whom you have joined together after hazard has put them asunder and done stunts with them."

"Very well; Victor Carden and his very lovely wife will be just the people."

"Is Victor married?" demanded Gatewood, astonished.

"No," said the Tracer demurely, "but he will be in time for that dinner." And he set the date for the end of the week in an amused voice, and rang off.

Then he glanced at the clock, touched an electric bell, and again unhooking the receiver of the telephone, called up the Sherwood Studios and asked for Mr. Carden.

"Is *this* Mr. Carden? Oh, good morning, Mr. Carden! This is Mr. Keen, Tracer of Lost Persons. Could you make it convenient to call—say in course of half an hour? Thank you.... What? ... Well, speaking with that caution and reserve which we are obliged to employ in making any preliminary statements to our clients, I think I may safely say that you have every reason to feel moderately encouraged."

"You mean," said Carden's voice, "that you have actually solved the proposition?"

"It has been a difficult proposition, Mr. Carden: I will not deny that it has taxed our resources to the uttermost. Over a thousand people, first and last, have been employed on this case. It has been a slow and tedious affair, Mr. Carden—tedious for us all. We seldom have a case continue as long as this has; it is a year ago to-day since you placed the matter in our hands....What? Well, without committing myself, I think that I may venture to express a carefully qualified opinion that the solution of the case is probably practically in the way of being almost accomplished! ... Yes, I shall expect you in half an hour. Good-by!"

The Tracer of Lost Persons' eyes were twinkling as he hung up the receiver and turned in his revolving chair to meet the pretty young woman who had entered in response to his ring.

"The Carden case, if you please, Miss Smith," he said, smiling to himself.

The young woman also smiled; the Carden case had become a classic in the office. Nobody except Mr. Keen had believed that the case could ever be solved.

"Safe-deposit box 108923!" said Miss Smith softly, pressing a speaking tube to her red lips. In a few moments there came a hissing thud from the pneumatic tube; Miss Smith unlocked it and extracted a smooth, steel cylinder.

"The combination for that cylinder is A-4-44-11-X," observed the Tracer, consulting a cipher code, "which, translated," he added, "gives us the setting combination, One, D, R-R,-J-'24."

Miss Smith turned the movable disks at the end of the cylinder until the required combination appeared. Then she unscrewed the cylinder head and dumped out the documents in the famous Carden case.

"As Mr. Carden will be here in half an hour or so I think we had better run over the case briefly," nodded the Tracer, leaning back in his chair and composing himself to listen. "Begin with my preliminary memorandum, Miss Smith."

"Case 108923," began the girl. Then she read the date, Carden's full name, Victor Carden, a terse biography of the same gentleman, and added: "Case accepted. Contingent fee, $5,000."

"Quite so," said Mr. Keen; "now, run through the minutes of the first interview."

And Miss Smith unrolled a typewritten scroll and read:

"Victor Carden, Esquire, the well-known artist, called this evening at 6.30. Tall, well-bred, good appearance, very handsome; very much embarrassed. Questioned by Mr. Keen he turned pink, and looked timidly at the stenographer (Miss Colt). Asked if he might not see Mr. Keen alone, Miss Colt retired. Mr. Keen set the recording phonograph in motion by dropping his elbow on his desk."

A brief *résumé* of the cylinder records followed:

"Mr. Carden asked Mr. Keen if he (Mr. Keen) knew who he (Mr. Carden) was. Mr. Keen replied that everybody knew Mr. Carden, the celebrated painter and illustrator who had created the popular type of beauty known as the 'Carden Girl.' Mr. Carden blushed and fidgeted. (Notes from *Mr. Keen's Observation Book, pp. 291-297.*) Admitted that he was the creator of the 'Carden Girl.' Admitted he had drawn and painted that particular type of feminine beauty many times. Fidgeted some more. (*Keen's O. B., pp. 298-299.*) Volunteered the statement that this type of beauty, known as the 'Carden Girl,' was the cause of great unhappiness to himself. Questioned, turned pinker and fidgeted. (*K. O. B., page 300.*) Denied that his present trouble was caused by the model who had posed for the 'Carden Girl.' Explained that a number of assorted models had posed for that type of beauty. Further explained that none of them resembled the type; that the type was his own creation; that he used models merely for the anatomy, and that he always idealized form and features.

"Questioned again, admitted that the features of the 'Carden Girl' were his ideal of the highest and loveliest type of feminine beauty. Did not deny that he had fallen in love with his own creation. Turned red and tried to smoke. (*K. O. B., page 303.*) Admitted he had been fascinated himself with his own rendering of a type of beauty which he had never seen anywhere except as rendered by his own pencil on paper or on canvas. Fidgeted. (*K.*

O. B., page 304.) Admitted that he could easily fall in love with a woman who resembled the 'Carden Girl.' Didn't believe she ever really existed. Confessed he had hoped for years to encounter her, but had begun to despair. Admitted that he had ventured to think that Mr. Keen might trace such a girl for him. Doubted Mr. Keen's success. Fidgeted (*K. O. B., page 306*), and asked Mr. Keen to take the case. Promised to send to Mr. Keen a painting in oil which embodied his loftiest ideal of the type known as the 'Carden Girl.' (*Portrait received; lithographs made and distributed to our agents according to routine, from Canada to Mexico and from the Atlantic to the Pacific.*)

"Mr. Keen terminated the interview with characteristic tact, accepting the case on the contingent fee of $5,000."

"Very well," said the Tracer, as Miss Smith rolled up the scroll and looked at him for further instructions. "Now, perhaps you had better run over the short summary of proceedings to date. I mean the digest which you will find attached to the completed records."

Miss Smith found the paper, unrolled it, and read:

"During the twelve months' investigation and search (*in re Carden*) seven hundred and nine young women were discovered who resembled very closely the type sought for. By process of elimination, owing to defects in figure, features, speech, breeding, etc., etc., this list was cut down to three. One of these occasionally chewed gum, but otherwise resembled the type. The second married before the investigation of her habits could be completed. The third is apparently a flawless replica of Mr. Carden's original in face, figure, breeding, education, moral and mental habits. (*See Document 23, A.*)"

"Read Document 23, A," nodded Mr. Keen.

And Miss Smith read:

ROSALIND HOLLIS, M. D.

Age	24
Height	5 feet 9 inches
Weight	160 pounds
Hair	Thick, bright, ruddy golden, and inclined to curl.
Teeth	Perfect
Eyes	Dark violet-blue
Mouth	Perfect
Color	Fair. An ivory-tinted blonde.
Figure	Perfect
Health	Perfect
Temper	Feminine

Habits   Austere, with a resolutely suppressed capacity for romance.
Business   None
Profession Physician
Mania   A Mission

"NOTE.—Dr. Rosalind Hollis was presented to society in her eighteenth year. At the end of her second season she withdrew from society with the determination to devote her entire life to charity. Settlement work and the study of medicine have occupied her constantly. Recently admitted to practice, she spends her mornings in visiting the poor, whom she treats free of all charge; her afternoons and evenings are devoted to what she expects is to be her specialty: the study of the rare malady known as Lamour's Disease. (*See note on second page.*)

"It is understood that Dr. Hollis has abjured the society of all men other than her patients and such of her professional *confrères* as she is obliged to consult or work with. Her theory is that of the beehive: drones for mates, workers for work. She adds, very decidedly, that she belongs to the latter division, and means to remain there permanently.

"NOTE (*Mr. Keen's O. B., pp. 916-18*).—Her eccentricity is probably the result of a fine, wholesome, highly strung young girl taking life and herself too seriously. The remedy will be the *Right Man.*"

"*Exactly,*" nodded Mr. Keen, joining the tips of his thin fingers and partly closing his eyes. "Now, Miss Smith, the disease which Dr. Hollis intends to make her specialty—have you any notes on that?"

"Here they are," said Miss Smith; and she read: "Lamour's Disease; the rarest of all known diseases; first discovered and described by Ero S. Lamour, M.D., M.S., F.B.A., M.F.H., in 1861. Only a single case has ever been observed. This case is fully described in Dr. Lamour's superb and monumental work in sixteen volumes. Briefly, the disease appears without any known cause, and is ultimately supposed to result fatally. The first symptom is the appearance of a faintly bluish circle under the eyes, as though the patient was accustomed to using the eyes too steadily at times. Sometimes a slight degree of fever accompanies this manifestation; pulse and temperature vary. The patient is apparently in excellent health, but liable to loss of appetite, restlessness, and a sudden flushing of the face. These symptoms are followed by others unmistakable: the patient becomes silent at times; at times evinces a weakness for sentimental expressions; flushes easily; is easily depressed; will sit for hours looking at one person; and, if not checked, will exhibit impulsive symptoms of affection for the opposite sex. The strangest symptom of all, however, is the physical change in the patient, whose features and figure, under the trained eye of the observer, gradually from day to day assume the symmetry and charm of a beauty almost unearthly, sometimes accompanied by a spiritual pallor which is unmistakable in confirming the diagnosis, and which, Dr. Lamour believes, presages the inexorable approach of immortality.

"There is no known remedy for Lamour's Disease. The only case on record is the case of the young lady described by Dr. Lamour, who watched her for years with unexampled patience and enthusiasm; finally, in the interest of science, marrying his patient in order to devote his life to a study of her symptoms. Unfortunately, some of these disappeared early—within a week—but the curious manifestation of physical beauty remained, and continued to increase daily to a dazzling radiance, with no apparent injury to the patient. Dr. Lamour, unfortunately, died before his investigations, covering over forty years, could be completed; his widow survived him for a day or two only, leaving sixteen children.

"Here is a wide and unknown field for medical men to investigate. It is safe to say that the physician who first discovers the bacillus of Lamour's Disease and the proper remedy to combat it will reap as his reward a glory and renown imperishable. Lamour's Disease is a disease not yet understood—a disease whose termination is believed to be fatal—a strange disease which seems to render radiant and beautiful the features of the patient, brightening them with the forewarning of impending death and the splendid resurrection of immortality."

The Tracer of Lost Persons caressed his chin reflectively. "*Exactly*, Miss Smith. So this is the disease which Dr. Hollis has chosen for her specialty. And only one case on record. *Ex*actly. Thank you."

Miss Smith replaced the papers in the steel cylinder, slipped it into the pneumatic tube, sent it whizzing below to the safe-deposit vaults, and, saluting Mr. Keen with a pleasant inclination of her head, went out of the room.

The Tracer turned in his chair, picked up the daily detective report, and scanned it until he came to the name Hollis. It appeared that the daily routine of Rosalind Hollis had not varied during the past three weeks. In the mornings she was good to the poor with bottles and pills; the afternoons she tucked one of Lamour's famous sixteen volumes under her arm and walked to Central Park, where, with democratic simplicity, she sat on a secluded bench and pored over the symptoms of Lamour's Disease. About five she retired to her severely simple apartments in the big brownstone office building devoted to physicians, corner of Fifty-eighth Street and Madison Avenue. Here she took tea, read a little, dined all alone, and retired about nine. This was the guileless but determined existence of Rosalind Hollis, M.D., according to McConnell, the detective assigned to observe her.

The Tracer refolded the report of his chief of detectives and pigeonholed it just as the door opened and a tall, well-built, attractive young man entered.

Shyness was written all over him; he offered his hand to Mr. Keen with an embarrassed air and seated himself at that gentleman's invitation.

"I'm almost sorry I ever began this sort of thing," he blurted out, like a big schoolboy appalled at his own misdemeanors. "The truth is, Mr. Keen, that the prospect of actually seeing a 'Carden Girl' alive has scared me through and through. I've a notion that my business with that sort of a girl ends when I've drawn her picture."

"But surely," said the Tracer mildly, "you have some natural curiosity to see the living copy of your charming but inanimate originals, haven't you, Mr. Carden?"

"Yes—oh, certainly. I'd like to see one of them alive—say out of a window, or from a cab. I should not care to be too close to her."

"But merely seeing her does not commit you," interposed Mr. Keen, smiling. "She is far too busy, too much absorbed in her own affairs to take any notice of you. I understand that she has something of an aversion for men."

"Aversion!"

"Well, she excludes them as unnecessary to her existence."

"Why?" asked Carden.

"Because she has a mission in life," said Mr. Keen gravely.

Carden looked out of the window. It was pleasant weather—June in all its early loveliness—the fifth day of June. The sixth was his birthday.

"I've simply got to marry somebody before the day after to-morrow," he said aloud—"that is, if I want my legacy."

"What!" demanded the Tracer sharply.

Carden turned, pink and guilty. "I didn't tell you all the circumstances of my case," he said. "I suppose I ought to have done so."

"*Exactly*," said the Tracer severely. "Why is it necessary that you marry somebody before the day after to-morrow?"

"Well, it's my twenty-fifth birthday—"

"Somebody has left you money on condition that you marry before your twenty-fifth birthday? Is that it, Mr. Carden? An uncle? An imbecile grandfather? A sentimental aunt?"

"My Aunt Tabby Van Beekman."

"Where is she?"

"In Trinity churchyard. It's too late to expostulate with her, you see. Besides, it wouldn't have done any good when she was alive."

The Tracer knitted his brows, musing, the points of his slim fingers joined.

"She was very proud, very autocratic," said Carden. "I am the last of my race and my aunt was determined that the race should not die out with me. I don't want to marry and increase, but she's trying to make me. At all events, I am not going to marry any woman inferior to the type I have created with my pencil—what the public calls the 'Carden Girl.' And now you see that your discovery of this living type comes rather late. In two days I must be legally married if I want my Aunt Tabby's legacy; and to-day for the first time I hear of a girl who, you assure me, compares favorably to my copyrighted type, but who has a mission and an aversion to men. So you see, Mr. Keen, that the matter is perfectly hopeless."

"I don't see anything of the kind," said Mr. Keen firmly.

"What?—do you believe there is any chance—"

"Of your falling in love within the next hour or so? Yes, I do. I think there is every chance of it. I am sure of it. But that is not the difficulty. The problem is far more complicated."

"You mean—"

"*Exactly*; how to marry that girl before day after to-morrow. That's the problem, Mr. Carden!—not whether you are capable of falling in love with her. I have seen her; I *know* you can't avoid falling in love with her. Nobody could. I myself am on the verge of it; and I am fifty: you can't avoid loving her."

"If that were so," said Carden gravely; "if I were really going to fall in love with her—I would not care a rap about my Aunt Tabby and her money—"

"You ought to care about it for this young girl's sake. That legacy is virtually hers, not yours. She has a right to it. No man can ever give enough to the woman he loves; no man has ever done so. What *she* gives and what *he* gives are never a fair exchange. If you can balance the account in any measure, it is your duty to do it. Mr. Carden, if she comes to love you she may think it very fine that you bring to her your love, yourself, your fame, your talents, your success, your position, your gratifying income. But I tell you it's not enough to balance the account. It is never enough—no, not all your devotion to her included! You can never balance the account on earth—all you can do is to try to balance it materially and spiritually. Therefore I say, endow her with *all* your earthly goods. Give all you can in every way to lighten as much as possible man's hopeless debt to all women who have ever loved."

"You talk about it as though I were already committed," said Carden, astonished.

"You are, morally. For a month I have, without her knowledge, it is true, invaded the privacy of a very lovely young girl—studied her minutely, possessed myself of her history, informed myself of her habits. What excuse had I for this unless I desired her happiness and yours? Nobody could offer me any inducement to engage in such a practice unless I believed that the means might justify a moral conclusion. And the moral conclusion of this investigation is your marriage to her."

"Certainly," said Carden uneasily, "but how are we going to accomplish it by to-morrow? How is it going to be accomplished at all?"

The Tracer of Lost Persons rose and began to pace the long rug, clasping his hands behind his back. Minute after minute sped; Carden stared alternately at Mr. Keen and at the blue sky through the open window.

"It is seldom," said Mr. Keen with evident annoyance, "that I personally take any spectacular part in the actual and concrete demonstrations necessary to a successful conclusion of a client's case. But I've got to do it this time."

He went to a cupboard, picked out a gray wig and gray side whiskers and deliberately waved them at Carden.

"You see what these look like?" he demanded.

"Y-yes."

"Very well. It is now noon. Do you know the Park? Do you happen to recollect a shady turn in the path after you cross the bridge over the swan lake? Here; I'll draw it for you. Now, here is the lake; here's the esplanade and fountain, you see. Here's the path. You follow it—so!—around the lake, across the bridge, then following the lake to the right—so!—then up the wooded slope to the left—so! Now, here is a bench. I mark it Number One. *She* sits there with her book—there she is!"

"If she looks like *that*—" began Carden. And they both laughed with the slightest trace of excitement.

"Here is Bench Number Two!" resumed the Tracer. "Here you sit—and there you are!"

"Thanks," said Carden, laughing again.

"Now," continued the Tracer, "you must be there at one o'clock. She will be there at one-thirty, or earlier perhaps. A little later I will become benignly visible. Your part is merely a thinking part; you are to do nothing, say nothing, unless spoken to. And when you are spoken to you are to acquiesce in whatever anybody says to you,

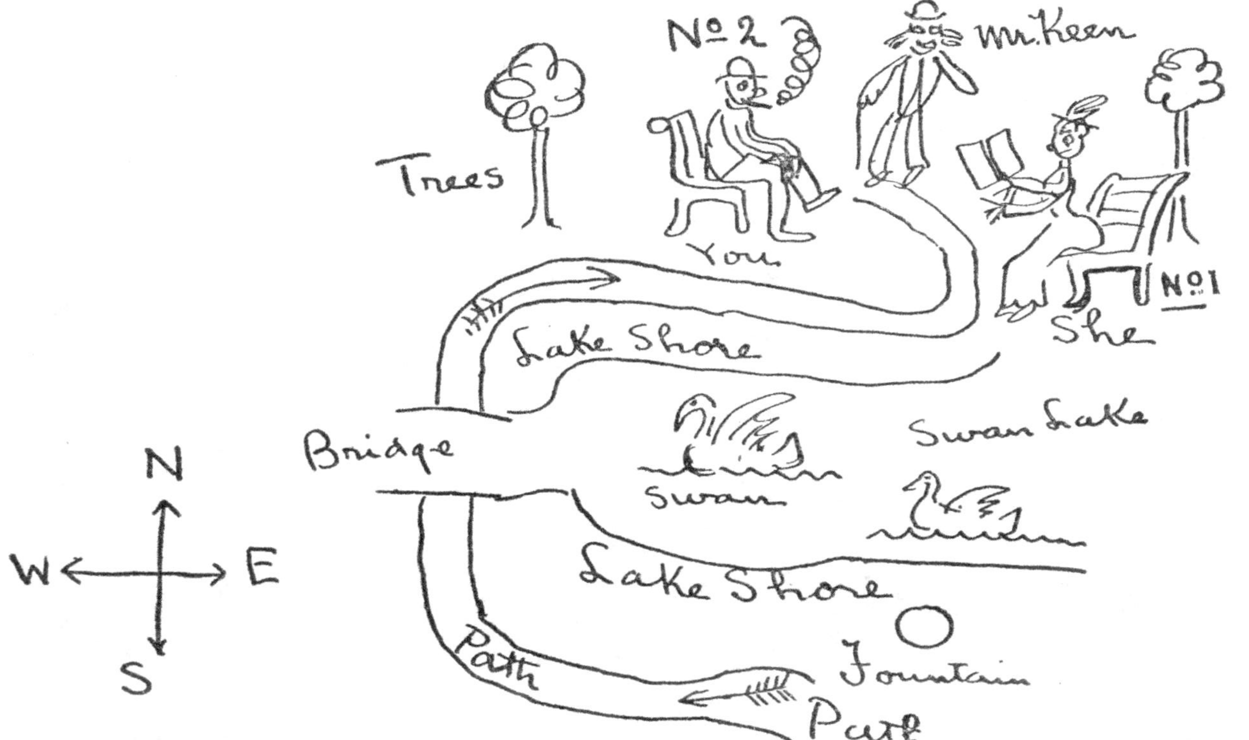
No. 2
Mr. Keen
Trees
You
She
No. 1
Lake Shore
Bridge
Swan Lake
Swan
Lake Shore
Fountain
Path
Path
N
W
E
S

and you are to do whatever anybody requests you to do. And, above all, don't be surprised at *anything* that may happen. You'll be nervous enough; I expect that. You'll probably color up and flush and fidget; I expect that; I count on that. But don't lose your nerve entirely; and don't think of attempting to escape."

"Escape! From what? From whom?"

"From her."

"*Her?*"

"Are you going to follow my instructions?" demanded the Tracer of Lost Persons.

"I—y-yes, of course."

"Very well, then. I am going to rub some of this under your eyes." And Mr. Keen produced a make-up box and, walking over to Carden, calmly darkened the skin under his eyes.

"I look as though I had been on a bat!" exclaimed Carden, surveying himself in a mirror. "Do you think any girl could find any attraction in such a countenance?"

"*She* will," observed the Tracer meaningly. "Now, Mr. Carden, one last word: The moment you find yourself in love with her, and the first moment you have the chance to do so decently, make love to her. She won't dismiss you; she will repulse you, of course, but she won't let you go. I know what I am saying; all I ask of you is to promise on your honor to carry out these instructions. Do you promise?"

"I do."

"Then here is the map of the rendezvous which I have drawn. Be there promptly. Good morning."

CHAPTER XXII

At one o'clock that afternoon a young man earnestly consulting a map might have been seen pursuing his solitary way through Central Park. Fresh green foliage arched above him, flecking the path with fretted shadow and sunlight; the sweet odor of flowering shrubs saturated the air; the waters of the lake sparkled where swans swept to and fro, snowy wings spread like sails to the fitful June wind.

"This," he murmured, pausing at a shaded bend in the path, "must be Bench Number One. I am not to sit on that. This must be Bench Number Two. I *am* to sit on that. So here I am," he added nervously, seating himself and looking about him with the caution of a cat in a strange back yard.

There was nobody in sight. Reassured, he ventured to drop one knee over the other and lean upon his walking stick. For a few minutes he remained in this noncommittal attitude, alert at every sound, anxious, uncomfortable, dreading he knew not what. A big, fat, gray squirrel racing noisily across the fallen leaves gave him a shock. A number of birds came to look at him—or so it appeared to him, for in the inquisitive scrutiny of a robin he fancied he divined sardonic meaning, and in the blank yellow stare of a purple grackle, a sinister significance out of all proportion to the size of the bird.

"What an absurd position to be in!" he thought. And suddenly he was seized with a desire to flee.

He didn't because he had promised not to, but the desire persisted to the point of mania. Oh, how he could run if he only hadn't promised not to! His entire being tingled with the latent possibilities of a burst of terrific speed. He wanted to scuttle away like a scared rabbit. The pace of the kangaroo would be slow in comparison. What a record he could make if he hadn't promised not to.

He crossed his knees the other way and brooded. The gray squirrel climbed the bench and nosed his pockets for possible peanuts, then hopped off hopefully toward a distant nursemaid and two children.

Growing more alarmed every time he consulted his watch Carden attempted to stem his rising panic with logic and philosophy, repeating: "Steady! my son! Don't act like this! You're not obliged to marry her if you don't fall in love with her; and if you do, you won't mind marrying her. That is philosophy. That is logic. Oh, I wonder what will have happened to me by this time to-morrow! I wish it were this time to-morrow! I wish it *were* this time next month! Then it would be all over. Then it would be—"

His muttering speech froze on his lips. Rooted to his bench he sat staring at a distant figure approaching—the figure of a young girl in a summer gown.

Nearer, nearer she came, walking with a free-limbed, graceful step, head high, one arm clasping a book.

That was the way the girls he drew would have walked had they ever lived. Even in the midst of his fright his artist's eyes noted that: noted the perfect figure, too, and the witchery of its grace and contour, and the fascinating poise of her head, and the splendid color of her hair; noted mechanically the flowing lines of her gown, and the dainty modeling of arm and wrist and throat and ear.

Then, as she reached her bench and seated herself, she raised her eyes and looked at him. And for the first time in his life he realized that ideal beauty was but the pale phantom of the real and founded on something more than imagination and thought; on something of vaster import than fancy and taste and technical skill; that it was founded on Life itself—on breathing, living, palpitating, tremulous Life!—from which all true inspiration must come.

Over and over to himself he was repeating: "Of course, it is perfectly impossible that I can be in love already. Love doesn't happen between two ticks of a watch. I am merely amazed at that girl's beauty; that is all. I am merely astounded in the presence of perfection; that is all. There is nothing more serious the matter with me. It isn't necessary for me to continue to look at her; it isn't vital to my happiness if I never saw her again.... That is—of course, I should like to see her, because I never did see living beauty such as hers in any woman. Not even in my pictures. What superb eyes! What a fascinately delicate nose! *What* a nose! By Heaven, that nose *is* a nose! I'll draw noses *that* way in future. My pictures are all out of drawing; I must fit arms into their sockets the way hers fit! I must remember the modeling of her eyelids, too—and that chin! and those enchanting hands—"

She looked up leisurely from her book, surveyed him calmly, absent-eyed, then bent her head again to the reading.

"There *is* something the matter with me," he thought with a suppressed gulp. "I—if she looks at me again—with those iris-hued eyes of a young goddess—I—I think I'm done for. I believe I'm done for anyway. It seems rather mad to think it. But there is something the matter—"

She deliberately looked at him again.

"It's all wrong for them to let loose a girl like that on people," he thought to himself, "all wrong. Everybody is bound to go mad over her. I'm going now. I'm mad already. I know I am, which proves I'm no lunatic. It isn't her beauty; it's the way she wears it—every motion, every breath of her. I know exactly what her voice is like. Anybody who looks into her eyes can see what her soul is like. She isn't out of drawing anywhere —physically or spiritually. And when a man sees a girl like that, why—why there's only one thing that can happen to him as far as I can see. And it doesn't take a year either. Heavens! How awfully remote from me she seems to be."

She looked up again, calmly, but not at him. A kindly, gray-whiskered old gentleman came tottering and rocking into view, his rosy, wrinkled face beaming benediction on the world as he passed through it—on the sunshine dappling the undergrowth, on the furry squirrels sitting up on their hind legs to watch him pass, on the stray dicky-bird that hopped fearlessly in his path, at the young man sitting very rigid there on his bench, at the fair, sweet-faced girl who met his aged eyes with the gentlest of involuntary smiles. And Carden did not recognize him!

Who could help smiling confidently into that benign face, with its gray hair and gray whiskers? Goodness radiated from every wrinkle.

"Dr. Atwood!" exclaimed the girl softly as she rose to meet this marvelous imitation of Dr. Austin Atwood, the great specialist on children's diseases.

The old man beamed weakly at her, halted, still beaming, fumbled for his eyeglasses, adjusted them, and peered closely into her face.

"Bless my soul," he smiled, "our pretty Dr. Hollis!"

"I—I did not suppose you would remember me," she said, rosy with pleasure.

"Remember you? Surely, surely." He made her a quaint, old-fashioned bow, turned, and peeped across the walk at Carden. And Carden, looking straight into his face, did not know the old man, who turned to Dr. Hollis again with many mysterious nods of his doddering head.

"You're watching him, too, are you?" he chuckled, leaning toward her.

"Watching whom, Dr. Atwood?" she asked surprised.

"Hush, child! I thought you had noticed that unfortunate and afflicted young man opposite."

Dr. Hollis looked curiously at Carden, then at the old gentleman with gray whiskers.

"Please sit down, Dr. Atwood, and tell me," she murmured. "I have noticed nothing in particular about the young man on the bench there." And she moved to give him room; and the young man opposite stared at them both as though bereft of reason.

"A heavy book for small hands, my child," said the old gentleman in his quaintly garrulous fashion, peering with dimmed eyes at the volume in her lap.

She smiled, looking around at him.

"My, my!" he said, tremblingly raising his eyeglasses to scan the title on the page; "Dr. Lamour's famous works! Are *you* studying Lamour, child?"

"Yes," she said with that charming inflection youth reserves for age.

"Astonishing!" he murmured. "The coincidence is more than remarkable. A physician! And studying Lamour's Disease! Incredible!"

"Is there anything strange in that, Dr. Atwood?" she smiled.

"Strange!" He lowered his voice, peering across at Carden. "Strange, did you say? Look across the path at that poor young man sitting there!"

"Yes," she said, perplexed, "I see him."

"*What* do you see?" whispered the old gentleman in a shakily portentous voice. "Here you sit reading about what others have seen; now what do you, see?"

"Why, only a man—rather young—"

"No *symptoms?*"

"Symptoms? Of what?"

The old gentleman folded his withered hands over his cane. "My child," he said, "for a year I have had that unfortunate young man under secret observation. He was not aware of it; it never entered his mind that I could be observing him with minutest attention. He may have supposed there was nothing the matter with him. He was in error. I have studied him carefully. Look closer! *Are* there dark circles under his eyes—or are there not?" he ended in senile triumph.

"There are," she began, puzzled, "but I—but of what interest to me—"

"Compare his symptoms with the symptoms in that book you are studying," said the old gentleman hoarsely.

"Do you mean—do you suppose—" she stammered, turning her eyes on Carden, who promptly blushed to his ears and began to fidget.

"*Every symptom*," muttered the old gentleman. "Poor, poor young man!"

She had seen Carden turn a vivid pink; she now saw him fidget with his walking stick; she discovered the blue circles under his eyes. Three symptoms at once!

"Do you believe it *possible?*" she whispered excitedly under her breath to the old gentleman beside her. "It seems incredible! Such a rare disease! Only one single case ever described and studied! It seems impossible that I could be so fortunate as actually to see a case! Tell me, Dr. Atwood, do you believe that young man is really afflicted with Lamour's Disease?"

"There is but one way to be absolutely certain," said the old gentleman in a solemn voice, "and that is to study him; corroborate your suspicions by observing his pulse and temperature, as did Dr. Lamour."

"But—how can I?" she faltered. "I—he would probably object to becoming a patient of mine—"

"Ask him, child! Ask him."

"I have not courage—"

"Courage should be the badge of your profession," said the old gentleman gravely. "When did a good physician ever show the white feather in the cause of humanity?"

"I—I know, but this requires a different sort of courage."

"How," persisted the old gentleman, "can you confirm your very natural suspicions concerning this unfortunate young man unless you corroborate your observations by studying him at close range? Besides, already it seems to me that certain unmistakable signs are visible; I mean that strange physical phase which Dr. Lamour dwells on: the symmetry of feature and limb, the curiously spiritual beauty. Do you not notice these? Or is my sight so dim that I only imagine it?"

"He is certainly symmetrical—and—in a certain way—almost handsome in regard to features," she admitted, looking at Carden.

"Poor, poor boy!" muttered the old gentleman, wagging his gray whiskers. "I am too old to help him—too old to dream of finding a remedy for the awful malady which I am now convinced has seized him. I shall study him no more. It is useless. All I can do now is to mention his case to some young, vigorous, ambitious physician—some specialist—"

"Don't!" she whispered almost fiercely, "don't do that, Dr. Atwood! I want him, please! I—you helped me to discover him, you see. And his malady is to be my specialty. Please, do you mind if I keep him all to myself and study him?"

"But you refused, child."

"I didn't mean to. I—I didn't exactly see how I was to study him. But I must study him! Oh, I *must!* There will surely be some way. Please let me. You discovered him, I admit, but I will promise you faithfully to devote my entire life to studying him, as the great Lamour devoted his life for forty years to his single patient."

"But Dr. Lamour married his patient," said the Tracer mildly.

"He—I—that need not be necessary—"

"But if it should prove necessary?"

"I—you—"

"Answer me, child."

She stared across at Carden, biting her red lips. He turned pink promptly and fidgeted.

"He *has* got it!" she whispered excitedly. "Oh, *do* you mind if I take him for mine? I am perfectly wild to begin on him!"

"You have not yet answered my question," said the old gentleman gravely. "Do you lack the courage to marry him if it becomes necessary to do so in order to devote your entire life to studying him?"

"Oh—it *cannot* be necessary—"

"You lack the courage."

She was silent.

"Braver things have been done by those of your profession who have gone among lepers," said the old gentleman sadly.

She flushed up instantly; her eyes sparkled; her head proudly high, delicate nostrils dilated.

"I am not afraid!" she said. "If it ever becomes necessary, I *can* show courage and devotion, as well as those of my profession who minister to the lepers of Molokai! Yes; I do promise you to marry him if I cannot otherwise study him. And I promise you solemnly to devote my entire life to observing his symptoms and searching for proper means to combat them. My one ambition in life is personally to observe and study a case of Lamour's Disease, and to give my entire life to investigating its origin, its course, and its cure."

The old gentleman rose, bowing with that quaintly obsolete courtesy which was in vogue in his youth.

"I am contented to leave him exclusively to you, Dr. Hollis. And I wish you happiness in your life's work—and success in your cure of this unhappy young man."

Hat in hand, he bowed again as he tottered past her, muttering and smiling to himself and shaking his trembling head as he went rocking on unsteady legs out into the sunshine, where the nursemaids and children flocked along the lake shore throwing peanuts to the waterfowl and satiated goldfish.

Dr. Hollis looked after him, her small hand buried among the pages of her open book. Carden viewed his disappearing figure with guileless emotions. He was vaguely aware that something important was about to happen to him. And it did before he was prepared.

CHAPTER XXIII

When Rosalind Hollis found herself on her feet again a slight sensation of fright checked her for a moment. Then, resolutely suppressing such unworthy weakness, the lofty inspiration of her mission in life dominated her, and she stepped forward undaunted. And Carden, seeing her advance toward him, arose in astonishment to meet her.

For a second they stood facing each other, he astounded, she a trifle pale but firm. Then in a low voice she asked his pardon for disturbing him.

"I am Rosalind Hollis, a physician," she said quietly, "and physicians are sometimes obliged to do difficult things in the interest of their profession. It is dreadfully difficult for me to speak to you in this way. But"—she looked fearlessly at him—"I am confident you will not misinterpret what I have done."

He managed to assure her that he did not misinterpret it.

She regarded him steadily; she examined the dark circles under his eyes; she coolly observed his rising color under her calm inspection; she saw him fidgeting with his walking stick. She *must* try his pulse!

"Would you mind if I asked you a few questions in the interest of science?" she said earnestly.

"As a m-m-matter of fact," he stammered, "I don't know much about science. Awfully glad to do anything I can, you know."

"Oh, I don't mean it that way," she reassured him. A hint of a smile tinted her eyes with brilliant amethyst. "Would you mind if I sat here for a few moments? *Could* you overlook this horrid unconventionality long enough for me to explain why I have spoken to you?"

"I could indeed!" he said, so anxiously cordial that her lovely face grew serious and she hesitated. But he was standing aside, hat off, placing the bench at her disposal, and she seated herself, placing her book on the bench beside her.

"Would you mind sitting here for a few moments?" she asked him gravely.

Dazed, scarcely crediting the evidence of his senses, he took possession of the end of the bench with the silent obedience of a schoolboy. His attitude was irreproachable. She was grateful for this, and her satisfaction with herself for not having misjudged him renewed her confidence in him, in herself, and in the difficult situation.

She began, quietly, by again telling him her name and profession; where she lived, and that she was studying to be a specialist, though she did not intimate what that specialty was to be.

Outwardly composed and attentively deferential, his astonishment at times dominated a stronger sentiment that seemed to grow and expand with her every word, seizing him in a fierce possession absolutely and hopelessly complete.

The bewildering fascination of her mastered him. No cool analysis of what his senses were confirming could be necessary to convince him of his condition. Every word of hers, every gesture, every inflection of her sweet, clear voice, every lifting of her head, her eyes, her perfectly gloved hands, only repeated to him what he knew was a certainty. Never had he looked upon such physical loveliness; never had he dreamed of such a voice.

She had asked him a question, and, absorbed in the pure delight of looking at her, he had not comprehended or answered. She flushed sensitively, accepting his silence as refusal, and he came out of his trance hastily.

"I beg your pardon; I did not quite understand your question, Miss Hollis—I mean, Dr. Hollis."

"I asked you if you minded my noting your pulse," she said.

He stretched out his right hand; she stripped off her glove, laid the tip of her middle finger on his wrist, and glanced down at the gold watch which she held.

"I am wondering," he said, laughing uncertainly, "whether you believe me to be ill. Of course it is easy to see that you have found something unusual about me—something of particular interest to a physician. Is there anything very dreadful going to happen to me, Dr. Hollis? I feel perfectly well."

"Are you sure you feel well?" she asked, so earnestly that the smile on his lips faded out.

"Absolutely. Is my pulse queer?"

"It is not normal."

He could easily account for that, but he said nothing.

She questioned him for a few minutes, noted his pulse again, looked closely at the bluish circles under his eyes. Naturally he flushed up and grew restless under the calm, grave, beautiful eyes.

"I—I have an absolutely new and carefully sterilized thermometer—" She drew it from a tiny gold-initialed pocket case, and looked wistfully at him.

"You want to put that into my mouth?" he asked, astonished.

"If you don't mind."

She held it up, shook it once or twice, and deliberately inserted it between his lips. And there he sat, round-eyed, silent, the end of the thermometer protruding at a rakish angle from the corner of his mouth. And he grew redder and redder.

"I *don't* wish to alarm you," she was saying, "but all this is so deeply significant, so full of vital interest to me—to the world, to science—"

"*What* have I got, in Heaven's name?" he said thickly, the thermometer wiggling in his mouth.

"Ah!" she exclaimed with soft enthusiasm, clasping her pretty ungloved hands, "I cannot be sure yet—I dare not be too sanguine—"

"Do you mean that you *want* me to have something queer?" he blurted out, while the thermometer wiggled with every word he uttered.

"N-no, of course, I don't *want* you to be ill," she said hastily. "Only, if you *are* ill it will be a wonderful thing for me. I mean—a—that I am intensely interested in certain symptoms which—"

She gently withdrew the glass tube from his lips and examined it carefully.

"*Is* there anything the matter?" he insisted, looking at the instrument over her shoulder.

She did not reply; pure excitement rendered her speechless.

"I seem to *feel* all right," he added uneasily. "If you really believe that there's anything wrong with me, I'll stop in to see my doctor."

"Your doctor!" she repeated, appalled.

"Yes, certainly. Why not?"

"Don't do that! Please don't do that! I—why I discovered this case. *I* beg you most earnestly to let me observe it. You don't understand the importance of it! You don't begin to dream of the rarity of this case! How much it means to me!"

He flushed up. "Do you intend to intimate that I am afflicted with some sort of rare and s-s-trange d-d-disease?" he stammered.

"I dare not pronounce upon it too confidently," she said with enthusiasm; "I have not yet absolutely determined the nature of the disease. But, oh, I am beginning to hope—"

"Then I *am* diseased!" he faltered. "I've got *something* anyhow; is that it? Only you are not yet perfectly sure what it is called! Is that the truth, Miss Hollis?"

"How can I answer positively until I have had time to observe these symptoms? It requires time to be certain. I do not wish to alarm you, but it is my duty to say to you that you should immediately place yourself under medical observation."

"You think that?"

"I do; I am convinced of it. Please understand me; I do not pronounce upon these visible symptoms; I do not express an unqualified opinion; but I could be in a position to do so if you consent to place yourself under my observations and care. For these suspicious symptoms are not only very plainly apparent to me, but were even noted by that old gentleman whom you may perhaps have observed conversing with me."

"Yes, I saw him. Who is he?"

"Dr. Austin Atwood," said the girl solemnly.

"Oh! And you say he also observed something queer about me? What did he see? Are there spots on me? Am I turning any remarkable color? Am I—" And in the very midst of his genuine alarm he suddenly remembered the make-up box and what the Tracer of Lost Persons had done to his eyes. Was *that* it? Where was the Tracer, anyway? He had promised to appear. And then Carden recollected the gray wig and whiskers that the Tracer had waved at him from the cupboard, bidding him note them well. *Could* that beaming, benignant, tottering old gentleman have been the Tracer of Lost Persons himself? And the same instant Carden was sure of it, spite of the miraculous change in the man.

Then logic came to his aid; and, deducing with care and patience, an earnest conviction grew within him that the dark circles under his eyes and the tottering old gentleman resembling Dr. Austin Atwood had a great deal to do with this dreadful disease which Dr. Hollis desired to study.

He looked at the charming girl beside him, and she looked back at him very sweetly, very earnestly, awaiting his decision.

For a moment he realized that she had really scared him, and in the reaction of relief an overwhelming desire to laugh seized him. He managed to suppress it, to compose himself. Then he remembered the Tracer's admonition to acquiesce in everything, do what he was told to do, not to run away, and to pay his court at the first decent opportunity.

He had no longer any desire to escape; he was quite willing to do anything she desired.

"Do you really want to study me, Dr. Hollis?" he asked, feeling like a hypocrite.

"Indeed I do," she replied fervently.

"You believe me worth studying?"

"Oh, truly, truly, you are! You don't suspect—you cannot conceive how important you have suddenly become to me."

"Then I think you had better take my case, Dr. Hollis," he said seriously. "I begin now to realize that you believe me to be a sort of freak—an afflicted curiosity, and that, in the interest of medicine, I ought to go to an asylum or submit myself to the ceaseless observation of a competent private physician."

"I—I think it best for you to place yourself in my care," she said. "Will you?"

"Yes," he said, "I will. I'll do anything in the world you ask."

"That is very—very generous, very noble of you!" she exclaimed, flushing with excitement and delight. "It means a great deal to me—it means, perhaps, a fame that I scarcely dared dream of even in my most enthusiastic years. I am too grateful to express my gratitude coherently; I am trying to say to you that I thank you; that I recognize in you those broad, liberal, generous qualities which, from your appearance and bearing, I—I thought perhaps you must possess."

She colored again very prettily; he bowed, and ventured to remind her that she had not yet given him the privilege of naming himself.

"That is true!" she said, surprised. "I had quite forgotten it." But when he named himself she raised her head, startled.

"Victor Carden!" she repeated. "You are the *artist*, Victor Carden!"

"Yes," he said, watching her dilated eyes like two violet-tinted jewels.

For a minute she sat looking at him; and imperceptibly a change came into her face, and its bewildering beauty softened as the vivid tints died out, leaving her cheeks almost pale.

"It is—a pity," she said under her breath. All the excitement, all the latent triumph, all the scarcely veiled eager enthusiasm had gone from her now.

"A pity?" he repeated, smiling.

"Yes. I wish it had been only an ordinary man. I—why should this happen to you? You have done so much for us all—made us forget ourselves in the beauty of what you offer us. Why should this happen to *you!*"

"But you have not told me yet what has happened to me, Miss Hollis."

She looked up, almost frightened.

"*Are* you our Victor Carden? I do not wish to believe it! You have done so much for the world—you have taught us to understand and desire all that is noble and upright and clean and beautiful!—to desire it, to aspire toward it, to venture to live the good, true, wholesome lives that your penciled creations must lead—*must* lead to wear such beautiful bodies and such divine eyes!"

"Do *you* care for my work?" he asked, astonished and moved.

"I? Yes, of course I do. Who does not?"

"Many," he replied simply.

"I am sorry for them," she said.

They sat silent for a long while.

At first his overwhelming desire was to tell her of the deception practiced upon her; but he could not do that, because in exposing himself he must fail in loyalty to the Tracer of Lost Persons. Besides, she would not believe him. She would think him mad if he told her that the old gentleman she had taken for Dr. Atwood was probably Mr. Keen, the Tracer of Lost Persons. Also, he himself was not absolutely certain about it. He had merely deduced as much.

"Tell me," he said very gently, "what is the malady from which you believe I am suffering?"

For a moment she remained silent, then, face averted, laid her finger on the book beside her. "That," she said unsteadily.

He read aloud: "Lamour's Disease. A Treatise in sixteen volumes by Ero S. Lamour, M.D., M.S., F.B.A., M.F.H."

"All that?" he asked guiltily.

"I don't know, Mr. Carden. Are you laughing at me? Do you not believe me?" She had turned suddenly to confront him, surprising a humorous glimmer in his eyes.

"I really do not believe I am seriously ill," he said, laughing in spite of her grave eyes.

"Then perhaps you had better read a little about what Lamour describes as the symptoms of this malady," she said sadly.

"Is it fatal?" he inquired.

"Ultimately. That is why I desire to spend my life in studying means to combat it. That is why I desire you so earnestly to place yourself under my observation and let me try."

"Tell me one thing," he said; "is it contagious? Is it infectious? No? Then I don't mind your studying me all you wish, Dr. Hollis. You may take my temperature every ten minutes if you care to. You may observe my pulse every five minutes if you desire. Only please tell me how this is to be accomplished; because, you see, I live in the Sherwood Studio Building, and you live on Madison Avenue."

"I—I have a ward—a room—fitted up with every modern surgical device—every improvement," she said. "It adjoins my office. *Would* you mind living there for a while—say for a week at first—until I can be perfectly certain in my diagnosis?"

"Do you intend to put me to bed?" he asked, appalled.

"Oh, no! Only I wish to watch you carefully and note your symptoms from moment to moment. I also desire to try the effects of certain medicines on you—"

"What kind of medicines?" he asked uneasily.

"I cannot tell yet. Perhaps antitoxin; I don't know; perhaps formalin later. Truly, Mr. Carden, this case has taken on a graver, a more intimate significance since I have learned who you are. I would have worked hard to save any life; I shall put my very heart and soul into my work to save you, who have done so much for us all."

The trace of innocent emotion in her voice moved him.

"I am really not ill," he said unsteadily. "I cannot let you think I am—"

"Don't speak that way, Mr. Carden. I—I am perfectly miserable over it; I don't feel any happiness in my discovery now—not the least bit. I had rather live my entire life without seeing one case of Lamour's Disease than to believe you are afflicted with it."

"But I'm not, Miss Hollis!—really, I am not—"

She looked at him compassionately for a moment, then rose.

"It is best that you should be informed as to your probable condition," she said. "In Lamour's works, volume nine, you had better read exactly what Lamour says. Do you mind coming to the office with me, Mr. Carden?"

"Now?"

"Yes. The book is there. Do you mind coming?"

"No—no, of course not." And, as they turned away together under the trees: "You don't intend to begin observing me this afternoon, do you?" he ventured.

"I think it best if you can arrange your affairs. Can you, Mr. Carden?"

"Why, yes, I suppose I can. Did you mean for me to begin to occupy that surgical bedroom at once?"

"Do you mind?"

"N-no. I'll telephone my servants to pack a steamer trunk and send it around to your apartment this evening. And—where am I to board?"

"I have a dining room," she said simply. "My, apartment consists of the usual number of servants and rooms, including my office, and my observation ward which you will occupy."

He walked on, troubled.

"I only w-want to ask one or two things, Dr. Hollis. Am I to be placed on a diet? I hate diets!"

"Not at once."

"May I smoke?"

"Certainly," she said, smiling.

"And you won't p-put me—send me to bed too early?"

"Oh, no! The later you sit up the better, because I shall wish to take your temperature every ten minutes and I shall feel very sorry to arouse you."

"You mean you are coming in to wake me up every ten minutes and put that tube in my mouth?" he asked, aghast.

"Only every half-hour, Mr. Carden. Can't you stand it for a week?"

"Well," he said, "I—I suppose I can if *you* can. Only, upon my honor, there is really nothing the matter with me, and I'll prove it to you out of your own book."

"I wish you could, Mr. Carden. I should be only too happy to give you back to the world with a clear bill of health if you can convince me I am wrong. Do you not believe me? Indeed, indeed I am not selfish and wicked enough to wish you this illness, no matter how rare it is!"

"The rarer a disease is the madder it makes people who contract it," he said. "I should be the maddest man in Manhattan if I really did have Lamour's malady. But I haven't. There is only one malady afflicting me, and I am waiting for a suitable opportunity to tell you all about it, but—"

"Tell me now," she said, raising her eyes to his.

"Not now."

"To-night?"

"I hope so. I will if I can, Miss Hollis."

"But you must not fear to tell a physician about anything which troubles you, Mr. Carden."

"I'll remember that," he said thoughtfully, as they emerged from the Park and crossed to Madison Avenue.

A moment later he hailed a car and they both entered.

CHAPTER XXIV

No, there could be no longer any doubt in her mind as she went into her bedroom, closed the door, and, unhooking the telephone receiver, called up the great specialist in rare diseases, Dr. Austin Atwood, M.S., F.B.A., M.F.H.

"Dr. Atwood," she said with scarcely concealed emotion, "this is Dr. Rosalind Hollis."

"How-de-do?" squeaked the aged specialist amiably.

"Oh, I am well enough, thank you, doctor—except in spirits. Dr. Atwood, you were right! He *has* got it, and I am perfectly wretched!"

"*Who* has got *what?*" retorted the voice of Atwood.

"The unfortunate young gentleman we saw today in the Park—"

"What park?"

"Why, Central Park, doctor—"

"Central Park! *I* haven't been in Central Park for ten years, my child."

"Why, Dr. Atwood!—A—is this Dr. Austin Atwood with whom I am talking?"

"Not the least doubt! And you are that pretty Dr. Hollis—Rosalind Hollis, who consulted me in those charity cases, are you not?"

"I certainly am. And I wanted to say to you that I have the unfortunate patient now under closest observation here in my own apartment. I have given him the room next to the office. And, doctor, you were perfectly right. He shows every symptom of the disease—he is even inclined to sentimentalism; he begins to blush and fidget and look at me—a—in that unmistakable manner—not that he isn't well-bred and charming—indeed he is most attractive, and it grieves me dreadfully to see that he already is beginning to believe himself in love with the first person of the opposite sex he encounters—I mean that he—that I cannot mistake his attitude toward me—which is perfectly correct, only one cannot avoid seeing the curious infatuation—"

"*What* the dickens is all this?" roared the great specialist, and Dr. Hollis jumped.

"I was only confirming your diagnosis, doctor," she explained meekly.

"What diagnosis?"

"Yours, doctor. I have confirmed it, I fear. And the certainty has made me perfectly miserable, because his is such a valuable life to the world, and he himself is such a splendid, wholesome, noble specimen of youth and courage, that I cannot bear to believe him incurably afflicted."

"Good Heavens!" shouted the doctor, "*what* has he got and *who* is he?"

"He is Victor Carden, the celebrated artist, and he has Lamour's Disease!" she gasped.

There was a dead silence; then: "Keep him there until I come! Chloroform him if he attempts to escape!"

And the great specialist rang off excitedly.

So Rosalind Hollis went back to the lamp-lit office where, in a luxurious armchair, Carden was sitting, contentedly poring over the ninth volume of Lamour's great treatise and smoking his second cigar.

"Dr. Atwood is coming here," she said in a discouraged voice, as he rose with alacrity to place her chair.

"Oh! What for?"

"T-to see you, Mr. Carden."

"Who? Me? Great Scott! I don't want to be slapped and pinched and polled by a man! I didn't expect that, you know. I'm willing enough to have you observe me in the interest of humanity—"

"But, Mr. Carden, he is only called in for consultation. I—I have a dreadful sort of desperate hope that perhaps I may have made a mistake; that possibly I am in error."

"No doubt you are," he said cheerfully. "Let me read a few more pages, Dr. Hollis, and then I think I shall be all ready to dispute my symptoms, one by one, and convince you what really is the trouble with me. And, by the way, did Dr. Atwood seem a trifle astonished when you told him about me?"

"A trifle—yes," she said uncertainly. "He is a very, very old man; he forgets. But he is coming."

"Oh! And didn't he appear to recollect seeing me in the Park?"

"N-not clearly. He is very old, you know. But he is coming here."

"*Exactly*—as a friend of mine puts it," smiled Carden. "May I be permitted to use your telephone a moment?"

"By all means, Mr. Carden. You will find it there in my bedroom."

So he entered her pretty bedroom and, closing the door tightly, called up the Tracer of Lost Persons.

"Is that you, Mr. Keen? This is Mr. Carden. I'm head over heels in love. I simply must win her, and I'm going to try. If I don't—if she will not listen to me—I'll certainly go to smash. And what I want you to do is to prevent Atwood from butting in. Do you understand? ... Yes, Dr. Austin Atwood. Keep him away somehow.... Yes, I'm here, at Dr. Hollis's apartments, under anxious observation.... She is the *only* woman in the world! I'm mad about her—and getting madder every moment! She is the most perfectly splendid specimen of womanhood—*what?* Oh, yes; I rang you up to ask you whether it was you in the Park to-day?—that old gentleman—*What!* Yes, in Central Park. Yes, this afternoon! No, he didn't resemble you; and Dr. Hollis took him for Dr. Atwood.... What are you laughing about? ... I can *hear* you laughing.... *Was* it you? ... What do I think? Why, I don't know exactly what to think, but I suppose it must have been you. Was it? ... Oh, I see. You don't wish me to know. Certainly, you are quite right. Your clients have no business behind the scenes. I only asked out of curiosity.... All right. Good-by."

He came back to the lamp-lit office, which was more of a big, handsome, comfortable living room than a physician's quarters, and for a moment or two he stood on the threshold, looking around.

In the pleasant, subdued light of the lamp Rosalind Hollis looked up and around, smiling involuntarily to see him standing there; then, serious, silent, she dropped her eyes to the pages of the volume he had discarded—volume nine of Lamour's great works.

Even with the evidence before her, corroborated in these inexorably scientific pages which she sat so sadly turning, she found it almost impossible to believe that this big, broad-shouldered, attractive young man could be fatally stricken.

Twice her violet eyes stole toward him; twice the thick lashes veiled them, and the printed pages on her knee sprang into view, and the cold precision of the type confirmed her fears remorselessly:

"The trained scrutiny of the observer will detect in the victim of this disease a peculiar and indefinable charm—a strange symmetry which, on closer examination, reveals traces of physical beauty almost superhuman—"

Again her eyes were lifted to Carden; again she dropped her white lids. Her worst fears were confirmed.

Meanwhile he stood on the threshold looking at her, his pulses racing, his very soul staring through his eyes; and, within him, every sense clamoring out revolt at the deception, demanding confession and its penalty.

"I can't stand this!" he blurted out; and she looked up quickly, her face blanched with foreboding.

"Are you in pain?" she asked.

"No—not that sort of pain! I—*won't* you please believe that I am not ill? I'm imposing on you. I'm an impostor! There's nothing whatever the trouble with me except—something that I want to tell you—if you'll let me—"

"Why should you hesitate to confide in a physician, Mr. Carden?"

He came forward slowly. She laid her small hand on the empty chair which faced hers and he sank into it, clasping his restless hands under his chin.

"You are feeling depressed," she said gently. Depression was a significant symptom. Three chapters were devoted to it.

"I'm depressed, of course. I'm horribly depressed and ashamed of myself, because there is nothing on earth the matter with me, and I've let you think there is."

She smiled mournfully; this was another symptom of a morbid state. She turned, unconsciously, to page 379 to verify her observation.

"See here, Miss Hollis," he broke out, "haven't I any chance to convince you that I am not ill? I want to be honest without involving a—a friend of mine. I can't endure this deception. Won't you let me prove to you that these symptoms are—are only significant of something else?"

She looked straight at him, considering him in silence.

"Let us begin with those dark circles under my eyes," he said desperately. "I found some cold-cream in my room and—look! They are practically gone! At any rate, if there is a sort of shadow left it's because I use my eyes in my profession."

"Dr. Lamour says that the dark circles disappear, anyway," said the girl, unconvinced. "Cold-cream had nothing to do with it."

"But it *did!* Really it did. And as for the other symptoms, I—well, I can't help my pulses when y-you t-t-touch me."

"Please, Mr. Carden."

"I don't mean to be impertinent. I am trying my hardest to tell the truth. And my pulses *do* gallop when you test them; they're galloping now! This very moment!"

"Let me try them," she said coolly, laying her hand on his wrist.

"Didn't I say so!" he insisted grimly. "And I'm turning red, too. But those symptoms mean something else; they mean *you!*"

"Mr. Carden!"

"I can't help saying so—"

"I know it," she said soothingly; "these sentimental outbursts are part of the disease—"

"Good Heavens! *Won't* you try to believe me! There's nothing in the world the matter with me except that I am—am—p-p-perfectly f-f-fascinated—"

"You must struggle against it, Mr. Carden. That is only part of the—"

"It isn't! It isn't! It's you! It's your mere presence, your personality, your charm, your beauty, your loveliness, your—"

"Mr. Carden, I beg of you! I—it is part of my duty to observe symptoms, but—but you are making it very hard for me—very difficult—"

"I am only proving to you that it isn't Lamour's Disease which does stunts with my pulses, my temperature, my color. I'm not morbid except when I realize my deception. I'm not depressed except when I think how far you are from me—how far above me—how far out of reach of such a man as I am—how desperately I—I—"

"D-don't you think I had better administer a s-s-sedative, Mr. Carden?" she said, distressed.

"I don't care. I'll take anything you give me—as long as *you* give it to me. I'll swallow pint after pint of pills! I'll fletcherize 'em! I'll luxuriate in poison—anything—"

She was hastily running through the pages of the ninth volume to see whether the symptoms of sentimental excitement ever turned into frenzy.

"What can you learn from that book?" he insisted, leaning forward to see what she was reading. "Anyway, Dr. Lamour married his patient so early in the game that all the symptoms disappeared. And I believe the trouble with his patient was my trouble. She had every symptom of it until he married her! She was in love with him, that is absolutely all!"

Rosalind Hollis raised her beautiful, incredulous eyes.

"What do you mean, Mr. Carden?"

"I mean that, in my opinion, there's no such disease as Lamour's Disease. That young girl was in love with him. Then he married her at last, and—presto!—all the symptoms vanished—the pulse, the temperature, the fidgets, the blushes, the moods, the whole business!"

"W-what about the strangely curious manifestations of physical beauty—superhuman symmetry, Mr. Carden?"

"Do you notice them in *me?*" he gasped.

"A—yes—in a m-modified measure—"

"In *me?*"

"Certainly!" she said firmly; but the slow glow suffusing her cheeks was disconcerting her. Then his own face began to reflect the splendid color in hers; their eyes met, dismayed.

"There are sixteen volumes about this disease," she said. "There *must* be such a disease!"

"There is," he said. "I have it badly. But I never had it before I first saw you in the Park!"

"Mr. Carden—this is the wildest absurdity—"

"I know it. Wildness is a symptom. I'm mad as a hatter. I've got every separate symptom, and I wish it was infectious and contagious and catching and fatal!"

She made an effort to turn the pages to the chapter entitled "Manias and Illusions," but he laid his hand across the book and his clear eyes defied her.

"Mr. Carden—"

Her smooth hand trembled under his, then, suddenly nerveless, relaxed. With an effort she lifted her head; their eyes met, spellbound.

"*You* have *every* symptom," he said unsteadily—"every one! What have you to say?"

Her fascinated eyes held his.

"What have you to say?" he repeated under his breath—"you, with every symptom, and your heavenly radiant beauty to confirm them—that splendid youthful loveliness which blinds and stuns me as I look—as I speak—

as I tell you that I love you. That is my malady; that is the beginning and the end of it; love!"

She sat speechless, immovable, as one under enchantment.

"All my life," he said, "I have spent in painting shadows. But the shadows were those dim celestial shapes cast by your presence in the world. You tell me that the world is better for my work; that I have offered my people beauty and a sort of truth, which they had never dreamed of until I revealed it? Yet what inspired me was the shadow only, for I had never seen the substance; I had never believed I should ever see the living source of the shadows which inspired me. And now I see; now I have seen with my own eyes. Now the confession of faith is no longer a blind creed, born of instinct. You live! You are you! What I believed from necessity I find proved in fact. The occult no longer can sway one who has seen. And you, who, without your knowledge or mine, have always been the one and only source of any good in me or in my work—why is it strange that I loved you at first sight?—that I worshiped you at first breath?—I, who, like him who raises his altar to 'the unknown god,' raised my altar to truth and beauty? And a miracle has answered me."

She rose, the beautiful dazed eyes meeting his, both hands clasping the ninth volume of Lamour's great monograph to her breast as though to protect it from him—from him who was threatening her, enthralling her, thrilling her with his magic voice, his enchanted youth, the masterful mystery of his eyes. What was he saying to her? What was this mounting intoxication sweeping her senses—this delicious menace threatening her very will? What did he want with her? What was he asking? What was he doing now—with both her hands in his, and her gaze deeply lost in his—and the ninth volume of Lamour on the floor between them, sprawling there, abandoned, waving its helpless, discredited leaves in air—discredited, abandoned, obsolete as her own specialty—her life's work! He had taken that, too—taken her life's work from her. And in return she was holding nothing!—nothing except a young man's hands—strong, muscular hands which, after all, were holding her own imprisoned. So she had nothing in exchange for the ninth volume of Lamour; and her life's work had been annihilated by a smile; and she was very much alone in the world—very isolated and very youthful.

After a while she emerged from the chaos of attempted reflection and listened to what he was saying. He spoke very quietly, very distinctly, not sparing himself, laying bare every deception without involving anybody except himself.

He told her the entire history of his case, excluding Mr. Keen in person; he told her about his aunt, about his birthday, about his determination to let the legacy go. Then in a very manly way he told her that he had never before loved a woman; and fell silent, her hands a dead weight in his.

She was surprised that she could experience no resentment. A curious inertia crept over her. She was tired of expectancy, tired of effort, weary of the burden of decision. Life and its problems overweighted her. Her eyes wandered to his broad young shoulders, then were raised to his face.

"What shall we do?" she asked innocently.

Unresisting, she suffered him to explain. His explanation was not elaborate; he only touched his lips to her hands and straightened up, a trifle pale.

After a moment they walked together to the door and he took his hat and gloves from the rack.

"Will you come to-morrow morning?" she asked.

"Yes."

"Come early. I am quite certain of how matters are with me. Everything has gone out of my life—everything I once cared for—all the familiar things. So come early, for I am quite alone without you."

"And I without you, Rosalind."

"That is only right," she said simply. "I shall cast no more shadows for you…. Are you going? … Oh, I know it is best that you should go, but— "

He halted. She laid both hands in his.

"We both have it," she faltered—"every symptom. And—you will come early, won't you?"

THE END

The Tree of Heaven
By Robert W. Chambers

To My Friend
Austin Corbin

CHAPTER I

THE CARPET OF BELSHAZZAR

We all were glad to see him; on his return he had found us all his friends. Nobody had spoken to him about his abrupt departure from New York; nobody had mentioned Westover; nothing connected with that episode was even hinted at by any of us, I believe, during his short sojourn among us. It was he himself who spoke of it first.

Of course during his absence we had followed his career; many among us had read and tried to understand what he had written in his three world-famous volumes, "Occult Philosophy," "The Weight of Human Souls," and "The Interstellar Laws of Psychic Phenomena."

It seemed, at times, here to us in America, that it was impossible that the man we had known so well could have become the great Psychic Scientist who had written these three astounding works—who now occupied the Chair of Psychical Philosophy in the great University of Trebizond—the man who was the confidential adviser of the Shah of Persia, the mentor of the Ameer of Afghanistan, the inspirer of the greatest diplomat of all the East—the late Akhound of Swat.

As he sat there in his immaculate evening dress, bronzed, youthful looking, presiding so quietly at the little dinner which he had given to us as a half-formal, half-intimate leave-taking before he sailed, it seemed to us incredible that this man, now on his return journey to Trebizond *via* Lhassa, could be the beloved and dreaded arbiter of Asiatic politics—the one white man in all the Orient who had ever been wholly respected, and absolutely feared by the temporal and spiritual heads of nations, religions, clans, and sects.

That, of course, he was what is popularly known as an adept, we supposed. What his wisdom, his insight, his amazing knowledge of the occult might include, we preferred, rather uncomfortably, not to conjecture.

There is, naturally, in all of us a childlike desire to hear of marvels; there is also a stronger and more childish desire to see miracles performed.

I am quite sure that we all hoped he might perhaps care to do something for us—merely to convince us. And at first, I know that many among us, seated there in the private room at the Lenox Club, felt a trifle ill at ease and a little in awe of this man with whom we were at such close quarters.

There was nothing particularly remarkable about the dinner; it was the usual excellent affair one might expect at the Lenox; the wines perfect, the service flawless.

And now, smoking our cigars, lounging in groups over the flower-laden table, we fell into the old, intimate, easy channels of conversation, chatting of past days, of our hopes and ambitions.

And our host, quiet, self-contained, pushed back his chair, looking somewhat curiously, I thought, from one to the other. And I thought, too, as his pleasant bronzed features changed from a faint smile to a graver expression, and then reverted to the smile for a moment, that he seemed to see something in each of us that was perhaps hidden from ourselves—that, as his eyes swept us, he was not only capable of reading much of what was not understood by us, but also something in the hidden future which awaited each of us.

So strongly did this idea begin to take hold of me that it began to make me uneasy. I felt, too, that others among us harbored that same idea—for the conversation was less accented now, and intermittent; voices had fallen to a lower, quieter pitch; and after a little nobody spoke.

Then I saw that we all were looking straight at our host, as though under some subtle and fascinated compulsion.

He sat very still; his composure appeared a trifle forced, as though he had voicelessly summoned us to concentrate upon him our attention, and was now searching for the exact words for some statement which he had meant to make to us all.

After a moment a slight flush crept over his handsome face. He said:

"You fellows are very good to come here and let me take leave of you so pleasantly. You have been very kind to me since I have come again among you. The sort of friendship that asks nothing but takes a man for granted is a good sort. "Helmer,"—he looked at the sculptor Helmer—"I shall see you soon again." We all turned in surprise to Helmer, who seemed as surprised as we were. "I shall see you sooner than you expect.... Smith!"—he smiled at J. Abingdon Smith, 3d—"some day you will uproot a Tree of Dreams, but not the dream, Smith; that will become very real when you awake—as true"—and he turned to the man on his left—"as true as a dream which you shall dream under the Sign of Venus."

We sat there breathless, expectant. He was doing something after all; he was prophesying, in a curious sort of manner, probably speaking in symbols. And though we could not understand, we listened while the little shivers fluttered our pulses.

Then he looked at Edgerton, smiling; and Edgerton flushed up and looked back at him, almost defiantly.

"Edgerton," he said, "don't worry too much. What is not to be settled in court can sometimes be settled—*ex curia*." And to the young man on his right: "Doctor, don't overwork. If you do you will learn a stranger truth than is locked up among the molecules and atoms in your laboratory!"

Then he leaned across the table and laid one hand on Leeds's shoulder. "I congratulate you," he said, smiling; "you've got a good-natured ghost following you about. But he'll leave you if you turn idle. And don't be afraid, my boy."

"I'm not afraid," said young Leeds, rather pallid, but straightening up in his chair.

Our host laughed; then his face changed, and he raised his eyes to Shannon:

"Where is Harrod?" he asked slowly.

"At Bar Harbor," replied Shannon, "I believe."

"I thought so. And—remember one thing—there is a certain law which governs the validity of a check drawn to a man's order when that check has been signed by a man no longer living. But, Shannon, the intention is the important thing in such a matter."

"What, exactly, do you mean?" asked Shannon, astonished.

But our host had already turned to Escourt:

"Captain," he said, "you sail—when?"

"I have no sailing orders," laughed Escourt.

"Not yet?" Our host looked quietly at the young officer. "Well, it isn't the length of a voyage that counts, Escourt—nor the size of the troopship. No; you will anchor, some day, in a smaller craft than you started in, in the Port of the Golden Pool."

Escourt, still smiling, waited; but our host sat silent, head bent, one hand on the edge of the tablecloth.

"Not one of you," he said, without raising his eyes, "not one among you but who shall come face to face with what you still consider miracles.... Even Hildreth, yonder"—Hildreth jumped—"even Hildreth shall learn from the Swastika."

"Swa—swat? What—what?" stammered Hildreth.

"Nothing to alarm you," smiled the other; then again the swift shadow fell across his face.

"Not one man among you who has not proven his friendship for me," he said, looking up and around. And to me he added: "You must prove it still further by telling fearlessly to the world what there will be to tell after I have gone, and after my words have been proven—the words I have spoken here to-night—and which no one among you understands.... But you all will understand them. And when the last man among you has understood"—turning again to me—"you must bear witness to the world, bear witness in printed page and over your own signature. Do you promise?"

"Yes," I said.

Then very quietly he looked around the table, and leaned forward, regarding each man in turn.

"I think," he said, "that it is time you understood exactly the facts about which you have forborne to question me. And I mean to tell you before we part; I mean to tell you the truth concerning Westover and—all that happened.... And when you know these facts, then you may begin to surmise why I went to Trebizond, why I remain, and—and—*what miracle of happiness I have found there—for the third time reincarnated.*"

He leaned back in his chair; his clear eyes became fixed and dreamy. Then he began to speak, in a low voice, as though to himself:

Time, and the funeral of Time, alas!—and the Old Year's passing-bell! Whistles from city and river, deep horns sounding from the foggy docks; and under my window a voice and a song—ah! that young voice in the street below calling me through the falling snow!

If it be true that Time makes all hurts well, I do not know; and "a thousand years in Thy sight is but as yesterday when it is passed, and as a watch in the night"; a thousand years! And this also is true; the flames of love make hot the furnace of Abaddon.

We were in the gallery as usual, Geraldine and I—the gallery where the carpets of the East were hung along the shadowy walls. For lately it was my pleasure to acquire rare rugs, and it was my profession to furnish expert opinion upon the age and origin of Oriental carpets, and to read and interpret the histories of forgotten emperors and the mysteries of long-forgotten gods from the colors and intricate flowery labyrinths tied in silk or wool to the warps of some dead sultan's lustrous tapestry.

Here in the long sky gallery hung my own rugs against the arabesque incrusted-ivory panels—Tabriz, Shiraz, Sehna, and Saruk—a somber blaze of color shot with fire—all rare, some priceless; Turkish Kulah, softly silky as a golden lion's hide, Persian Sehna, shimmering with rose and violet lights, fiercely brilliant rugs from Samarkand, superbly flowered, secreting deep in every floral thicket traceries of the ancient Mongol conqueror; Feraghans glowing like jewel-sewn velvets set with the Herati and the lotus—symbols of Egypt or of China, as you please to interpret the oldest pattern in the world.

Far in the gallery's amber-tinted gloom the red of Ispahan dominated, subduing fiery vistas to smoldering harmony through which, like a vast sapphire set in opals, glimmered the superb lost Persian blue.

There was one other rug, an Eighur, the famous so-called "Babilu," or

"Carpet of Belshazzar"; but it hung alone in imperial magnificence behind the locked doors of a marble room, which it seemed to fill with a soft luster of its own, radiating from the mystic "Tree of Heaven" woven in its center.

We were, as I say, in this gallery; Geraldine poring over an illuminated volume on cuneiform inscriptions, I, with pad and pencil, idly shifting and reshifting the Kufic key to the ancient cipher, which always left me stranded where I had begun with the stately repetition:

> "King of Kings—
> King of Kings—
> King of Kings—"

As for Westover, my cousin, he was, as usual, in the laboratory fussing with his venomous extracts—an occupation which, to my dismay, he had taken up within the year, working, as he explained, on the theory that every poison has its antidote. Yet it seemed to me that he was more anxious to invent some new and subtle toxic than to devise the remedy.

From where I sat I could not see him, but the crystalline tinkle of his glass retorts and bottles distracted my attention from the penciled calculations. Without moving my head, I glanced across the room at Geraldine. She looked up immediately, raising her level eyebrows in mute inquiry as though I had moved or spoken; then, realizing that I had not, she bent above the book once more, the warm color stealing to her cheeks.

Within the year a wordless intimacy had grown up between us; we never understood it, never acknowledged it, and at times it disconcerted us.

I sat silent, tracing with my pencil series after series of futile Kufic combinations with the cuneiforms, but ever the first turn of the ancient key creaked in my ears,

> "King of Kings—
> King of Kings—"

until the triverbal reiteration wore on my nerves.

Geraldine leaned back abruptly, closing her book.

"I'm tired and nervous," she said. "You may wear out your eyes and temper if you choose—and you're doing the latter, for I'm as restless as an eel. Besides, I'm lonely, and I'm going back to the East—if you'll come, too."

I laughed, understanding what she meant by the "East."

"Will you come with me?" she insisted.

"Yes," I said, "whenever you are ready."

She sprang to her feet, scattering the illuminated pages over the floor, and stood an instant facing me, tall, dark-eyed, smiling, brushing back the lustrous hair from her cheeks.

"Where is Jim?" she asked—although we both knew.

"In the laboratory," I replied mechanically. Still busy with her hair, she regarded me dreamily out of those dark, sweet eyes of hers.

"It would be wonderful," she mused, "if Jim should find an antidote to death; but I wish it were not necessary to kill so many little helpless creatures. Did you hear that pitiful sound in there yesterday? Was it something he was killing?"

"I don't know," I said. And after a silence: "What are you going to do?"

She shook her head vaguely and leaned against the window, looking out into the rain.

"Shall we go back to our inscriptions?" I suggested.

She shook her head again. After a while she turned away from the window, stifling a dainty yawn, and stretched out, languidly straightening up to the full height of her young body.

"I feel stupid," she said; "I'm tired of cryptograms and the pages of dusty books. I'm tired of the rain, too. The languor of April is in me. I'm homesick for lands I never knew. So come back to the East with me, Dick."

She held out her hand to me with a confident little smile; and knowing what she meant, I acquiesced in her caprice, and conducted her solemnly to the piano, leaving her before it.

She stood there for a space, musing, her lovely head bent; then, still standing, she struck a sequence of chords—chords pulsating with color; and through them flashed strange little trills like threads of tinsel.

"This is an Eighur carpet I am dreaming of," she murmured, as the music swelled, glowing as tints and hues glow in the old dyes of the East.

Wave on wave of color seemed to spread from the keys under her fingers; she looked back at me over her shoulder with a warning nod.

"I shall begin to weave very soon. Khiounnou horsemen may appear and frighten me for a moment—but I shall finish. Listen! I am at the loom."

Seating herself, she developed out of the flowing, somber harmony a monotonous minor theme, suddenly checked by a distant rattle like the clatter of nomad lances on painted stirrups; then she picked up the thread of the melody again, dropped it, breathless for a moment's quivering silence, resumed it, twisting it into delicate arabesques, threading it across the dull, rich harmonies, at first slowly, then faster, faster, swift as the flying fingers of a nomad maid tying fretted silver in a Ghiordes knot. The whirring tempo was the cadence of the loom; soft feathery notes flew like carded wool; thicker, duller, softer grew the fabric, dense, silky, heavily lustrous.

Suddenly she broke the thread off short, the whole fabric falling with a muffled shock.

"Why did you do that?" I demanded wrathfully.

"The rug is woven; the weaver is dead," she said.

"Oh, go on, Geraldine," I insisted; "don't stop half way in a thing like that. It's the East—it's the real East, I tell you. How you do it—you who have never seen the East—Heaven only knows!"

"U Allah Aalem," she murmured; "it's in me." Then she looked back at me, laughing. "Centuries ago you and I heard that music along the Arax—or I sang it among the Tcherkess roses for you, perhaps—perhaps in the gardens of Trebizond."

"That might explain it," I said gravely. Lately she had found pleasure in a fancy that she and I had lived together in the East, centuries since, and that we were soon to return forever.

"You and I," she mused, touching the keys lightly—"and Jim, of course," she added.

"Of course," I said.

She dropped her head, striking chord on chord with nervous precision; and hanging in the wake of every ringing harmony a frail melody floated like the Chinese cloud band in a Kirman tapestry.

"What's that air?" I asked, fascinated.

"I don't know; it sounds pagan, doesn't it?—like the wicked beauty of Babylon. Do you hear how it beats on and on like the rhythm of naked feet—little, delicate, naked feet ablaze with gems—the feet of Herodiade perhaps—thud—thud—tching!—don't you hear them, Dick? And now listen to those silky, flowery trills! They're Asiatic; ancient Cathay is awaking—camel bells in the hazar of the Golden Emperor! Hark!—now you hear trumpets, don't you? Well, of course that must be the Mongols marching with the Prince of the Vanguard. Hark! How savagely the brutal Afghan theme breaks in with its fierce trampling and the staccato echo of Tekke drums! It's frightening me out of the East. I think we had better come home, Dick," she added, mischievously running into the latest popular street song.

"How on earth could you do that!" I exclaimed wrathfully. "You're a futile mixture of feather brain and genius!"

But where was the genius hidden under that laughing and exquisite mask confronting me? Suddenly the delicate mask became grave.

"Let me laugh when I can, Dick," she said. "It is not often I laugh."

I was silent.

"Of course you may be horrid if you choose," she observed with a shrug, running a brilliantly inane series of trills from end to end of the keyboard.

"But it's no use scolding, for I won't study, I won't compose, I won't 'try to do something,' and I won't be serious. I'm shallow, I'm frivolous, I've the soul of a Trebizond dancing girl, and I like it. Now what are you going to do?"

"I'm going out," I said ungraciously.

"Oh—alone?"

"Not if you'll come. It's stopped raining. Will you come? Oh, get your hat, Geraldine, and stop that torment of idiotic trills!"

"If Jim doesn't mind, I think I'll go and sit in the laboratory with him," she observed carelessly.

I looked at her without comment.

"I have a curious idea," she continued, "that he might like to have me around to-day while he is working."

I stared at her, but there was no bitterness in her tranquil smile as she leaned forward, resting her elbows on the polished rosewood case.

"So I won't go with you, Dick," she said slowly.

One of those intervals of restless silence, which within the year we had learned to dread, menaced us now. Mute, motionless, I watched the soft color deepening in her face, then, impatient, roused myself and walked over to the laboratory. Westover looked up as I pushed aside the screen.

"Will you drive with us?" I asked. "The sun's out."

He declined, peering at me through his glass mask.

"Come on, Jim," I urged. "You've inhaled enough poison for one day. Take off your mask and wash your hands and drive us out to High Bridge. I'll telephone to the stable if you say the word, and they'll hook up the new four. Is it a go?"

"No," he said coldly, and turned on his heel, lifting a test tube to the light.

He was more taciturn and a trifle uglier than usual. I watched him for a moment warming the test tube over a burner, then without further parley replaced the screen, closed the double glass doors, and walked back to Geraldine.

"Doesn't Jim care to come?" she asked.

I said that her husband appeared to be absorbed in his work.

"Very well," she said, with airy composure; "trot along, Dicky—and if you see a bunch of jonquils growing on Fifth Avenue, you may pick them for me—or for that pretty girl you met at Lakewood—"

"I'll send you a bunch as big as a bushel."

"A bushel of flowers is as compromising as a declaration," she said. "Send them to her."

"There's only one way to settle it," I said; "I'll send them to the loveliest girl in the world—shall I?"

She assented, laughing uncertainly.

"I think I'll pay Jim a little call," she said, rising from the piano and walking slowly toward the laboratory.

A few moments later as I passed down the broad stairway I heard West-over's penetrating voice: "Let that glass tube alone, Geraldine! Why the devil can't you keep your hands off things when you come in here?"

I lingered for a while in the hallway, thinking that she might change her mind and come down, for she had left the laboratory to her husband, and I heard her moving about in her own apartment. She did not come, and after a little while I left the house, a sense of apprehension depressing me.

The asphalt of Fifth Avenue was still wet with the first warm rain of April, but the sun glittered on window and pavement and flashed along the polished panels of carriages crowding the avenue from curb to curb. A breath of spring had set the sparrows chattering and chirping; the movement of the throng, the bright gowns, the fresh faces of young girls, and the endless façades of glass reflecting it—all were pleasant to me, a man sensitive to impressions.

And so in the pale sunshine I sauntered on through the throng, now idling curiously by some shop window whither a display of jewels or curios attracted me, now strolling on again content with the soft color in sky and sunlight.

I found a florist whose shop windows were filled with thickets of fragrant, fragile spring flowers; and every little scented blossom that I touched, choosing the freshest, nodded to the voiceless cadence of a name repeated—and: "Geraldine! Geraldine!" they nodded, so confidently, so sweetly, that what was I to do but send them to her?

And so I sauntered on again, threading the throng, half-minded to turn back, yet ever tempted on by idleness, until above me the twin spires of the cathedral glimmered, all silvered in the shimmering blue.

Halting, undecided, I presently became aware of an old man, his withered hands crossed before him, standing quite patiently under the cathedral terrace. Before him on the sidewalk rested a basket draped with a brilliant rug or two and heaped with tawdry rubbish—scarlet fezzes, slippers of spangled leather, tasseled charms of gilt, flimsy striped fabrics—all the worthless flummery known as "Oriental" to the good peoples of the West.

Few stopped to look; no one bought. As I passed him his dimmed gaze met mine; all the wistfulness of the very poor, all the mystery of the very, very old, was in his eyes. Moved by impulse, perhaps, I spoke to him in a low voice, using the Turkish language.

A dull animation came into his misty eyes.

"Allahou Ekber," he muttered, in a trembling voice; "it is sweet to hear your words, my son."

"Mussulman," I said, "who are you who recite the Tekbir here under the spires of a Roman church?"

"Is there harm in bearing witness to the glory of God here under the minarets of your cathedral?" he asked humbly.

"Spire and minaret are one to Him," I said. "Who are you, Mussulman?"

"My name is Khassar," he said; "my nation Eighur; my Iort is the Issig-Kul; Baïon-Aoul my clan. I am an Eighur Turk, a Khodja; and I am able to write the Turkish language in Arabic and in Eighur-Mongol characters."

"Reverend father," I said, full of astonishment and pity, "how should a Khodja of the Baïon-Aoul come to this? Even the Tekrin horseman halts at the sea."

"It is written," he said feebly, "that we belong to God and we return to Him."

Troubled, I stood there on the sidewalk, oblivious of the knot of idlers around us, curious to hear two men so different conversing in a common tongue.

I wished to give him something, yet did not venture to humiliate him without pretense of buying.

"Here is my card," I said, "on which is written my name and where I live. Bring me these rugs to-night, ata, I wish to buy."

"You do not desire them," he said, shaking his head. "You know the East; you understand these rugs; you know they are worthless, acid-washed, singed, rubbed with pumice, smoked—every vile Armenian practice used! You know the dyes are aniline; that they are loosely tied, hastily and flimsily woven by Armenian dogs and sons of dogs. You mean kindness; you have done me enough by speaking to me."

He passed his trembling hand over his ragged beard.

"You who know carpets and love them," he quavered; "listen attentively. I have a strip to show—not here—but I could bring it."

"Bring it," I said gently.

He fumbled in the pocket of his tattered coat and presently brought to light a scrap of paper on which was scrawled some Persian characters.

"It is such a carpet as I have never seen," he said; "there is nothing in our history or our traditions to teach us the meaning of this carpet—nothing save that it is an Eighur rug inscribed in Persian and in an unknown script. I have traced the characters in a single cartouche. Read, my son."

And I read, translating freely:

"Ten thousand thousand stars shine down on Babylon. The desert well

reflects but one."

"I will bring the carpet," he said, after a silence. "I do not know its value; it has no beauty any longer; only the ghost of ancient splendor remains in the thin knots clinging to warp and weft. And it is old, my son, older than tradition. Upon it there is not one sign to teach us the mystery of its meaning."

He peered at me with his old, sad eyes, earnestly.

"I will bring it," he said. "Go with Ali, thou fair comrade of Hassan."

"May the Blessed Companions intervene for you," I said.

And so we parted, gravely and with circumstance, I to stroll homeward, touched, musing curiously upon this carpet of which a nomad Mussulman could make nothing. The Persian verse from the cartouche interested me, too, the refrain lingering persistently in my memory:

"Ten thousand thousand stars shine down on Babylon. The desert well reflects but one."

Never before, save on the imperial carpet known as Belshazzar's Rug, had I encountered any inscription mentioning Babylon. So, at the first glance, the nomad's rug should have some value. But speculation was futile—surely I ought to have learned that if unnumbered disappointments could teach me anything.

Thinking of these things, I passed along the noble avenue, retracing my steps to the big dusky house standing alone, with two old trees to guard it—relics, like the mansion, of the great city's infancy—the last old dwelling left marooned amid the arid wastes of commerce. Here my cousin and his wife lived with me in winter; I with them at their Lenox home in summer.

A brougham or two at the curb before the house warned me of clients waiting or of visitors for Geraldine—doubtless the latter, for it was now past five.

Under the circumstances I went in to second Geraldine—for Westover never troubled himself to be civil to her friends.

There were people there, and tea—and a pretty, wordless welcome from Geraldine.

The violet-tinted April dusk brought candlelight; people went away and others came; then, one by one, they left, and we were alone, Geraldine and I—and the new moon shining through the frail curtains. For a long time we talked together, aimlessly, of this and that which mattered nothing to anybody. A maid entered to draw the curtains. When she left, Geraldine laughed and picked up a cluster of yellow jonquils.

"Your courage failed you, after all," she said; "the loveliest woman in the world must go without my flowers to-night."

"She has them," I retorted.

"Do you mean me, Dick?" she said under her breath.

"Did you doubt it?"

She bowed her head. Silence, ever waiting to ensnare us, crept like a shadow in between us. And I would not have it.

"An old man is to bring a rug to-night," I said abruptly.

Geraldine stirred in her armchair, repeating in a low voice:

"Ten thousand thousand stars shine down on Babylon. The desert well reflects but one. Abaddon none."

Bolt upright in my chair I listened, incredulous of my own ears.

"Where on earth did you hear that?" I demanded.

"I read it on Belshazzar's Rug in cuneiform with the Kufic key," she answered, watching me.

"You—all alone—interpreted that?" I asked, astounded.

"Yes. It is the cuneiform inscription in the gold cartouche."

Profound astonishment left me silent. She lay back in her chair with a little laugh of pure excitement.

"After you went out," she said, "I was horribly lonely, and I thought of you, and then I thought about the work you loved—the cuneiforms—and—as Jim did not seem to need me in the laboratory—I thought to myself: 'Suppose—suppose by luck I could unravel the inscription on the gold cartouche! Dick would be the happiest man in the world.' And then—your—your flowers came, and I sat for a while alone with them. Then, on impulse, I jumped up and took the Kufic tables and all the combinations that you and I had tried together, and I slipped upstairs to the marble room and knelt down before Belshazzar's Rug. O Dick! the Tree of Heaven seemed to quiver in every jeweled branch and leaf!—it was only the draught from the closing door that moved the rug, but the mystic tree swayed there as the folds of the carpet moved, and I seemed to feel the mystery of the Prophet's Paradise stealing into me, penetrating me like the incense of forbidden wine—and I felt very Eastern and very pagan, kneeling there.

"It was strange, too; the intricate Kufic key seemed to be falling into place of its own impulse, symbol after symbol promising a linked symmetry of sense, until, almost before I was conscious of the miracle, it had been wrought there in the marble room; and my eyes were opened; and I, kneeling before the Tree of Heaven, read quite clearly what is written in the gold cartouche on the great carpet of Belshazzar. Dick! I prayed so hard that I might read it. And I have read it—for *you!*"

In the eloquence of her emotion she had risen, holding out both hands to me; I caught them, crushing them to my lips.

Ominous pulsating silence grew between us; her fingers relaxed and her hands fell from my lips. The stillness, intense, absolute, became a tension, a growing resistless force pressing us apart, slowly, inexorably driving me back step by step against the silk-hung wall, which I reached for, groping, steadying myself.

Never before had we been so swayed, so thrilled; never before had we been so reckless of the peril. Over us a magic snare had fallen, and we had evaded it—an unseen and delicate web, enmeshing us, drawing us together limb to limb, body to body, soul to soul, there on the kindling edges of destruction.

She sank back into the deep seat by the window, her white hands tightening on the gilded foliation of the chair's carved arms. And I saw how pale her face was and how her dark eyes were fixed steadily upon the floor as though destruction was a pit whose edge lay at her feet.

Presently I became aware that the world outside the curtained windows was moving still—had perhaps never halted on its way to wait upon our fate. And, crossing the room, I raised the shade and saw the new moon, low in the sky, kneeling amid the watching stars. Yellow rays from a street lamp illuminated the old trees' foliage, edging with palest fire the tracery of newborn leaves, tufting each stem and twig, exquisite, delicately formal as the leafy labyrinths of the Tree of Heaven spreading above the flowery field of Belshazzar's Rug.

Khassar the nomad had come and gone, and his rug hung in the marble room, pale as the tinted shadow cast by the great carpet of Belshazzar.

The nomad's rug was clean but very ancient, and so worn, so time-eaten to the very warp, that the Kherdeh was all but obliterated in the metnih. But outside of that, between the outside band and the ara, or central line, there were traces of ancient glory and dimmed outlines of design; and I saw the twelve cartouches inscribed alternately in Persian and in cuneiform characters. There, too, were the worn remains of floral thickets haunted of beast and bird, intricate allegories, chronicles in color and symbol, every leaf, every blossom, every creature fraught with mystic meaning; and there also, still faintly to be made out, the shadowy foliage of the Tree of Heaven.

"How much did you pay for that ghost of a rug?" demanded Westover, who had followed me upstairs after dressing for dinner.

When I told him he shrugged his shoulders, but made no comment. A moment later Geraldine entered, and his small eyes, no longer furtive, became fixed and dull.

"They say in the East," I remarked, "that when all color is gone from an Eighur rug a lost soul takes it for its abode. Eighur women are supposed to have souls occasionally, and to lose them now and then."

"There are plenty of lost souls in town," observed Westover; "no doubt you'll have your choice of tenants for your carpet—or," he added, staring at space, "if you like I'll provide you."

I did not understand his remark, but it left a vaguely sinister impression. Geraldine, standing between us, her white fingers linked behind her, looked up at me very gravely.

"Do you know," she said, "that I am convinced that I wove that rug some centuries ago?"

"I have no doubt of it," I replied, smiling.

"Do you doubt it, Jim?" she asked gayly.

He did not reply.

"As a matter of fact," I said, "it was always believed that a young girl who dared to weave the Tree of Heaven into an Eighur carpet died when her task was ended—her entire physical and spiritual vitality entering into the sacred tree and infusing it with mystic splendor."

"Oh, I died as you say," observed Geraldine gravely.

"I don't see that you infused much physical or spiritual splendor into that rug," observed Westover.

"I must die again, you know, Jim, and bring its vanished beauty back," she said gayly. "Shall I, Dick?—and leave you a priceless carpet as my bequest and monument?"

Westover turned on his heel, fidgeting with his collar. Recently his neck had grown fat behind the ears.

A few moments later dinner was announced.

We lingered late over dinner, I remember. Jim drank heavily—a habit which both Geraldine and I had long since left unnoticed, she shrinking from the sullen rebuff certain to follow even a playful protest, I understanding the utter hopelessness of interference. His mind, already shaken, would one day shatter, and the dreadful price be paid.

As he sat there sousing walnuts in port, in his altered features and swollen hands I seemed to divine something malicious and patient and powerful—that indescribable physical menace one feels in the inert brooding eye of the mentally and spiritually crippled.

When Geraldine rose he stood up unsteadily. After she had gone he lighted a cigar and turned his bloodshot eyes on me.

"Is that wine expensive?" he demanded, pointing to Geraldine's half-empty glass.

"Rather," I said.

He picked up the glass, examined it, sniffing at the contents.

"It's poor claret," he said. "Taste it. It's pure poison, I tell you."

"I'm sorry," I said indifferently.

Again he sniffed it. "Faugh!" he sneered, and threw it into the fireplace behind him. Then he got on his feet, heavily, muttering to himself, and stumbled off through the drawing-room.

For a while I sat there amid the shaded candles, staring at space. But I could not read the future pictured there amid the empty chairs and the flowers, already drooping in each crystal vase.

When at length I roused myself and went upstairs, passing her apartment I heard her singing to herself, and I wondered that she could.

I paused on the gallery stairway to listen; and she could not have heard my footsteps on the thick deep carpeting, yet she came to the door and opened it, looking up at me where I stood.

"You are going to the marble room. May I come and help you?" she asked sweetly. And as I was silent, she said again: "Let me be happy, won't you, Dick? Let me be where you are."

"Have I ever avoided you, Geraldine?"

I descended the steps, she laid her hand lightly on my arm, and together we mounted the stairway toward the gallery.

"I was singing a Hillah tent song when you passed," she said, "partly because I was lonely, and partly"—she hesitated, looking around at me—"partly because I've come to the conclusion, Dick, that I was once at Belshazzar's feast in Cadimirra—for there's a great deal of wickedness in me—you'd never believe it, would you?"

She smiled at me so innocently, so adorably, that I laughed outright.

"I've heard that the maids of Babilu-Ki had a bowing acquaintance with the devil," I said. "Even an Eighur girl nodded pleasantly to Erlik now and then—according to the chronicles of the Tekrins."

"Oh, they surely did," she said. And, "Thank you, Dick," she added, as we reached the gallery; "when I am an old woman you must help me up the steep places."

"It is you who help me," I said lightly.

She stood, resting her arm on the table while I gathered up the mass of papers containing our cuneiform combinations and the Kufic key.

"All that is useless," she said suddenly. Her manner and smile had altered.

I looked up in surprise, and at the same instant she pushed the papers from beneath my hands.

"The memory of things forgotten centuries ago has returned to me," she said feverishly. "I am a pagan again. It was Istar who first taught my hands to weave and my fingers to tie the Sehna knot. I wove that carpet; what I have woven there I can read. Why do you laugh? Will you believe me if I translate the mystery of each inscription as easily as I read the gold cartouche? Come; we shall never need those papers again."

What new caprice was this? She was smiling, almost fixedly, and I thought that there was something in her overflushed face and in the star-like brilliancy of her eyes not quite normal. At the same moment the electric lights in the laboratory went out. Westover was evidently in there. I waited, expecting him to appear, but he did not. Again I reached for the papers, but Geraldine scattered them with a quick sweep of her hand.

"Won't you believe me? Won't you let me try?" she repeated almost impatiently.

With a quick movement she bent forward past me and shut off the lights in the gallery where we stood. Another second, and the lights in the marble room broke out fiercely; and there, full in the dazzling glory, I saw the great carpet of Belshazzar hanging, and beside it the Eighur rug—a pallid shadow on the wall.

Geraldine, hands clasped to her scarlet mouth, dark eyes fixed, moved forward slowly, opalescent tints flashing on her smooth bare arms and shoulders, her head a delicate silhouette against the glare.

I followed, pausing at her side, and we stood silently before the miracle, the great folds gently stirring in some unfelt current; and I saw the upper branches of the Tree of Heaven sway, and a thousand leaves, all glistening, quiver and subside.

"One can almost hear the rustling of the leaves," I whispered.

"I hear more than that," she murmured. "I hear my soul bidding me good-by."

She smiled dreamily, turning to the faded Eighur carpet, and stepping back one pace, dropped her left arm, clasping my hand in hers.

"It was I who wove that carpet—I, maid of the Issig-Kul—and it was you, beloved of Hassan, who inspired it."

"What are you saying, Geraldine?" I began uneasily; "where did you ever hear my name linked with the name of Hassan?"

Her palm was burning hot, her eyes too bright. The fever of caprice possessed her, and her imagination was running riot.

There was a silence, through which a distant sound penetrated—the faint ring of glass somewhere in the laboratory. Westover was tying on his crystal mask.

She heard it, too, and she turned, looking me full in the eyes.

"Dick," she said, "he has slain my body. My soul is bidding me good-by."

"It is my own that he is dragging to destruction, not yours," I muttered.

But she only clasped my hand tighter, the fixed smile stamped on her lips.

"Listen," she whispered, raising her arm. "This is what is written in the rose cartouche on the Eighur carpet that I made:

> '*Roses of Babylon: Ashes of roses in Abaddon.*'

Love and its awful penalty, Dick—and the warning I wove, coffined in cryptogram! Listen again. The cartouche below was once topaz—for I wove it—I!

> '*All Paradise the cost:*
> *Warp and weft for souls so lost.*'

—Mine, Dick, mine!—lost in loving as I loved, centuries since. I have no soul; I have never had any since I lost it then. It is there, tenanting the phantom of an Eighur carpet. Do you not understand? There is my faded monument and refuge—that magic-woven sanctuary—that hiding place from hell!"

Her little feverish fingers tightened convulsively in mine; the color flamed in her cheeks. Suddenly she crushed our clasped hands to her heart, and I felt it leaping madly.

"Geraldine," I stammered, "what is all this ghastly nonsense? Are you ill?"

"Listen! Listen!" she whispered; "the next cartouche was blue—the lost Persian blue! I know; why should I not know—I who wove it centuries ago? And thus it reads, O thou whom I loved to my destruction—thou whom I love!

> '*Time and the Guest*
> *Shall meet me twice—once East, once West.*'

"Ah, prophetess was I by Istar's favor—seeing I died for love. Do you not understand, Dick? Time and the Guest!—the Guest is Death—the Guest we all must entertain one day—and I twice—once in the East, once here in the West—here, now!"

"Geraldine, are you mad?" I whispered; "look at me!—turn and look at me, I say!"

But she shivered in my arms, whispering that she was ransoming her soul and mine. A distant sound broke from the laboratory, and we listened.

"Hush, beloved," she said breathlessly; "the last cartouche is black! And this is written there:

> '*Soul, lotus-sealed,*
> *Receive—thy—Paradise—*'"

Her voice died out; a terrible pallor struck her face; she swayed where she stood, the smile frozen on her bloodless lips.

As I caught her to me, her head fell straight back and her body sank a dead weight in my arms. Then a dreadful thing occurred; the faded ancient tapestry glowed out like a live ember, kindling from end to end, brighter, fiercer, flaming into living fire; and the phantom Tree of Heaven, flashing, superbly jeweled, burst into magnificent florescence.

Blinded, almost stupefied, I staggered back, but the straining cry died in my throat as a voice is strangled in dreadful dreams. Again I strove to shout. The rug, glowing like a living ember, slowly faded before my eyes. Suddenly the last spark went out in a shower of whitening ashes.

Again I strove to cry out: "Jim! Jim!" but my lips stiffened with horror as I listened. For he was somewhere there in the darkness, laughing.

"It was in her wine," he chuckled—"and I saw her kiss the glass and look at you!—and you, there, staring at nothing! Stare at it now!"

And again: "Do you think I have never watched her?—and you? Now she's in hell, and we'll race for her on even terms once more."

Silence: a low, insane laugh, cut by a report and the crash of glass as he fell, shattering his masked face upon the floor.

After a long while I spoke, listening intently. Then I took up my burden.

And there was no sound save the soft stirring of her silken gown as I bore her through the darkness, my cold lips pressed to hers.

He has never returned to America, but now that the time has come for me to fulfill my part, I do so, setting down what I know and what occult in formation I have received in letters from him, of the strange fate which overtook, separately, each and every man present at that farewell dinner at the Lenox Club.

My own fate is stranger still—to record these facts and take my position as his historian and his disciple.

CHAPTER II

THE SIGN OF VENUS

In the card room the game, which had started from a chance suggestion, bid fair to develop into an all-night séance: the young foreign diplomat had shed his coat and lighted a fresh cigar; somebody threw a handkerchief over the face of the clock, and a sleepy club servant took reserve orders for two dozen siphons and other details.

"That lets me out," said Hetherford, rising from his chair with a nod at the dealer. He tossed his cards on the table, settled side obligations with the man on his left, yawned, and put on his hat.

Somebody remonstrated: "It's only two o'clock, Hetherford; you have no white man's burden sitting up for you at home."

But Hetherford shook his head, smiling.

So a servant removed his chair, another man cut in, the dealer dealt cards all around. Presently from somewhere in the smoke haze came a voice, "Hearts." And a quiet voice retorted, "I double it."

Hetherford lingered a moment, then turned on his heel, sauntered out across the hallway and down the stairs into the court, refusing with a sign the offered cab.

Breathing deeply, yawning once or twice, he looked up at the stars. The night air refreshed him; he stood a moment, thoughtfully contemplating his half-smoked cigar, then tossed it away and stepped out into the street.

The street was quiet and deserted; darkened brownstone mansions stared at him through somber windows as he passed; his footsteps echoed across the pavement like the sound of footsteps following.

His progress was leisurely; the dreary monotony of the house fronts soothed him. He whistled a few bars of a commonplace tune, crossed the deserted avenue under the electric lamps, and entered the dimly lighted street beyond.

Here all was silence; the doors of many houses were boarded up—sign that their tenants had migrated to the country. No shadowy cat fled along the iron railings at his approach; no night watchman prowled in deserted dooryards or peered at him from obscurity.

Strolling at ease, thoughts nowhere, he had traversed half the block, when an opening door and a glimmer of light across the sidewalk attracted his attention.

As he approached the house from whence the light came, a figure suddenly appeared on the stoop—a girl in a white ball gown—hastily descending the stone steps. Gaslight from the doorway tinted her bared arms and shoulders. She bent her graceful head and gazed earnestly at Hetherford.

"I beg your pardon," she almost whispered; "might I ask you to help me?"

Hetherford stopped and wheeled short.

"I—I really beg your pardon," she said, "but I am in such distress. Could I ask you to find me a cab?"

"A cab!" he repeated uncertainly; "why, yes—I will with pleasure—" He turned and looked up and down the deserted street, slowly lifting his hand to his short mustache. "If you are in a hurry," he said, "I had better go to the nearest stables—"

"But there is something more," she said, in a tremulous voice; "could you get me a wrap—a cloak—anything to throw over my gown?"

He looked up at her, bewildered. "Why, I don't believe I—" he began, then fell silent before her troubled gaze. "I'll do anything I can for you," he said abruptly. "I have a raincoat at the club—if your need is urgent—"

"It is urgent; but there is something else—something more urgent, more difficult for me to ask you. I must go to Willow Brook—I must go now, to-night! And I—I have no money."

"Do you mean Willow Brook in Westchester?" he asked, astonished. "There is no train at this hour of the morning!"

"Then—then what am I to do?" she faltered. "I cannot stay another moment in that house."

After a silence he said: "Are you afraid of anybody in that house?"

"There is nobody in the house," she said with a shudder; "my mother is in Westchester; all the household are there. I—I came back—a few moments ago—unexpectedly—" She stammered and winced under his keen scrutiny; then the pallor of utter despair came into her cheeks, and she hid her white face in her hands.

Hetherford watched her for a moment.

"I don't exactly understand," he said gently, "but I'll do anything I can for you. I'll go to the club and get my raincoat; I'll go to the stables and get a cab; I haven't any money with me, but it would take only a few minutes for me to drive to the club and get some.... Please don't be distressed; I'll do anything you desire."

She dropped her arms with a hopeless gesture. "But you say there is no train!"

"You could drive to the house of some of your friends—"

"No, no! Oh, my friends must never know of this!"

"I see," he said gravely.

"No, you don't see," she said unsteadily. "The truth is that I am almost frightened to death."

"Can you not tell me what has frightened you so?"

"If I tried to tell you, you would think me mad—you would indeed—"

"Try," he said soothingly.

"Why—why, it startled me to find myself in this house," she began. "You see, I didn't expect to come here; I didn't really want to come here," she added piteously. "Oh, it is simply dreadful to come—like this!" She glanced fearfully over her shoulder at the lighted doorway above, then turned to Hetherford as though dazed.

"Tell me," he said in a quiet voice.

"Yes—I'll tell you. At first it was all dark—but I must have known I was in my own room, for I felt around on the dresser for the matches and lighted a candle. And when I saw that it was truly my own room, and when I caught sight of my own face in the mirror, it terrified me—" She pressed her fingers to her cheeks with a shudder. "Then I ran downstairs and lighted the gas in the hall and peered into the mirror; and I saw a face there—a face like my own—"

Pale, voiceless, she leaned on the bronze balustrade, fair head drooping, lids closed.

Presently, eyes still closed, she said: "You will not leave me alone here—will you—" Her voice died to a whisper.

"No—of course not," he replied slowly.

There was an interval of silence; she passed her hand across her eyes and raised her head, looking up at the stars.

"You see," she murmured, "I dare not be alone; I *dare* not lose touch with the living. I suppose you think me mad, but I am not; I am only stunned. Please stay with me."

"Of course," he said in a soothing voice. "Everything will come out all right—"

"Are you sure?"

"Perfectly. I don't quite know what to say—how to reassure you and offer you any help—"

He fell silent, standing there on the sidewalk, worrying his short mustache. The situation was a new one to him.

"Suppose," he suggested, "that you try to take a little rest. I'll sit down on the steps—"

She looked at him in wide-eyed alarm. "Do you mean that I should go into that house—alone!"

"Well—you oughtn't to stand on the steps all night. It is nearly three o'-

clock. You are frightened and nervous. Really you must go in and—"

"Then you must come, too," she said desperately. "This nightmare is more than I can endure alone. I'm not a coward; none of my race is. But I need a living being near me. Will you come?"

He bowed. She turned, hastily gathering her filmy gown, and mounted the shadowy steps without a sound; and he followed leisurely, even perhaps warily, every sense alert.

He was prepared to see the end of this encounter—see it through to an explanation if it took all summer. Of the situation, however, and of her, he had so far ventured no theory. The type of woman and the situation were perfectly new to him. He was aware that anything might happen in New York, and, closing the heavy front door, he was ready for it.

The hall gas jets were burning brightly, and in the darkened drawing-room he could distinguish the heavy outlines of furniture cased in dust coverings.

She asked him to strike a match and light the sconces in the drawing-room, and he did so, curiosity now thoroughly aroused.

As the gas flared up, shrouded pictures and furniture sprang into view surrounding him, and in the dusk of the room beyond he saw a ray of light glimmering on the foliated carving of a gilded harp.

Slowly he turned to the girl beside him. A warm shadow dimmed her delicate features, yet they were the loveliest he had ever looked upon.

Suddenly he understood the mute message of her eyes: "My imprudence places me at your mercy."

"Your helplessness places me at yours," he said aloud, scarcely conscious that he had spoken.

At that a bright flush transfigured her. "I trusted you the moment I saw you," she said impulsively. "Do you mind sitting there opposite me? I shall take this chair—rather near you—"

She sank into an armchair; and, touched and a trifle amused, he seated himself, at a little nod from her, awaiting her further pleasure.

She lay there for a minute or two without speaking, rounded arms resting on the gilt arms of the chair, eyes thoughtfully studying him.

"I've simply got to tell you everything," she said at length.

"It can do no harm, I think," he replied pleasantly.

"No; no harm. The harm has been done. Yet, with you sitting there so near me, I am not frightened now. It is curious," she mused, "that I should feel no apprehension now. And yet—and yet—"

She leaned toward him, dropping her linked fingers in her lap.

"Tell me, did you ever hear of the Sign of Venus?—the *Signum Veneris?*" she asked.

"I've heard of it—yes," he replied, surprised. And as she said nothing, he went on: "The distinguished gentleman who occupies the chair of Applied Psychics at the university lectures on the Sign of Venus, I believe."

"Did you attend the lectures?" she asked calmly.

He said he had not, smiling a trifle.

"I did."

"They were probably amusing," he ventured.

"Not very. Psychic phenomena bored me; I went during Lent. Psychic phenomena—" She hesitated, embarrassed at his amusement. "I suppose you laugh at that sort of thing."

"No, I don't laugh at it. Queer things occur, they say. All I know is that I myself have never seen anything happen that could not be explained by natural laws."

"I have," she said.

He bent his head in polite acquiescence.

"I went to the lectures," she said. "I am not very intellectual; nothing he said interested me very much—which was, of course, suitable for a Lenten amusement."

She leaned a little nearer, small hands tightly interlaced on her knee.

"His lecture on the Sign of Venus was the last." She lifted a white finger, drawing the imaginary *Signum Veneris* in the air. Hetherford nodded gravely.

"The lecture," she continued, "ended with an explanation of the Sign of Venus—how, contemplating it by starlight, one might pass into that physical unconsciousness which leaves the mind free to control the soul."

She held out her left hand toward him. On a stretched finger a ring glistened, mounted with the Sign of Venus blazing in brilliants.

"I had this made specially," she said; "not that I had any particular desire to test it—no curiosity. It never occurred to me that here in New York one could—could—"

"What?" asked Hetherford dryly.

"—could leave one's own body at will."

"I don't believe it could be accomplished in New York," he said with great gravity. "And that's a pretty safe conclusion to come to, is it not?"

She dropped her eyes, silent for a moment, resting her delicate chin on the palm of her hand. Then she lifted her eyes to him calmly, and the direct beauty of her gaze disturbed him.

"No, it is not a safe conclusion to come to. Listen to me. Last night they gave a dance at the Willow Brook Hunt. It was nearly two o'clock this morning when I left the club house and started home across the lawn with my mother and the maid—"

"But how on earth could—" he began, then begged her pardon and waited.

She continued serenely: "The night was warm and lovely, and it was clear starlight. When I entered my room I sent the maid away and sat down by the open window. The scent of the flowers and the beauty of the night made me restless; I went downstairs, unbolted the door, and slipped out through the garden to the pergola. My hammock hung there, and I lay down in it, looking out at the stars."

She drew the ring from her finger, holding it out for him to see.

"The starlight caught the gems on the Sign of Venus," she said under her breath; "that was the beginning. And then—I don't know why—as I lay there idly turning the ring on my finger, I found myself saying, 'I must go to New York: I must leave my body here asleep in the hammock and go to my own room in Fifty-eighth Street.'"

A curious little chill passed over Hetherford.

"I said it again and again—I don't know why. I remember the ring glittered; I remember it grew brighter and brighter. And then—and then! I found myself upstairs in the dark, groping over the dresser for the matches."

Again that faint chill touched Hetherford.

"I was stupefied for a moment," she said tremulously; "then I suspected what I had done, and it frightened me. And when I lighted the candle, and saw it was truly my own room—and when I caught sight of my own face in the mirror—terror seized me; it was like a glimpse of something taken unawares. For, do you know that although in the glass I saw my own face, the face was not looking back at me." She dropped her head, crushing the ring in both hands. "The reflected face was far lovelier than mine; and it was mine, I think, yet it was not looking at me, and it moved when I did not move. I wonder—I wonder—"

The tension was too much. "If that be so," he said, steadying his voice—"if you saw a face in your mirror, the face was your own." He made an impatient gesture, rising to his feet at the same moment. "All that you have told me can be explained," he said.

"How can it? At this very moment I am asleep in my hammock."

"We will deal with that later," he said, smiling down at her. "Where is there a looking-glass?"

"There is one in the hallway." She rose, slipping the ring on her finger, and led the way to where an oval gilt mirror hung partly covered with dust cloths.

He cast aside the coverings. "Now look into the glass," he said gayly.

She raised her head and faced the mirror for an instant.

"Come here," she whispered; and he stepped behind her, looking over her shoulder.

In the glass, as though reflected, he saw her face, but *the face was in profile!*

A shiver passed over him from head to foot.

"Did I not tell you?" she whispered. "Look! See, the other face is moving, while I am still!"

"There's something wrong about the glass, of course," he muttered; "it's defective."

"But who is that in the glass?"

"It is you—your profile. I don't exactly understand. Good Lord! It's turning away from us!"

She shrank against the wall, wide-eyed, breathing rapidly.

"There is no use in our being frightened," he said, scarcely knowing what he uttered. "This is Fifty-eighth Street, New York, 1903." He shook his shoulders, squaring them, and forced a smile. "Don't be frightened; there's an explanation for all this. You are not asleep in Westchester; you are here in your own house. You mustn't tremble so. Give me your hand a moment."

She laid her hand in his obediently; it shook like a leaf. He held it firmly, touching the fluttering pulse.

"You are certainly no spirit," he said, smiling; "your hand is warm and yielding. Ghosts don't have hands like that, you know."

Her fingers lay in his, quite passive now, but the pulse quickened.

"The explanation of it all is this," he said: "You have had a temporary suspension of consciousness, during which time you, without being aware of what you were doing, came to town from Willow Brook. You believe you went to the dance at the Hunt Club, but probably you did not. Instead, during a lapse of consciousness, you went to the station, took a train to town, came straight to your own house—" He hesitated.

"Yes," she said, "I have a key to the door. Here it is. "She drew it from the bosom of her gown; he took it triumphantly.

"You simply awoke to consciousness while you were groping for the matches. That is all there is to it; and you need not be frightened at all!" he announced.

"No, not frightened," she said, shaking her head; "only—only I wonder how I can get back. I've tried to fix my mind on my ring—on the Sign of Venus—I cannot seem to—"

"But that's nonsense!" he protested cheerfully. "That ring has nothing to do with the matter."

"But it brought me here! Truly I am asleep in my hammock. Won't you believe it?"

"No; and you mustn't, either," he said impatiently. "Why, just now I explained to you   —"

"I know," she said, looking down at the ring on her hand; "but you are wrong—truly you are."

"I am not wrong," he said, laughing. "It was only a dream—the dance, the return, the hammock—all these were parts of a dream so intensely real that you cannot shake it off at once."

"Then—then *who* was that we saw in the mirror?"

"Let us try it again," he said confidently. She suffered him to lead her again to the mirror; again they peered into its glimmering depths, heads close together.

A second's breathless silence, then she caught his hand in both of hers with a low cry; for the strange profile was slowly turning toward them a face of amazing beauty—her own face transfigured, radiantly glorified.

"My soul!" she gasped, and would have fallen at his feet had he not held her and supported her to the stairs, where she sank down, hiding her face in her arms.

As for him, he was terribly shaken; he strove to speak, to reason with her, with himself, but a stupor chained body and mind, and he only leaned there on the newel post, vaguely aware of his own helplessness.

Far away in the night the bells of a church began striking the hour—one, two, three, four. Presently the distant rattle of a wagon sounded. The city stirred in its slumbers.

He found himself bending beside her, her passive hands in his once more, and he was saying: "As a matter of fact, all this is quite capable of an explanation. Don't be distressed—please don't be frightened or sad. We've both had some sort of hallucination, that's all—really that is all."

"I am not frightened now," she said dreamily. "I am quite sure that—that I am not dead. I am only asleep in my hammock. When I awake—"

Again, in spite of himself, he shivered.

"Will you do one more thing for me?" she asked.

"Yes—a million."

"Only one. It is unreasonable, it is perhaps silly—and I have no right to ask—"

"Ask it," he begged.

"Then—then, will you go to Willow Brook? Now?"

"Now?" he repeated blankly.

"Yes." She looked down at him with the shadow of a smile touching lips and eyes. "I am asleep in the hammock; I sleep very, very soundly—and very, very late into the morning. They may not find me there for a long while. So would you mind going to Willow Brook to awaken me?"

"I—I—but you do not expect me to leave you here and find you in Westchester!" he stammered.

"You need not go," she said quietly. "If you will telephone to the house and ask somebody to go out to the pergola—"

"No," he said, "I will go; I will go anywhere on earth for you."

He stood up, his senses in a whirl. She rose, too, leaning lightly on the balustrade.

"Thank you," she said sweetly. "When you awake me, give me this." She held out the *Signum Veneris*; and he took it, and bending his head slowly, raised it to his lips.

It was almost morning when he entered his own house. In a dull trance he dressed, turned again to the stairs, and crept out into the shadowy street.

People began to pass him; an early electric tram whizzed up Forty-second Street as he entered the railway station. Presently he found himself in a car, clutching his ticket in one hand, her ring in the other.

"It is I who am mad, not she," he muttered as the train glided from the station, through the long yard, dim in morning mist, where green and crimson lanterns still sparkled faintly.

Again he pressed the *Signum Veneris* to his lips. "It is I who am mad— love mad!" he whispered as the far treble warning of the whistle aroused him and sent him stumbling out into the soft fresh morning air.

The rising sun smote him full in the eyes as he came in sight of the club house among the still green trees, and the dew on the lawn flashed like the gems of the *Signum Veneris* on the ring he held so tightly.

Across the club house lawn stood another house, circled with gardens in full bloom; and to the left, among young trees, the white columns of a pergola glistened, tinted with rose from the early sun.

There was not a soul astir as he crossed the lawn and entered the garden, brushing the dew from overweighted blossoms as he passed.

Suddenly, at a turn in the path, he came upon the pergola, and saw a brilliant hammock hanging in the shadow.

Over the hammock's fringe something light and fluffy fell in folds like the billowy frills of a ball gown. He stumbled forward, dazed, incredulous, and stood trembling for an instant.

Then, speechless, he sank down beside her, and dropped the ring into the palm of her half-closed and unconscious hand.

A ray of sunlight fell across her hair; slowly her blue eyes unclosed, smiling divinely.

And in her partly open palm the Sign of Venus glimmered like dew silvering a budding rose.

CHAPTER III

THE CASE OF MR. HELMER

He had really been too ill to go; the penetrating dampness of the studio, the nervous strain, the tireless application, all had told on him heavily. But the feverish discomfort in his head and lungs gave him no rest; it was impossible to lie there in bed and do nothing; besides, he did not care to disappoint his hostess. So he managed to crawl into his clothes, summon a cab, and depart. The raw night air cooled his head and throat; he opened the cab window and let the snow blow in on him.

When he arrived he did not feel much better, although Catharine was glad to see him. Somebody's wife was allotted to him to take in to dinner, and he executed the commission with that distinction of manner peculiar to men of his temperament.

When the women had withdrawn and the men had lighted cigars and cigarettes, and the conversation wavered between municipal reform and *contes drolatiques*, and the Boznovian *attaché* had begun an interminable story, and Count Fantozzi was emphasizing his opinion of women by joining the tips of his overmanicured thumb and forefinger and wafting spectral kisses at an annoyed Englishman opposite, Helmer laid down his unlighted cigar and, leaning over, touched his host on the sleeve.

"Hello! what's up, Philip?" said his host cordially; and Helmer, dropping his voice a tone below the sustained pitch of conversation, asked him the question that had been burning his feverish lips since dinner began.

To which his host replied, "What girl do you mean?" and bent nearer to listen.

"I mean the girl in the fluffy black gown, with shoulders and arms of ivory, and the eyes of Aphrodite."

His host smiled. "Where did she sit, this human wonder?"

"Beside Colonel Farrar."

"Farrar? Let's see"—he knit his brows thoughtfully, then shook his head. "I can't recollect; we're going in now and you can find her and I'll—"

His words were lost in the laughter and hum around them; he nodded an abstracted assurance at Helmer; others claimed his attention, and by the time he rose to signal departure he had forgotten the girl in black.

As the men drifted toward the drawing-rooms, Helmer moved with the throng. There were a number of people there whom he knew and spoke to, although through the increasing feverishness he could scarce hear himself speak. He was too ill to stay; he would find his hostess and ask the name of that girl in black, and go.

The white drawing-rooms were hot and over-thronged. Attempting to find his hostess, he encountered Colonel Farrar, and together they threaded their way aimlessly forward.

"Who is the girl in black, Colonel?" he asked; "I mean the one that you took in to dinner."

"A girl in black? I don't think I saw her."

"She sat beside you!"

"Beside *me?*" The Colonel halted, and his inquiring gaze rested for a moment on the younger man, then swept the crowded rooms.

"Do you see her now?" he asked.

"No," said Helmer, after a moment.

They stood silent for a little while, then parted to allow the Chinese minister thoroughfare—a suave gentleman, all antique silks, and a smile "thousands of years old." The minister passed, leaning on the arm of the general commanding at Governor's Island, who signaled Colonel Farrar to join them; and Helmer drifted again, until a voice repeated his name insistently, and his hostess leaned forward from the brilliant group surrounding her, saying: "What in the world is the matter, Philip? You look wretchedly ill."

"It's a trifle close here—nothing's the matter." He stepped nearer, dropping his voice: "Catharine, who was that girl in black?"

"What girl?"

"She sat beside Colonel Farrar at dinner—or I thought she did—"

"Do you mean Mrs. Van Siclen? She is in white, silly!"

"No—the girl in black."

His hostess bent her pretty head in perplexed silence, frowning a trifle with the effort to remember.

"There were so many," she murmured; "let me see—it is certainly strange that I cannot recollect. Wait a moment! Are you sure she wore black? Are you *sure* she sat next to Colonel Farrar?"

"A moment ago I was certain—" he said, hesitating. "Never mind, Catharine; I'll prowl about until I find her."

His hostess, already partly occupied with the animated stir around her, nodded brightly; Helmer turned his fevered eyes and then his steps toward the cool darkness of the conservatories. But he found there a dozen people who greeted him by name, demanding not only his company but his immediate and undivided attention.

"Mr. Helmer might be able to explain to us what his own work means," said a young girl, laughing.

They had evidently been discussing his sculptured group, just completed for the new façade of the National Museum. Press and public had commented very freely on the work since the unveiling a week since; critics quarreled concerning the significance of the strange composition in marble. The group was at the same time repellent and singularly beautiful; but nobody denied its technical perfection. This was the sculptured group: A vaquero, evidently dying, lay in a loose heap among some desert rocks. Beside him, chin on palm, sat an exquisite winged figure, calm eyes fixed on the dying man. It was plain that death was near; it was stamped on the ravaged visage, on the collapsed frame. And yet, in the dying boy's eyes there was nothing of agony, no fear, only an intense curiosity as the lovely winged figure gazed straight into the glazing eyes.

"It may be," observed an attractive girl, "that Mr. Helmer will say with Mr. Gilbert,

> "'It is really very clever,
> But I don't know what it means.'"

Helmer laughed and started to move away. "I think I'd better admit that at once," he said, passing his hand over his aching eyes; but the tumult of protest blocked his retreat, and he was forced to find a chair under the palms and tree ferns. "It was merely an idea of mine," he protested, good-humoredly, "an idea that has haunted me so persistently that, to save myself further annoyance, I locked it up in marble."

"Demoniac obsession?" suggested a very young man, with a taste for morbid literature.

"Not at all," protested Helmer, smiling; "the idea annoyed me until I gave it expression. It doesn't bother me any more."

"You said," observed the attractive girl, "that you were going to tell us all about it."

"About the idea? Oh, no, I didn't promise that—"

"Please, Mr. Helmer!"

A number of people had joined the circle; he could see others standing here and there among the palms, evidently pausing to listen.

"There is no logic in the idea," he said, uneasily—"nothing to attract your attention. I have only laid a ghost—"

He stopped short. The girl in black stood there among the others, intently watching him. When she caught his eye, she nodded with the friendliest little smile; and as he started to rise she shook her head and stepped back with a gesture for him to continue.

They looked steadily at one another for a moment.

"The idea that has always attracted me," he began slowly, "is purely in-stinctive and emotional, not logical. It is this: As long as I can remember I have taken it for granted that a person who is doomed to die, never dies utterly alone. We who die in our beds—or expect to—die surrounded by the living. So fall soldiers on the firing line; so end the great majority—never absolutely alone. Even in a murder, the murderer at least must be present. If not, something else is there.

"But how is it with those solitary souls isolated in the world—the lone herder who is found lifeless in some vast, waterless desert, the pioneer whose bones are stumbled over by the tardy pickets of civilization—and even those nearer us—here in our city—who are found in silent houses, in deserted streets, in the solitude of salt meadows, in the miserable desola-tion of vacant lands beyond the suburbs?"

The girl in black stood motionless, watching him intently.

"I like to believe," he went on, "that no living creature dies absolutely and utterly alone. I have thought that, perhaps in the desert, for instance, when a man is doomed, and there is no chance that he could live to relate the miracle, some winged sentinel from the uttermost outpost of Eternity, putting off the armor of invisibility, drops through space to watch beside him so that he may not die alone."

There was absolute quiet in the circle around him. Looking always at the girl in black, he said:

"Perhaps those doomed on dark mountains or in solitary deserts, or the last survivor at sea, drifting to certain destruction after the wreck has foundered, finds death no terror, being guided to it by those invisible to all save the surely doomed. That is really all that suggested the marble—quite illogical, you see."

In the stillness, somebody drew a long, deep breath; the easy reaction fol-lowed; people moved, spoke together in low voices; a laugh rippled up out of the darkness. But Helmer had gone, making his way through the half light toward a figure that moved beyond through the deeper shadows of the foliage—moved slowly and more slowly. Once she looked back, and he followed, pushing forward and parting the heavy fronds of fern and palm and masses of moist blossoms. Suddenly he came upon her, stand-ing there as though waiting for him.

"There is not a soul in this house charitable enough to present me," he began.

"Then," she answered laughingly, "charity should begin at home. Take pity on yourself—and on me. I have waited for you."

"Did you really care to know me?" he stammered.

"Why am I here alone with you?" she asked, bending above a scented mass of flowers. "Indiscretion may be a part of valor, but it is the best part of—something else."

That blue radiance which a starless sky sheds lighted her white shoulders; transparent shadow veiled the contour of neck and cheeks.

"At dinner," he said, "I did not mean to stare so—but I simply could not keep my eyes from yours—"

"A hint that mine were on yours, too?"

She laughed a little laugh so sweet that the sound seemed part of the twilight and the floating fragrance. She turned gracefully, holding out her hand.

"Let us be friends," she said, "after all these years."

Her hand lay in his for an instant; then she withdrew it and dropped it caressingly upon a cluster of massed flowers.

"Forced bloom," she said, looking down at them, where her fingers, white as the blossoms, lay half buried. Then, raising her head, "You do not know me, do you?"

"Know you?" he faltered; "how could I know you? Do you think for a moment that I could have forgotten you?"

"Ah, you have not forgotten me!" she said, still with her wide smiling eyes on his; "you have not forgotten. There is a trace of me in the winged figure you cut in marble—not the features, not the massed hair, nor the rounded neck and limbs—but in the eyes. Who living, save yourself, can read those eyes?"

"Are you laughing at me?"

"Answer me; who alone in all the world can read the message in those sculptured eyes?"

"Can you?" he asked, curiously troubled.

"Yes; I, and the dying man in marble."

"What do you read there?"

"Pardon for guilt. You have foreshadowed it unconsciously—the resurrection of the soul. That is what you have left in marble for the mercilessly just to ponder on; that alone is the meaning of your work."

Through the throbbing silence he stood thinking, searching his clouded mind.

"The eyes of the dying man are your own," she said. "Is it not true?"

And still he stood there, groping, probing through dim and forgotten corridors of thought toward a faint memory scarcely perceptible in the wavering mirage of the past.

"Let us talk of your career," she said, leaning back against the thick foliage—"your success, and all that it means to you," she added gayly.

He stood staring at the darkness. "You have set the phantoms of forgotten things stirring and whispering together somewhere within me.

Now tell me more; tell me the truth."

"You are slowly reading it in my eyes," she said, laughing sweetly. "Read and remember."

The fever in him seared his sight as he stood there, his confused gaze on hers.

"Is it a threat of hell you read in the marble?" he asked.

"No, nothing of destruction, only resurrection and hope of Paradise. Look at me closely."

"Who are you?" he whispered, closing his eyes to steady his swimming senses. "When have we met?"

"You were very young," she said under her breath—"and I was younger—and the rains had swollen the Canadian river so that it boiled amber at the fords; and I could not cross—alas!"

A moment of stunning silence, then her voice again: "I said nothing, not a word even of thanks when you offered aid.... I—was not too heavy in your arms, and the ford was soon passed—soon passed. That was very long ago." Watching him from shadowy sweet eyes, she said:

"For a day you knew the language of my mouth and my arms around you, there in the white sun glare of the river. For every kiss taken and re-taken, given and forgiven, we must account—for every one, even to the last.

"But you have set a monument for us both, preaching the resurrection of the soul. Love is such a little thing—and ours endured a whole day long! Do you remember? Yet He who created love, designed that it should last a lifetime. Only the lost outlive it."

She leaned nearer:

"Tell me, you who have proclaimed the resurrection of dead souls, are you afraid to die?"

Her low voice ceased; lights broke out like stars through the foliage around them; the great glass doors of the ballroom were opening; the il-luminated fountain flashed, a falling shower of silver. Through the outrush of music and laughter swelling around them, a clear far voice called "Françoise!"

Again, close by, the voice rang faintly, "Françoise! Françoise!"

She slowly turned, staring into the brilliant glare beyond.

"Who called?" he asked hoarsely.

"My mother," she said, listening intently. "Will you wait for me?"

His ashen face glowed again like a dull ember. She bent nearer, and caught his fingers in hers.

"By the memory of our last kiss, wait for me!" she pleaded, her little hand tightening on his.

"Where?" he said, with dry lips. "We cannot talk here!—we cannot say here the things that must be said."

"In your studio," she whispered. "Wait for me."

"Do you know the way?"

"I tell you I will come; truly I will! Only a moment with my mother—then I will be there!"

Their hands clung together an instant, then she slipped away into the crowded rooms; and after a moment Helmer followed, head bent, blinded by the glare.

"You are ill, Philip," said his host, as he took his leave. "Your face is as ghastly as that dying vaquero's—by Heaven, man, you *look* like him!"

"Did you find your girl in black?" asked his hostess curiously.

"Yes," he said; "good night."

The air was bitter as he stepped out—bitter as death. Scores of carriage lamps twinkled as he descended the snowy steps, and a faint gust of music swept out of the darkness, silenced as the heavy doors closed behind him.

He turned west, shivering. A long smear of light bounded his horizon as he pressed toward it and entered the sordid avenue beneath the iron arcade which was even now trembling under the shock of an oncoming train. It passed overhead with a roar; he raised his hot eyes and saw, through the tangled girders above, the illuminated disk of the clock tower—all distorted—for the fever in him was disturbing everything—even the cramped and twisted street into which he turned, fighting for breath like a man stabbed through and through.

"What folly!" he said aloud, stopping short in the darkness. "This is fever—all this. She could not know where to come—"

Where two blind alleys cut the shabby block, worming their way inward from the avenue and from Tenth Street, he stopped again, his hands working at his coat.

"It is fever, fever!" he muttered. "She was not there."

There was no light in the street save for the red fire lamp burning on the corner, and a glimmer from the Old Grapevine Tavern across the way. Yet all around him the darkness was illuminated with pale unsteady flames, lighting him as he groped through the shadows of the street to the blind alley. Dark old silent houses peered across the paved lane at their aged counterparts, waiting for him.

And at last he found a door that yielded, and he stumbled into the black passageway, always lighted on by the unsteady pallid flames which seemed to burn in infinite depths of night.

"She was not there—she was never there," he gasped, bolting the door and sinking down upon the floor. And, as his mind wandered, he raised his eyes and saw the great bare room growing whiter and whiter under the uneasy flames.

"It will burn as I burn," he said aloud—for the phantom flames had crept into his body. Suddenly he laughed, and the vast studio rang again.

"Hark!" he whispered, listening intently. "Who knocked?"

There was some one at the door; he managed to raise himself and drag back the bolt.

"You!" he breathed, as she entered hastily, her hair disordered and her black skirts powdered with snow.

"Who but I?" she whispered, breathless. "Listen! do you hear my mother calling me? It is too late; but she was with me to the end."

Through the silence, from an infinite distance, came a desolate cry of grief—"Françoise!"

He had fallen back into his chair again, and the little busy flames enveloped him so that the room began to whiten again into a restless glare. Through it he watched her.

The hour struck, passed, struck and passed again. Other hours grew, lengthening into night. She sat beside him with never a word or sigh or whisper of breathing; and dream after dream swept him, like burning winds. Then sleep immersed him so that he lay senseless, sightless eyes still fixed on her. Hour after hour—and the white glare died out, fading to a glimmer. In densest darkness, he stirred, awoke, his mind quite clear, and spoke her name in a low voice.

"Yes, I am here," she answered gently.

"Is it death?" he asked, closing his eyes.

"Yes. Look at me, Philip."

His eyes unclosed; into his altered face there crept an intense curiosity. For he beheld a glimmering shape, wide-winged and deep-eyed, kneeling beside him, and looking him through and through.

CHAPTER IV

THE TREE OF DREAMS

It was a slim, well-groomed, top-hatted, frock-coated Smith who entered his private office that morning; it was a very different species of Smith who left stealthily by a back corridor an hour later, a shabby-genteel Smith whose cravatless collar was fastened with a democratic bone collar button—whose clean but shapeless trousers bagged and flapped in the June breeze—who gazed out at Broadway from under the faded brim of a cheap felt hat—who, as he forced his pace from a Fifth Avenue saunter into a Third Avenue hustle, thrust both thin, clean hands into his trousers pockets and satisfied himself that every cent which he meant to spend for a week was there in the shape of ten one-dollar bills.

At Wall Street he adjusted his glasses and peered about with pleasant, near-sighted eyes to discover the policeman at the crossing in order to avoid him. Once beyond the financial zone downtown he had no fear of being recognized by anybody; his features, he was modestly persuaded, resembled the typical features of about fifty per cent of the male inhabitants of Manhattan, although those same features had been public and newspaper property for three years now—ever since his father, J. Abingdon Smith, 2d, had faded heavenward, leaving the enormous fortune in Manhattan real estate to his only son, J. Abingdon Smith, 3d.

He was still a young man, thin of hair, nearsighted, endowed with sufficient intelligence to enable him to turn over his inherited fortune, legitimately increased, to any heir he might have if he should ever marry. Had he resembled Smith the first, or Smith the second, he would have done this as a matter of family routine—married the sort of girl that generations of Smiths found inoffensive enough to marry; produced one heir, and, when the proper time arrived, would have in his turn decorously and formally faded heavenward—leaving a J. Abingdon Smith, 4th, to follow his example.

But Smith had inherited from his mother a thin but deep streak of romantic sentiment. This vein ran clean through him, and might have manifested itself in almost any form along the line of least resistance, had it not been half imbedded in a stratum of negative platitudes inherited from his emotionless father.

As he stood in his shabby clothes, near the new Hall of Records, waiting for a Fourth Avenue car, a slender, blue-eyed girl, passing, looked up at him with such a frank, sweet gaze that he missed his next breath and then made up for it by breathing twice too quickly. He had an idea that he had seen her before, but finally decided he hadn't.

To be loved for himself alone was one of his impractical ideas, born of the maternal sentimental streak; but, for years, the famous Smith fortune, its enormous holdings in realty, the doings of the Smiths, their shrewd sales, purchases, leases, improvements, their movements, their personal affairs, their photographed features had been common property and an unfailing source of news for the press; and he knew perfectly well that, however honest and theoretically disinterested a girl might be, the courtship of a J. Abingdon Smith, of whatever vintage, could not help representing a bunch of figures that no human being in shape of a female biped could avoid seeing, no matter how tightly she closed her innocent eyes. Thinking of these things, he calmly encountered the curious eyes of the conductor as he boarded a crowded car.

The blue-eyed girl also got in, but Smith, on the back platform, did not see her.

"That fellow," said the conductor to the grip-man, as he swung off the front platform after collecting a fare, "is a ringer for J. Abingdon Smith, the millionaire."

And the conductor was not the only one; several passengers were amused by the resemblance this near-sighted, shabby young man bore to the features that every newspaper had made familiar to the submerged tenth, the frantically swimming twentieth, and the marooned remainder of the great unwashed.

Half an hour later Smith said to the conductor: "Would you be kind enough to stop here?"

"Certainly, Mr. Smith," said the conductor, meaning a joke.

Smith ambled along, intent upon his own business. The blue-eyed girl had preceded him in the same direction; but as he entered the main doorway of the Smith model tenement houses, which formed almost a complete quadrangle around the block, he was not aware that she was on the iron and concrete stairway, three stories above him, and was still climbing heavenward.

When he reached his room, which he had paid for in advance, he found that his trunk and furniture had arrived. The air in the room was close; he opened the window.

For a while he bustled busily about, arranging the meager furniture. The narrow iron bed he dragged into a corner by the window, pushed the washstand against the opposite wall and hung a ninety-eight-cent mirror over it. He laid a strip of carpet in the center of the floor, placed a pine table upon it, and then, picking up the only chair, distractedly began traveling about with it, trying the effect, first in one corner, then in another.

At this juncture Kerns, his agent, general estate manager, and boyhood friend, slipped into the room on tiptoe, carefully closing the door behind him.

"*I* don't know where to put it," Smith said, pausing to settle his refractory glasses and glance suspiciously at Kerns out of pleasant, near-sighted eyes. "When they have only one chair where do they usually put it, Tommy?"

"When they get down to one chair they usually put it in the stove," said Kerns.

"What? They do? That's another point, Kerns; we've got to give them free furniture somehow; I mean for the same rent. You figure it up; cut out something or other—" He gazed vaguely about the bare walls as though contemplating their possible economic elimination. Then, he looked at the floor; but his tenants, being wingless, required something to stand on. "Could we give them bed, tables, and chair, and cut out that gas range?" he suggested.

"Not unless you throw in a stove," said Kerns, trying to look serious. "And if you do that, they'll keep their coal in the bath tubs, as before."

Smith began to remove the contents of a shabby little trunk. First, there were shaving utensils, which he placed in a row on the unpainted washstand, then a tin pitcher and wash basin, a cake of soap, and last, some cheap towels.

"I've a notion that I've too much crockery," he said, gazing about. "Do you think I've overdone it? I don't need two plates—do I? And all that tinware—do I? What the deuce are you grinning at?" he added, diving into his battered trunk again and emerging with both arms full of tinware. These utensils he hung upon nails above the sink in the corner, arranging them with care.

"That's the place for pots and pans, isn't it, Kerns?" he said, backing off to observe the effect. Then, by chance, he caught sight of himself in the ninety-eight-cent mirror, and a slight flush of embarrassment rose to his cheeks.

"Do I look like a respectable man out of work?" he asked. "Tell me the truth."

"Exactly," replied Kerns; "you look like what you are—a well-meaning gentleman, permanently unemployed—and likely to remain so. In other words, dear friend, you resemble a Lulu bird of leisure."

"Do you mean to say I look like myself?" demanded Smith innocently. "Do I seem to be made up for a part? There was an impudent conductor who called me Smith. Don't you suppose he did it in joke? And—a—a girl—who looked at me—er—"

"Because you're a winner. Because a Smith ill dressed is half confessed; because a Smith in any other clothes would look as neat; because a Sm—"

Smith's brows contracted, but lifelong endurance of Kerns's raillery had habituated him to disregard such gibes.

"John Abingdon," continued Kerns, "I've inspected these barracks of yours to-day because you insisted; I've met you here because you told me to; but it's all portentous and top-heavy nonsense on your part, and it's my business to say so whether it makes you fidgety and sulky or not."

"We won't start that line of discussion again," said Smith, "because, Kerns, outside of your own harmless routine, you're so densely ignorant that I am continually ashamed of you. What do you know about humanity?"

"I thought you weren't going to start that thing going," yawned Kerns.

"You started it yourself," said Smith.

"All right, then; I'll go on. Haven't I told you a thousand times that, if you are anxious to know how your tenants live, I can tell you, or any of your collectors or your brokers, or even your janitors. Every time you do a thing without my advice you mess matters. You insisted on giving them bath tubs, and they used them for coal, and I had to straighten that out by taking away their cook stoves and substituting gas ranges and ovens. You insisted on inserting rotary ventilators in every window, and the noise of the wheels kept your tenants awake at night; and, when they don't sleep, they fight. Besides, they all caught cold, and there are a dozen enraged Hibernians suing you now. If you could only know what I know and see what I've seen—"

"I've told you a hundred times, Tom, that I don't intend to slop over and bestow charity; but I do want to know what are my just obligations to my tenants, and how I can place them in a better position."

He was somewhat heated when he finished, and stood touching his forehead with his handkerchief.

"Toot! Toot!" said Kerns plaintively, backing toward the door. "The next stop is Chautauqua. Go it your own way, Smithy; I'm about due at the club for luncheon."

The door slammed as the wash basin struck it; Smith glared at the dent in the woodwork, prepared to hurl the coffeepot. But Kerns did not come back; and, after a while, he replaced the coffeepot, searched his trunk for a collar, buttoned it to his flannel shirt, and, picking up his hat, went out into the hallway.

And there he encountered the slender girl with the blue eyes.

There was something very innocent in her confident, fearless gaze; as he passed her, lifting his hat, he bade her good day in his pleasant voice. Her quaintly impersonal nod in acknowledgment pleased him.

"Just what I thought," he reflected, as he descended the stairs: "the poor are always nice to each other; they're frank and human, unspoiled by our asinine code of conventions. If I'd worn a top hat that girl would have looked the other way; if I'd noticed her she'd have been defiant or sullen or saucy."

And while he trudged about, purchasing groceries for his luncheon, he looked out upon the world through optimistic glasses, smiling, warmhearted, pleased with himself and everybody he encountered.

He was hungry—it being long past his regular luncheon time—an hour from which he had not varied half a dozen times in a dozen years.

As he ascended the iron stairs of his lodging house once more he counted over the little packages of groceries piled up in his arms—butter, salt, sugar, a bottle of milk, tea, coffee, rolls, and eggs. "Probably too much," he reflected; "I'll have to go about among these people and find out what they eat— Good Heavens! that is awful!"

In his own hallway a khamsin gust of cabbage smote him with its answer to his question, and he shuddered. He forced his door in with the point of his knee, made his way to the table, and dropped the packages. Then, producing a match box, he advanced blithely toward the gas range.

"The first thing to do is to start that exceedingly convenient machine and get action at once," he continued, turning on the gas and lighting a match. "Cooking coffee and eggs is nothing to any man who has ever camped out in the woods—"

Flash!—bang! went the gas range; and Smith executed what his office boys might have characterized as a "quick get-away."

"W-what a perfectly ghastly species of range," he stammered, "g-going off in a man's face like a t-t-ten-inch shell!" He sat down in the only chair, breathed hard, and stared at the range; then, suddenly afraid that gas might be pouring into the room, he crept toward it, lighted another match, and extended his arm like the hero touching off a magazine in the ship's hold.

Bang! repeated the gas range emphatically.

"W-well, this is a pleasant situation!" he breathed, wringing his slightly scorched fingers. "Am I expected to fry my eggs over a volcano?"

Hesitating, he wiped his glasses, affixed them, and gazed earnestly at the range. Very gingerly he tiptoed toward it and, with a sudden dash, turned off the gas.

For a while he alternately stood in front of it and walked all around it. He looked at his coffee and eggs—he could not eat them raw. It was now long after his usual luncheon hour, and he began to feel famished.

"The trouble is that I don't know how to get the proper spark," he reflected; but, driven by necessity, he turned on the gas once more, and, lighting a match, applied it. There was no explosion this time; a bluish flame played all over the machine for a few seconds, sank, rose, subsided, and went out. In vain he lighted match after match. He got no more flame.

"This is a disgracefully run house!" he exclaimed aloud. "It's high time I heard something about it! Here I am two hours late and can't get enough heat to cook an egg!"

Very angry, he marched out on a hunt for the janitor; but, after climbing up and down stairs and making inquiries on every landing, he had come no nearer to discovering the janitor. A gentleman named Dugan thought that the janitor might be engaged in tenpins at Bauer's popular corner resort. Smith repaired thither, but could not discover him. Another gentleman, named Clancy, emerging from the two-room apartment adjoining Smith's, came in at Smith's invitation and rubbed a flat, rough thumb up and down the range. Then he departed, scratching his head and advising further search for the janitor.

"Ye cud cook a bit an' a sup on our own range," he said, "but th' ould woman do be bilin' shirrts."

When Mr. Clancy had departed Smith spent ten more minutes tinkering with the range, growing hungrier and hungrier every second. But, hungry, angry and discouraged as he was, he obstinately refused to consider a restaurant as even a temporary solution. Once more he set off down the endless iron and concrete stairway to hunt up the janitor; and, returning unsuccessful, encountered the janitor on his own landing. The janitor was talking to the girl with the blue eyes.

"Please don't let me interrupt you," said Smith; "it's only that I can't work my range."

"You are not interrupting," said the girl with the blue eyes. "My ceiling is beginning to fall, that is all."

"I'll have that attended to at once!" exclaimed Smith, forgetting his role of tenant—"that is," he added, in confusion, "the janitor will notify M—, the agent. You will, won't you?" he continued, turning to the janitor, whose face had been growing redder and redder as he grew madder and madder.

"Where do you think you are?" he demanded. "In the Waldorf? An' who do you think you are, young man? John D.? or the Dutch Emp'ror? Or do you think you're J. Abingdon Smith, the owner of this here plant, because you look like his grandfather's hired man?"

"Not at all," said Smith, turning red. "I had no intention of interfering."

"Well, you go and sit on your range and keep it warm till I get a gasfitter, see!" growled the janitor; "an' mebbe he'll fix it to-night," he said, looking back malevolently over his shoulder as he descended the stairs, "an' mebbe he'll fix it next month. You mind your business, young man, an' I'll mind yours."

Smith, tingling all over, looked after him, but his anger passed with a shrug and a short laugh as he realized that the rebuke had been in a fashion his own fault.

He had made a step across the hallway toward his own room, when he remembered the girl with the blue eyes.

"I'm sorry I caused any unpleasantness," he said. "I hope the janitor won't visit his petty tyranny on you."

"I don't think he will; I— Can't you make your range burn properly?"

"No," he said, smiling. "It blew up three times, and now it has retired from active business. I believe it has become permanently extinct."

"Perhaps," she ventured, "you are not accustomed to gas ranges. Are you?"

"No, but I've got to learn to manage them if I'm to do any cooking." He thought she meant to speak again, but, as she said no more, he turned to his own door. Behind him a hesitating voice began:

"You may use my range to cook on—until your own is repaired, if you wish—"

"That's awfully nice of you," he said, gratefully surprised. "I've only a couple of eggs to fry—or boil—and a little coffee, but I didn't like to ask you—"

"You didn't. *I* asked *you*," she said. "You are quite welcome." And, as he still hesitated: "I really don't mind," she said. "I can take my work somewhere else while you are cooking."

"No, no," he protested, beginning to realize the inconvenience he was causing her; but she nodded impatiently and, stepping back into her room, began to gather up into a writing portfolio a mass of scattered papers.

A few moments later he appeared in the open doorway, his arms piled high with the paper packages containing groceries. She looked up at him, her hands full of inky papers. Unbidden laughter was sparkling in her blue eyes.

"The range is ready," she said, schooling her voice. "You may begin at once. I shall be gone in a second." And she began to rummage furiously among the papers.

Sidelong glances she could not help casting at his culinary preparations. She saw him ruin two eggs, and hid her face in the table drawer where she was searching for that elusive something.

"No use trying to fry those eggs," he observed, gazing at the disintegrating yolks.

"You could scramble them," she suggested, raising her pretty head. Her face was delicately flushed; a bright strand of hair, loosened, fell like a tendril across one pink cheek.

"To scramble an egg," he said slowly, as though attempting to recall some intricate evolution in cookery—"To *scramble* an egg, you stir it round and round, I believe."

"And to scramble two eggs," she said almost hysterically, "you stir them both round and round."

"But," he added thoughtfully, "*how* to get them into the pan. I suppose one pours them in—"

"Don't! Please don't! You have put no butter in yet," she said; but he had already poured a spoonful into the pan, where it began to char and sputter and smoke.

She laid aside her portfolio and papers, removed the smoking pan, scraped it, tinkered with it, and then, preparing it properly, poured in the remainder of the eggs.

"It's awfully good of you. I'm ashamed of myself," he muttered; "but, please—*please* don't mind about the coffee. I can do that, I'm sure."

"It will take only a moment," she said. "You are not accustomed to—to—gas ranges, I see." Before he knew it his modest luncheon was ready. She swept the papers from the table, threw over it a white square of linen, and placed his luncheon under his mortified eyes.

"It will get cold if you attempt to carry it back to your room. You are quite welcome to eat it here, believe me. My range may fail me some day and I may have to beg a little fire at your door."

"You shall have oceans of it!" he cried gratefully.

"Thank you; and, please, begin. I am on my way out."

"Am I driving you away? I know I am—"

"No, really you are not. I work out of doors all I can. I was going out as soon as the janitor came to examine my ceiling." She raised her pretty eyes; he looked aloft.

"It's a leak," he said. "I'll have it fi—I mean I'll tell the jan— What I do mean," he said, "is that somebody ought to have it fixed."

"I think so, too," she said demurely, gathering up her portfolio and papers. At the doorsill she halted:

"But—but how—but who is going to lock my door?" she asked.

"Oh, I'd better take my luncheon into my own room!"

"No, no. Please sit down again. Please do so now! I can leave my key with you if you are going to be here."

He thought to himself, charmed, what touching confidence the poor have in each other's honesty.

She drew from her purse the door key and laid it beside his plate.

"If I don't hear you in the hallway, will you please knock?" he asked.

"I think you had better leave the key with the janitor," she said; then, thinking further along the same line: "or perhaps you had better hide it."

She stepped back into the hallway and looked all around; but no plausible hiding place presented itself. Then she gazed at him.

"I might leave it with my neighbor, Mrs. Clancy," he said with rare intelligence.

"No," she said with her pretty, fearless smile, "I will knock at your door and ask for it."

She was gone before he could rise again.

When he had finished he washed the dishes and did it thoroughly, restoring each to its shelf. His remaining groceries and his own tinware he carried into his own habitation, came back and locked her door, and then, lighting his pipe, began to prowl about the corridors.

Presently he fished out a pad and pencil, and, squatting down on the stairway, made some notes concerning the use of steel for doorsills and frames, and tiles or tassellated floors to replace the already worn and dirty planks of Southern pine.

"First of all, plenty of ventilation," he murmured. "Next, cleanliness; next, light.... I—I've a mind to complete the entire block—put up a big, square tower on that vacant lot—a big, clean, airy tower, ten stories—sixteen—twenty, by jingo!"

He seized his pad with enthusiasm and drew a plan of the block which he owned with the present model tenements on it and showing the vacant lot:

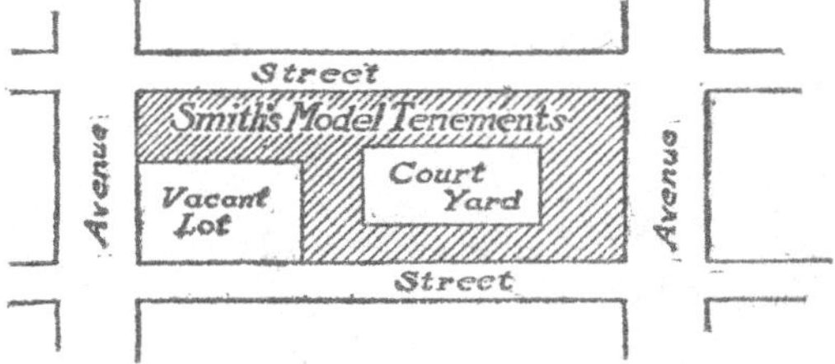

There were no windows giving on the vacant lot—nothing but blank brick walls.

"That's what I'll do," he thought. "I'll have my own way for once. I'll plan and design and build an absolutely beautiful and sanitary tower with a hundred rooms and two elevators in it, and Kerns can laugh if he wants to. What these people need is light and air—cheap light and cheap air. I'll just go down and take a look at that lot."

He pocketed pad and pencil, seized his hat, and, locking his door on the outside, ran down the stairs.

"You can't go into that lot," said the janitor. "No tenants ain't allowed in there by orders of Mr. Kerns."

"Well, can't I just look at it?"

"No," said the janitor. "An' lemme tell you something else. If you an' me is goin' to gee you'd better do less buttin' in an' less runnin' up an' downstairs. You butt in an' you run around like you was the Dutch Emp'ror. Say, what are you lookin' for, anyhow? If you're a spotter, say so; I ain't worryin'. If you're just loony you're in the wrong hotel."

"But, my good fellow—"

"Forget it!" retorted the janitor wrathfully. "*Your* good fellow! Look here, Percy, I ain't your good fellow, nor I ain't your dear old college chum, an' no buttin' in goes. See?"

"I'm not attempting to offend you!" exclaimed Smith desperately.

"That's all right, too," said the janitor unconvinced. "You seen me talkin' to Miss Stevens an' you make a play like you owned the buildin'. 'Here, me good man,' sez you, 'fix this an' fix that, an' be d—d quick about it, too,' sez you—"

"I didn't," retorted Smith indignantly; "at least I didn't mean to say—"

"What *you* are," interrupted the janitor deliberately, "God knows an' I don't. You may be makin' phony stuff up there fur all I know."

"What's phony stuff?" demanded Smith, getting hotter.

"Look into the dictionary, Clarence," retorted the janitor, and slammed the door of his office in Smith's face.

"That man," thought Smith to himself, as he started up the stairs, "is a singularly impudent man, but he's probably faithful enough. I shall not do anything about it. But I wish I could get into my vacant lot."

The remainder of the afternoon he spent drawing magnificently un-buildable plans for his tower.

Then he pulled his chair out into the fire escape and sat there through the sunset hour and into the smoky June twilight.

Suddenly, as he sat there, dreaming, a faint sound at his door brought him to his feet and into the room.

"I *beg* your pardon," he said. "I was out on the fire escape. *Did* you knock more than once?"

"It doesn't matter," she said, smiling under the shadow of her big straw hat and taking her key from him.

"I'm terribly sorry," he repeated, "and I really am very grateful for letting me cook on your range—"

"Is yours fixed yet?" she asked diffidently.

"By George!" he said. "I'd forgotten that! But it doesn't matter," he added, determined to dine on the remainder of his rolls and milk, for he simply would not begin by running to a restaurant at the first mishap.

She hesitated, not knowing whether again to offer her salt and fire; then, finding it too difficult, she said "Good night" in a low voice, and crossed the hallway to her own abode. And there she sat down, fair face tense, gaze concentrated on space, her big straw hat still on her head, her portfolio and papers in her lap.

Minutes ticked away on the little nickel alarm clock. She pondered on, and, sometimes, her straight, delicate brows contracted, and, sometimes, her teeth worried the edge of her lower lip; and once she smiled and lifted her eyes as though she could see through her closed door into his room across the hall.

After that she rose, made her toilet, cooked her own supper; and when, at length, the dishes had been laid away and her pretty hands rinsed, carefully examined, and soothed with glycerine and cream of almonds—luxuries she preferred to a varied menu—she laid a pile of yellow manuscript paper on her table, and, dipping her pen into the ink, began to scribble like mad. For, at last, her chance in life had come.

Meanwhile, Smith, doggedly munching his buttered rolls, drank his milk and considered plans for doing good to his tenants without either injuring their self-respect or bankrupting himself.

"Buy up block after block, cover 'em with handsome sanitary tenements, with a big, grassy court and a fountain in the middle—that's the decent and self-respecting way to invest one's surplus! That's the only way a rich man can keep his own respect and administer his stewardship. I'd be ashamed to make any more money! I won't! I'd be ashamed to keep what I have if I didn't use the income to help somebody. Clean, airy, sunny homes—within the means of the poorest working people! It can be done without making it a charity. It's got to be done. I'm going to build that tower—if my janitor ever lets me into the lot—"

After he had completed his ablutions and was ready for bed he stood a moment at the open window looking out over the city.

"That girl—she was *very* nice to me.... I've the oddest notion that I've seen her before ... somewhere. Wonderfully—ah—decorative—her eyes— a graceful way of—er—moving."

He lay down on his bed and pulled up the sheet.

A few minutes later he murmured drowsily: "Build handsome tower— spite of Kerns.... Nobody pay rent.... 'Strordinary eyes that girl ... pretty blue—very blue for—a—a girl.... 'Strordinary rot I'm talking.... G'night, Smith; ... night!"

The next morning a pessimistic gasfitter repaired Smith's range. That night it blew up again. Two days later it was again in commission, then remained quiescent for a week. After that the range worked fitfully, intimidating Smith until it had him so thoroughly cowed that he never attempted to light it except with the match inserted in the end of a broom handle. Between the range and the cookery he was almost famished.

However, it was a matter of too little importance to disturb him in his purpose; the days were full days indeed, no matter how empty he went. Hour after hour he sat cramped over the table, drawing impossible plans and elevations for the completion of his model tenements. Hour after hour he tramped the hot streets in search of likely sites for further philanthropic operations.

Almost every morning and evening he was sure to encounter his blue-eyed neighbor on the landing or stairs; and, after a while, he began to spend a few minutes of the day in looking forward to these brief meetings.

Matters were not going very well with his blue-eyed neighbor; but he didn't know it. Her work, always precarious and dependent on the whims of several underpaid people, was not sufficient to keep her very well nourished during the hot months of midsummer. She defaulted on the July payment for her small piano, and they took it away. The little desk went later; an armchair followed.

Alone in her room, palely considering the why and wherefore of the disagreeable, she invariably almost fell a prey to temptation; but, so far, the victory had remained with her. Temptation came when somebody refused her work or when somebody removed an article of furniture for nonpayment of the installment due, and the temptation confronted her in the shape of a packet of yellow manuscript.

She was the author of the manuscript; it lay in a drawer of her table.

Sometimes, when they frightened her by giving her no work or by lugging off a chair, she would sit down, white and desperate, and take out her manuscript and read it through.

She knew where she could place it in an hour. She had been promised a permanent position on the strength of just such work. It was well done, of its sort. It fairly bristled with double-leaded headlines; it was yellow enough for the yellowest—a "beat," a "scoop," a story that would be copied in every newspaper of the country. The title of it was "A Millionaire in Disguise." The subject, Smith. She had only to show it to the city editor who had promised to take her on the first time she displayed any ability. All she had to do was to tuck the yellow sheets under her arm and start downtown, and that would end all this removing of furniture and scarcity of foodstuffs—all this sleeplessness, this perplexed dismay—all these heavy-hearted journeys to the offices of the fashion papers where sometimes she was paid for her articles on domestic affairs and sometimes not.

After these experiences she usually returned to the temptation of her yellow manuscript, read it through, wept a little, cast it from her into the table drawer once more, and buried her face in her slim hands. Later, she usually dried her eyes, hurriedly gathered up her papers and portfolio, and, locking the door on the outside, descended to the cellar.

In this profound crypt a small iron door and a few stone steps ascending permitted her access to the vacant lot which the janitor had forbidden

Smith to enter. And here she was accustomed to sit in the long, rank grass under a big ailantus tree, writing for the fashion papers, to which she contributed such predigested pabulum as the weak-minded might assimilate. In this manner she paid for lodging, board, and almond cream.

Meanwhile, she was growing shyer and more formal with Smith when they chanced to meet on stairs or landing. Beginning with the politely pleasant exchange of a few words concerning the initial episode which had excused their acquaintance, they had ventured on a little laughter at his expense—a shade less of the impersonal. But, little by little, the pretty, fearless gaze which he found so attractive changed to something more reserved and far less expressive. Her laughter, always edging lips and eyes, her untroubled voice, with its winningly careless sweetness, changed, too. He noticed this. Sometimes he wondered whether she was quite well. He had been aware from the first that she did not belong in her surroundings any more than did he, and at times he speculated on the subject, wondering what crumbling of her social and financial fabric had landed her here on her own resources, stranded along the outer edges of things.

One scorching day he had been drawing an elevation for his tower, which partook impartially of the worst in both Manhattan, Gothic, and Chinese architecture—a new crinkle in his theory being that the poor had a right to the best in art, and that they should have it in spite of Kerns. For an hour he had been trying to estimate the cost of such a masterpiece, and had grown cross and discouraged in the effort.

July was fast going. August already had been discounted by the monthly magazines; he had purchased one which contained an article on concrete construction, and, tired of his sweltering room, he put on his hat, pocketed the magazine, and went out to seek a bit of shade in Central Park.

As he passed his neighbor's door he glanced at it a trifle wistfully. He had not seen her now for nearly a week. He actually missed her, even though now she seldom seemed to have the leisure or inclination to chat with him.

The last time, he reflected, that they had exchanged a dozen words, he had, lured by her receptively intelligent attitude, drifted into an almost enthusiastic dissertation upon model lodgings for the poor. He had kept her standing before her door for almost half an hour while he, forgetting everything except the subject and the acquiescence of his audience, had aired his theories with a warmth and brilliancy which, later, it slightly astonished him to remember.

Since that they had exchanged scarcely a word. And now, as he passed her door, he looked wistfully at it, thinking of his slender neighbor.

And, thinking of her, he descended the stairs, and, still immersed in this agreeable reverie, he did not notice that he had passed the ground floor and was descending the cellar stairs, until he came to in front of an iron door. This seemed unfamiliar. He took out his handkerchief to rub his glasses, looked around at the furnaces and coal bins, passed his hand over his eyes, replaced the glasses, gazed at the iron door which was partly ajar, and caught a glimpse of green grass outside.

"I'll bet that's my vacant lot," he said aloud, and, opening the door, he ascended the stone steps into his own property.

There was green grass everywhere; south and west a high board fence; north and east the brick, windowless, rearward cliffs of the tenements; in the middle of the lot an ailantus tree in full foliage.

And, under it, a young girl lying in the grass, her wide straw hat hanging from a leafy branch above. Even before he stirred in his tracks she sat up, instinctively looking across the grass at him. It was his duty to make his excuses and go. But, for almost the first time in his life, he deliberately neglected duty.

"So this is where you come every day to work out of doors!" he exclaimed, smiling, as he halted beside her where she remained, seated in the grass, looking up at him.

There was color in her face and in his, too. He had had absolutely no idea how pleasant it could be to meet his neighbor again after so many days— seven in number—but a great many all the same.

Then he told her, laughingly, how he came to discover the cellar door that led to Paradise. "Paradise," he repeated; "for, you see, the Tree of Ten Thousand Dreams is here. Did you know that the ailantus tree is the Chinese Tree of Paradise—the fabled Tree of Dreams? Have you never heard of the Feng-Shui? Dragons live deep in the earth among the tree roots. You didn't know that, did you?"

"No," she said, smiling, "I didn't know that."

He looked at her. Her manner was not very cordial, and he decided not to ask permission to seat himself just yet. But he had nothing in particular to say to her and he was very anxious to say it.

"The Fung-Hwang also perches in the branches of the Dream Tree," he continued, for lack of a better topic; "it's an imperial as well as a celestial tree. Are you interested in Chinese mythology? If you are not, it's all right, because I am interested in anything you like."

She looked up at the foliage above her. "It is a curious tree," she said. "In early June these branches were full of great olive and rose-colored moths, enormous ones, flopping about at sunset like big, soft bats. In the daytime they hang to the leaves and bark, wings wide—such beautiful, such miraculous wings—set with silvery quarter-moons!"

She raised both hands to the nape of her neck to smooth and secure her hair—a most fascinating gesture, he thought, watching her seated there in the grass, slim and graceful as the lovely lotus-bearing goddess, Kwan-Yin.

"Silvery quarter-moons," she repeated, "and now, look! The silver has changed into metal pendants!" She pointed upward where, among the foliage, shining, white cocoons swung from silk-wound stems, each wrapped in its single green leaf.

"Wonderful fairy fruit your Tree of Dreams bears!" he said. "And how thickly it hangs! I don't know much about such things. I was inclined to be fond of all that until I read some modern nature books. So I fell back on real myths again."

She began to laugh and, meeting in her eyes all the old-time friendliness, he ventured to ask if he might seat himself.

"Yes," she said gravely, "but I must be going."

"Then I don't care to stay here," he said, unprepared to hear himself utter any such sentiment. His astonishment at himself overcame even the reaction which turned his face red. She, too, surprised, looked at him unconvinced.

"What have I to do with it?" she inquired.

"The fact is," he said impressively, as though the intelligence were well worth sharing with her, "I have been rather lonely."

"Have you?" she asked, wide-eyed. "So have I. But I usually am."

"I wish you had said so!"

"How could I? And to whom?"

They said nothing more for a while. The sunlight, filtering through the Tree of Dreams, glimmered on her hair. Her eyes, darker in the shadow, dwelt tranquilly upon the waste of thick, tall grass which the languid breezes furrowed now and then.

"Do you mind my offering you my friendship?" he asked at length; "for that's what I'm doing."

"No, I don't mind," she replied listlessly. "Other men have done that."

"Will you accept—this time?"

"Shall I?" she asked, raising her clear eyes. "Shall I? I have been here two years—and I have made no friends."

She folded her unringed hands on her knees, examined them with calm inattention, and said: "After a while, I suppose, a girl becomes partly stupefied under the strain of it all—the tension of self-respecting silence. Two years of self-suppression! Even pickpockets receive a sentence more humane. Shall I try your remedy?"

"It would be very jolly to see each other, now and then," he said, so pleasantly that she smiled at his simplicity.

"What about the conventions?" she inquired, amused. "Still, after all, what has a girl to do with conventions who lives as I live? Her problem is a great deal simpler than to bother with usages." There was a defiant smile hovering about eyes and lips—a hint of recklessness in the bright color rising under his gaze: "A girl can't live and flourish on silence."

"You always hurry past me when we meet—"

"But surely you didn't expect me to invite you to a seat on the stairs, did you?"

"I wish you had."

"Then why didn't *you* invite *me?*" she asked with a gay audacity new to him. For, in the summer sunshine of the moment, she was forgetting all except the pleasure of the moment and its pretense that the old order of things had returned. Sunshine and green grass and the sophisticated city breeze in the leaves above—youth, and ardent health, and one of her own kind to speak to after the arid silence of these sad months—what wonder that she willfully forgot? What wonder that she dared to breathe and laugh again, drifting and relaxing in the moment's merciful relief from a tension that had benumbed her to the verge of actual stupidity?

Afterwards, in her room, the relaxed strain tightened again. She realized their acquaintance was only an episode—she knew his advent here was but a caprice. But it was an interim that gave her a chance—a brief vacation in which she might breathe for a moment before the inevitable returned again to submerge her. And she meant to enjoy it with all her heart—every moment, every atom of sunshine, every bright second of respite from what she actually dared look forward to no longer.

That first meeting under the ailantus tree was only one of a sequence.

At first, when he came sauntering across the grass, she politely laid aside her work—dissertation on flounces and napkins and old mahogany and the care of infants, and what Heppelwhite knew about table legs, and why Sheraton is usually saluted as Chippendale.

Later, she continued her work unembarrassed as long as she was able to concentrate her mind under the agreeable little shock of pleasure which his advent always brought to her.

"How did you find out all about such things?" he asked curiously, looking over her manuscripts with her shrugged permission.

"All about what things?"

"These—ah—crooked-legged tables and squatty chairs?"

"I had them—once."

"I see," he said gravely. Then, with embarrassed hesitation, but very nicely: "There must have been a pretty bad smash-up?"

She nodded.

"Ah—I'm awfully sorry! Hope it's going to come out all right—some day."

"Thank you." But she continued to be brief and uncommunicative, never volunteering anything.

In the days when she became accustomed to his coming to find her under the tree, she ventured to continue her writing, merely greeting him with a nod of confidence and pleasure. And so he fell into the habit of bringing his own impossible plans and elevations to the vacant lot. And often, biting her pencil reflectively, she would cast side glances at him where he lay, flat in the grassy shade, drawing board under his nose, patiently constructing lines and angles and Corinthian capitals and Romanesque back doors. He was a very, very poor draughtsman; even she could see that.

"I'm doing this for a man who means to build a big tower on this lot," he explained cheerfully. "I've a notion he will be delighted with this plan of mine."

"Oh, is he going to cut down your Tree of Dreams!" she exclaimed, raising her eyes in dismay.

He looked up at the tree, then at her. "By Jove! It is a pity, isn't it?" he said, "after the jolly hours we have spent out here."

"Perhaps he won't build his tower until after—after—"

"After what?"

"After we—you and I have forgotten all about this tree—" She hesitated. Then calmly—"and each other. Which, of course," she laughed, "means no tower at all."

He sat so long silent, preoccupied with his drawing, looking at it half dreamily, that she thought he had forgotten her rather foolish observations.

But he hadn't; for he said in a troubled voice: "There's a way—a way of taking up big trees. I'll ask him to do it. I don't want it chopped down."

"You're afraid of angering the dragon!" she said, laughing. "What use could such a man have for an old ailantus tree? Besides, where could he plant it?"

"There's a place I know of," he said. "I'll speak to him…. No; it wouldn't do to have our Tree of Dreams cut down—"

"It's not *my* tree," she said, looking down at her pencil; "it's yours."

"It is yours," he insisted. "You found it, and I found you under it."

"Oh, it's mine because I found it?" she mocked gayly, "and, I suppose, I'm yours because you found me under it."

Her tongue had run away that time. She checked her badinage, picked up her pencil with an admirable self-possession that admitted nothing, and scribbled away in calm insouciance. Only the heightened brilliancy of her cheeks could have undeceived the adept. Smith was no adept; besides, he was thinking of other matters.

"Do you know," he said solemnly, "that I am going away for about a week?"

She congratulated him without raising her head from her writing pad. That was pure instinct, for the emotion she had detected in Smith's voice was perfectly apparent in his features.

Smith gazed at her for a long time, during which she grew busier and busier with her pencil, and more oblivious of him.

The intellectual processes of Smith were, at times, childlike in their circuitous simplicity. "Do you think I'm a good draughtsman?" he asked.

"I don't know; are you?" she asked, numbering a fresh sheet of her pad.

"Why, you've seen my drawing!" he reminded her, a little hurt. "I think I am a good draughtsman. I could probably earn about a hundred and twenty dollars a month."

"You are very fortunate," she murmured, rubbing out a sentence.

"A hundred and twenty dollars a month is enough for anybody to marry on," he continued. "Don't—you think so?"

"It is probably sufficient," she said carelessly.

"Do *you* think it is?"

"I haven't considered such matters very seriously," she said. "It will be time when I am earning a hundred and twenty dollars a month. And I'm not likely to earn it if you continue to interrupt me."

Smith turned red; presently he tucked his drawing board under his arm and stood up.

"I'm going," he said. "Good-by."

She nodded her adieux pleasantly, scarcely raising her head from her work.

But when Smith had disappeared she straightened up with a quick, indrawn breath and stared across the grass at the blank, brick walls. After a long while she dropped her tired shoulders back against the trunk of the Tree of Dreams, reclining there inert, blue eyes brooding in vacancy.

Meanwhile, Smith had locked up his room, gone home for the first time in two months, telephoned for a stateroom on the Western Limited, and sent for Kerns, who presently arrived in an electric cab.

"I'm going to Illinois," said Smith, "to-night."

"The nation must know of this," insisted Kerns; "let me telegraph for fireworks."

"There'll be fireworks," observed Smith—"fireworks to burn, presently. I'm going to get married to a working girl."

"Oh, piffle!" said Kerns faintly; "let's go and sit on the third rail and talk it over."

"Not with *you*, idiot. Did you ever hear of Stanley Stevens, who tried to corner wheat? I think it's his daughter I'm going to marry. I'm going to Chicago to find out. Good heavens, Kerns! It's the most pitiful case, whoever she is! It's a case to stir the manhood in any man. I tell you it's got to be righted. I am thoroughly stirred up, and I won't stand any nonsense from you."

Kerns looked at him. "Smith," he pleaded in sepulchral tones; "Smithy! For the sake of decency and of common sense—"

"Exactly," nodded Smith, picking up his hat and gloves; "for the sake of decency and of common sense. Good-by, Tommy. And—ah!"— indicating a parcel of papers on the desk—"just have an architect look over these sketches with a view to estimating the—ah—cost of construction. And find some good landscape gardener to figure up what it will cost to remove a big ailantus tree from New York to the Berkshires. You can tell him I'll sue him if he injures the tree, but that I don't care what it costs to move it."

"Smith!" faltered Kerns, appalled, "as mad as Hamlet!"

"It's one of my ambitions to be madder," retorted Smith, going out and running nimbly downstairs.

"Help!" observed Kerns feebly as the front door slammed. And, as nobody responded, he sat down in the bachelor quarters of J. Abingdon Smith, a prey to melancholy amazement.

When Smith had been gone a week Kerns wrote him, when he had been gone two weeks he telegraphed him, when the third week ended he telephoned him, and when the month was up he prepared to leave for darkest Chicago; in fact he was actually leaving his house, suit case in hand, when Smith drove up in a hansom and gleefully waved his hand.

Smith beckoned him to enter the cab. "I'm going home to put on my old clothes," he said. "It's all right, Tom. I've been collecting old furniture, tons of antique chairs and things. They were pretty widely scattered at the sale two years ago—"

"What sale, in the name of sanity?" shouted Kerns.

"Why, when Stanley Stevens failed to corner wheat he shot his head off before they pounced on his effects. I managed to find most of the things. I've sent them to my place, Abingdon, and now I'm going to ask her to marry me."

"Oh, are you?"

"Certainly. And, Kerns, if she will have me it will be for my own sake. Do you know what she thinks? She thinks I'm a draughtsman at thirty dollars a week. Isn't it delightful? Isn't it perfectly splendid?"

"Dazzling," whispered Kerns, unable to utter another word.

Smith's progress was certainly rapid. When he arrived at the door of his tenement lodgings he fairly soared up the stairs, flight on flight, until he came to the top.

The door of his neighbor's room stood open and he impulsively crossed the hallway, but there were only two men there moving out a table, and his slender blue-eyed neighbor was nowhere visible.

"What's that for?" he inquired. "Is Miss Stevens moving?"

"No, but her table is," said one of the men.

Something about the proceeding kept Smith silent. He saw one of the men drop his end of the table, close the door, lock it, and hang the key on a nail outside.

"That isn't safe," said Smith. "I'll take charge of the key until Miss Stevens returns."

He unhooked it, and, turning, let himself into his own room, but left the door ajar.

Two flights down the table drawer dropped out, dumping a pile of yellow manuscript on the stairs.

"Glory!" panted one of the movers; "that's hers. Take it up and leave it with the guy in the glasses, Bill."

And so it happened that Smith, standing outside on his fire escape for a breath of air, returned to find a mass of yellow manuscript littering his bed.

Wondering, he picked up the first sheet, saw his own name in her handwriting, stared, and sat down in astonishment to read. Suddenly his face burned fiery red, and, as long as he sat there, the deep color remained throbbing, scorching him anew with every page he turned.

After a long while he dropped the sheets and returned to the first page. It was dated in June, the day after his arrival.

He was slowly beginning to understand the matter now. He was beginning to realize that this manuscript had been placed in his room by mistake; that it had never been intended for him to read; that, if it had been written with a purpose, it had never been used for any purpose.

Then he remembered the moving of her table. Clearly the men had found it and, as he had assumed possession of her key, no doubt they had returned and flung the papers on his bed.

"In that case," said Smith thoughtfully, "I think I'll go down to the ailantus tree, and see if, by any chance, she is there."

She was there, seated in a chair, very intent on her writing pad. He was quite near her before she noticed him, and then she seemed dazed for a moment, rising and holding out her hand mechanically, looking at him in silence as he held her fingers imprisoned.

"I did not think you would return," she said. "It is a month—at least—"

"Are you glad to see me?"

"Of course," she said simply, reseating herself. "Have you been well?"

"Yes; and you?"

"Perfectly, thank you."

He looked around at the long grass withered in patches; at the leafless tree. "Do you remember our first encounter here?" he said.

"Perfectly. You told me that there was a dragon under the tree, and a Chinese bird sat in its branches. That was in August, I think. This is November. Look up at the branches. All the leaves are gone. Only the silvery cocoons are hanging in clusters everywhere." And, bending slowly above her work again, "When are you going to turn our Tree of Dreams into a tower of bricks?"

But he only sat silent, smiling, watching her white fingers flying over the pad on her knees.

"I wonder," she said carelessly, "how long you are going to stay here this time."

"I wonder, too," he said.

"Don't you know?" she asked, raising her eyes and laughing faintly.

"No, I don't. Besides, why should I leave this lodging house? I like it."

"Can't you afford to leave—after all that lucrative tower designing?"

He said, looking at her deliberately: "You know perfectly well that I can afford to."

Something in the quiet voice and gaze of the man startled her, but only a delicate glow of rising color in her cheeks betrayed any lack of self-possession. "I don't think I understand you," she said.

"I think you do," he insisted, seating himself at her feet in the grass.

She wrote a word or two on her pad, then looked down to meet his changed smile. A moment more, and she resumed her work in flushed confusion.

"You know who I am," he said calmly. "I didn't think you did until an hour ago. Shall I tell you what happened an hour ago?"

She managed to meet his gaze without expression, but she did not answer.

"Then I will tell you what happened," he continued.

"Some men carried out a table from your room. A few moments later one of the men deposited a lot of loose manuscript which he had, I suppose, found in the table drawer. This all occurred while I was out on the balcony. When I returned to the room I found the papers on my bed. I could not avoid seeing my own name at the head of this breezy newspaper article. It is very cleverly written."

Wave after wave of scarlet flooded her face.

"So you have known who I am all this time?" he nodded slowly.

"Y-yes."

"It was a good chance—a legitimate chance for an article. You thought so, and you wrote it. The papers would have given it three columns and double leads…. Why didn't you use it?"

The tears flashed in her eyes. "I did not use it for the same reason that I am here with you now! Some things can be done, and some cannot. Good-by."

"Good-by?" he repeated slowly.

He stepped back; she passed before him, halted, turned, and spoke again, steadying her voice which broke deliciously in spite of her: "I did not mean to ridicule you. When I wrote that article I had known you only a day or two—and I was desperate—frightened—half-starved. The chance came, and I took it—or tried to. But I couldn't. I never could have. So— that is all."

"I knew all that, too," he said. "I only thought I'd speak of it. I wanted to ask you something else —"

She had halted.

"Ask it," she said, exercising every atom of self-command.

"Won't you turn around?"

"No. I—I cannot. What is it you wish, Mr. Smith?"

"Ah—about this tree. It's to be taken up, I believe. They've a method of doing it, you know. I—ah—have considered arrangements."

She made no movement.

"Fact is," he ventured, "I've a sort of a country place in the Berkshires. Do you think that our tree would do well in the Berkshires?"

"I don't know, Mr. Smith."

"Oh, I thought, perhaps, you'd be likely to know!"

There was a pause of a full minute. "Is that all?" she asked, turning toward him with tear-flushed self-possession—but she had no idea that he was so close to her—no idea of what he was doing with her hands so suddenly imprisoned in his.

"Can you stand such a-a m-man as I am?" he stammered, the ancestral sentimental streak in the ascendency. "Would yo—ah—mind marrying me?"

Her face was pale enough now.

"Do you mean you love me?" she said, dazed. And the next moment she had released her hands, stepping toward the tree.

"Yes, I mean that," he repeated; "I love you."

"But—but I do not love you, Mr. Smith—"

"I—I know it. P-perhaps you could try. D-do you mind trying—a little—"

He had followed her to the ailantus. She retreated, facing him, and now stood backed up against the tree, her hands flat against the trunk behind her.

"Couldn't you try?" he asked. "I love you—I love you dearly. I know you're younger—I know you think me m-more or less of a—"

"I don't!"

"I suppose I really haven't many brains," he said; "but yours are still intact."

Her blue eyes filled and grew starry.

"Did you read that entire article?" she asked unsteadily—"*did* you?"

"Yes—in bits—before I knew you had not meant me to.... I guess I am the sort of a man you make fun of—"

Her eyes met his fairly for a moment, were lowered, then again raised. Something within them gave him courage, or perhaps the splendid rising color in her face, or perhaps the provocation of her mouth. And he kissed her. She did not stir; her lips were stiffly unresponsive.

But when, once more, he bent above her, she caught both his hands with a sob and met his lips with heart and soul, closing her wet eyes.

"D-darling," said J. Abingdon Smith, bending his head over hers where it lay buried in his shoulder, "I don't mind being an ass—really I don't—"

Her hands crushed his, signaling silence.

"It isn't the funny things you wrote about me," he persisted; "but I really am that sort of a man. And likely to continue. You don't care, do you, dear?"

"W-when I love you!" she sobbed; "how can you say such things! D-do you think I'd love an idiot?"

He was discreetly silent for a while, then: "Anyway, I've found all your furniture—the bandy-legged chairs and things," he whispered cheerfully. "They are waiting for you at—a—Abingdon—a place I have in the country. Are you pleased?"

She lifted her face and made an effort to speak.

"Never mind," he said, dizzy with happiness, "we'll talk it over to-morrow. I think," he added, "that I'll have the men here to-morrow to remove our tree. There's a splendid place for it on the lawn."

She turned, her hands clasped in his, and looked up at the Tree of Dreams. Then, very gently, she bent and laid her lips against the bark.

CHAPTER V

THE BRIDAL PAIR

"If I were you," said the elder man, "I should take three months' solid rest."

"A month is enough," said the younger man. "Ozone will do it; the first brace of grouse I bag will do it—" He broke off abruptly, staring at the line of dimly lighted cars, where negro porters stood by the vestibuled sleepers, directing passengers to staterooms and berths.

"Dog all right, doctor?" inquired the elder man pleasantly.

"All right, doctor," replied the younger; "I spoke to the baggage master."

There was a silence; the elder man chewed an unlighted cigar reflectively, watching his companion with keen narrowing eyes.

The younger physician stood full in the white electric light, lean head lowered, apparently preoccupied with a study of his own shadow swimming and quivering on the asphalt at his feet.

"So you fear I may break down?" he observed, without raising his head.

"I think you're tired out," said the other.

"That's a more agreeable way of expressing it," said the young fellow. "I hear"—he hesitated, with a faint trace of irritation—"I understand that Forbes Stanly thinks me mentally unsound."

"He probably suspects what you're up to," said the elder man soberly.

"Well, what will he do when I announce my germ theory? Put me in a strait-jacket?"

"He'll say you're mad, until you prove it; every physician will agree with him—until your radium test shows us the microbe of insanity."

"Doctor," said the young man abruptly, "I'm going to admit something—to *you*."

"All right; go ahead and admit it."

"Well, I *am* a bit worried about my own condition."

"It's time you were," observed the other.

"Yes—it's about time. Doctor, I am seriously affected."

The elder man looked up sharply.

"Yes, I'm—in love."

"Ah!" muttered the elder physician, amused and a trifle disgusted; "so that's your malady, is it?"

"A malady—yes; not explainable by our germ theory—not affected by radio-activity. Doctor, I'm speaking lightly enough, but there's no happiness in it."

"Never is," commented the other, striking a match and lighting his ragged cigar. After a puff or two the cigar went out. "All I have to say," he added, "is, don't do it just now. Show me a scale of pure radium and I'll give you leave to marry every spinster in New York. In the mean time go and shoot a few dozen harmless, happy grouse; they can't shoot back. But let love alone.... By the way, who is she?"

"I don't know."

"You know her name, I suppose?"

The young fellow shook his head. "I don't even know where she lives," he said finally.

After a pause the elder man took him gently by the arm: "Are you subject to this sort of thing? Are you susceptible?"

"No, not at all."

"Ever before in love?"

"Yes—once."

"When?"

"When I was about ten years old. Her name was Rosamund—aged eight. I never had the courage to speak to her. She died recently, I believe."

The reply was so quietly serious, so destitute of any suspicion of humor, that the elder man's smile faded; and again he cast one of his swift, keen glances at his companion.

"Won't you stay away three months?" he asked patiently.

But the other only shook his head, tracing with the point of his walking stick the outline of his own shadow on the asphalt.

A moment later he glanced at his watch, closed it with a snap, silently shook hands with his equally silent friend, and stepped aboard the sleeping car.

Neither had noticed the name of the sleeping car.

It happened to be the *Rosamund*.

Loungers and passengers on Wildwood station drew back from the platform's edge as the towering locomotive shot by them, stunning their ears with the clangor of its melancholy bell.

Slower, slower glided the dusty train, then stopped, jolting; eddying circles of humanity closed around the cars, through which descending passengers pushed.

"Wildwood! Wildwood!" cried the trainmen; trunks tumbling out of the forward car descended with a bang!—a yelping, wagging setter dog landed on the platform, hysterically grateful to be free; and at the same moment a young fellow in tweed shooting clothes, carrying gripsack and gun case, made his way forward toward the baggage master, who was being jerked all over the platform by the frantic dog.

"Much obliged; take the dog," he said, slipping a bit of silver into the official's hand, and receiving the dog's chain in return.

"Hope you'll have good sport," replied the baggage master. "There's a lot o' birds in this country, they tell me. You've got a good dog there."

The young man smiled and nodded, released the chain from his dog's collar, and started off up the dusty village street, followed by an urchin carrying his luggage.

The landlord of the Wildwood Inn stood on the veranda, prepared to receive guests. When a young man, a white setter dog, and a small boy loomed up, his speculative eyes became suffused with benevolence.

"How-de-do, sir?" he said cordially. "Guess you was with us three year since—stayed to supper. Ain't that so?"

"It certainly is," said his guest cheerfully. "I am surprised that you remember me."

"Be ye?" rejoined the landlord, gratified. "Say! I can tell the name of every man, woman, an' child that has ever set down to eat with us. You was here with a pair o' red bird dawgs; shot a mess o' birds before dark, come back pegged out, an' took the ten-thirty to Noo York. Hey? Yaas, an' you was cussin' round because you couldn't stay an' shoot for a month."

"I had to work hard in those days," laughed the young man. "You are right; it was three years ago this month."

"Time's a flyer; it's fitted with triple screws these days," said the landlord. "Come right in an' make yourself to home. Ed! O Ed! Take this bag to 13! We're all full, sir. You ain't scared at No. 13, be ye? Say! if I ain't a liar you had 13 three years ago! Waal, now!—ain't that the dumbdest— But you can have what you want Monday. How long was you calkerlatin' to stay?"

"A month—if the shooting is good."

"It's all right. Orrin Plummer come in last night with a mess o' pa'tridges. He says the woodcock is droppin' in to the birches south o' Sweetbrier Hill."

The young man nodded, and began to remove his gun from the service-worn case of sole leather.

"Ain't startin' right off, be ye?" inquired his host, laughing.

"I can't begin too quickly," said the young man, busy locking barrels to stock, while the dog looked on, thumping the veranda floor with his plumy tail.

The landlord admired the slim, polished weapon. "That's the instroo-ment!" he observed. "That there's a slick bird dawg, too. Guess I'd better fill my ice box. Your limit's thirty of each—cock an' pa'tridge. After that there's ducks."

"It's a good, sane law," said the young man, dropping his gun under one arm.

The landlord scratched his ear reflectively. "Lemme see," he mused; "wasn't you a doctor? I heard tell that you made up pieces for the papers about the idjits an' loonyticks of Rome an' Roosia an' furrin climes."

"I have written a little on European and Asiatic insanity," replied the doctor good-humoredly.

"Was you over to them parts?"

"For three years." He whistled the dog in from the road, where several yellow curs were walking round and round him, every hair on end.

The landlord said: "You look a little peaked yourself. Take it easy the fust, is my advice."

His guest nodded abstractedly, lingering on the veranda, preoccupied with the beauty of the village street, which stretched away westward under tall elms. Autumn-tinted hills closed the vista; beyond them spread the blue sky.

"The cemetery lies that way, does it not?" inquired the young man.

"Straight ahead," said the landlord. "Take the road to the Holler."

"Do you"—the doctor hesitated—"do you recall a funeral there three years ago?"

"Whose?" asked his host bluntly.

"I don't know."

"I'll ask my woman; she saves them funeral pieces an' makes a album.... Friend o' yours buried there?"

"No."

The landlord sauntered toward the barroom, where two fellow taxpayers stood shuffling their feet impatiently.

"Waal, good luck, Doc," he said, without intentional offense; "supper's at six. We'll try an' make you comfortable."

"Thank you," replied the doctor, stepping out into the road, and motioning the white setter to heel.

"I remember now," he muttered, as he turned northward, where the road forked; "the cemetery lies to the westward; there should be a lane at the next turning—"

He hesitated and stopped, then resumed his course, mumbling to himself: "I can pass the cemetery later; she would not be there; I don't think I shall ever see her again.... I—I wonder whether I am—perfectly—well—"

The words were suddenly lost in a sharp indrawn breath; his heart ceased beating, fluttered, then throbbed on violently; and he shook from head to foot.

There was a glimmer of a summer gown under the trees; a figure passed from shadow to sunshine, and again into the cool dusk of a leafy lane.

The pallor of the young fellow's face changed; a heavy flush spread from forehead to neck; he strode forward, dazed, deafened by the tumult of his drumming pulses. The dog, alert, suspicious, led the way, wheeling into the bramble-bordered lane, only to halt, turn back, and fall in behind his master again.

In the lane ahead the light summer gown fluttered under the foliage, bright in the sunlight, almost lost in the shadows. Then he saw her on the hill's breezy crest, poised for a moment against the sky.

When at length he reached the hill, he found her seated in the shade of a pine. She looked up serenely, as though she had expected him, and they faced each other. A moment later his dog left him, sneaking away without a sound.

When he strove to speak, his voice had an unknown tone to him. Her upturned face was his only answer. The breeze in the pine tops, which had been stirring lazily and monotonously, ceased.

Her delicate face was like a blossom lifted in the still air; her upward glance chained him to silence. The first breeze broke the spell: he spoke a word, then speech died on his lips; he stood twisting his shooting cap, confused, not daring to continue.

The girl leaned back, supporting her weight on one arm, fingers almost buried in the deep green moss.

"It is three years to-day," he said, in the dull voice of one who dreams; "three years to-day. May I not speak?"

In her lowered head and eyes he read acquiescence; in her silence, consent.

"Three years ago to-day," he repeated; "the anniversary has given me courage to speak to you. Surely you will not take offense; we have traveled so far together!—from the end of the world to the end of it, and back again, here—to this place of all places in the world! And now to find you here on this day of all days—here within a step of our first meeting place—three years ago to-day! And all the world we have traveled over since, never speaking, yet ever passing on paths parallel—paths which for thousands of miles ran almost within arm's distance—"

She raised her head slowly, looking out from the shadows of the pines into the sunshine. Her dreamy eyes rested on acres of golden-rod and hillside brambles quivering in the September heat; on fern-choked gullies edged with alder; on brown and purple grasses; on pine thickets where slim silver birches glimmered.

"Will you speak to me?" he asked. "I have never even heard the sound of your voice."

She turned and looked at him, touching with idle fingers the soft hair curling on her temples. Then she bent her head once more, the faintest shadow of a smile in her eyes.

"Because," he said humbly, "these long years of silent recognition count for something! And then the strangeness of it!—the fate of it—the quiet destiny that ruled our lives—that rules them now—now as I am speaking, weighting every second with its tiny burden of fate."

She straightened up, lifting her half-buried hand from the moss; and he saw the imprint there where the palm and fingers had rested.

"Three years that end to-day—end with the new moon," he said. "Do you remember?"

"Yes," she said.

He quivered at the sound of her voice. "You were there, just beyond those oaks," he said eagerly; "we can see them from here. The road turns there—"

"Turns by the cemetery," she murmured.

"Yes, yes, by the cemetery! You had been there, I think."

"Do you remember that?" she asked.

"I have never forgotten—never!" he repeated, striving to hold her eyes to his own; "it was not twilight; there was a glimmer of day in the west, but the woods were darkening, and the new moon lay in the sky, and the evening was very clear and still."

Impulsively he dropped on one knee beside her to see her face; and as he spoke, curbing his emotion and impatience with the subtle deference which is inbred in men or never acquired, she stole a glance at him; and his worn visage brightened as though touched with sunlight.

"The second time I saw you was in New York," he said—"only a glimpse of your face in the crowd—but I knew you."

"I saw you," she mused.

"Did you?" he cried, enchanted. "I dared not believe that you recognized me."

"Yes, I knew you.... Tell me more."

The thrilling voice set him aflame; faint danger signals tinted her face and neck.

"In December," he went on unsteadily, "I saw you in Paris—I saw only you amid the thousand faces in the candlelight of Notre Dame."

"And I saw you.... And then?"

"And then two months of darkness.... And at last a light—moonlight— and you on the terrace at Amara."

"There was only a flower bed—a few spikes of white hyacinths between us," she said dreamily.

He strove to speak coolly. "Day and night have built many a wall between us; was that you who passed me in the starlight, so close that our shoulders touched, in that narrow street in Samarcand? And the dark figure with you—"

"Yes, it was I and my attendant."

"And ... you, there in the fog—"

"At Archangel? Yes, it was I."

"On the Goryn?"

"It was I.... And I am here at last—with you. It is our destiny."

So, kneeling there beside her in the shadow of the pines, she absolved him in their dim confessional, holding him guiltless under the destiny that awaits us all.

Again that illumination touched his haggard face as though brightened by a sun ray stealing through the still foliage above. He grew younger under the level beauty of her gaze; care fell from him like a mask; the shadows that had haunted his eyes faded; youth awoke, transfiguring him and all his eyes beheld.

Made prisoner by love, adoring her, fearing her, he knelt beside her, knowing already that she had surrendered, though fearful yet by word or gesture or a glance to claim what destiny was holding for him—holding securely, inexorably, for him alone.

He spoke of her kindness in understanding him, and of his gratitude; of her generosity, of his wonder that she had ever noticed him on his way through the world.

"I cannot believe that we have never before spoken to each other," he said; "that I do not even know your name. Surely there was once a corner in the land of childhood where we sat together when the world was younger."

She said, dreamily: "Have you forgotten?"

"Forgotten?"

"That sunny corner in the land of childhood."

"Had you been there, I should not have forgotten," he replied, troubled.

"Look at me," she said. Her lovely eyes met his; under the penetrating sweetness of her gaze his heart quickened and grew restless and his uneasy soul stirred, awaking memories.

"There was a child," she said, "years ago; a child at school. You sometimes looked at her; you never spoke. Do you remember?"

He rose to his feet, staring down at her.

"Do you remember?" she asked again.

"Rosamund! Do you mean Rosamund? How should you know that?" he faltered.

The struggle for memory focused all his groping senses; his eyes seemed to look her through and through.

"How can you know?" he repeated unsteadily.

"You are not Rosamund.... Are you? ... She is dead. I heard that she was dead.... *Are you Rosamund?*"

"Do you not know?"

"Yes; you are not Rosamund.... What do you know of her?"

"I think she loved you."

"Is she dead?"

The girl looked up at him, smiling, following with delicate perception the sequence of his thoughts; and already his thoughts were far from the child Rosamund, a sweetheart of a day long since immortal; already he had forgotten his question, though the question was of life or death.

Sadness and unrest and the passing of souls concerned not him; she knew that all his thoughts were centered on her; that he was already living over once more the last three years, with all their mystery and charm, savoring their fragrance anew in the exquisite enchantment of her presence.

Through the autumn silence the pines began to sway in a wind unfelt below. She raised her eyes and saw their green crests shimmering and swimming in a cool current; a thrilling sound stole out, and with it floated the pine perfume, exhaling in the sunshine. He heard the dreamy harmony above, looked up; then, troubled, somber, moved by he knew not what, he knelt once more in the shadow beside her—close beside her.

She did not stir. Their destiny was close upon them. It came in the guise of love.

He bent nearer. "I love you," he said. "I loved you from the first. And shall forever. You knew it long ago."

She did not move.

"You knew I loved you?"

"Yes, I knew it."

The emotion in her voice, in every delicate contour of her face, pleaded for mercy. He gave her none, and she bent her head in silence, clasped hands tightening.

And when at last he had had his say, the burning words still rang in her ears through the silence. A curious faintness stole upon her, coming stealthily like a hateful thing. She strove to put it from her, to listen, to remember and understand the words he had spoken, but the dull confusion grew with the sound of the pines.

"Will you love me? Will you try to love me?"

"I love you," she said; "I have loved you so many, many years; I—I am Rosamund—"

She bowed her head and covered her face with both hands.

"Rosamund! Rosamund!" he breathed, enraptured.

She dropped her hands with a little cry; the frightened sweetness of her eyes held back his outstretched arms. "Do not touch me," she whispered; "you will not touch me, will you?—not yet—not now. Wait till I understand!" She pressed her hands to her eyes, then again let them fall, staring straight at him. "I loved you so!" she whispered. "Why did you wait?"

"Rosamund! Rosamund!" he cried sorrowfully, "what are you saying? I do not understand; I can understand nothing save that I worship you. May I not touch you?—touch your hand, Rosamund? I love you so."

"And I love you. I beg you not to touch me—not yet. There is something—some reason why—"

"Tell me, sweetheart."

"Do you not know?"

"By Heaven, I do not!" he said, troubled and amazed.

She cast one desperate, unhappy glance at him, then rose to her full height, gazing out over the hazy valleys to where the mountains began, piled up like dim sun-tipped clouds in the north.

The hill wind stirred her hair and fluttered the white ribbons at waist and shoulder. The goldenrod swayed in the sunshine. Below, amid yellow treetops, the roofs and chimneys of the village glimmered.

"Dear, do you not understand?" she said. "How can I make you understand that I love you—too late?"

"Give yourself to me, Rosamund; let me touch you—let me take you—"

"Will you love me always?"

"In life, in death, which cannot part us. Will you marry me, Rosamund?"

She looked straight into his eyes. "Dear, do you not understand? Have you forgotten? I died three years ago to-day."

The unearthly sweetness of her white face startled him. A terrible light broke in on him; his heart stood still.

In his dull brain words were sounding—his own words, written years ago: "When God takes the mind and leaves the body alive, there grows in it, sometimes, a beauty almost supernatural."

He had seen it in his practice. A thrill of fright penetrated him, piercing every vein with its chill. He strove to speak; his lips seemed frozen; he stood there before her, a ghastly smile stamped on his face, and in his heart, terror.

"What do you mean, Rosamund?" he said at last.

"That I am dead, dear. Did you not understand that? I—I thought you knew it—when you first saw me at the cemetery, after all those years since childhood.... Did you not know it?" she asked wistfully. "I must wait for my bridal."

Misery whitened his face as he raised his head and looked out across the sunlit world. Something had smeared and marred the fair earth; the sun grew gray as he stared.

Stupefied by the crash, the ruins of life around him, he stood mute, erect, facing the west.

She whispered, "Do you understand?"

"Yes," he said; "we will wed later. You have been ill, dear; but it is all right now—and will always be—God help us! Love is stronger than all— stronger than death."

"I know it is stronger than death," she said, looking out dreamily over the misty valley.

He followed her gaze, calmly, serenely reviewing all that he must re- nounce, the happiness of wedlock, children—all that a man desires.

Suddenly instinct stirred, awaking man's only friend—hope. A lifetime for the battle!—for a cure! Hopeless? He laughed in his excitement. De- spair?—when the cure lay almost within his grasp!—the work he had given his life to! A month more in the laboratory—two months—three—perhaps a year. What of it? It must surely come—how could he fail when the work of his life meant all in life for her?

The light of exaltation slowly faded from his face; ominous, foreboding thoughts crept in; fear laid a shaky hand on his head which fell heavily for- ward on his breast.

Science and man's cunning and the wisdom of the world!

"O God," he groaned, "for Him who cured by laying on His hands!"

Now that he had learned her name, and that her father was alive, he stood mutely beside her, staring steadily at the chimneys and stately dor- mered roof almost hidden behind the crimson maple foliage across the val- ley—her home.

She had seated herself once more upon the moss, hands clasped upon one knee, looking out into the west with dreamy eyes.

"I shall not be long," he said gently. "Will you wait here for me? I will bring your father with me."

"I will wait for you. But you must come before the new moon. Will you? I must go when the new moon lies in the west."

"Go, dearest? Where?"

"I may not tell you," she sighed, "but you will know very soon—very soon now. And there will be no more sorrow, I think," she added timidly.

"There will be no more sorrow," he repeated quietly.

"For the former things are passing away," she said.

He broke a heavy spray of golden-rod and laid it across her knees; she held out a blossom to him—a blind gentian, blue as her eyes. He kissed it.

"Be with me when the new moon comes," she whispered. "It will be so sweet. I will teach you how divine is death, if you will come."

"You shall teach me the sweetness of life," he said tremulously.

"Yes—life. I did not know you called it by its truest name."

So he went away, trudging sturdily down the lane, gun glistening on his shoulder.

Where the lane joins the shadowy village street his dog skulked up to him, sniffing at his heels.

A mill whistle was sounding; through the red rays of the setting sun people were passing. Along the row of village shops loungers followed him with vacant eyes. He saw nothing, heard nothing, though a kindly voice called after him, and a young girl smiled at him on her short journey through the world.

The landlord of the Wildwood Inn sat sunning himself in the red evening glow.

"Well, doctor," he said, "you look tired to death. Eh? What's that you say?"

The young man repeated his question in a low voice. The landlord shook his head.

"No, sir. The big house on the hill is empty—been empty these three years. No, sir, there ain't no family there now. The old gentleman moved away three years ago."

"You are mistaken," said the doctor; "his daughter tells me he lives there."

"His—his daughter?" repeated the landlord. "Why, doctor, she's dead." He turned to his wife, who sat sewing by the open window: "Ain't it three years, Marthy?"

"Three years to-day," said the woman, biting off her thread. "She's buried in the family vault over the hill. She was a right pretty little thing, too."

"Turned nineteen," mused the landlord, folding his newspaper reflectively.

The great gray house on the hill was closed, windows and doors boarded over, lawn, shrubbery, and hedges tangled with weeds. A few scarlet poppies glimmered above the brown grass. Save for these, and clumps of tall wild phlox, there were no blossoms among the weeds.

His dog, which had sneaked after him, cowered as he turned northward across the fields. Swifter and swifter he strode; and as he stumbled on, the long sunset clouds faded, the golden light in the west died out, leaving a calm, clear sky tinged with faintest green.

Pines hid the west as he crept toward the hill where she awaited him. As he climbed through dusky purple grasses, higher, higher, he saw the new moon's crescent tipping above the hills; and he crushed back the deathly fright that clutched at him and staggered on.

"Rosamund!"

The pines answered him.

"Rosamund!"

The pines replied, answering together. Then the wind died away, and there was no answer when he called.

East and south the darkening thickets, swaying, grew still. He saw the slim silver birches glimmering like the ghosts of young trees dead; he saw on the moss at his feet a broken stalk of golden-rod.

The new moon had drawn a veil across her face; sky and earth were very still.

While the moon lasted he lay, eyes open, listening, his face pillowed on the moss. It was long after sunrise when his dog came to him; later still when men came.

And at first they thought he was asleep.

CHAPTER VI

EX CURIA

And now, at his attorney's request, and before his report was made, they decided to run through the documents in the case once more, reviewing everything from the very beginning. So young Courtlandt, his attorney, lighted a cigar and unwrapped the pink tape from the bundle of papers.

There was enough daylight left to read by, for wall and ceiling still bore the faded imprint of the red winter sunset. Edgerton sat before the fire, his well-shaped head buried in his hands; Courtlandt, lounging on a sofa by the window, unfolded the first paper, puffed thoughtfully at his cigar, and presently began to read without inflection or apparent interest:

December 24, 1902.

JOHN EDGERTON, Esq.

Sir: My client, Michael Innis, is seriously ill, and I am writing you on his behalf and at his urgent solicitation.

It would appear that, during the panic of 1884, my client came to your father's assistance, at a time when your father's financial ruin, involving also, I believe, the ruin of many of his friends, was apparently only a question of hours.

It would also appear that, upon your father's death, you wrote Mr. Innis, voluntarily assuming your father's unpaid obligations. (Copy of your letter herewith inclosed.)

It further appears that Mr. Innis, accepting the assurance of your personal gratitude, generously offered to wait for the sums due him, permitting you to pay at your own convenience. (Copy of Mr. Innis's letter inclosed herewith.)

In the conclusion of this last letter (No. 2 on file) Mr. Innis mentions his lifelong respect for your father and his family, humorously drawing the social distinction between the late Winthrop Edgerton, Esq., and Michael Innis, the Tammany contractor; and rather wistfully contrasting the future prospects of Mr. Edgerton's son, yourself, and the chances of the child of Michael Innis.

To this letter you replied (copy herewith), repeating in a manly fashion your assurance of gratitude, holding yourself at the service of Mr. Innis.

Now, sir, if your assurances meant more than mere civility, you have an opportunity to erase the deep obligations that your father assumed.

Mr. Innis is a man broken in mind and body. His fortune was invested, against my advice, in Madagascar Railways. To-day he could not realize a thousand dollars from the investment.

For twenty years his one absorbing passion has been the education and fitting of his only child for a position in the world which he himself could never hope to attain. Wealth and education, linked with an agreeable personality, may go anywhere in this century. And his daughter has had the best that Europe can afford.

Within a month all is changed. Sir, it is sad to see the stricken man lying here, watching his daughter.

And now, knowing that impending dissolution is near, terror of the future for her has wrung an appeal from him to you—a strange appeal, Mr. Edgerton. Money alone is little; he asks more; he asks your protection for her—not the perfunctory protection of a guardian for a ward, but the guidance of a father, the companionship of a brother, the loyalty of a husband.

The man is blinded by worship of his own child; your father's son represents to him all that is noblest, most honorable, most desirable in the world.

Sir, this is a strange request, an overdrawn draft upon your gratitude, I fear. Yet I write you as I am bidden. An answer should be returned by cable with as little delay as possible. He will live until he receives it. Marriage by proxy is legal. Special dispensation is certain.

I am, sir, with great respect,
Your very humble servant,
WILLIAM CAMPBELL.

Att'y and Counselor at Law,
7 rue d'Issy.

When Courtlandt finished reading he folded the letter, glancing across at Edgerton: "That was written two years ago to-day, you remember?—this foreclosure of his mortgage upon your gratitude!"

"I remember," said Edgerton.

"From the gratitude of the conscientious, good Lord deliver us!" murmured Courtlandt, unfolding another paper. "This is a copy of the asinine cablegram you sent, without consulting me." And he read:

INNIS,
23 rue d'Abdul Hamid, Paris.
I assume all responsibility for your daughter's future. Utterly impossible for me to leave New York. If you believe marriage advisable, arrange for special dispensation and ceremony by proxy.
JOHN EDGERTON.

Courtlandt rose and walked over to the fire where Edgerton was sitting. His client raised his head, eyes a trifle dazed from the pressure of his fingers on the closed lids.

"What the merry deuce did you send that cable for?" muttered Courtlandt under his breath.

"I don't know—a debt of gratitude—and he did not want it paid in money. I—an appeal like that had to be honored, you see. I was ashamed to haggle at the day of reckoning. A man cannot appraise his own gratitude."

"Such things cannot be asked of gratitude," growled the attorney. "The business of the world is not run on impulse! What is gratitude?"

"It is not gratitude if it asks that question," returned Edgerton; "and I fear that after all it was not exactly gratitude. Gratitude gives; a debt of honor exacts. There is no profit in following this line further, is there, Billy?"

"No," assented Courtlandt, "unless it's going to help us disentangle the unfortunate affair." He unfolded another paper. "It's too dark to read," he observed, leaning forward into the firelight. The red reflection of the coals played over his face and the black-edged notepaper he was scanning. And he read, slowly:

January 3, 1903.

DEAR MR. EDGERTON: For your very gentle letter to me I beg to thank you; I deeply appreciate your delicacy at a time when kindness is most needed. Had you not written as you have, I should have found it difficult to discuss a situation which I am only just beginning to realize must be as embarrassing to you as it is to me.

In the grief and distress which overwhelmed me when I was so suddenly summoned from the convent to find my father so ill, I did not, could not realize the step I was asked to take. All I knew was that he desired it, begged for it, and it meant to me nothing—this ceremony which made you my husband—nothing except a little happiness for the father I loved.

He made the responses for you, I kneeling at his bedside, scarce able to speak in my grief. There were two brief ceremonies, the civil and religious. He died very quietly that night.

Pray believe me that I understand how impossible it is for you to leave affairs of importance to come to Paris at this time. My aunt, who is with the Ursulines, has received me. It is very quiet, very peaceful; I have opportunity for meditation, and for studies which I left uncompleted. Mr. Campbell, whom you have so considerately retained for my legal guidance, is kind and tactful. He has, I believe, communicated with you in regard to the most generous provision you have made for me. Pray believe that I require very, very little. I regret the loss of my father's fortune only because it should have perhaps compensated you a trifle for your kindness to my father in his last hours.

I hesitate—I feel the greatest reluctance and delicacy in addressing you upon a matter that troubles me. It is this, Mr. Edgerton: if, through gratitude to my father for service done your father, you offered to become responsible for me, perhaps—I do not know—perhaps, as you have done me the honor of protecting me with your name, it is all that could be expected—and I hasten to assure you that I am content. Indeed, had I realized, had I even begun to comprehend what I was doing— Yet what could I do but obey him at such a time?

So, if you think it well that we remain apart for a while, I am content and happy to obey your wishes. Your name, which I now bear, I honor; your wishes, monsieur, are my commands.

With gratitude, confidence, and respect, I remain,

Faithfully yours,

KATHLEEN INNIS EDGERTON.

Convent of the Ursulines,
rue Daumont.

Courtlandt refolded the letter, and sat rubbing his eyes. "For Heaven's sake let's have a light!" he grumbled, leaning over and pushing the electric button.

The light broke out overhead, flooding the library, glistening among gay evergreen wreaths tied with bunches of Christmas holly which hung against the library windows.

Edgerton raised his pale face, then his head sank on his breast; he folded his arms, gazing absently into the fire. "Go on," he said.

So Courtlandt read other letters from Mrs. Edgerton, brief notes, perfunctory, reserved, and naïve; and he read letters from Campbell, the attorney, acknowledging provisions made for his young client.

When he finished he refolded all the papers, retied them with pink tape, and laid them on the table at Edgerton's elbow. "Now," he said, "comes the question. You have arrived at the conclusion that Mrs. Edgerton desires and deserves her freedom. And you want to know what I think."

"Yes," said Edgerton.

"You gave me a month to look up the matter."

"Yes, a month."

"And now you want me to report, don't you, Jack?"

Edgerton glanced up. "If you're ready," he said.

"I'm ready. First I want to ask you a question. Is there any woman you have met, before or since your marriage, whom you might fall in love with if you were free to do so?"

"No, I believe not—I don't know. I am—I was not actuated by selfishness."

"All right. Still, you are capable of loving somebody, are you not?"

"I fancy so. I should like to have a chance to marry—for love."

"But you never met the right one?"

"There is—I have caught a glimpse—once—one woman—"

"Is that all?" laughed Courtlandt. "That's not enough to bowl you over."

"It was almost enough!" retorted Edgerton. Through his voice rang an undertone of impatience. His attorney looked up quickly.

"Oh, is it as serious as that? No wonder you want your freedom! Who is the woman?"

"I don't know what you mean," retorted the younger man sullenly. "I told you that I saw a woman once, whom I should like to have had a chance to see again. What of it? I never shall."

"When was this, Jack?"

"Yesterday—if you want to know."

"Where?"

"Driving in the park."

"Who is she?"

"You could answer that question," said Edgerton, wheeling around on his friend. "You were driving with her."

Courtlandt stared, slowly turning redder and redder.

"You wanted to know," observed Edgerton, eying him. "It means nothing, of course—I was riding along the bridle path and I caught a glimpse of you, and I saw her face. I thought her beautiful, that's all. Drop the subject."

"Certainly," answered Courtlandt. He opened his match box and relighted his cigar; then he fell to musing, breaking the burnt match up into little pieces and tossing the morsels, one by one, into the fire.

"Jack," he drawled, still busy with the match, "you gave me a month to report upon this matter concerning the dissolution of your marriage. It might interest you to learn the first step I took."

"What was it?" inquired Edgerton, raising his troubled eyes.

"I went to Paris."

"To—to see—"

"Certainly, to see Mrs. Edgerton."

The men's eyes met; the lawyer shrugged his shoulders.

"Mrs. Edgerton is very inexperienced, very young," he said. "She is, of course, a Catholic. But if she desired her freedom a thousand times as fervently as you might desire yours, the law of her religion bars her way. You knew that of course."

"I thought—sometimes—" began the other.

"You are wrong."

Edgerton stared into the glowing coals.

"So you left it to me to see what could be done," added the attorney dryly. Edgerton assented.

"Well," said Courtlandt, "I shouldn't have accepted such a commission had I not known it was quite unselfish on your part. You told me that her letters to you were pitifully loyal and conscientious; that you felt like a jailer watching an innocent life prisoner; that if you only knew how to do it you would give her the liberty God meant her to enjoy—liberty to love and be loved. And you allowed me a month to find the way to settle this wretched affair."

"Yes. Is there a way?"

"Only one," replied Courtlandt gravely. He rose, offering his hand.

Edgerton also rose, tall, clean cut, closely cropped hair just tinged with gray at the temples.

"Only one way," repeated Courtlandt deliberately, "and that is for you to discuss the situation with Mrs. Edgerton."

"What!" exclaimed Edgerton sharply, dropping his friend's hand. "You know I can't leave town to go to Paris."

Courtlandt coolly consulted his watch. "I neglected to say that Mrs. Edgerton is in town. I believe"—he glanced at his watch again, then closed it with a snap—"I suggested that she waive ceremony and meet us here."

"Here!" muttered Edgerton. "Wait a moment, will you? Do you mean to say that she is coming here *to-night?*"

"Why not?" said Courtlandt, his gray eyes narrowing. "If she chooses to accept my advice, if she is woman enough to overlook what is due her from her husband, why should she not come here as freely as you come?"

"Are you my attorney or hers?" demanded the other in astonishment.

"Yours, Jack—acting for your interest—which is hers, too—which must be hers. Where is your sense of honor? Where is your sense of justice? Has the glimpse of a woman's face in the park seared your eyes? Is it true that an indifferent man can be just, but a man in love is a partisan? You could be coldly considerate and deal out passionless justice until yesterday. Now for the first time the fetters gall you. Is this the crisis where you flinch?"

He stood, jerking on his gloves, scanning Edgerton's face.

"I told her that the proper place to discuss the situation was under her own roof; and I am right. Do you consider a public hotel the suitable environment for such a conference? Her pride and intelligence comprehended me. That's all I have to say."

"Why did you not tell me before this that she was in town? I understand the requirements of civilization, do I not?"

"I did not tell you, because we landed only yesterday morning."

"She came over with *you?*"

"On my advice and at my earnest solicitation."

Edgerton stared at him, tugging at his short mustache.

"What are we to discuss?" he demanded sullenly. "As she is Catholic we cannot discuss divorce. We could, of course, come to some conclusion concerning a *modus vivendi*."

"I expect you to come to some such conclusion. Two years ago you were twenty-eight—an oversensitive young man, impulsive, illogical, and morbid concerning personal obligations. Without consulting your legal adviser you perpetrated a crime—for it is criminal to parody the highest safeguard to civilization—marriage. It was a crime; your wife is your accomplice—*particeps criminis*, my friend. Neither you nor she deserves mercy."

He turned away, buttoning his gloves.

"It's touched your temples with gray," he observed. "You have learned something at thirty, Jack, even if it's cost you what you think a *mésalliance*."

As he stepped to the door a maid appeared with a card on a salver. Edgerton glanced at it, then looked straight into Courtlandt's eyes.

"I'm sorry I needed this lesson in decency," he said. "It was all right for you to administer it. You need not worry; I understand that I am at my wife's disposal, not she at mine. I've kept my medicine waiting for two years, that's all."

"Oh, you're getting on," observed Courtlandt carelessly. "Good night— I've a word to say to Mrs. Edgerton before I go."

"You mean to stay, don't you?" began the other, flushing up. "It would be less trying for her—"

But Courtlandt hurried off down the stairs, muttering vaguely of engagements for Christmas Eve, leaving Edgerton staring after him through the dimly lighted hallway.

He heard Courtlandt enter the drawing-room; he could distinguish the quick, low exchange of greeting; then he went down slowly, steadying himself by the banisters.

A young girl in furs turned toward him as he entered; he caught a glimpse of blue eyes, a glint of bright hair framed in fluffy fur; he heard Courtlandt's cool, easy voice presenting him to his wife; he took the slim gloved hand outstretched, held it stupidly until it was withdrawn; then Courtlandt's voice again, promising to return, and exacting her promise to wait here for him if he should be detained.

"I'm sorry I can't remain and dine with you and Mr. Edgerton on this night before Christmas," added Courtlandt blandly, making for the door.

"Oh!" she said, surprised, "I did not understand that Mr. Edgerton invited us."

The color stung Edgerton's face, and he said in a low voice: "You are at home, madam; it is for you to invite us. Perhaps Mr. Courtlandt will stay if you ask him; I will if you ask me."

She gave him a confused, brilliant little smile, a delicate tint mounting to her cheeks.

"Thank you," she said; "you—everybody is so delightful to me. Will you stay, Mr. Courtlandt? I—we beg of you! No? Then, until I—until we have the pleasure—at nine, I believe?" From force of habit she turned to the dazed maid, who also instinctively recognized authority, and opened the door which a second later closed upon the most profoundly excited young attorney in Manhattan.

Mrs. Edgerton raised her blue eyes to her husband as a maid relieved her of her furs and little gilt-edged tricorne.

"I—I wonder if you are as embarrassed as I am?" she said, laughing and touching her golden hair with a frank side glance at the mirror.

"Dreadfully embarrassed," admitted Edgerton, scarcely conscious of what he uttered; oblivious, too, of the usages of civilization until she sank into an armchair with a shy "May I?"

"It is for me to ask the privilege," he said, biting his lip.

"Oh, if you please?"—she smiled, with a gesture toward the chair beside her.

Seated there with him under the crystal chandelier, she fell silent, meeting his gaze at moments with a questioning smile, partly confident, partly uncertain.

"I saw you in the park yesterday," he said under his breath, never taking his eyes from her.

"I saw you, too," she replied quickly. "You rode a bay. I never imagined—" she bent her head, thoughtfully studying the arabesques on the rug. "You ride very well," she added. Then, after a moment's silence: "And you remembered me?"

"I recognized you at once," he said, "the instant I entered this room. It was that which startled me—made me appear stupid—"

"You did not appear stupid—"

"I was awkward, dumb—"

"I chattered sufficiently for two. Indeed, I was not at all composed."

"Did—did you recognize me at once?"

She looked at him, she glanced at the rug, her blue eyes grew vague, lost in retrospective reverie.

He did not repeat the question, but asked her how long it was since she had been in America. "Oh, many years—I was only three when my father went to France." Then the warm color came into her face and she clasped her hands impulsively. "I do not believe," she said, "that I have conveyed to you in letters my deep appreciation of your loyalty to me. I—I did not know how to express it—I do not now. Believe me, monsieur, it does exist!"

"What have you to thank me for?" he asked almost brusquely. Then, in a rush of bitterness: "Your sentiments honor yourself, not me, madam. For two years I have been responsible for your happiness. What have I done to secure it?"

She turned a trifle pale, unprepared for such a question. But she answered very sweetly: "You left me guarded by the honor of your own name. I have never wanted for anything; I have had the quiet and seclusion I desired. What more is there, Mr. Edgerton?"

And as he remained silent, she raised her head with a gay little smile: "You could not leave your affairs to come to France; you did not suggest that I come to New York. How could I know that I should—"

"What?" he urged.

But she closed her red lips, sitting mute, suddenly shy again.

After a moment she said: "*Mais*—he is absent a long while, Mr. Courtlandt."

"He isn't coming until nine o'clock," said Edgerton. He glanced across at the clock. It was half-past seven.

"So, in the meanwhile, we are to discuss matters of importance," she suggested seriously. "Mr. Courtlandt said so. What, monsieur, are we to discuss?"

"There is absolutely nothing that I know of to discuss," replied Edgerton slowly.

"Nothing?" she inquired, wide-eyed and innocent.

"Nothing, except your wishes, and they admit of no discussion. You are at home now."

"But I—but I am staying at the Holland—" Edgerton touched a button; a servant appeared.

"Mrs. Edgerton's luggage is at the Holland," he said quietly. "Telephone for it."

Mrs. Edgerton half rose from her chair; then, meeting her husband's grave eyes, she sank back, crimson to the temples.

"We are merely about to exchange quarters," he said pleasantly. "I shall be most comfortable at the Holland."

"Oh, you shall not!—no, it is all wrong!" she pleaded, the color fading in her face. "I cannot come into your house—into your life—"

"It is your house," he said gently. "Still, if—if you don't mind—there is a better way still of arranging matters. I have a whole floor on the third story; and perhaps you might not mind if I retain it. I promise," he added, laughing, "to be a model tenant and not keep coal in my bath tub!"

She laughed, too, a little uncertainly.

"You are so generous—so kindly," she said. "How can you endure to have a perfectly silly girl march into your house—"

"*Your* house!"

"*Your* house! Carry it by assault, capture the nicest suite, and drive you to the roof among the sparrows! No, it is shameful! More than that, it is absurd!"

"I never have occupied the rooms on the second floor," he protested. "They have been vacant since I took this house."

"Truly?"

"Truly. They are too pretty for a man who smokes a pipe—all rococo, and furniture with beagle legs, you know."

"For whom were they intended?" she asked innocently.

He reddened. "I bought the house after our wedding," he hesitated; "then, afterwards, from your letters, I fancied that you might prefer to remain abroad. So I said nothing."

She bent her head. "I—I thought it fairer—to you," she said in a low voice. "I would have come had you asked me. I—how was I to know, Mr. Edgerton?"

They sat silent, eyes bent on the floor. Presently he went on: "So I had that suite fixed up for you. And I moved upstairs. I am very happy that you are to occupy it."

"Do you *really* desire it?"

"You have no idea how pretty it is," he urged.

"Is it so pretty?"

"Come up and look at it!"

She sprang to her feet on the impulse, smiling, confident of his kindness. And they mounted the stairs together, *sans façon*, arriving on the second floor breathless.

"Oh," she cried softly, as she entered, "it is perfectly charming!" She stood a moment, gazing around, then with a delightful gesture bade him enter.

"Is this really mine?" she repeated. "How delicious!" She passed from room to room, pausing before bits of furniture that attracted her, touching and lifting the silver on dresser and table. "My own initials!" she said under her breath. "And what is this?" laying her white fingers on a jewel case. "Am I to open it? Really! Oh, the beauty of it all! I—I am perfectly overwhelmed, *mons*—Mr. Edgerton!" And she sat down on the edge of the bed, pressing her hands to her eyes.

A maid came to the door; the luggage from the Holland had arrived. Presently two burly expressmen entered, staggering under the first of a series of trunks. Her maid directed the men; Mrs. Edgerton sat, hands folded, smiling, blue eyes a trifle dim, while her husband, standing beside her, watched the operations.

The silvery chime of a clock sounded, striking eight times, and on either side of the dial gilt cupids fluttered their burnished wings.

"Impossible!" exclaimed Edgerton. Then with a laugh almost boyish, he said: "We're supposed to dine at eight."

She looked vacantly at her husband. "Dinner already! Can it be possible time has flown like that? And I—behold me! Have I time to dress?"

"Time is yours to dispose of," he said, smiling back into her eyes; "all here are yours to dispose of as you see fit."

"Even you, monsieur?" She laughed in her excitement and happiness, not weighing words and their meaning until their echo returned again to appall her—while her maid aided her to dress—and the echo of his answer, too, rang persistently in her ears: "Yes, to pardon, to dispose of, to command, always, as long as I have life to serve you."

And now she was ready, smiling nervously back at her own flushed reflection in the mirror—a young girl stirred to the soul by kindness, almost intoxicated at a glimpse of her own undreamed-of beauty, surprised there in the depths of the mirror.

The banisters were decorated with twisted ropes of evergreens; she descended slowly, cheeks burning, eyes fixed steadily on her husband, who stood motionless below to receive her. A tiny light here and there caught the thick tendrils of her heavy burnished hair and glimmered on her smooth, full neck and arms.

At the foot of the stairs she paused, made him a low reverence, then, gathering her silken train, she looked fearlessly into his face and laid her hand lightly in his.

So, moving serenely side by side, they passed under holly and mistletoe and ropes of evergreen, through the long drawing-room, through the music room, slowly, more slowly, until the great velvet hangings barred their way.

There they paused, turning face to face, her small hand scarcely touching his.

"Can you forgive me?" he asked under his breath.

"Forgive you?" she repeated tremulously; "can do—more than that.... Ask me."

But there was no time, for the butler, bowing, had drawn the portieres to the full length of the golden cords.

CHAPTER VII

THE GOLDEN POOL

So the doctor, finding his patient's quarters untenanted for the first time in many months, hastened downstairs and out to the veranda, where he discovered a lean, soldierly looking young fellow clad in fishing coat fussing with rod and reel.

"Oho, my enterprising friend!" he said. "What mischief are you hatching now?"

"I'm going to try for your big trout in the Golden Pool," said his patient calmly.

This unlooked-for energy appeared to embarrass the doctor. His grim mouth tightened.

"Don't go now," he said; "it's too late in the morning."

"I'm going anyhow," retorted his patient.

"Don't be obstinate; that fish won't rise till evening."

"I know it, but I'm going."

"Against my orders!" demanded the exasperated doctor.

"With pleasure," replied the young man gayly.

"And it's your own doing, too. Do you remember what you said last night?"

"I said I saw a big fish rising in that pool," growled the doctor.

"Exactly; and that has done more to brace me up than all your purple pills for peculiar people."

"Don't go to the Golden Pool *now!*" said the doctor with emphasis. "I have a particular reason for making this request."

"What reason?"

"I won't tell you."

"You're after that fish yourself! No, you don't!"

"That's idiotic."

"Well, anyhow, good-by."

"You shan't!" exclaimed the doctor wrathfully. "Give me that rod!"

But his patient clung to the rod, laughing.

"Now what the devil possesses you to make for the Golden Pool at this particular minute?" demanded the vexed doctor. "You've been an invalid for a year and more, and up to this moment you've done what I told you."

His patient continued to laugh—that same light-hearted, infectious laugh which the doctor had not heard in many a month, and he looked at him keenly.

"All the same, you're not well yet, and you know it," he said.

"My aversion to women?"

"Partly."

"You mean my memory still fails me? Well, then, what do you think happened this morning?"

"What?" inquired the doctor sulkily.

"This: I went out to the stables and recognized Phelan and Riley! How's that for a start? Then"—he glanced across the lawn where an old gardener pottered about among the petunias—"there's Dawson, isn't it? And this is my own place—Gleniris! Isn't it? Besides," he added, "my aversion to women is disappearing; I saw a girl on the lawn from my window this morning. Who is she?"

"Was she dressed in white?" asked the doctor.

"Don't remember."

"You never before saw her?"

"No—I don't know. I didn't see her face."

"So it seems you can't recollect the back of a relative or a neighbor! Now what do you think of yourself?"

"Relative? Nonsense," he laughed; "I haven't any. As for the neighbors, give me time, for Heaven's sake! I'm doing beautifully. There are millions of things that set me thinking and worrying now—funny flashes of memory—hints of the past, vague glimpses that excite me to effort; but nothing—absolutely nothing—yet of that blank year. Was it a year?"

"More; never mind that!"

"How long was it?" asked his patient wistfully.

"Sixteen months."

"You said I was shot, I think."

"No, I didn't. You think you were, but it was done with a Malay kris. Now, what can you remember about it?"

The young man stood silent, fumbling with his rod.

"And you tell me you're cured!" observed the doctor sarcastically, "and you can't even recollect how you got swiped with a Malay kris!"

"I might if I could see the Malay—or the kris." The doctor, who had begun to pace the veranda, halted and glanced sharply at his patient.

"The best way to remember things is to see 'em? Is that your idea?"

"I think so. It's true I've seen Phelan many times without remembering him, but to-day I recognized him. Isn't that good medicine?"

The doctor thought a moment, fished out his watch from the fob pocket, regarded it absently, and came down the steps to the lawn, where his patient stood making practice casts with his light bamboo rod.

"I'll tell you why I didn't want you to go to the Golden Pool," he said.

"Well, why?"

"Poachers," replied the doctor, watching him. "They fish in the pools, and they use your canoe, and they even have the impudence to go bathing in the Golden Pool.... I didn't want you to worry."

"I think the poacher I catch will do the worrying," said the young man, laughing. "Is that all?"

"That is all. Go ahead if you want to. If you run across that girl invite her to dinner. She's a friend of mine." And the doctor walked off, shoving his hands deep into his capacious pockets.

His patient reeled in the line, smiling to himself, and started off across the meadow at a good swinging pace. He entered the forest by the meadow bridge, where a lank yokel was mowing grass.

"Mornin'!" ventured the native, with a doubtful grin of recognition.

"Look here," said the young man, halting in the path of the scythe, "ought I to know your name? Tell me the truth."

"I cal'late yew orter," replied the yokel. "I've been chorin' for yew close tew ten year."

A shadow fell over the master's lean face, and he went on through the underbrush, muttering to himself, passing his thin hand again and again across his forehead.

"Oh, well, I'll stick to it," he said aloud; "a man can't dance on a broken leg nor think with a broken head; they've got to be mended first—well mended."

Walking on through the fragrant forest, the shadow of care slipped from his face again, leaving it placid once more. The scent of the June woods, the far, dull throbbing of a partridge drumming in leafy depths, the happy sighing of a woodland world astir, all these were gentle stimulants to that sanity toward the shadowy borders of which he had so long been struggling from the region of dreadful night.

Spreading branches, dew-spangled, slapped his face as he passed; the moist rich odor of clean earth filled throat and lungs; a subdued, almost breathless expectancy brooded in the wake of the south wind.

When he emerged from the forest and entered the long glade, mountain and thicket were swimming in crystalline light; ferns hung weighted with dew; the outrush of bird music was incessant.

Far in the wet woods he could hear the river flowing—or was it the breeze freshening in the pines?

Listening, enraptured, boyish recollections awoke, and he instinctively took his bearings from the blue peak in the east. So the Ousel Pool lay to the west. He would fish that uncertain water later; but first the Golden

Pool, where the great trout had been seen, rising as recklessly as a minnow in a meadow brook.

Now, all excitement and expectancy, he waded on, knee-deep in drenched grasses, watching the soft mothlike flutter of the bluebirds among the iris. They had always hovered over this spot in June, he remembered now. Truly summer skies were healing him of his hurt; he recognized the belt of blue-beech saplings all crossbarred with sunlight, and he heard the familiar rush of waters below.

Suddenly, beyond the sprayed undergrowth, he caught a glow of color, a glimpse of that rich sunny foliage which gave the Golden Pool its name; and now the familiar water lay glimmering before him through the trees, and he began the descent, stepping quietly as a deer entering a strange covert.

At the water's edge he paused, cautiously; but there was no canoe lying under the alders. Memory halted short, then began groping backward through the years.

Where was the canoe? There had always been one here—in his boyhood and ever since—up to that obscured and cloudy space of time

He dropped to his knees and parted the leafy thicket with his hands. There was no canoe there, nothing except a book lying on a luncheon basket; and—what was this?—and this?

He stared stupidly for a moment, then rose and stepped through the thicket to the edge of the water. A canoe glittered out there, pulled up on a flat, sunny rock in midstream, and upon the rock lay a girl in a dripping bathing dress drying her hair in the sun.

Instantly an odd sense of it all having happened before seized him—the sun on the water, the canoe, the slim figure lying there. And when she indolently raised her hand, stifling a dainty yawn, and stretched her arms luxuriously, it seemed to him the repetition of a forgotten scene too familiar to surprise him.

Then, as she sat up, leisurely twisting her sun-bronzed hair, a chance turn of her head brought him into direct line of vision. They stared at one another across the sunny water.

For one second the thought flashed on him that he knew her; then in the same moment all that had seemed familiar in the situation faded into strangeness and apprehension, and he was aware that he had never before looked upon her face.

Yet, curiously enough, his long and melancholy aversion to women had not returned at sight of her. She had risen in surprise, wide dark eyes on him; and he spoke immediately, saying he had not meant to disturb her, and that she was quite welcome to use the canoe.

Her first stammered words annoyed him. "Did the doctor—come with you? Are you—are you alone?"

"I suppose the entire countryside knows I have been ill," he said; "but I'm perfectly able to be about without a doctor." He began to laugh. "But those are not the questions. The questions are what are people doing in these woods with luncheon baskets and summer novels, and how am I to fish this pool if people swim in it; and how am I to fish at all if an attractive stranger takes possession of my canoe?"

"I—I had no idea you were coming here," she faltered. "I bathe here every morning, and then I lunch here and read."

He laughed outright at her innocent acknowledgment of the trespass.

"I have a clear case against you," he said. "Haven't you read all my notices nailed up on trees? '*Warning! All trespassers will be dealt with to the full extent of the law*'—and much more to similar effect? And do you know what a very dreadful thing it is to be dealt with to the full extent of the law?"

"But—I am not—not trespassing," she said. "Can you not remember?"

"I'm afraid I can't," he replied, smiling; "I'm afraid I have a clear case against you. The doctor warned me that trespassers were about."

"Did he know you were coming *here?*" she asked incredulously.

"He did. And I'm afraid somebody has been caught *in flagrant délit!* What do you think?"

He stood there, amused, curiously noting the play of emotions over her delicate features. Consternation, dismay, had given place to quick resentment; that in turn died out, leaving something of comprehension in her perplexed face.

"So he sent you to catch a trespasser?" she said.

"I was coming to fish. Well, yes; he said I might find one."

"A trespasser? A stranger?" She hesitated; there was hurt astonishment in her voice. Suddenly her face took a deeper flush, as though she had come to an unexpected decision; her entire manner changed to serene self-possession. "What are you going to do with me?" she asked curiously.

"I'm afraid I can't put you in jail," he admitted. "You see, there's no punishment for swimming in favorite trout pools and spoiling a man's morning sport. Now, if you had only thought of catching one of my trout I could arrange to have you imprisoned."

"Please arrange it immediately, then," she said, lifting an enormous trout from the canoe and holding it up by the gills with both hands.

"Good Lord," he gasped, "it's the big one!" And he sat down suddenly on a log.

Her smiling defiance softened a trifle. "Did you really wish to catch this fish very much?" she asked. "I—I never supposed you would come here—to-day."

"The enormity of your crime stuns me," he said. "First you invade my domain, then you abstract my canoe, then you swim in my favorite pool, then you catch the biggest fish that ever came out of it."

"No," she said, "I was not such a goose as to swim first. I caught the fish first."

"Recount to me the battle," he said with a groan. "Fish like that only rise once in a lifetime. Tell me how you—but that's useless. It was the usual case of a twig and a bent pin, I suppose?"

She smiled uncertainly, and lifted a rod from the canoe.

"By Jove, that looks like one of my rods!" he exclaimed. "Where did you get it?"

Her eyes were bright with excitement; she shook her head, laughing.

"Are you in league with my doctor? Who are you?" he insisted.

"Only a poacher," she admitted. "I creep about and lurk outside windows where doctors talk in loud voices about big trout they have seen. Then—I go and catch them."

They were both laughing now; she standing beside the canoe, rod in hand, he balanced on a rock opposite.

Yet, even while laughing, his thin face sobered, darkening as though a gray shadow had crept across it.

"Are you a neighbor of mine?" he asked. "If you are, you will know why I ask it. If you are not, never mind," he added wearily.

She shook her head. His face cleared.

"I thought you were not a neighbor; I was certain that I had never seen you—as certain as a man can be awakening from—from illness, with his mind—his memory—shaky—almost blank." He bent his head, gazing into the water. Then he looked up. "You know the doctor? I think I saw you on the lawn this morning."

"Are you sure you have never before seen me?" she asked, with a ghost of a smile.

"I thought at first—for an instant—the canoe on the rock, and the sunshine, and you—" He fell silent, groping through the darkened corridors of thought for the key to memory.

In the sunlit hush a rippling noise sounded far out across the pool; then up out of the glassy water shot a sinuous shape, dark against the sun—a fish in silhouette, curving over with a flapping splash. Widening circles spread from a center where a few bubbles floated; the pool became placid once more—a mirror for the tapestry of golden thickets set with the heavenly hue above.

The long-dormant passion which sleeps but never dies awoke in him; the flush on his lean cheeks deepened as he turned and looked across the pool where the pretty intruder stood watching him, an eager question dancing in her eyes.

"I'd like to try," he said. "Do you mind?"

"Tell me what to do."

"Paddle very quietly over here—very carefully and without a splash. Can you do it?"

She loosened the canoe noiselessly, a lithe figure in her wet brown skirt and stockings. The mellow glow enveloped her as she moved into the shadows; and she seemed, in the soft forest light, part of the woodland harmony, blending with it as tawny-tinted shadows blend.

The canoe slipped into the pool; she knelt in the stern; then, with one silent push, sent it like an arrow across the water. He caught and steadied the frail craft; she stepped from it and sprang without a sound into the green shadows beside him.

He was muttering to himself: "I've forgotten some things—but not how to throw a fly, I think. Let us see—let us see."

She stood motionless as he embarked, watching him raise his rod and send the tiny brightly colored flies out over the water. The delicate accuracy seemed to fascinate her; her dark eyes followed the long upward loop of the back cast, the whistling flight of the silken line, the instant's suspense as the leader curved, straightened out, and fell, dropping three flies softly on the still surface of the pool.

As the canoe drifted nearer, nearer to the spot where the trout had leaped, the sharp dry click of the reel, the windlike whistle of the line, grew fainter. Suddenly, far ahead of the floating flies, a dark lump broke the water; there came a spatter of spray, a flash of pink and silver, and that was all—all, though for two hours the silken line darted out across the water, and many feathered flies of many hues fell vainly across the glassy mirror of the Golden Pool.

She was still standing in the same place when he returned. He drew a long deep breath of disappointment as he stepped ashore, and she echoed his sigh. The tension had ended.

"Showed color, but wouldn't fight," he said in a low voice. "Biggest trout I ever saw."

"Can't you possibly do something?" she asked tremulously.

"Not now; I must rest him. You can't force a fish like that by persistent worry. There's a chance he may come again; he's not serious yet. I dare not bother him for an hour or two."

He looked into her sensitive face; then, suddenly conscious of its youthful beauty, he fell silent, reeling in his wet line inch by inch.

Through the heated stillness dragon flies darted; the mounting perfume of brake and fern, the almost imperceptible odor of earth and water, seemed to envelop him in a delicate spell, soothing, healing, while pulseless moments drifted away in the smooth flow of a summer hour.

The rod slipped from his hand; his musing eyes rested on her. She was seated on a mossy log, head bent, slender stockinged feet trailing in the pool.

"All this has happened before," he said quietly. But there was no conviction in his voice.

She raised her dreamy eyes, the color came and went in throat and cheeks; through her half-parted lips the breath scarcely stirred.

He rose with a restless laugh, and stood a moment, his thin hand pressed across his forehead. Her eyes fell, were lifted to his, then fell again.

"Can't you help me?" he said wistfully.

"Can you not remember?" she breathed.

"Then we—we have known one another. Have we?"

"I once knew a friend of yours—a close friend—named Escourt."

"Escourt," he repeated blankly.

And after a long silence he turned away with a gesture that seemed to frighten her. But into her face came a flash of determination, reddening her cheeks again.

"It does not matter," she said; "nothing matters on a summer day like this.... I did not mean to trouble you."

He turned in his steps and stood looking at her.

"You say my friend's name *was* Escourt? Is my friend dead?"

"Please don't let it matter."

"It does matter. I—it is a fancy, perhaps, but the name of Escourt was once familiar—and pleasant. It is not your name, is it?"

"Yes," she said.

At last he began fretfully: "That is the strangest thing in the world. I have never before seen you, and yet I am perfectly conscious that your name has haunted me for years. Escourt—*Escourt!*—for years, I tell you," he went on in a sort of impatient astonishment; "ever since I can remember anything I can remember that name."

"And my first name?" Flushed, voice scarcely steady, she avoided his troubled gaze.

And as he did not answer, she said: "You once knew my husband. Can you not remember?"

He shook his head, studying her intently.

"No," he said in a dull voice, "I have forgotten; I have been very ill. The name troubles me; it is strange how the name troubles me."

"If it troubles you, let us talk of other things, will you?" she asked, almost timidly. "I did not think to awaken the memory of anything sad."

"It is not sad," resting his sunken, perplexed eyes on her; "it is something intimate—almost part of my life that I seem to have forgotten—" His hand sought the same spot over his right eye. "What were we doing when you interrupted everything?" His wandering glance fell on the canoe and the rod lying in the bottom, and his face cleared.

"I ought to be worrying that trout again," he said. "You won't go away, will you?"

"No; but I wish you would go," she said, laughing; "I'd dress if you would give me half an hour."

"You won't go—you will wait?" he repeated almost childishly.

"Yes, I will wait."

She shook her head, watching him embark; standing there looking out across the water where the paddle bubbles marked his course long after the canoe had vanished around the curved shore of the Golden Pool.

Suddenly her eyes filled; but she set her lips resolutely, groping with white hands for her knotted hair; the heavy shining twist, loosened, fell, veiling face and shoulders—a golden mask for sorrow and falling tears.

It was high noon when his far hail brought her to the water's edge, and she answered with a clear, prettily modulated call.

"Do you observe?" she asked, as he climbed the bank; and she made a little gesture of invitation toward a white napkin spread upon the moss.

A jug of milk, lettuce, bread, and a great bunch of hothouse grapes—and a hostess in a summer gown, smiling an invitation; what wonder that the haggard lines in his visage softened till something of the afterglow of youth lay like a ray of sun across his face.

"This is perfectly charming," he said, dropping to his knees beside her. "I—I am very happy that you waited for me."

She sat silent for a moment, with lowered eyes, then raised them shyly. "Let us eat bread and salt together, will you?—that nothing break our friendship."

"From your hands," he said.

She leaned over, took a tiny pinch of salt between her thumb and forefinger, and offered it to him on a bit of bread. He gravely broke the bread, returned half to her, and they ate, watching one another in silence.

"By the bread and salt I have shared with you," he said, half seriously, half smiling, "I promise to cherish this forest friendship. Let this day begin it."

"Let it," she said.

"Let pleasant years continue it."

"Yes—the coming years. So be it."

"Let nothing end it—nothing—not even—"

"Nothing—and, amen," she said faintly.

Again, unbidden, the ghosts of the past stirred, whispering together within him; echoes of unquiet days awoke, blind consciousness of that somber year where darkness dwelt, where memory lay slain forever.

She sat watching him there on the moss, supporting her weight on one arm.

"I am striving," he said, "to trace my thoughts." There was dull apology in his voice. "All this is not accident—you and I here together. I am haunted by something long forgotten, something that I am almost conscious of. When your voice sounds I seem to be quivering on the verge of memory.... Do you know what it is I have forgotten?"

She trembled to her lips. "Have you forgotten?"

"Yes—a great deal. Is it you I have forgotten?"

"Try to remember," she said under her breath.

"Remember? God knows I am trying. Begin with me, will you?"

"Yes; let us begin together. You were hurt."

"Yes, I was hurt."

"In a battle."

"I was hurt in a skirmish."

"Where?" she whispered.

"Why, on the Subig," he answered, surprised; "I was in the Philippine scouts."

He sat bolt upright, electrified, and struck his knee sharply with the flat of his wasted hand.

"Do you know," he said excitedly, "that until this very instant I have not thought of the Philippine scouts. Isn't that extraordinary?"

She strove to speak; her breast rose and fell, and she closed her lips convulsively.

He sat there, head drooping, passing his hand repeatedly across the scar over his right temple. She waited, whitening under the tension. His face became placid; he looked up at her; and a smile touched her wet lashes in response.

The contentment of convalescence seemed to banish his restlessness; her voice broke the silence, and its low, even tones satisfied the half-aroused longing for dead echoes.

So the ghost of happiness arose and sat between them; and she lay back, resting against a tree, smiling replies to his lazy badinage. And after a long while her laughter awoke to echo his, laughter as delicate as the breeze stirring her bright hair.

And afterward, long afterward, when the sunshine painted orange patches on the westward tree trunks and a haze veiled the taller spires, she reminded him of the great trout; but he would not go without her; so together they descended to the stream's edge.

Floating in the canoe there through the mellow light, he remembered that he had left his rod ashore, but would not go back, and she laughed outright, through the thread of the song she had been humming:

> "Fate is a dragon,
>> Faith the slim shape that braves it:
> Hope holds the stirrup-cup—
>> Drain it who craves it."

She smiled, singing carelessly:

> "Who art thou, young and brave?
> *La vie est un sommeil; l'amour en est le rêve!*"

"There is more," he said, watching her intently.
"How do you know?"
"I know that song. *I remember it, and there is more to it!*"
"Is it this, then?" and she sang again:

> "Life is but slumber,
>> Love the sad dream that haunts it,
> Death is thy waking gift;
>> Take it who wants it!

> "Who art thou, young and brave?
> *La vie est un sommeil; l'amour en est le rêve!*"

He sat for a long while, very still, head buried in his hands. A violet mist veiled water and trees; through it the setting sun sent fiery shafts through the mountain cleft. And when the last crimson shaft was sped and tree and water faded into darker harmony, the canoe had drifted far downstream, and now lay still in the shoreward sands; and they stood together on the water's edge.

Her fingers had become interlocked with his; she half withdrew them, eyes lowered.

"It is strange that our names should be the same," he said.

"Is your name Escourt, too?" she faltered.

"Yes; I know it now.... I have been ill—very ill. God alone knows what my hurt has done to me. There is a doctor at the house; he's been with me for a long time—a long time. I—I wonder why? I wonder if it was because I had forgotten—even my own name.... Who are you who bear my name? "

She swayed almost imperceptibly where she stood; he lifted both her hands and laid them against his lips, looking deep into her eyes.

"Who are you, bearing my name?" he whispered. "Unclose your eyes."

In the twilight her dark eyes opened; she was in his arms now, her head fallen a little backward, yielding to his embrace crushing her.

"Try—try to remember—before you kiss me," she breathed. "I wish you to love me—I desire it—but not like this. Oh, try to remember before— before it is too late!"

"I do remember!—Helen! Helen!"

Her lips on his stifled the cry; a long sigh, a sob, and she lay quivering in her husband's arms.

CHAPTER VIII

OUT OF THE DEPTHS

Dust and wind had subsided; there seemed to be a hint of rain in the starless west.

Because the August evening had become oppressive, the club windows stood wide open as though gaping for the outer air. Rugs and curtains had been removed; an incandescent light or two accentuated the emptiness of the rooms; here and there shadowy servants prowled, gilt buttons sparkling through the obscurity, their footsteps on the bare floor intensifying the heavy quiet.

Into this week's-end void wandered young Shannon, drifting aimlessly from library to corridor, finally entering the long room where the portraits of dead governors smirked through the windows at the deserted avenue.

As his steps echoed on the rugless floor, a shadowy something detached itself from the depths of a padded armchair by the corner window, and a voice he recognized greeted him by name.

"You here, Harrod!" he exclaimed. "Thought you were at Bar Harbor."

"I was. I had business in town."

"Do you stay here long?"

"Not long," said Harrod slowly.

Shannon dropped into a chair with a yawn which ended in a groan.

"Of all God-forsaken places," he began, "a New York club in August."

Harrod touched an electric button, but no servant answered the call; and presently Shannon, sprawling in his chair, jabbed the button with the ferrule of his walking stick, and a servant took the order, repeating as though he had not understood: "Did you say two, sir?"

"With olives, dry," nodded Shannon irritably. They sat there in silence until the tinkle of ice aroused them, and—

"Double luck to you," muttered Shannon; then, with a scarcely audible sigh: "Bring two more and bring a dinner card." And, turning to the older man: "You're dining, Harrod?"

"If you like."

A servant came and turned on an electric jet; Shannon scanned the card under the pale radiance, scribbled on the pad, and handed it to the servant.

"Did you put down my name?" asked Harrod curiously.

"No; you'll dine with me—if you don't mind."

"I don't mind—for this last time."

"Going away again?"

"Yes."

Shannon signed the blank and glanced up at his friend. "Are you well?" he asked abruptly.

Harrod, lying deep in his leather chair, nodded.

"Oh, you're rather white around the gills! We'll have another."

"I thought you had cut that out, Shannon."

"Cut what out?"

"Drinking."

"Well, I haven't," said Shannon sulkily, lifting his glass and throwing one knee over the other.

"The last time I saw you, you said you would cut it," observed Harrod.

"Well, what of it?"

"But you haven't?"

"No, my friend."

"Can't you stop?"

"I could—now. To-morrow—I don't know; but I know well enough I couldn't day after to-morrow. And day after to-morrow I shall not care."

A short silence and Harrod said: "That's why I came back here."

"What?"

"To stop you."

Shannon regarded him in sullen amazement.

A servant announcing dinner brought them to their feet; together they walked out into the empty dining room and seated themselves by an open window.

Presently Shannon looked up with an impatient laugh.

"For Heaven's sake let's be cheerful, Harrod. If you knew how the damned town had got on my nerves."

"*That's* what I came back for, too," said Harrod with his strange white smile. "I knew the world was fighting you to the ropes."

"It is; here I stay on, day after day, on the faint chance of something doing." He shrugged his shoulders. "Business is worse than dead; I can't hold on much longer. You're right; the world has hammered me to the ropes, and it will be down and out for me unless— "

"Unless you can borrow on your own terms?"

"Yes, but I can't."

"You are mistaken."

"Mistaken? Who will—"

"I will."

"You! Why, man, do you know how much I need? Do you know for how long I shall need it? Do you know what the chances are of my making good? *You!* Why, Harrod, I'd swamp you! You can't afford—"

"I can afford anything—now."

Shannon stared. "You have struck something?"

"Something that puts me beyond want." He fumbled in his breast pocket, drew out a portfolio, and from the flat leather case he produced a numbered check bearing his signature, but not filled out.

"Tell them to bring pen and ink," he said.

Shannon, perplexed, signed to a waiter. When the ink was brought, Harrod motioned Shannon to take the pen. "Before I went to Bar Harbor," he said, "I had a certain sum—" He hesitated, mentioned the sum in a low voice, and asked Shannon to fill in the check for that amount. "Now blot it, pocket it, and use it," he added listlessly, looking out into the lamp-lighted street.

Shannon, whiter than his friend, stared at the bit of perforated yellow paper.

"I can't take it," he stammered; "my security is rotten, I tell you—"

"I want no security; I—I am beyond want," said Harrod. "Take it; I came back here for this—partly for this."

"Came back here to—to—help *me!*"

"To help you. Shannon, I had been a lonely man in life; I think you never realized how much your friendship has been to me. I had nobody—no intimacies. You never understood—you with all your friends—that I cared more for our casual companionship than for anything in the world."

Shannon bent his head. "I did not know it," he said.

Harrod raised his eyes and looked up at the starless sky; Shannon ate in silence; into his young face, already marred by dissipation, a strange light had come. And little by little order began to emerge from his whirling senses; he saw across an abyss a bridge glittering, and beyond that, beckoning to him through a white glory, all that his heart desired.

"I was at the ropes," he muttered; "how *could* you know it, Harrod? I—I never whined—"

"I know more than I did—yesterday," said Harrod, resting his pale face on one thin hand.

Shannon, nerves on edge, all aquiver, the blood racing through every vein, began to speak excitedly: "It's like a dream—one of the blessed sort—Harrod! Harrod!—the dreams I've had this last year! And I try—I try to understand what has happened—what you have done for me. I can't—I'm shaking all over, and I suppose I'm sitting here eating and drinking, but—"

He touched his glass blindly; it tipped and crashed to the floor, the breaking froth of the wine hissing on the cloth.

"Harrod! Harrod! What sort of a man am I to deserve this of you? What can I do—"

"Keep your nerve—for one thing."

"I will!—you mean *that!*" touching the stem of the new glass, which the waiter had brought and was filling. He struck the glass till it rang out a clear, thrilling, crystalline note, then struck it more sharply. It splintered with a soft splashing crash. "Is *that* all?" he laughed.

"No, not all."

"What more will you let me do?"

"One thing more. Tell them to serve coffee below."

So they passed out of the dining room, through the deserted corridors, and descended the stairway to the lounging room. It was unlighted and empty; Shannon stepped back and the elder man passed him and took the corner chair by the window—the same seat where Shannon had first seen him sitting ten years before, and where he always looked to find him after the ending of a business day. And continuing his thoughts, the younger man spoke aloud impulsively: "I remember perfectly well how we met. Do you? You had just come back to town from Bar Harbor, and I saw you stroll in and seat yourself in that corner, and, because I was sitting next you, you asked if you might include me in your order—do you remember?"

"Yes, I remember."

"And I told you I was a new member here, and you pointed out the portraits of all those dead governors of the club, and told me what good fellows they had been. I found out later that you yourself were a governor of the club."

"Yes—I was."

Harrod's shadowy face swerved toward the window, his eyes resting on the familiar avenue, empty now save for the policeman opposite, and the ragged children of the poor. In August the high tide from the slums washes Fifth Avenue, stranding a gasping flotsam at the thresholds of the absent.

"And I remember, too, what you told me," continued Shannon.

"What?" said Harrod, turning noiselessly to confront his friend.

"About that child. Do you remember? That beautiful child you saw? Don't you remember that you told me how she used to leave her governess and talk to you on the rocks—"

"Yes," said Harrod. "*That*, too, is why I came back here to tell you the rest. For the evil days have come to her, Shannon, and the years draw nigh. Listen to me."

There was a silence; Shannon, mute and perplexed, set his coffee on the window sill and leaned back, flicking the ashes from his cigar; Harrod passed his hands slowly over his hollow temples: "Her parents are dead; she is not yet twenty; she is not equipped to support herself in life; and— she is beautiful. What chance has she, Shannon?"

The other was silent.

"What chance?" repeated Harrod. "And, when I tell you that she is un- suspicious, and that she reasons only with her heart, answer me—what chance has she with a man? For you know men, and so do I, Shannon, so do I."

"Who is she, Harrod?"

"The victim of divorced parents—awarded to her mother. Let her par- ents answer; they are answering now, Shannon. But their plea is no con- cern of yours. What concerns you is the living. The child, grown to wom- anhood, is here, advertising for employment—here in New York, asking for a chance. What chance has she?"

"When did you learn this?" asked Shannon soberly.

"I learned it to-night—everything concerning her—to-night—an hour be- fore I—I met you. *That* is why I returned. Shannon, listen to me attentively; listen to every word I say. Do you remember a passing fancy you had this spring for a blue-eyed girl you met every morning on your way downtown? Do you remember that, as the days went on, little by little she came to re- turn your glance?—then your smile?—then, at last, your greeting? And do you remember, once, that you told me about it in a moment of depression— told me that you were close to infatuation, that you believed her to be everything sweet and innocent, that you dared not drift any farther, know- ing the chances and knowing the end—bitter unhappiness either way, whether in guilt or innocence—"

"I remember," said Shannon hoarsely. "But that is not—cannot be—"

"That is the girl."

"Not the child you told me of—"

"Yes."

"How—when did you know—"

"To-night. I know more than that, Shannon. You will learn it later. Now ask me again, what it is that you may do."

"I ask it," said Shannon under his breath. "What am I to do?"

For a long while Harrod sat silent, staring out of the dark window; then, "It is time for us to go."

"You wish to go out?"

"Yes; we will walk together for a little while—as we did in the old days, Shannon—only a little while, for I must be going back."

"Where are you going, Harrod?"

But the elder man had already risen and moved toward the door; and Shannon picked up his hat and followed him out across the dusky lamp-lighted street.

Into the avenue they passed under the white, unsteady radiance of arc lights which drooped like huge lilies from stalks of bronze; here and there the front of some hotel lifted like a cliff, its window-pierced façade pulsating with yellow light, or a white marble mass, cold and burned out, spread a sea of shadow over the glimmering asphalt. At times the lighted lamps of cabs flashed in their faces; at times figures passed like spectres; but into the street where they were now turning were neither lamps nor people nor sound, nor any light, save, far in the obscure vista, a dull hint of lightning edging the west.

Twice Shannon had stopped, peering at Harrod, who neither halted nor slackened his steady, noiseless pace; and the younger man, hesitating, moved on again, quickening his steps to his friend's side.

"Where are—are you going?"

"Do you not know?"

The color died out of Shannon's face; he spoke again, forming his words slowly with dry lips:

"Harrod, why—why do you come into this street—to-night? What do you know? *How* do you know? I tell you I—I cannot endure this—this tension—"

"*She* is enduring it."

"Good God!"

"Yes, God is good," said Harrod, turning his haggard face as they halted. "Answer me, Shannon, where are we going?"

"To—her. You know it! Harrod! Harrod! How did you know? I—I did not know myself until an hour before I met you; I had not seen her in weeks—I had not dared to—for all trust in self was dead. To-day, downtown, I faced the crash and saw across to-morrow the end of all. Then, in my journey hellward to-night, just at dusk, we passed each other, and before I understood what I had done we were side by side. And almost instantly—I don't know how—she seemed to sense the ruin before us both—for mine was heavy on my soul, Harrod, as I stood, measuring damnation with smiling eyes—at the brink of it, there. And she knew I was adrift at last."

He looked up at the house before him. "I said I would come. She neither assented nor denied me, nor asked a question. But in her eyes, Harrod, I saw what one sees in the eyes of children, and it stunned me.... What shall I do?"

"Go to her and look again," said Harrod. "*That* is what I have come back to ask of you. Good-by."

He turned, his shadowy face drooping, and Shannon followed to the avenue. There, in the white outbreak of electric lamps, he saw Harrod again as he had always known him, a hint of a smile in his worn eyes, the well-shaped mouth edged with laughter, and he was saying: "It's all in a lifetime, Shannon—and more than you suspect—much more. You have not told me her name yet?"

"I do not know it."

"Ah, she will tell you if you ask! Say to her that I remember her there on the sea rocks. Say to her that I have searched for her always, but that it was only to-night I knew what to-morrow she shall know—and you, Shannon, you, too, shall know. Good-by."

"Harrod! wait. Don't—don't go—"

He turned and looked back at the younger man with that familiar gesture he knew so well.

It was final, and Shannon swung blindly on his heel and entered the street again, eyes raised to the high lighted window under which he had halted a moment before. Then he mounted the steps, groped in the vestibule for the illuminated number, and touched the electric knob. The door swung open noiselessly as he entered, closing behind him with a soft click.

Up he sped, mounting stair on stair, threading the narrow hallways, then upward again, until of a sudden she stood confronting him, bent forward, white hands tightening on the banisters.

Neither spoke. She straightened slowly, fingers relaxing from the polished rail. Over her shoulders he saw a lamplighted room, and she turned and looked backward at the threshold and covered her face with both hands.

"What is it?" he whispered, bending close to her. "Why do you tremble?

You need not. There is nothing in all the world you need fear. Look into my eyes. Even a child may read them now."

Her hands fell from her face and their eyes met, and what she read in his, and he in hers, God knows, for she swayed where she stood, lids closing; yielding hands and lips and throat and hair. She cried, too, later, her hands on his shoulders where he knelt beside her, holding him at arm's length from her fresh young face to search his for the menace she once had read there. But it was gone—that menace she had read and vaguely understood, and she cried a little more, one arm around his head pressed close to her side.

"From the very first—the first moment I saw you," he said under his breath, answering the question aquiver on her lips—lips divinely merciful, repeating the lovers' creed and the confession of faith for which, perhaps, all souls in love are shriven in the end.

"Naida! Naida!"—for he had learned her name and could not have enough of it—"all that the world holds for me of good is here, circled by my arms. Not mine the manhood to win out, alone—but there is a man who came to me to-night and stood sponsor for the falling soul within me.

"How he knew my peril and yours, God knows. But he came like Fate and held his buckler before me, and he led me here and set a flaming sword before your door—the door of the child he loved—there on the sea rocks ten years ago. Do you remember? He said you would. And he is no archangel—this man among men, this friend with whom, unknowing, I have this night wrestled face to face. His name is Harrod."

"*My* name!" She stood up straight and pale, within the circle of his arms; he rose, too, speechless, uncertain—then faced her, white and appalled.

She said: "He—he followed us to Bar Harbor. I was a child, I remember. I hid from my governess and talked with him on the rocks. Then we went away. I—I lost my father." Staring at her, his stiffening lips formed a word, but no sound came.

"Bring him to me!" she whispered. "How can he know I am here and stay away! Does he think I have forgotten? Does he think shame of me? Bring him to me!"

She caught his hands in hers and kissed them passionately; she framed his face in her small hands of a child and looked deep, deep into his eyes: "Oh, the happiness you have brought! I love you! You with whom I am to enter Paradise! Now bring him to me!"

Shaking, amazed, stunned in a whirl of happiness and doubt, he crept down the black stairway, feeling his way. The doors swung noiselessly; he was almost running when he turned into the avenue. The trail of white lights starred his path; the solitary street echoed his haste, and now he sprang into the wide doorway of the club, and as he passed, the desk clerk leaned forward, handing him a telegram. He took it, halted, breathing heavily, and asked for his friend.

"Mr. Harrod?" repeated the clerk. "Mr. Harrod has not been here in a month, sir."

"What? I dined with Mr. Harrod here at eight o'clock!" he laughed.

"Sir? I—I beg your pardon, sir, but you dined here alone to-night—"

"Send for the steward!" broke in Shannon impatiently, slapping his open palm with the yellow envelope. The steward came, followed by the butler, and to a quick question from the desk clerk, replied: "Mr. Harrod has not been in the club for six weeks."

"But I dined with Mr. Harrod at eight! Wilkins, did you not serve us?"

"I served you, sir; you dined alone—" The butler hesitated, coughed discreetly; and the steward added: "You ordered for two, sir—"

Something in the steward's troubled face silenced Shannon; the butler ventured: "Beg pardon, sir, but we—the waiters thought you might be—ill, seeing how you talked to yourself and called for ink to write upon the cloth and broke two glasses, laughing like—"

Shannon staggered, turning a ghastly visage from one to another. Then his dazed gaze centered upon the telegram crushed in his hand, and shaking from head to foot, he smoothed it out and opened the envelope.

But it was purely a matter of business; he was requested to come to Bar Harbor and identify a useless check, drawn to his order, and perhaps aid to identify the body of a drowned man in the morgue.

CHAPTER IX

THE SWASTIKA

This is rather a curious story—not nearly as artistic as if it were fiction. Fact seldom is artistic.

One thing is certain: Hildreth had never before heard of a swastika; he had heard of Judge Grey, one of the Mixed Tribunal, and he knew that the Sarna came from that magistrate as a wedding gift to his father; but he never for one moment connected anything that ever happened in the Orient with his stenographer and private secretary. Nor did he suspect—but this story is running away from me backward.

Reclining in his uncle's emblazoned armchair, the tips of his fingers joined, young Hildreth gazed meditatively at the ceiling through the drifting haze of his cigar. On the ceiling several delicately tinted Cupids were attempting to asphyxiate one another with piles of roses. The room and its furniture also were gayly ornamental after the style popularly imputed to Louis XIV, that monarch being in no condition to deny the accusation. There was a view through one door into a rococo library, through another into a breakfast room, and through the windows into a snowstorm at Thirtieth Street and Fifth Avenue. However, the ensemble did not appear illogical if you turned your back to the window; besides, there was the stenographer to look at. But Hildreth was gazing fixedly at the ceiling through the stratified mist from his cigar.

The youthful stenographer, dimpled chin on hand, drummed softly with her pencil tip and watched him sidewise out of two very beautiful eyes. Her cuffs were as immaculate as her cool, white skin; her head, with its thick, bright hair, harmonized with other pretty things; and I do not think that Louis XIV would have repudiated her, at any rate.

Hildreth blew ring after ring of smoke at the ceiling, passing his hand, at intervals, through his hair, which was rather short and inclined to curl.

"Miss Grey," he said, "can't you think of anything else that rhymes with 'tin'?"

"Gin, din, thin," suggested the stenographer, referring to a rhyming dictionary.

"We've used 'din' and 'thin' already in the second verse; don't you remember? And we can't use 'gin' in any combination whatever; I've tried it. Isn't there anything else you can think of?"

"Sin?" she inquired demurely.

"'Sin,'" he repeated. "'Sin' sounds interesting. We need something to flavor the poem. Do you believe that you and I could make any proper use of 'sin'?"

She appeared doubtful.

"Let us see, anyway. Read what you've taken," he said, composing himself to listen to his own lines with the modest resignation of the true poet.

And the girl sorted her notes and read softly:

> "Behold them packed so snug within
> Their air-tight box of shining tin—
>   Hildreth's Honey Wafers!
>
> "Ready for breakfast, lunch or din-
> Ner; crisp and fresh and sweet and thin—
>   Hildreth's Honey Wafers!"

She raised her blue eyes, looking at him inquiringly over the penciled sheets of manuscript.

"There ought to be another verse," he mused.

"Don't you think so?"

"I think two verses of this kind are sufficient, Mr. Hildreth."

"You are mistaken; the poem is still incomplete. The first verse, you see, is an impression—a sort of word-picture of the tin box—a kind of prologue to prepare people for what is inside the box in the second verse. In the second I explain that Hildreth's Honey Wafers are all ready to eat, and I excite people's appetites. Now, the third verse must gratify them. Don't you see?"

"Is it not good advertising to break off abruptly and leave the public hungry?"

"No; that's only good literature; but in advertising you must not leave your public discontented. People like to look at pictures of other people who are enjoying something to repletion—pitching into a generous trough of breakfast food, or pausing to savor the delicious after-effects of a nerve tonic. Besides," he added moodily, puffing his cigar, "my uncle requires three verses, and that settles it. What was that rhyme you suggested?"

"I—I ventured to suggest 'sin.'"

"'Sin,'" he repeated thoughtfully, pinching his chin and staring at the snowy roofs across Thirtieth Street. "Well, how would this do for the third verse?

> "They invigorate the hair and clear the skin,
> And promote happiness in this world of sin—
> Hildreth's Honey Wa—"

"But you have the meter all wrong again," she expostulated. "You never pay any attention to the meter."

"Oh, you can fix that as you fixed the other verses!"

"Besides, is it really true that Hildreth's Honey Wafers do all those things?"

He began an elaborate argument to prove that falling hair and poor complexion were caused by improper nourishment, and that the wafers were proper nourishment; but presently his voice dwindled to a grumble. He relighted his cigar, looking at her askance.

"We might say," he resumed, "using poetic license:

> "Into this world of crime and sin
> Like an angel above was wafted the box of tin;
> Hildreth's Ho—"

She shook her head:

"Why not?" he asked.

"You can't compare a tin box to an angel above—and you can't waft a tin box, you know—"

"Yes, I can. Poets' license—"

"That is one of the troubles with your verses, Mr. Hildreth—there is so much license and so little—so—little—"

"You are rather rough on me," he said, coloring up.

"I don't mean to be; I only try to help you."

"I know it; you are very kind—very amiable. I am perfectly aware that a stenographer's duties do not include literary criticism. I ought to be ashamed to ask your aid, but if I don't have it I'm done for."

"But I give it most freely, Mr. Hildreth."

"I know you do, and I'm also aware that I am imposing on you most shamefully. After this week we'll let my verses go as I compose them. It will probably put me out of business, but I can't help that."

"Mr. Hildreth, we simply cannot let your verses go unedited."

He looked at her for a moment in silence. "Can't you stand my verses?" he inquired. And, as she made no reply: "If you can't—if they are really as bad as that, why, the public is going to recoil, too, and I'll doubtless ruin the business for my uncle. He has no more idea of good poetry than I have. I'll ruin him; and our rivals, The Bunsen's Baby Biscuit Company, will call me blessed!"

"Your uncle writes you that he likes the advertising verses you send him," she interrupted cheerily. "He tells you that the verses have made the wafers worth a fortune."

"Yes, but you always have revised my verses, and he doesn't know that. Every poem I've done for the Honey Wafers Company you've revised. It is you who have made them sell all over this continent."

"What of it?" she answered, amused, "as long as your uncle is satisfied. I don't mind the trouble of editing your verses—truly I don't." She rested her cheek on her wrist, playing the while with her pencil. "I am very happy to do what I can, Mr. Hildreth. Shall we try once more?"

She seemed to grow more disturbingly pretty every day; he permitted himself to look at her long enough to remember that he had something else to do. "Din, pin, gin, sin," he repeated sullenly. "What the mischief am I to write, anyway?"

"I don't think we can use 'sin,' do you?" she asked, lifting her blue eyes.

Perhaps he found inspiration in them; he looked at them hard; an inward struggle set his mouth in an uncompromising line. And this is what he evolved:

> "Bright as blue eyes that are innocent of sin
> Is the box of tin they're packed in—
> Hildreth's Honey W—"

"You *can't* compare a tin box to blue eyes, Mr. Hildreth! You surely must admit that."

"Tin is bright, isn't it? Blue eyes are bright, aren't they? Well, if one's bright and the others are—"

She shook her head slowly; her eyes had softened to a violet tint. He noticed that phenomenon, but he did not know that he had noticed it. His brows met in a frown of intense intellectual concentration; for five full minutes he remained rigid in the agony of composition, then, with a long breath, he delivered himself of another verse:

> "Soft as the color of blue violets that grow in
> The woods, is perfume from the box of tin!
> Hil—"

"Oh, dear!" said the stenographer with a sudden little indrawing of her breath.

"If you want to laugh," he said, flushing, "go ahead. I'm not sensitive."

"I had no desire to laugh, Mr. Hildreth; it's far beyond a laughing matter."

He regarded her gloomily, relighted his cigar, and gazed out of the frosty window. After a moment a smile twitched his mouth.

"I suppose it's not good—that last idea about ingrowing violets—"

She laughed: she could not help it; he laughed, too.

"How long have we been working together?" he asked, leaning back in his chair. He knew, but he wanted to know whether *she* knew.

She knew, but she pretended to think very hard before answering, laying her pencil thoughtfully across her lips, immersed in calculation.

"It must be nearly a month, Mr. Hildreth."

"Impossible!" he exclaimed, pretending surprise.

"Almost," she insisted. "Let me see; I came to you on the fifth—"

"The ninth," he said quickly. He was easily beguiled.

"*Was* it the ninth?" she asked wonderingly—though what there was to wonder at is not clear, the date signalizing nothing in particular except the day they first laid eyes on one another. "I believe it was the ninth, after all. That would make it almost a month—"

"Exactly a month," he said triumphantly. "This is our first anniversary—

and *you* didn't know it!"

He stopped; he hadn't meant to use words of that sort. People employ such expressions for other matters, not to commemorate the date of a purely business engagement.

"What you mean to say, Mr. Hildreth, is that I have been in your employment exactly a month," she said with amiable indifference.

"Exactly," he repeated, opening the inlaid cover of a rococo desk and bringing forth a package. Then he rose to his feet and made her a bow, full of the charm of good breeding: "May I venture to offer a little gift in memory of the fortunate event?"

She stood up, surprised, quiet, a trifle perplexed.

"What fortunate event, Mr. Hildreth?"

"The annivers—the—pleasant occasion—" He floundered, and she let him. It irritated him to flounder, for his intentions were above reproach.

"What I mean to say is simple enough," he snapped. "You've practically written my poems for me, and you didn't have to, but if you hadn't I either should have ruined my uncle's business or lost my job, and I'm grateful, and I wanted to give you something to show it—these books—"

She took them, a trifle uncertain, but guided by inherited instinct. She looked at the beautifully bound and dreadfully expensive volumes. The constraint lasted only a second; she thanked him, glanced at the title-page, where he had written the date and her name, but not his own. His good taste appealing to her, she smiled at him in a delightfully friendly fashion; and the charm of the transfiguration so occupied him that, finding himself staring, he neutralized the rudeness by closing his eyes with a wise look as though intent on pursuing elusive rhymes for commercial purposes.

She seated herself at her little flyaway gilded desk once more; he relapsed into his chair and sat there drumming with his fingers on the golden foliations of the carved arms.

She had, instinctively, picked up her pencil and pad, ready for dictation when the sacred fire should blaze up in him. The fire, however, appeared to be out. There was not a sputter.

"And in all this time," he mused, continuing his cogitations aloud, "you have never asked me why, in the name of common decency, I insisted on trying to be a poet!"

As she made no reply:

"Have you?" he repeated.

"Of *course* I haven't—"

"Is it because you are too civil to hurt a man's feelings?"

"It is because I am employed by you, Mr. Hildreth—"

"Because you are employed by me? Nonsense! That's no reason why I should torture a cultivated ear with unspeakable rhymes. I wonder, Miss Grey, what you really think of me?"

She could have told him that she didn't think of him at all except in a business sense, which would have been an untruth, but the proper answer for him. She thought of several answers, all reserved, indifferent, discouraging the faintest hint of intimacy, and therefore suitable. Then she said: "Would it interest you to know what your stenographer thinks about you?"

He said it would interest him excessively, and he desired information.

"I think," she said, not looking at him but at her pencil, with which she was tracing arabesques on the pad, "I think that you could do some things much better than—others. Oh, dear! that sounds like Tupper—but it's true."

"You mean I'd make a better bandit, for example, than I do a poet?"

"I don't know what qualification you have for the career you suggest," she replied demurely.

"I understand you," he said; "it's as simple as those profound lines:

> "'A fool is bent upon a twig, but wise men shun a bandit;
> Which is really very clever if you only understand it.'"

That's what you intended to say, wasn't it?"

They were both laughing, she with more reserve than he.

"If a bandit's life is not a happy one, what must a poet's life resemble?" he demanded. "Why, it's a perfect—but the word is inadequate, Miss Grey. Did you ever for one mad moment suppose that I wrote rhymes for the pleasure it gave me?"

"No," she said, "I didn't."

"Or did you imagine I was infatuated with the notion that my rhymes gave pleasure to others?"

She laughed such a care-free laugh—so sweet, so entirely gay and innocent—that he said impulsively: "I wish you'd let me tell you how it is. I do so hate to appear a fool to you."

Something checked her mirth, yet it scarcely could be what he said, for his speech and manner were quite free from offense.

"May I tell you?" he asked, conscious of the shadow of constraint between them.

There was something in her silent acquiescence which hinted: "My time is yours, Mr. Hildreth; but, considering the strictly business footing of our relations, hadn't you better begin to make your third verse?" And no doubt the slight impatient movement of his shoulders meant: "No, I won't begin my third verse; I desire to unburden to you a soul too long misunderstood." But the interpretation of her silence and his shrug are purely speculative on my part.

"I'd quit this verse making in a moment if I could," he said; "but it's my livelihood. I always loathed poetry, even my own; but I've simply got to earn my living."

"Surely," she said, with an instinctive glance around the exceedingly ornate apartment, "it would be silly for you to give up making advertising verses for your uncle as long as—as—"

"As long as it permits me to live like this? Do you suppose that this is *my* apartment?—that anything in it belongs to me?—that my income from my wafer poetry would even pay for a single week's rent here? There's the ghastly mockery of it. Why, my salary is just twice what yours is: in other words, I divide with you every week."

She regarded him with amazement.

"Apartment, servants—everything belongs to my uncle. My uncle has views," he said, waving his hand. "Unfortunately, one of his views is how to bring up his only nephew. Just fancy a man fresh from Harvard flung neck and heels into his uncle's wafer business on thirty dollars a week!"

"Dreadful," she motioned with her lips.

"Neck and heels! He said I was to find no favors, no privileges; that I must begin at the lowest rung of the ladder, and, as he knew of nothing lower than poetry, he set me to work writing Honey Wafer ads. I'm to be promoted next year to be the artist that draws pictures for the ads. After that I shall advance through the baking, packing, and truck departments until I become a traveling salesman. Meanwhile, I've emerged from my cheap boarding house to keep his servants busy till he returns."

She sat very still, watching him with her beautiful, serious young eyes.

"Then, some day, I'm to be taken into the concern and become a partner if—"

"If?"

"If I don't marry."

"Oh!" she said faintly.

"But if I *do*—"

There was an ominous pause; then she repeated calmly:

"If you *do?*"

"I'm down and out, and he leaves about five millions to the Society for Psychical Research. A nice position for me if I should ever fall in love, isn't it?"

The pause was longer this time.

"The Society for Psychical Research," she repeated under her breath.

"Yes. You know—they investigate spooks, and tip tables, and go into trances, and see blond gentlemen coming over the ocean to marry you, and dark ladies hiding around the corner."

"Is he interested in such things—your uncle?"

"Mad about them. He's up at his country place now with a bunch of Columbia professors and Sixth Avenue clairvoyants, engaged in crystal-gazing experiments. Later he's going to lecture about 'em at Columbia University."

"What is crystal gazing?" she asked innocently.

"To tell you the truth, I don't know exactly. My uncle and a fat clairvoyant in a pink teagown sit at a table and squint into a big globe made of rock crystal; and he tells me that he can sit in his chair up there at Adrintha Lodge and see, in the crystal, everything that he wants to see—including how I'm behaving myself down here in town. He told me that if I ever—ever kissed anybody he'd see it and discharge me."

"Does he say he can see *you?*"

"He does."

"And everything you are doing?"

"Every blessed thing."

"Do you believe it?" she asked anxiously.

"No, of course not. But I let him think he has me scared to death."

She leaned forward on the table, clasping both hands under her chin.

"Is that what keeps you on your best behavior?"

It was rather a curious thing to say.

"Suppose," she added, "that your uncle was looking into his crystal at this very minute. I think, if you please, we'd better stop talking and begin our work.... Don't you? I think we ought at least to *look* as though we were busy."

"You don't believe that he could see us, do you?" demanded Hildreth.

"No; ... but suppose he could? Don't you think I'd better copy your verses—or be doing something—"

She hastily placed a sheet of paper in the machine, slid it into place, and struck several keys. It was quite unconscious on her part, but when, a moment later, she turned the sheet over she found that she had written his name about sixty times. The portent of this, however, did not then strike her.

Somewhere in the room little silvery chimes sounded the hour.

"Can it be two o'clock already?" she exclaimed.

He examined his watch in assumed surprise.

"Why, we are just in time!" he said hazily.

"Yes, Mr. Hildreth—in time for what?"

"You—you won't be offended—where anything but offense is meant—will you?"

She had risen to face him; he, rather red about the ears, began by making a mess of what he was saying; and when she had grasped the import of it she let him go on making a mess until his irritation straightened out matters.

"It's only that you've been so kind to help me do all that advertising poetry, and I'm so tremendously grateful, and it's our first annivers—our—er—the occasion— You know what I mean. So please stay to luncheon. Will you?"

"Please don't ask me, Mr. Hildreth—"

"Yes, I will! You simply can't be offended; you simply cannot mistake my attitude, my meaning—"

"I am not offended. You are very thoughtful—amiable—but I think I ought to go—"

"Our anni—the date, you know—just to celebrate a purely business arrangement which has been so delight—so profitable to me, I mean—"

"No, I could not stay, Mr. Hildreth—"

"But it's partly for business purposes," he explained anxiously. "Why, you must know, Miss Grey, that more business is transacted at luncheon than before or after. That's what great financiers do; they say to the head of a department: 'Lunch with me, Mr. So-and-so.' And Mr. So-and-so understands at once."

"Does that great financier ever say: 'Lunch with me, *Miss* So-and-so'?"

"Yes, often and often. And *she* understands!"

"Are you sure she does?"

"I am. Please let me be sure."

"Mr. Hildreth, I should—should like to—there, I admit it! But it is not *convenable*. I know it; you know it; it is *not* the thing for us to do. I have no business here except as your stenographer. I could not accept."

"Because you are a stenographer?"

"If I were not in your employment I should not be here with you. You know that."

"But I should perhaps be at your house if—"

"You are speculating in impossibilities." She bent her head, smiling across the table at him, and dropping her hand on the books he had given her. "Your kindness must have some bounds; let it end in these bindings; I—I shall remember it with each leaf I turn." And as he said nothing, but looked rather miserable, she added: "Won't you?"

There was another interval of silence; she considered his face anew. The unhappiness in it was evident.

"Do you really want me ... to talk business?"

"I want you to stay. Will you?"

She did not answer, though a little tremor touched her lips.

"That's jolly!" he said gayly, and touched an electric button behind him. And a moment later a maid in cap and apron respectfully piloted her out of sight.

About half past two a Japanese butler served them in the colonial breakfast room, and she laughed at the little silver trifle she found beside her plate—a tiny type-machine made to hold scents in microscopic crystal vials. Her initials were engraved upon it.

"You see," he said, "*I* do not regard our poetical partnership lightly, even if you do. What you have done for me is going to enable me to enter the firm one day—aided by your editing my verses."

"I never before understood," she admitted, "why you advertised for a stenographer who was a graduate of Barnard College. And—when I applied to you I was perfectly astonished when you asked me so anxiously whether I could rhyme and draw pictures."

He examined his grape fruit and extracted a minted cherry with great care. Presently he swallowed it.

"I knew from the first instant I saw you that my chance in life had come," he observed.

"You didn't know it before you questioned me."

"Yes, I did."

"How?"

He looked up at her: "I don't know *how* I knew it." She was apparently interested in the aroma of her wine. "But I knew it," he ended.

The vintage was doubtless worthy of the serious attention she gave it.

"Do you know what wine that is?" he asked, amused.

"Yes; it is Sarna," she said simply.

"How did you know?" he exclaimed in amazement.

She lifted the glass with a pretty gesture: "Are you so astonished that your stenographer knows the rarest wine in the world—and the legend concerning it? A most inappropriate wine for such a luncheon, Mr. Hildreth—"

"You are a constant series of endless astonishments to me," he said. "Where on earth you ever heard of Sarna—and how you should have known it when you saw it—this wine so rare that but one in ten thousand experts ever heard of it—"

"Why did you have it served?" she asked directly. "Do you know what this wine of Sarna signifies? Do you know every drop is worth ten times its weight in gold? Do you know there are not three other bottles of it known in the world?"

"I knew all that. I believed that Sarna alone was worthy of—of"—he met her level gaze—"of our first anniversary."

"No; it is inappropriate," she replied steadily. "Do you not know the legend?"

"It is the only wine not forbidden by the Koran. Is that what you mean? Or do you mean—" He hesitated.

"Yes, that. The last Khedive emptied the last glass of the last but three bottles remaining in all the world while his bride's lips were still wet with the dew of Sarna. It is the custom of Emperors and Sultans—ask me for how long, and my answer is: as long as the saros; compute it, oh, Heaven-born!" She crossed her pretty hands below her throat, a smile, half gay, half tender, parting her lips.

"How did *you* know such things?" he asked.

"My father was a judge of the Mixed Tribunal," she answered gravely. "My mother was married there; I was born in Cairo."

"Fate!" he said excitedly—"sheer Fate! My father was the ex-Confederate, Hildreth Pasha, of the Khedival Court! The Sarna—that bottle cradled there—came from a judge of the Mixed Tribunal! Shall not their children touch the same glass?"

They both were excited, flushed, a little bewildered.

"Do you know the custom?" he asked recklessly.

"Y-es." She held up one slender finger; her mother's betrothal ring, set with the diamond scarab, sparkled on the white skin; and she drew the thin circlet from her finger and held it suspended over the glass of golden Sarna. The single brilliant flashed and flashed as though the sacred beetle were struggling to be free.

"Shall I?"

"Try it," he laughed. "Who knows what sign of fortune the dead Sultans may send?"

"They—they only send a sign to—to brides—"

"I know it. Try!"

"But the mechanism is unknown to me; it is not possible that a bath of this scented wine could start it—"

"Try!"

There was a glimmer, a little clinking splash in the slim wineglass. They inspected the ring lying in the amber wine; they glanced at one another rather foolishly. Then, looking at him, she raised the glass, tasted, passed it to him. He tasted, his eyes on her, and set the half-empty glass before her.

"I—I believe there's something happening to that ring," said Hildreth suddenly, rising and passing around the table to her side.

Breathless, they bent over the glass, heads close together.

"Doesn't it look to you as though that diamond scarab were moving?" he said in a low voice.

"Yes; but it can't be—*how* can it—"

"Look!"

"Oh—h!" she whispered—"see! It—it's alive! It is unfolding arms and legs like a crab."

"What on earth—" he stammered, but got no further, for the girl caught him by the arm: "Look! Look! *The swastika!* It means fortune! It means—it means—"

His hand shook as he lifted the glass and reversed it. A shower of perfumed wine sprinkled the lace centerpiece; the mystic swastika, glittering, magnificent, fell heavily upon the mahogany—a dull, gem-incrusted lump of purest gold.

"What is it?" he gasped. "I thought it was alive, like one of those jeweled Egyptian beetles! I thought those things were legs!"

"It is the swastika," she whispered, laying it in her pink palm. "Who wears it shall always—" She stopped short, hesitated, then the color in her face deepened, and she looked up over her shoulder at him. "Will you do something for me?" she asked.

"Yes."

"Wear this. Will you?" She drew her tiny handkerchief from her sleeve, tore a shred of cambric from it, passed it through the swastika, and, before he knew what she meant to do, had tied it to his lapel.

"Just to see what happens," she said, laughing almost hysterically. If there was the slightest chance of any luck in the world she wished it to be his. It was all she had to give.

"You resign your chance of fortune to me?" he asked curiously—and, as she only nodded: "There is but one happiness Fortune can bring me. Are you willing to trust it to me?"

Before she could reply a maid appeared with a telegram; he asked her pardon, and opened it. Twice he read it, read it again, nodded a dazed dismissal to the maid, read it again very carefully, and finally, with a smile that was somewhat sickly, handed it across the table to her.

What she read was this:

> ADRINTHA LODGE,
> MOHAWK COUNTY, NEW YORK.
> JOHN HILDRETH: I know what you're up to, and you had better stop.
>
> PETER HILDRETH.

"Peter Hildreth," she repeated blankly.

"My uncle."

"But—but what does he mean?"

"That's what I'd like to know," said the young fellow uneasily.

"Is he in the habit of telegraphing you?"

"No, he isn't; he never did such a thing."

She turned the yellow leaf of paper over and over thoughtfully. Then he suddenly encountered her disturbed gaze.

"He says that he knows what you're up to, and you'd better stop," she said. "What are you up to, Mr. Hildreth?"

"Up to? Absolutely nothing! I'm fairly tingling with the consciousness of innocence, righteousness, and good intentions. *I* don't know what that old crank means—any more than you know."

"I—I am dreadfully afraid that *I* know what he means."

"What?"

"I think he means me."

"You! Why?"

"Because I'm here—here lunching with you. He might draw—dreadful conclusions."

"What on earth do you mean, Miss Grey? He never even heard of you. How can he know you are here?"

"Suppose—suppose he is—is looking into his crystal!"

A sudden silence fell, lasting until the coffee was served.

"It is nonsense to suppose that people can do such things," said Hildreth abruptly.

"What things?" she asked, watching him set fire to a cigarette.

"Such things as looking into crystals and seeing nephews. Anyway, what is there to see?" He waved his hands as though scattering suspicion to the four winds. "What is there to see except a future financier and his principal chief of department at a purely business luncheon—"

"With silver souvenirs and Sarna," she murmured.

They laughed, feeling the constraint subsiding once more.

"Please let us talk a little business—for form's sake, if nothing else," she said.

"All right; your salary is to be increased—"

"Mr. Hildreth, you cannot afford any extravagances, and you know it."

"I am not going to let you write my verses, and profit by it to your exclusion! Besides, this swastika is going to enable me to afford anything, I understand."

"But you already divide your salary with me. You can't do more!"

"Yes, I can."

"No, no, no! Wait until you are promoted to be the advertising artist. Wait until the swastika begins to help us—you."

"No; because then you'll have to draw all my pictures for me, and your salary must be increased again."

"At that rate," she said, laughing, "I'll be half partner when you are."

"Full partner—if the swastika knows its business. I—I—wish he didn't have that crystal up there at Adrintha. I've a mind to buy a rabbit's foot. With a rabbit's foot and a swastika we ought to checkmate any crystal-gazing, pink-eyed clairvoyants."

"But—what have they to do with us?" she asked gently.

What he was about to say he only half divined—for she was bewilderingly pretty—and perhaps she dimly foresaw it, too, for they both flushed with a sudden constraint that was abruptly broken by the entrance of the maid with another telegram.

"What the deuce—" stammered Hildreth, tearing open the yellow envelope; and he read:

ADRINTHA LODGE.

JOHN HILDRETH: watching you in my crystal. If you want the Society for Psychical Research to become my heirs, do exactly what you're doing with that girl.

PETER HILDRETH.

"Is—is it anything alarming?" asked the pretty stenographer as he crumpled the paper.

"Alarming? I don't know—no! What the mischief has got into that uncle of mine?"

"Is it from *him?*" she asked, turning pale.

"Yes—it is. But if he thinks he can make me believe that he sees me in his dinky little crystal—"

"Oh, don't talk that way," she pleaded; "there may be things that we don't understand happening all the while—"

"There can't be!"

For a while she was dumb, mutely refusing to be reassured, and presently, rising from the table, they passed into the gay little room where her desk stood.

The fire was glowing very brightly in the carved fireplace of golden and pearl-tinted onyx. He drew up his uncle's great chair for her; she shook her head and looked meaningly at her pad and pencil, but after a silent struggle with indecision and inclination she seated herself by the gilt fender, pretty hands folded in acquiescence.

"Now," he said, "let us speak of those things that *have* come true."

"What has come true, Mr. Hildreth?"

"You."

The slightest of rose tints touched her cheeks. "Did you believe me unreal?" she asked.

He was leaning forward, looking up into her face, which reflected the pink light of the fire. And what he started to say Heaven alone knows, for his voice was dreadfully unsteady. However, it ceased quickly enough when the maid knocked rather loudly and presented a third telegram to her disconcerted master; and this was what he read:

> ADRINTHA LODGE.
>
> JOHN HILDRETH: If you kiss that girl you're talking to I'll disinherit you.
>
> PETER HILDRETH.

Stunned, the young man sat for a moment, vacant eyes fixed on the writing that alternately blurred and sprang into dreadful distinctness under his gaze. Presently he heard a voice not much like his own saying: "It's nonsense; things like this don't happen in 1907 in the borough of Manhattan. Why, that's Fifth Avenue out there, and there's Thirtieth Street, too; besides, the town's full of police; and they pinch star-readers and astrologers these days. Anyway, we have the swastika, and it will put any Sixth Avenue astrologer out of business—"

"I—I don't think I quite understand you," faltered the girl.

He looked at her; the scared expression died out.

"I'll get my uncle on the long-distance 'phone in a moment," he said irritably. "Then we'll clear up this business. Meanwhile—" He twisted up the telegram as though to cast it on the coals.

"Let me see it," she said calmly.

"I—it is—no—I can't—"

"Then it concerns *me?*"

He was silent.

"Very well," she said. "Don't burn it; leave it for a moment."

He laid the telegram on the arm of his chair. "It's more crystal-gazing," he said, trying to laugh easily, and failing. "It is rather extraordinary, too. But—see here, Miss Grey, it's utter nonsense to believe that my uncle can actually see us here in this room!

"I concede that it is rather odd, even, perhaps, exceedingly remarkable," he added slowly; "but I cannot believe that *my* uncle, two hundred miles north of us, can see you and me in his confounded crystal. My explanation of his telegrams is this: he has merely taken the precaution, at intervals, to try to frighten me, assuming that I am in mischief. It's coincidence—"

"Mr. Hildreth!"

"Not that I admit for one moment that you and I *are* in mischief!" he explained hastily.

"But *I* admit it. It is all wrong, and we both know it. If I am not here officially I ought not to be here at all."

"Can't I talk to you except on business?"

"Why should you?"

"Because I want to—because it is pleasant—because it's the pleasantest thing that has ever come into my life!"

"That cannot be," she said, paling. "You know many people, you go everywhere—everywhere that I do not—"

"If I were not an advertising poet at thirty dollars a week," he said, "I'd not care where my uncle left his millions. I'd do what I pleased—what I ought to do—what any man with a grain of sense would do."

"What would you do, Mr. Hildreth?"

"Make love to the girl I love, and not be scared away like a rabbit!"

She was still paler when she said: "Are you—in love, then?"

"Yes; but I can't tell her."

She was silent, staring into the fire.

"I can't tell her, can I? I have nothing to offer—nothing except a prospect of losing my expectations. A man can't tell a girl that he loves her under such circumstances, can he?"

"I—don't know."

"Do you suppose a—a girl like that would wait for him—until he got into the firm?"

"If she loved him," said Miss Grey in a low voice, "there is absolutely no telling what that girl might do."

"Suppose," he said carelessly, "for the sake of illustration, that I was, at this moment, with that girl. For example"—he waved his hand airily—"for example, suppose you were that girl. Now, suppose that I told her I loved her; do you imagine that uncle of mine could see what I was about—if I worked the swastika on him vigorously?"

"I don't know," she said, staring at the fire, "how to work the swastika."

"If you—if you would consent to aid me—just a little," he ventured, "I could soon prove whether it was safe to speak to the—the other girl."

"How, Mr. Hildreth?"

"By just—just pretending that you were that other girl."

"You mean that you might practice a declaration—test it—on me? Just to see how it might affect your uncle?"

"Yes," he said eagerly, "and if my uncle doesn't telegraph again that he disowns me, why, I'll know that his other telegrams were merely coincidences!"

"And if he *does* telegraph that he has seen—everything—in his crystal?"

"Why—we'll have to wait—"

"The *other* girl and you? I see. You and I can truthfully deny our apparent guilt, can't we? ... I will do what I can, Mr. Hildreth."

She stood up, one little hand on the back of the chair. He hesitated, then picked up the last telegram, opened it, and handed it to her, reading it again over her shoulder:

"If you kiss that girl you're talking to I'll disinherit you."

A bright blush stained her skin.

"It is only—only to test his power," he managed to say, but the thumping of his heart jarred his speech and scared him into silence.

"You—is it necessary to kiss me?"

"Yes—absolutely."

She met his gaze, standing erect, one hand on the chair. Then she drew a long breath as he lifted her hand; her eyes closed. He said: "I love you— I loved you the moment I saw you—a month ago!" This was no doubt a mistake; he was mixing the two girls. "What do I care for a crystal-squinting uncle, or for those accursed Honey Wafer verses? If he's looking at us now let us convince him; shall we—sweetheart?"

She unclosed her eyes. "Am I to play my part when you speak to me like that? I don't know how—"

"Do what I do," he stammered; and he encircled her slender waist and kissed her until, cheeks aflame, she swayed a moment in his arms, freed herself, and sank breathless into the chair, covering her face. And he knelt beside her by the gilt fender, his lips to her fingers, stammering words that almost stunned her and left her faint with their passion and sweetness:

"You must have known that it was you I loved—that *you* were that *other* girl. You must have seen it a thousand times!"

She was crying silently; she could not speak, but one arm tightened around his neck in tremulous assent.

The telephone bell had been ringing for some time in their ears, deaf to all sounds except each other's whispers; but at length he stumbled to his feet, cleared his eyes of enchantment, and made his way across the room to the receiver.

"What the deuce is the matter?"

"Who?"

"Oh, is that you, Uncle Peter?"

"Yes, I did get your telegrams, but I thought—"

"You mean to say you can *see us now?*"

"No, I don't deny it; I did kiss her."

"Because I love her!"

"I can't help it; you can do as you please. And I may as well tell you that I'm not afraid of your professors, or clairvoyants, or your crystals, because I've got a swastika—"

"Yes, a swastika!"

"You don't know what a swastika is? Well, let me tell you it's about five thousand times more powerful than a rabbit's foot.... What? ... Yes, I'll hold the wire till you look it up in the dictionary."
A throbbing silence. Then:
"Yes, Uncle Peter, I'm here."

"Very well; I'm sorry you're angry, and I regret that you're not afraid of the swastika. I am quite willing to trust to it; the swastika gave me the girl I love. And, by the way, Uncle Peter, didn't you write me that my advertising poems made a fortune for you out of your wafers? ... All right; I only wanted to confess that she, not I, wrote them."

"Don't believe it? Why, I could no more write those charming verses than *you* could!"

"You may imagine that with her talent and mine, and the swastika working away for us, we are not going to starve—"

"That's just what we intend to do. Bunsen's Baby Biscuit Company will appreciate our talents. Besides, she can draw—"

"You can call it blackmail if you choose. But what do you offer us to refuse advances from Bunsen?"

"No, I won't consider it. My price is full partnership in the Hildreth's Honey Wafer Company, a cordial blessing from you, use of your apartments for a year, and the same old cozy place in your testament."

"Yes, in return we will write your poetry and draw your pictures for you. And, besides, we'll name after you our first—"
"Jack!" she exclaimed, aghast.
"Dearest, for Heaven's sake let me deal with him!" whispered Hildreth; then he shouted through the transmitter:
"Is it all right, Uncle Peter?"

"I promise you—*we* promise you that we will name him Peter! If you don't, by Heaven, I'll name him Bunsen—"

"That's all right, but we're desperate. Peter or Bunsen; take your choice!"

"Yes; and I'll have his photograph taken for Bunsen, and under it I'll print: 'A Bunsen's Baby Biscuit Boy!'"

"Don't use such language; they'll cut us off!"

"What?"

"Good! All right, Uncle Peter, you're a brick. But—just one thing more; please put that crystal away for an hour or two—"

"Because we'd like a little privacy!"

"Of course I shall. Long engagements are foolish—"
"Jack!"
"Dearest, you know they are," he said, turning toward her. "Shall I tell him in a week?"
Her blue eyes filled; again the little tremor of acquiescence set her red mouth quivering.
"In a week, Uncle Peter!" he shouted.

"What? I'll ask her. Hold the wire."
And to her he said: "Sweetheart, our kind Uncle Peter desires to say something civil to you. I—I think it may be something about a check. Will you speak to him?"
She rose and came toward him; he handed her the receiver; she raised her

head, and he bent his. They kissed—while his uncle waited.

Then she raised the receiver to her pretty ear, and said, very softly:
"Hello! Hello, Uncle Peter!"

CHAPTER X

THE GHOST OF CHANCE

As young Leeds entered the imposing bronze and marble portico of the Algonquin Trust Building, where he had a studio on the top floor, the elevator boy handed him a telegram and he opened it with instinctive foreboding of trouble. Meanwhile, the Ghost of Chance, which had followed him into the building, looked over his shoulder at the telegram.

There was evidently trouble enough in it; he had turned rather white as he stood there, eyes riveted on the yellow paper. Minute after minute sped; the elevators whizzed up and down in their gilded cages; people passed and repassed; the ornamental marble pavement of the rotunda echoed the clatter of footsteps. Several people he knew nodded to him as they entered or left the elevators: an architect domiciled on the top floor in the east wing, McManus, of the Belden Building and Construction Company; young Farren, private Secretary to De Peyster Thorne, president of the great Algonquin Trust Company, and director of about everything worth directing in the five boroughs.

"Mr. Farren!" called out Leeds; and, as that suave man checked his speed, wheeled, and came back, "Mr. Farren, could I see Mr. Thorne for half a second?"

Farren's eyes narrowed thoughtfully. "If it's a favor you want to ask, don't ask it now—"

"It is, and I've got to—"

"Better not; he's in a devilish humor; he'd foreclose on his own grandmother to-day."

"But I can't wait! I'll use your telephone while you're taking my card."

Farren shrugged, turned, and led the way across the rotunda, ushered Leeds into the outer office, and took his card. Leeds went to a desk and used the telephone vigorously until Farren reappeared, nodding; and Leeds walked into the president's private room. De Peyster Thorne, handsome, rather too elaborately groomed, and ruddier of face and neck than usual, looked up to return the young man's greeting with an expressionless word and nod. He did not see the Ghost of Chance standing at Leeds's elbow.

"I'm awfully sorry," said Leeds, "but I don't see how I can finish the key panel on time, Mr. Thorne."

"Why not?" said Thorne, a darker flush mounting his heavy face and neck.

"I've a telegram this moment from my model; she's ill. I telephoned for another, but there's scarcely a chance I can get one I want. Something went wrong with the colors yesterday and I scraped out all I had done, expecting to finish to-day with a drier, dry to-morrow, and have Mr. McManus set the key panel in the ballroom Thursday morning. Now, I've probably got to spend to-day chasing up a red-haired model; and if I do, I cannot finish by Thursday. Couldn't you give me one day more?"

"Mr. Leeds," said Thorne, biting off his words unpleasantly, "a contract is a contract. Can you fulfill yours?"

"I've told you," began Leeds, astonished—for never before had Thorne looked or spoken in that way—"I told you that my model—"

"Can you keep your contract?" repeated Thorne sharply.

"There's a ghost of a chance if I can get a proper model," replied Leeds, keeping his temper.

"Then you'd better take that ghost of a chance, Mr. Leeds. On reflection it will occur to you that my housewarming can scarcely be postponed to suit your rather erratic convenience. If the key panel is not in place, the room will be as attractive as a man in evening clothes without a collar. I'd rather tear out the entire frieze, and call the contract void!—and I'll do it, too, if the contract is not fulfilled."

"Is that the language you employ in all your commercial transactions?" asked Leeds without a trace of the passion that clutched at him.

"It is. An artist is as amenable to the commercial code of responsibility as any man I deal with—I don't care a damn who he is or how he likes it.... Is there anything more I can do for you, Mr. Leeds?"

"No," said Leeds thoughtfully, "unless you choose to take a kindergarten course in the elements of decency."

Leaving the door ajar as he went out, and far too amazed and furious to notice Mr. Farren, the amused secretary, he crossed the corridor, followed by the Ghost of Chance, entered an elevator, and shot up to the top floor. Black rage and astonishment still possessed him when he met McManus in the hall, and he would have passed on with a nod and a scowl had that genial Irishman permitted.

"Phwat the divil's up now, Misther Leeds?" inquired the big contractor and builder. "I'll lay twinty to wan ye've joost come from Thorne."

Leeds laid his hand on the door knob of his studio.

"I have; I—I'm not in very good humor, Mr. McManus—" He jerked open the door and started to enter.

"Hould on!—don't be runnin' away. Sure haven't I come from him meself—an' kept me temper, too, Irish that I am! Phwat's wrong betchune you an' Misther Thorne an' the hydrant?"

"Nothing much; my model is ill and I can't promise to give you that key panel to set. Thorne said—one or two things—oh, I can't talk about it; he said one or two things—"

"Bedad, thin, he said a dozen things to me; an' me as cool as a Waldorf julep, an' he dammin' the gildin' whin I asked f'r the sivinth installment due this day. 'It's an expert I'll have f'r to examine it,' sez he. 'Projooce the wad,' sez I, 'an' afther that I'll talk talks to anny expert ye name.' An' he had to."

Leeds's heart turned heavy. "I don't know what Thorne means to do," he said. "I'm not much on contracts; I've done my best. I suppose he will rip it out if he wants to. If he does, and if he cancels the contract, it will about ruin me. I never had but four other commissions; it cost me more to execute them than I was paid."

The big Irishman studied the younger man with keen, kindly eyes. He knew what Leeds's frieze really was—a piece of work that for sheer inspired beauty had not its equal in modern mural art. He knew—even his artisans knew. And he knew, also, that in this fifth essay, a young man, of whom the public had already heard, was stepping half unconsciously into the highest place in the Western world of art. All this McManus was shrewdly aware of, and he was aware, too, that Leeds was more or less conscious of it, and that Thorne was utterly unconscious that, in his new house, the golden ballroom already contained the mural masterpiece of the twentieth century—an exquisite, gay riot of color and design, so lovely, so fresh, that, concealed under the miracle of its simplicity, the marvelous technical perfections of color, drawing, and composition were almost unnoticed in the blinding brilliancy of the *ensemble*.

"Did that red-necked madman say he'd rip it out?" inquired McManus, his fiery blue eyes aglitter.

"That's what he said. I don't know whether the work is good or bad; I'm two years stale on it. I could paint a better one now. But if he holds me to the letter of the contract and throws back two years' work on my hands, what can I do? I—I never imagined he was that sort of a man; I knew he didn't care much for painting—his architects got him to give me the work—my first commission that promised any profit—"

Something tightened in his throat, and he turned his head sharply to the window of the corridor.

"Arrah, thin," said McManus hastily, "don't be frettin'. G'wan, now, an' paint like the divil. Give him anny ould thing f'r to ploog the key. Sure, 'tis his fri'nds will tell him fasht enough the bargain he's got in a frieze—a frieze, begob! that no man twist the two poles can paint like you!—an' that's the truth, Misther Leeds, though ye don't know it, bein' modestlike an' misthrustin' av the powers God sinds ye. Ploog him up with a key panel—anny ould daub, I tell ye!—f'r to clinch the contract come pay-day! An' I'll set it accordin' to conthract Thursday comin'; an' afther he's opened his big gilt house to the millionaires he consorts with, an' afther the bunch has christened their muddy wits with the j'yful juice, go to him quietlike, yer foot in yer hand an' the tongue in the cheek o' ye, an' say modestlike: 'Wisha, sorr, me mastherpiece is not quite to me likin'; an' I'm thinkin' to add a few millions to its value wid a stroke av a badger brush.'"

The big Irishman laughed heartily and laid an enormous paw on Leeds's shoulder—a gesture so kindly that the familiarity seemed without offense.

"Phwat does the like o' youse care for Mr. Thorne an' his big red neck an' the pants o' him wid the creases, an' his collar buttoned by his valley? F'r all his scarf pin an' his shiny shoes an' his Thrust Company an' his millions, I seen a bit of a lass give him the frozen face an hour ago."

Leeds looked up curiously.

"Arrah, thin, that's what crazed him. I was there in his office discoorsin' on conthracts, pwhen the dure opened an' a young lady sthepped in—not seein' me pwhere I sat behind the dure.

"'Naida!' sez he, joompin' up, the Burrgundy flush on the face an' neck av him.

"'I came to tell you that I can't do it,' sez she, her purty face like a rose in blush. 'I'm sorry,' she sez, 'but I thought you ought to be told, an' I drove downtown in a hurry,' sez she, 'f'r to tell you,' she sez, 'that I was not in me right mind when you asked me to marry you,' sez she. 'So I'm sorry— I'm so sorry,' she sez, an' good-by!' an' wid that the breath stopped in her an' she gulped, scairtlike.

"'*Phwat!*' sez he, bitin' the worrud in two halves. An' she gulped an' shook her head.

"Wid that he began in a wild way, clane forgettin' me in the corner, me hat on me two knees; an' the young lady was a bit wild, too, bein' very young an' excited; an' there they had it like John Drew an' his leadin' lady—quietlike an' soft-spoken, but turrible as a dress-shirt drama, till she said: 'No! No! No!' wid a little sob, an' out o' the dure an' off, he afther her. Sorra the sight av her he got, with Farren hunting her, an' himself ridin' up an' down in the cages when the porther tould him she'd dodged an' gone up to the top floor."

"So that was why he was so ugly," said Leeds curiously.

"It was. He was smooth enough till the lass came in an' left him her sweet little mitten. But whin he came back, red as a bottle o' Frinch wine, an' the two eyes o' him like black holes burnt in a blanket—save us! All that was close an' hard an' mean an' sly an' bitter an' miserly came out in the man, an' the way he talked to me av honest work done wud stir the neck hair on a fightin' pup. I was wild; but I sez to meself, lave him talk his talk; it's all wan on pay-day. An' so it is, Misther Leeds; it is so. G'wan into ye're workshop, an' shpit on ye're hands, an' we'll ploog that key space by 5 P.M., come Thursday, bad cess to the bad, an' luck to the likes of us, glory be!"

Leeds stood half inside his threshold, the edge of the open door grasped in his hand, gazing thoughtfully at the floor.

"All right, McManus," he said quietly; "I'll do what I can to save my bread, but"—he looked straight at the Irishman—"it's bitter bread we learn to eat sometimes—we who are employed."

"Troth, I've swallyed worse nor that; I have so, Misther Leeds. Bide the time, sorr. An' phwin it comes!—paste him wan."

"Oh, I'll have forgotten him by that time," said Leeds, laughing, as Mc-Manus, with a significant and powerful gesture, turned on his broad heel and strode off toward his own rooms, where Kenna, his partner, had been making frantic signals to him for the last five minutes.

Leeds entered his studio, the Ghost of Chance at his heels, closing the door behind him. Through the golden gloom of the room his huge picture loomed up, somber in the subdued light; an aromatic odor of wet colors and siccatif hung in the air.

First, he laid aside his overcoat and hat, unhooked from a door peg a short painting blouse and pulled it over his head; then he moved about briskly, opening ventilators to air the place, manipulating the curtains for top and side lights, dragging the carved mahogany model stand into the position marked by the chalk crosses on the polished floor. Presently he touched a spring; the top shade rolled up with a click; a flood of pure north light fell upon the gorgeous colors of the canvas. He began to adjust the delicate machinery of the complex easel, turning a silver screw to regulate the pitch of the heavy canvas, twisting a cogwheel here, a lever there, until he had brought that part of the canvas within reach whereon he expected to work.

He was one of those modest, dissatisfied young men who can never be content with the work done, perfectly aware of possibilities not yet attained, willing to try for them, vaguely confident of attaining them; a young man who would go far—*had* gone far—farther than he realized. Yet, although the critics were joyously bellowing his praises as *the* coming man, his work so far had barely given him a living.

He required great surfaces to cover, and the beauty of the results was apparent in the new marble library, the Hotel Oneida, the Theater Regent, and the new Brooklyn Academy of Music. Superb color, faultless taste, vigor, delicacy—all were his. The technique that sticks out like dry bones, the spineless lack of construction, fads, pitiful eccentricities to cover inability—nothing of these had ever, even in his student days, threatened him with the pitfall of common disaster. Nor was there in his work the faintest hint of physical weakness—nothing unwholesome, smug, suggestive— nothing sugary, nothing insincerely brutal; perhaps because he was a very normal young man, inclined to normal pleasures, and worldly enough to conform to the civilized code outside the barriers of which genius is popularly supposed to pasture.

And still, with all this, he had been paid so little for his work heretofore, and to produce his work had cost him so much in materials and in model and studio hire, that he scarcely knew how to make both ends meet in the most cruelly expensive metropolis of all the world.

For the first time, when approached by Thorne, he had dared name a price for his work which might give him a decent profit when the last brush stroke was laid on; and, while Thorne's big new house slowly rose, stone on stone, overlooking the Park, he had worked on the frieze of life-size figures—two hundred in all—which was to complete the golden ballroom with an exquisite, springlike garland of youth and loveliness.

He had accepted Thorne's cut-throat, cast-iron contract with the deadly time clause; he had used up every second of time, shirking nothing, sparing no expense; making life-size study after study, scintillating with a cleverness that would not only have satisfied but turned the heads of ninety- nine painters in a hundred. But he was the hundredth.

He had given himself just time to complete his work and say: "I can do no better. I have done all that was in me." But, though he had foreseen trouble and delay from models, and the dozens of vexations artists fall heir to, he could not have foreseen that a young girl he never heard of should, at a critical moment, bring out a side of Thorne's character he did not suspect existed in him—the sharp, ugly brutality of wounded arrogance, which vents itself where opportunity offers; the fiercely sullen desire to hurt, to stamp its power upon those who have no defense.

And now, with the entire frieze all but completed, the man had suddenly snarled at him—for no reason on earth save a willingness to crush and dominate. There was not a day of grace named in the contract; there was no grace to be expected from Thorne, who cared no more for the frieze that hid part of his golden-lacquered paneling than for the gilded sconces below. If one or the other did not suit him, he'd tear them out without a word and cover the raw space with ten thousand dollars' worth of hot-house roses for his housewarming. Leeds understood that. He was beginning to appreciate the man. He must try to beat him.

He stood there confronting his defaced picture, examining it as keenly as a physician might inspect an interesting phase of human misfortune, pondering the remedy. And, as he stood, silent, preoccupied, his telephone bell rang, and he stepped to the receiver.

"Hello! Is this the Models' League?"

"Yes, James Leeds. Yes, I wanted a model with red hair, if possible, and good limbs."

"Well, that can't be helped. Send any model as close to Miss Clancey's type as you can. Send her now. She's to take a cab. I'm in a desperate hurry."

"Yes, Miss Clancey is ill. I want a girl of her type, but don't waste time hunting. Send me somebody at once."

"All right.... Good-by!"

He hung up the receiver, walked back to his canvas, and began to set a huge ivory-faced palette table, squeezing out tube after tube of color, rainbow fashion, ending in a curly mass of silver white. Then he uncorked a jar of turpentine, filled a bowl with it, and began searching among twisted tubes and scrapers for an ivory palette knife, whistling thoughtfully the while.

A slight sound behind one of the great screens attracted his attention, and he glanced up. Nothing stirred. He sorted some paint rags, and picked up a bottle of drying medium. As he held it to the light, again a sudden sound came from the screen; he turned squarely, surprised, and the same instant a girl stepped out and raised a pair of very lovely and frightened eyes to his.

"Do you want a model?" she asked sweetly, but unsteadily. "Because, if you do—   "

"Good Heavens!" he said, exasperated. "Have you been behind that screen all this, time while I've been telephoning for a model?"

"Ye-s. I—I came in. I heard you."

"But why didn't you come out? Why on earth—"

"I think I was a trifle frightened."

"Oh! ... I see ... you have never before posed?"

"Never. I—I really have not made up my mind to pose now. I suppose I had better do—do something. I've—the fact is, I've *got* to do something to earn my living."

She was red-haired, white-skinned, blue-eyed, shod and gloved to perfection, and plainly scared. He looked at her from head to foot.

"As a matter of fact," he said, delighted, "you are a sort of God-sent miracle. Whether you mean to pose or not for a living, I want you to pose for me to-day. Don't be frightened; sit down here in this chair. I'm in desperate need of somebody. Won't you help me?"

She looked at him in breathless silence.

"Won't you please sit here—just a moment?" he said.

She bent her head a trifle, and moved forward to the offered chair with a grace that claimed his instant and serious attention. But he had no time to wonder or speculate on the reasons for such a woman with such a presence being in his studio to seek employment; he took a chair opposite, scrutinizing her fresh young beauty with frank approval. Indeed, he heartily approved of everything about her—the masses of red-gold hair, the lovely azure-tinted eyes, the wonderfully paintable white skin.

"Your coloring—your figure—your hands are beautiful," he said slowly. "I can give you all day to-day, and I'll take all the time you can give me to-morrow. You see, that canvas must be finished to-day, be dry by to-morrow, and be delivered Thursday. Tell me, is it only head and shoulders and costume, or will you pose without drapery for—"

A bright flush stained her face. "I—I am not a model!" she stammered.

"Not a model," he repeated blankly. "Oh, no, of course not—I forgot."

"Did you—do I look like—" Words failed her; she glanced appalled at the canvas, then straight at him, self-possessed again, but paler.

"I can't help what you think of me," she said. "I am perfectly aware of my indiscretion—but your door was open and this—this is my hour of need."

"Certainly," he said, soothingly, "I see—"

"No, you don't see! I came in here to—to hide! By and by I shall go out." She sat up very straight. "I am determined," she said, "to remain concealed here until I can leave this building without annoyance. May I?" She ended so sweetly, so piteously, that Leeds caught his breath in astonishment.

"So—may I stay here for a while?"

"Well, there's a model coming to pose for that figure—if you refuse to pose—"

"Which figure?" demanded the girl.

"That one on the left—the one that is scraped down."

"You mean that I couldn't stay here while you painted?"

"I don't believe you would care to. You wouldn't bother me, but I don't think you'd care to."

"Why?" The blue eyes met his so purely, so fearlessly, that he gave her a frank and gentle answer.

"Oh! Then—then hadn't you better dismiss your model for the day?" she said, "because I've got to stay."

"But I can't. The paint on that canvas is exactly in the right condition, neither too wet nor too dry. I've simply got to use a drier, and paint on it now. That picture must be dry to-morrow."

"Must it—truly?"

"It certainly must!"

The girl rose, stood for a moment nervously twisting her veil up over her hat; then: "But I can't go! You don't understand. I've—I've run away!"

"Run away! From whom?"

"Somebody," she said vaguely, looking about the room. Suddenly he remembered the story McManus told. And he spoke of it, watching her curiously.

"Exactly," she said, nodding her pretty head, while the tint of excitement deepened on her cheeks, "I ran away from him! You know who I am, don't you? You know my sister, anyhow."

She hesitated, searching his face; then impulsively: "I usually decide all matters very quickly!" She made an impatient little gesture and seated herself, looking up at him with bright eyes and heightened color: "For three months I've stood it—"

"Stood what?"

"Being engaged. I had not really thought much about it—we're usually indifferent and obedient in my family—and no doubt I'd have gone on and married just as my sisters have—if something had not happened." She dropped her head, looking thoughtfully at the floor. Then: "I simply could not stand him, Mr. Leeds; I woke up this morning, understanding that I couldn't marry him. I was so excited—and dreadfully afraid of telling him—and I was so sorry for my mother, but I couldn't do it; I knew that, and it was time he knew, too.

"So I told my mother, and there was trouble, and I went out and found a cab and drove here as fast as I could, and I said: 'Mr. Thorne, I cannot do it!' You know what I said. That Irishman told you."

Leeds nodded.

"So that's all; I simply ran away from him; and I won't go home and live on my mother, because we are as poor as mice and rabbits, and if I don't marry Mr. Thorne my mother will probably expire of mortification, and if I don't marry *at all* by Monday next, I'll lose what my grandfather left me in a horrid will, which forces me to marry before I'm twenty-one—and *that's* next Monday. All my sisters did it—Mrs. Egerton, and Mrs. Clay-Dwyning, and another you don't know. But I won't, I won't, *I won't!* And my mother will probably starve unless I earn our living, so I'd better begin at once."

"I think you had, too," said Leeds gravely.

"Oh, I thought of that when I was running away from Mr. Thorne; and when he came up in one elevator, I came down; and when he came down I went up, and I turned into the first corridor I saw, and entered somebody's office and shut the door.

"A man came to ask me what I wanted. And I asked him if he required a stenographer, and he said he did—very offensively—so I marched out and walked about the hallways trying to find my way out. Then I heard Mr. Thorne's voice on the stairs, and I opened your door and hid. And before I had courage to leave, you came and talked and talked with that Irishman. And now what am I to do? You know who I am, and you know my sisters—or you did once, before you went abroad to study—for they've told me they knew you at Narragansett when you were a boy of twelve."

"Are *you* their little sister, Naida?" he asked curiously, when she stopped, clean out of breath, flushed and fascinating in her consternation.

"Yes; I'm Naida. Do you really remember me? I wish I could be civil and say the same to you, but I don't, Mr. Leeds, though since everybody says you are a very great artist, I pretend I do know you, and I say: 'Oh, yes, James Leeds; he was such a jolly fellow when he was a boy at Narragansett!'

"But I'm careful not to tell them that I was so little that you never even looked at me, or that I was so young I couldn't remember you. Oh, dear, what frauds we all are! And here I am, compromising myself and not caring, after having driven my mother distracted, jilted my fiancé, and beggared myself. I think I'd better pose for you."

"Will you?"

"Why, coward that I am, I don't want to face the consequences of my own deeds. But I won't go back after smashing the finances so dreadfully."

"Suppose you help me a little, then. And while you're helping me to avert financial ruin we'll talk of your future," he said laughingly.

She looked up quickly. "I heard what you and that Irishman were saying. Are you truly in trouble about your picture?"

"All kinds of trouble," he assented.

"Could I really help you?"

"Indeed you could."

"Of course, I would compromise myself, wouldn't I?" she asked innocently. "I've been doing it all day, haven't I?"

He sat there perplexed, fascinated, watching her in silence.

She shrugged her pretty shoulders. A rather valuable fur stole slipped down to the floor, and he picked it up and sat smoothing it and watching the exquisite color wane and deepen in her cheeks.

The telephone rang. He rose and set the receiver to his ear.

"No, that model won't do. You need not send anybody now; I have exactly the model I require. Good-by."

Turning to her he said: "You heard me say that I needed no model. Will you help me now? This is an hour of direst need with me."

"I—I don't know—"

"Will you? If you will, I will promise to help you—not to become an artist's model; that is silly. But I promise you, on my honor, that you shall have an offer which no woman need refuse; an offer suitable and honorable, where you may enjoy absolute independence and freedom from all annoyance, live your own life freely, without taxing your mother's resources, and without care or dread of importunities from anybody attempting to marry you. Will you?"

"If—if you could do *that* for me I'd be grateful enough to do anything for you," she said slowly.

The Ghost of Chance sat watching them. His job was nearly ended.

A curious exhilaration, a gayety rather foreign to Leeds's nature, took possession of him. He lifted a beautiful garment, all stiff with turquoise and gold, and held it toward her. He laid two jeweled sandals at her feet, pulled a table to the screen, and opened a box full of glittering gilded articles.

There was color enough in her face now, flooding it from brow to throat.

"Won't you help me?" he asked. "It is ruin for me if you don't."

She searched his face. There was nothing in the eyes that a woman might not look upon, might not meet with a smile, might not respond to. She measured him in breathless silence, red lips parted. He was her own kind.

"Will you?"

"Yes."

Then excitement transfigured him. She scarcely knew his face, lighted into quick enthusiasm.

"Never, never, have I had such a model!" he cried, delighted as a boy. "Never have I seen such color, such exquisite loveliness. Good Heavens! A man might really paint with you before him! Don't—don't look at me that way—don't be frightened. I'm simply astonished at my fortune—I don't mean to be rude—you know I don't!"

"Yes, I know it," she said tremulously.

"May I suggest how you should tie the sandals?"

"Am I to—to be barefooted?"

"With sandals, you know, and that gorgeous gold and blue Byzantine robe hung straight from the shoulders! Everything is here. I'll step out and smoke a cigarette. Will you knock when you are ready?"

She nodded, looking down at the crumpled heaps of gold and turquoise stuff.

Enchanted he saw her raise her pretty arms and begin to unpin her hat, with its floating veil. Then he went out.

For half an hour he walked the resounding corridor, smoking madly. Once or twice he doubted her—half convinced that she meant to lock him out—and the idea scared him. But at last a low knocking on the inside of the door summoned him; he entered, blinking in the flood of light after the darkness of the hallway, and the vision was revealed slowly to his dazzled eyes.

White—a trifle too pale; her eyes burned like azure stars under the gold-red glory of her hair, which fell in two loose, heavy braids straight down, framing her body from shoulders to hips. The rounded throat, the white arms glimmering along the seams of the blue and golden robe, the sandals accenting the snowy feet—and in her eyes the straight, fearless gaze of a child—left him mute, stunned, utterly spellbound, overwhelmed by a magic that sometimes wears another name.

She did not need to ask his criticism. The faint rose color came into her face again slowly.

She turned and mounted the model stand without a word, seating herself in the carved marble chair; and, glancing at the painted figure, let her arms fall in harmony with the drawing. Then she placed one little sandal-shod foot upon the silken cushion at her feet. When she looked up, with a pale smile, he had already begun to paint.

His hand, not steady at first—for a new emotion had given him new eyes—became steadier. Magnificent tints and hues grew upon the canvas, stiff gold folds and creases shimmered, framing the snowy contours of perfect arms.

The glory of hair, the wonder of wide azure-tinted eyes, the lips full scarlet, all took color and loveliness as his brushes flew. And into the picture came something else—a joyousness, a tint of youth and freshness, and something subtle, indefinable.

And now he seemed to hold the whole power of the world in his grasp. The color-wet point of every brush hovered, then left its message of beauty on an enchanted canvas. Power was his; he dominated; he could do anything, achieve anything—with her before him. Difficulties? There were none. He had but to wet a brush with purest tints, look her in the eyes, and the thing was wrought.

Twice she rested. He said nothing, nor did she, and, when she was ready, he went on. But already the work was done—finished! He lingered over it, thrilled, touching it here and there fearlessly, with the silent certainty of mastery.

At last he lay back on his chair, and the arm supporting his palette dropped to his side.

"Won't you have mercy?" she asked in a low voice.

"Are you tired? Oh, I am so sorry!" he cried, springing to his feet.

She rose. He held out his hand. She laid hers on his arm and descended.

"You are terribly tired!" he said anxiously, almost tenderly.

"No—but—I am a little—hungry."

He dragged out his watch. "Good Lord! It's four—almost dark!" he cried. "What a—a beast I am! I must be crazy!"

She stood smiling beside him, looking curiously at the picture in the fading light.

"Am I as—as glorious as that!" she said under her breath. It was not a question, besides he scarcely dared answer, for the magic was thick about him.

"Do you know," she said slowly, "there is something in that canvas that I have never before seen?"

"What is it?"

"The—the eyes you have given me—as though I had just opened them on paradise."

"They are like yours."

"But I—I never saw paradise. What a heavenly beauty you have given me. My soul was never as untroubled as is hers—the lovely, snowy, golden saint you have raised up on my shadow. What eyes do you see with to work such miracles?"

"You are the miracle. I never painted like that until you came."

She turned to look at him. And, perhaps, the magic light was strong enough to dazzle her, too, for she thought there was something in his eyes that he had painted into hers upon the canvas.

For a little while they stood silent. Then she raised her head. "And now?" she questioned.

"Now?"

"Yes. What am I to do?"

He gazed at her blankly. "You are not going away?"

"Your picture is finished."

"Yes, but where are you going?"

"Where?" She pressed her white hand over her brow. "I—I don't exactly know. I—I thought you had a plan—"

"As long as you have run away," he began slowly

"Yes? And as long as I have done all the dreadful things I have done. Go on!"

"All those dreadful things—"

"Yes; all those common horrid things. Go on."

"I—I think—"

"Yes—"

"That we—that we might further degrade ourselves by—"

"Yes—go on!"

"By taking tea together."

"Do you think so?"

"I do," he said solemnly.

She reflected for a moment. "But what after that?"

"We must consider the situation at the tea table," he said gravely. "We'll go out as soon as you can change your gown. And—is there any likelihood of our jumping any of your family if we go to Sherry's?"

"I'll risk it," she said slowly.

"Then," and he smiled at her through a rosy light which really didn't exist, "then I'll go out and smoke until you are ready."

And he did, no longer tormented with the fears of being locked out, and presently she opened the door and stood a moment on the threshold, looking at him.

"I wonder," she said, "if ever a girl has done as mad a thing as I have to-day?"

She stepped out and closed the door behind her.

"Listen," she said; "a thousand dreadful questions are on my lips—tortured pride refuses to ask for mercy—but—oh, I *do* care to know what you think of me!"

He told her as much as he dared tell, haltingly, stammering under the enchantment thickening always around them.

"You—you think—that?"

"More. May—shall I say—"

"Not—not now."

Dazed, their young heads turned, they descended the marble steps together.

Elevator boys, hall servants, the gorgeous porter in his green and gilt livery, stared at the runaway. She passed them, head high.

"There is going to be a great deal of trouble about nothing, I fear," she said softly, as they walked out into Fifth Avenue.

"I fear so," he mused.

"You—you will probably be evicted by Mr. Thorne when the porter tells him where I've been."

"Probably," he smiled.

"Where will you go when you are evicted?"

"Where are you going?"

She glanced at him sweetly. "To tea—with you."

"And after that?" he asked unsteadily.

But she pretended not to hear him, repeating, "To tea with the great artist, Mr. Leeds. Oh, you are surprised that I know how great you are? Did you think I didn't know? Dear me, don't my sisters talk of you as though our family discovered you?"

"That settles it then," he said, enchanted.

"What settles what, if you please?"

"My status. I'm one of your family and entitled to advise you."

A moment later two flushed young people entered Sherry's, utterly oblivious of cloak rooms, bellboys, and butlers, and instinctively chose a remote table secluded in a corner, banked high with verdure.

They may have had tea. They were so absorbed in talking to each other that they not only paid no attention to what they ordered, but did not notice whether they had eaten anything or not, when the early winter night found them on Fifth Avenue once more, strolling slowly uptown, absorbed in one another to the exclusion of time and similar unimportant trifles.

She was saying in that full-throated sweet voice, pitched a trifle lower than the roar of traffic, "Yes, I do trust you. I have been horrid and common and silly to go dashing around that trust company, but you are perfectly lovely to understand, and I'll do exactly what you tell me to do—except—"

"What?"

"Oh—you wouldn't ask me that!"

"What?"

"To—to marry *him*—"

"Good God," he breathed.

After a silence he said: "I have promised you an offer. But first you must go back as though nothing had happened."

"Yes, I will. There's no use in my going to a hotel like a silly, romantic creature, and starting out to look for work in the morning. Besides, my mother would be frantic and call up the police. Besides, I haven't enough money to really run away; I have only a dollar and some pennies."

"Home is the place for you," he said, laughing under his breath. "When am I to come to tell you about my plan for you?"

"You'd better hurry," she said sincerely. "I'll probably lose courage and be bullied into something or other if you don't."

"May I come to-morrow?"

"No; there's a luncheon I don't dare cut out, and in the evening there's a dance at the Carringtons'. Do you—do you ever go about? I go to the Lanarks' dance to-night—"

"I was asked to that dance, too—"

"Oh!" she cried enraptured, "*will* you come? Please—please! If you don't, I won't go. Mr. Thorne will be there, and between mamma and him I'll be driven into something before I know it. Will you?"

"Yes, I will. And I'll do more," he added under his breath; "I'll lay that offer before you."

"That will be perfectly delightful! You won't fail, will you? And"—she paused at the door of her own house and gave him a small gloved hand—"and I want to tell you how happy I am to have helped *you*, and how glad I am that you are able to keep to that wicked contract, and that I have had a perfectly lovely time, and I shall never—never forget how nice you have been even if I have behaved like a brainless ninny. And I am so glad you don't think me as horrid as I seemed to be. I was reckless for the first time in my life, and did all those desperate things because I've been—I've been a trifle unhappy."

And so he left her, the door opening to engulf her, she turning her pretty head to nod to him as it closed. And he went away soberly, walking up the dark avenue under the flaring electric lights, absorbed, almost stunned, by what had come so suddenly into a life that, but a few hours since, had seemed to him too full, too complete, to hold anything except the love he bore for his profession.

He dined at the club where he lived, read the evening papers, scarcely conscious of what he was reading, then went upstairs to his room, sat a long while on the bed's edge, staring at vacancy, and finally lay down, closing his eyes. The Ghost of Chance stood by the bed a moment, considering his victim.

Hour after hour he lay there, thinking as clearly as the tumult in his breast permitted. Later he bathed, dressed very carefully, and, descending, climbed into a hansom.

"I've a ghost of a chance," he muttered. "Thorne told me to take it once, and his advice was good. Now, I'll try it again—for I *have* got a ghost of a chance again, and I'll take that chance to-night!"

And so he came to the great house of the Lanarkses, overlooking the wintry park, and he climbed out of his humble hansom amid the clustering clatter of the rich and great and agreeable, and entered the house which he might not have troubled himself to enter, had a young girl with red hair and wonderful blue eyes not asked him.

After drifting about in the scented crush for half an hour, he caught a glimpse of her surrounded by a dozen men, among them a diplomat or two, and several attachés; and now, with the intention of claiming her, he marked her down in the glittering throng as carefully as he might have marked a flushed quail in a thicket of golden willow.

But when, pressing his way through barriers of black coats and threading half an acre of rustling silk and lace, he found the spot where he had expected to find her, she was no longer there; only the red fez of the Turkish Ambassador, nodding affably above the press, indicated that he had reached the spot upon the floor that he had aimed at.

Glancing up at the gilded musicians' gallery to verify his bearings, he struck a circle, as he would have done in the woods, and presently came across young Terriss, who was also in love with her—but Leeds did not know that.

"Thorne took her off," said Terriss sullenly. "They're in the conservatory. By the way, I didn't know you knew her."

"I do," growled Leeds.

"That pasty-white Russian prince, the fellow with a fat face and a thin nose splitting a brace of eyes too close together"—Terriss shrugged his shoulders—"he's hanging about, looking for her, too. Her mother steered him off. I suppose it will be announced to-night."

Leeds saw her mother and recalled himself to her memory, and her mother's cordiality surprised and flattered him until he found he could not get past her to the conservatory.

Meanwhile the musicians were playing away madly. He attempted to dodge her, affably explaining that it was his dance with her daughter.

"But Naida is not in here," said her mother, carefully riding him off.

"Terriss said—"

"Doubtless," continued her mother cheerfully, "Naida is waiting for you with Constance. Do you remember my daughter Constance? If you take me across, Mr. Leeds, we can find Naida."

Steered off, vaguely aware of too much sweetness in the matron's guileless smile, he looked back and beheld the girl he was seeking emerging from the thicket of palms with Thorne, followed by a heavy and very white young man, with rings on his fingers and under his eyes.

The girl looked at Leeds as though she had never before seen him. For a moment, as he instinctively stepped forward, they faced one another in silence. Then a faint recognition animated her eyes. She looked at Thorne, at the Russian, at her mother, then, as Leeds said a conventional but decisive word or two, she smiled, laid one hand on his shoulder as he encircled her waist with his right arm, nodded at her mother, and glided off into the glitter with a man who danced well enough to leave her indifferent and occupied with her own reflections.

How long she had been dancing with him she did not know, nor care, when his voice roused her from a meditation that had left her red mouth sullen and her eyebrows bent.

"What did you say?" she asked. "I beg your pardon—"

"Nothing. I wondered whether you were bored? I dance pretty well, you know."

"You dance very well. Do I look bored?"

"You certainly do."

"I am."

They swung out through the center of the perfumed crush a little recklessly, but with sufficient skill.

"I wish you would look at me—once," he said. "What has happened since we parted?"

She raised her eyes, amused. "The inevitable. I couldn't escape."

"I can't give you up yet to your own reflections," he said. "You dance too perfectly. What do you mean by the 'inevitable'?"

"Oh, it is not you or the dancing that I meant! You must not mind me; I am likely to say anything to-night."

"Anything?"

"Absolutely anything to anybody." She raised her eyes again to his face. It was a cleanly modeled countenance, rather lean—not at all like Thorne's or Prince Minksky's.

A vague feeling of being at home again after a foreign tour came over her, a comfortable sensation, lasting for a second—time enough to contrast his amiable features with the features of the man she had been with in the conservatory.

Constantly passing dancers nodded to them, exchanged a word or two or a brief smile—Terriss with a pretty girl who called her Naida, the British third secretary, very gay in his greeting, dozens and dozens, all whirling by; and through the brilliant glare, the scented breezy wavering scene, Leeds guided the girl with the ruddy gold hair and the sulky mouth—sulky, for she was preoccupied again, oblivious of all in her perfect grace and poise, swinging where he led, as easily, as unconsciously as a wind-blown bird floating half asleep in the flow of the upper air.

"If you are really too much bored," he breathed

She looked up disturbed. "I told you it was not you. You don't bore me. You don't know me well enough."

"Is there no chance that I might know you better?"

"No, no chance."

"May I try it?"

Her beautiful brows unbent. "Why, yes, try it; but I am not worth the effort."

"Very well. For this evening you and I will speak the absolute and unvarnished truth; shall we? You may ask me whatever you care to; I will ask you. Dare you?"

She had shaken her head first, but at the word "dare" her indifference changed to a slight amusement.

"Oh, I dare anything to-night," she said. "What question am I to answer?"

"Is it a bargain that we tell the truth?" he persisted.

"Certainly, if it amuses you. It won't amuse me."

"And I may venture to be cheerfully impertinent?"

She nodded, smiling.

"Then tell me why you asked me to come to this dance?"

She hesitated. A little more color crept into her face.

"Am I to answer truthfully?"

"You promised."

Then her entire personality changed with an impulse as illogical, as sudden as any caprice that ever swept over a heart too young to bear bitterness.

"I asked you," she said, "to come because—because I was happy with you to-day. But now—now it is too late. I am for sale once more.... Will you buy me?"

"Willingly," he returned, amazed but smiling.

"Too late," she said, looking up; "I have sold myself."

They were on the outer edge of the whirl now. Her hand slid from his shoulder, and she stepped back, flushed, brilliant-eyed, perfectly self-possessed.

"Thank you for offering to purchase," she laughed, looking him straight in the face. "Shall we finish the dance? I am ready."

"Let me see your card," he said coolly. She held out the cluster of ivory and gold filigree for his inspection.

"I thought you had undertaken to amuse me," she observed. "I didn't bargain to amuse you." Her blue eyes were too brilliant, her color almost feverish now.

"I am going to," he said. "But I warn you, you may not like it."

"Try. Perhaps I may."

"I'm going to rub out these names," he said, watching her.

"That will be deliciously rude and impertinent. Do it. Can you think of anything else?"

"Oh, yes!" he said, filling in the card with his own name.

"Let me see," she breathed, looking over his shoulder. "Delightful! Why, what you have done is exquisitely indecent, and will certainly involve us both in everything unpleasant. Now, what else are you going to do?"

"That sale," he reflected—"you remember?"

"Oh, yes!"

"It's canceled."

"No, it isn't," she said with a laugh ending in a little check. "But you may compromise me if you—if you can manage it. I'll flirt with you if you can keep the others off."

"I'll do my best," he said, looking at her, scarcely knowing what he was saying. "You danced too well for me to let you go when I bored you; now that I don't, do you think I shall let you go?"

She was on the verge of something—laughter or tears. He felt it, yet knew that she would not pass the verge.

"Now I have amused you a little," he said, "will you sit out the rest of this dance with me?"

"How can I help it? Your name has replaced the others."

He erased his name, and, from memory, filled in the other names in sequence. Then pocketing the tablets, he said airily: "Technically, I recover my self-respect—but, there's a second conservatory beyond this one where I may lose yours."

"I hope it is dark," she said calmly.

"It is. We'll go to the farthest corner."

Passing through palms and tree ferns, they heard the music behind them cease; and they moved a trifle more quickly.

"It's locked," he said.

"I don't care. Unlock it."

He turned the key. They entered. A few electric bulbs glimmered here and there, gilding thickets of blossoms. There were no chairs to be found, and he had started to return for them, when she called his attention to a green bench under a mass of flowering vines, and, seating herself, looked up at him expectantly.

"Now," he said, as he took his place beside her, "you may tell me anything or nothing, as you please. You are terribly excited—I'm rather excited, too. Every normal man is always reckless; every normal woman is, once in a lifetime. It's a crisis; you've reached it. I'm a decent sort of fellow—safer than the next man, maybe. And now I'm keyed up, ready to listen, ready to talk, seriously or frivolously—ready to make love—either way."

"Make love to me, *seriously?*" she said gayly. "Ah, but you are safe to say so—knowing that I am sold!" After a moment she looked up: "Why don't you ask me who bought me?"

"Oh, I know," he nodded.

"How do you know?"

"I saw your face—after the bargain."

The smile on her mouth remained, but he looked away, unable to meet her haunted eyes.

"Rub out these names," she said suddenly, offering to take the card again. And, as he made no movement, she suddenly tore it to pieces in her gloved hands and held the fragments toward him with a miserable little laugh. He took them, retaining her hand in his.

"You are the prettiest girl in the world," he said lightly. "Shall I tell you more?"

"Do you know that I am engaged to Mr. Thorne again?"

"But I am going to make love to you."

"But—I am really going to marry him—on Monday."

He laughed, looking her in the eyes.

"Do you not believe me?" she asked.

"No," he said, laughing.

"But it is true. I have put it off—I have waited until the last moment— you know what I said to-day—"

Incredulous, smiling, he recovered the hand she had withdrawn. She suffered it to lie in his, looking at him almost frightened.

"It is stupid not to believe me," she said. "Can't a man tell when a girl is speaking the truth? I tell you I must marry him on Monday, if I'm to get anything from my grandfather—"

His hand, holding hers, relaxed; he looked at her uneasily.

"All my sisters did the same thing," she went on—"all hung back until the last moment. Then, like me, deadly tired of the pressure, they gave in in a hurry. I'm the youngest and last—thank Heaven!"

"What is all this?" he demanded.

"Nothing—indolence—an idea that I might fall in love, perhaps—kept me from marrying."

Her voice trailed, vaguely reminiscent; she gazed at him with dimmed, speculative eyes, resting her chin on one curved wrist, elbow denting her silken knee.

"If a girl has a fool for a grandfather, what can she do? And I'm tired of the home pressure."

She bent her head, idly lifting finger after finger of the white gloved hand that lay passively in his palm.

"So there you are," she added; and, as he said nothing, she went on:

"Tuesday, I'm twenty-one. Isn't it absurd and dreadful? But there you are; I put it off and put it off, vowing and declaring I wouldn't marry just to inherit my part. Mother has wept most of this year; but I said 'No! no! no!' and I refused to be the victim of any grandfather, and I declined to consider his wishes, or Mr. Thorne's."

She shrugged her shoulders: "But—you see? Cupidity at the last moment!"

"Whose cupidity?" he asked coolly.

"Mine," she said, but he knew she was not truthful.

"That's all right," he observed cheerfully—"as long as it was not your family's." And, still smiling, he thought of her mother adroitly blocking his way until the daughter and the merchant had concluded the bargain and patched up a broken truce.

"It will be one of those 'married-while-you-wait' affairs," she said, watching him; "traveling clothes and a few of the family. Don't you want to come? You must come!" she added; "will you?"

"I have an idea," he said, with a curious stare, "that I may be present at your wedding."

"Good! Come with Jack Terriss and Prince Minsksky."

"Oh, do you already number me with the Jack Terrisses?" he drawled.

"Certainly. Am I not pretty? Wouldn't you kiss me if you—could? He always wants to; others have wanted to. Then I number you with the others; they were no more serious than you are."

"Is it they or you who are not serious?" he asked. "I think if you gave any of them the chance you have given Thorne—"

"Yes, but I don't love any of them. And Mr. Thorne is inevitable."

"I see," said Leeds carelessly. "So I am to say to-night: 'Much happiness!' and other stupidities. Am I not to say all these things?"

"Yes, if you like."

"But I won't."

"That would be rude, wouldn't it?" She looked up at him smiling, yet with something of concern, for he had both her hands now.

"Do you know what I am going to do?" he asked.

"No."

"I am going to make love to you at once."

"You may; I'm engaged."

He listened a moment; the music rang distantly; somebody was missing a dance with the woman whose gloved hands lay in his.

"If you are going to marry for pure cupidity, why not take me?" he asked. "Any man would do for your amiable grandfather—and it seems to be all the same to you."

"I did not know you well enough to ask you," she said audaciously.

"Would I have done as well as anybody?" he demanded.

"Yes, as well—for me. Mother prefers the inevitable one."

"Would I have done better than anybody—for *you?*" he persisted.

"Must I answer?"

"Yes; you have only fibbed once to-night."

"Then—I'd rather—not answer. Don't—don't pretend to be serious. Be as frivolous as you will; make love to me if you wish—only don't pretend."

"No, I won't pretend," he said. She looked at him; his face caught fire though he strove to speak gayly: "I never believed I should fall in love—like this—not even when I first met you. You are faultlessly beautiful, with your thick, ruddy-gold hair—the hair I painted into my picture—and I painted your splendid, innocent eyes, and that scarlet, sulky mouth—not sullen then, Naida. Had I known such things were bought and sold I should have bid—"

"Stop," she breathed.

"But all I should have offered was an ordinary heart—and you say that counts nothing against—other considerations."

"Nothing," she said, setting her lips.

"It counts nothing," he repeated, watching her.

"Nothing—absolutely nothing. Is this how you amuse me? Is this what you call making love?"

"Partly this," he said, "partly"—and he deliberately and unskillfully kissed her—"partly this."

She rose, blushing scarlet, whisking her hands from his. He stood up to confront her, rather white.

"You are too—" she began unsteadily.

"What?"

"Brutal. I have been kissed before—but not stupidly—as you did. It was almost an affront—if such a woman as I can be affronted." Cheeks and eyes were ablaze.

"I told you," he said between lips almost colorless, "that I should speak the truth. I do; I love you. Can you give me a ghost of a chance?"

"You are clumsy and silly," she said. "I—I was ready for almost any-thing—supposing you were clever enough to carry it all off lightly—"

"I can; I've kissed plenty of girls, but only one I've cared for—that's why I was so awkward; I was scared to death. Why on earth did I awake at the eleventh hour to find that I loved you!"

"You are imposing on us both," she said calmly. "Besides, I don't believe you've kissed very many girls. Jack Terriss says you have no use for them except as models."

"Jack's crazy. Girls? Why, the girls I've kissed," he explained blandly, "would fill that ballroom —"

"And overflow into this conservatory," she added, quietly curious, yet perfectly convinced now that his experience had been as limited as her own. For she had never before been kissed.

"If you'll let me show you—" he suggested.

"Show me what?"

"That I do know how to kiss a girl—"

She looked at him, then sat up straight, stripping off her gloves. Her face was hot; she used her fan.

He picked up one of her hands and she demurred, but he held to it with a fascinated determination that made a struggle unreasonable.

"What is the use," she said, "of kissing a girl who is engaged? No, I will *not!* I forbid you! I—*please* don't do—"

"Do what?" he asked.

"That! You have done it twice—when I asked you not to."

"Was I clumsy this time?"

"Yes!"

"Then—"

"No—no—no!" Hands locked, she bent backward, evading him breathlessly, yet looking into his eyes with a curiosity, a fear, and something else that no man had ever seen in her gaze—something that he saw, and which the scarlet mouth, no longer sulky, tremblingly confirmed.

"There is a chance—a ghost of a chance!" he said, steadying his voice.

"No—no! There is no chance—even if you did— "

"What?"

"Love me! No chance, no ghost of a chance. Release me—please—I beg you. Oh, won't you listen? You—you must not put your arm around me—"

The struggle was brief; she strained away from him desperately; and when he had her closer, she avoided his lips, hiding her face—and, as the hiding place happened to be, by some dreadful mistake, his shoulder, he drew her face upward and kissed her mouth again and again, until her head lay there quietly, eyes closed, wet lashes on her burning cheeks.

Then he used what voice he could command in a very manly and earnest fashion; and whether she heeded or whether even she heard was uncertain, for the tears kept her lashes wet, and her hands covered her face.

This was all very well, particularly when he drew one hand away, and her slim fingers closed convulsively over his. Between them they wrecked her delicate ivory fan, but neither seemed conscious of any loss.

"Now will you give me a ghost of a chance?" he whispered.

"I—I can't—"

"Look at me, Naida—"

"No."

"You must. I love you."

"How can you—a girl bought—sold—"

"I bid higher, dear."

"I know—my—my first kiss. You will not believe it—of a girl you kissed so easily. But it is—I have never before been kissed. But I can't take the price; I'm sold —You had better kiss me for all the years to come."

He bent his head; her eyes unclosed, and, looking up at him, she put both arms around his neck.

"You do love me," he breathed.

She only looked at him.

"You must!"

"I might—if there was time. How can I have time to love you?"

"Marry me; and you shall have years of time."

"But suppose I found I did not love you, silly?"

"You would be no worse off than if you married the inevitable."

Her head lay on his shoulder; she looked at him reflectively. "Suppose," she said, "suppose I marry neither of you—for a while—and let that wretched inheritance go!"

"For God's sake, let it go!" he said fiercely.

"Give me a ghost of a chance; that is all I ask—more than I dare hope."

"And—if I loved you—in the remote future, would you marry a penniless girl?"

"Will that penniless girl promise me?" he asked under his breath.

"No!" said her mother from the glass doorway. And they both stood up.

"The dishonorable part you have played," continued the quivering matron, "matches your lack of the elemental decencies, and your ignorance of the ordinary observances of conventional—" Fury choked her.

"I only desire to marry your daughter, madam."

"Naida!"

"Yes, mamma."

She hesitated, turned to the man beside her, and looked up at him.

"Good-by," she said; "don't forget."

Forget what, silly child? A flirt whom he had so easily kissed in a conservatory? Why, men find them everywhere—and not too difficult. Her first? Why, some man must be a coquette's first—and in her case it happened to be Leeds.

So she walked slowly to the door, and her mother took her arm, and she looked back at the man standing there, his hands fumbling the shreds of her broken fan.

"Good night!" she said; and to her mother: "You hurt my arm, dear."

"Are you mad?" hissed that horrified matron.

"Quite. I told him I was likely to do anything to-night."

"You have done it!"

"I hope so, mother."

"Hope what?"

"That I've made him love me."

"Merciful Heaven! What has—" She halted, turning her tall daughter to face her. "Is it champagne?" she demanded.

"No; do I look dreadfully mussed? Oh, well—it was my first kiss, you know. One doesn't understand how to take it coolly; I was very awkward—and fool enough to cry. My head aches. I fancy I look perfectly disreputable. Mother, will you—there he is now!—will you please keep off your Thornes and your Russians until I can escape? I will be in the dressing room—quite ready to go, mother dear."

"Naida," she said, her voice trembling, "I tell you now that if you are actually in love—"

"Yes, dear?"

"If you *are*, don't consider my—my wishes—"

"About Mr. Thorne?"

"About anybody—even a man disreputable enough to kiss you—"

"Any man—to save my inheritance, mother?"

"Any *eligible* man, we decided."

"Then it's got to be *somebody?*"

"It has, little daughter—unless we're a pair of fools!"

"Well, then—if it's to be a *man*, I think—I think—" She turned and looked back into the long conservatories. But what she thought she did not utter, for at that moment the Russian spied her and came up palled and speechlessly fierce. And she took his arm very sweetly.

"Now we'll dance until daylight if you desire," she said, heading him off in the midst of an astonished inquiry concerning her disappearance. "I think we had better have the jolliest time we can—while it lasts. Because," she added pensively, "I may run away from everybody some day. I'm quite likely to do anything, you know; am I not, mother?"

His alarm was so genuine that she threw back her head and laughed the most delicious and carefree laugh he had ever heard from her.

"Ah! It iss a pleasantry!" he said, inexpressibly relieved.

"Of course," she said gayly. "I shall keep my legacy and marry somebody—you or Thorne or somebody. Therefore, monsieur, I require sleep; therefore"—she dropped his arm and a courtesy at the same time—"adieu, monsieur."

"So soon, mademoiselle!"

"None too soon, monsieur. Mother! If you are ready? The prince is waiting to make his adieus."

An hour later her mother kissed her good night with the humble and modest conviction that she had done well by every daughter, and had garnered every penny with which that miserable will had tantalized her so long.

"Good night, Naida," she said affectionately. "De Peyster is a lovable fellow. If you can't love him you can't love anybody."

"I don't know; I'll see how I sleep, mother."

"What do you mean, Naida?" she asked anxiously.

"That's just it—I don't know exactly what I do mean. But I'll know if I don't sleep. Good night, mother. If I am not in my room in the morning you will know I have married—somebody."

"You—you wouldn't do—"

"Oh, you know I am likely to do anything! I wish I could guess what it is to be—the next thing I am destined to do."

She turned over in her great white bed, burying her hot cheeks in the pillow. She heard her mother leave the room; then her maid tiptoeing about, and presently the click of the electric button. She opened her eyes in darkness, and lying there fell a-thinking of the ghost of a chance a man had lost forever—or was it the man who had lost it? Was it not the maid after all?

"Men kiss pretty women when they can," she reasoned, raising her hands to her heated cheeks. "He meant nothing that he will not forget this time next month.... So *that* is how it feels to be kissed! And I sniveled.... dear me!

"Still—if I had only had time—I could have made him love me—I think.... But artists are notoriously inconstant.... and usually very poor. If I—I could have married him, I should have felt morally obliged to bring him something. So there you are; I didn't know he was like that or I might have hunted him up and given him a chance a year ago.... Why didn't he take it? He—it is impossible he could suddenly love me—now—at the last moment, when it's too late.... And I suppose it was abominable of him to have kissed me.... And he did it so frequently.... As a matter of fact, I, lying here, am a thoroughly kissed girl.... And I'm shamelessly indifferent to his guilt and mine. So—I think I'll sleep a little...."

But she couldn't.

"If I really find that I can't sleep," she said softly to herself, "I'm likely to do almost anything. I wonder whether *he* is asleep."

He was not; he was seated in a rather small, dark, and chilly room not half a mile uptown. Jaws set, chin on his clenched fist, looking into the hollow eyes of a ghost—the Ghost of Chance. But the ghost as yet had made no sign.

For a while she lay there, wide-eyed, restless, face and arms flushed, her heart quickening to the rapid rush of disordered thought hurrying her onward—whither, she scarcely knew, until she found herself standing before her mirror, the electric light flooding the room once more.

"I can't lie there," she said to herself; "I can't sleep; it seems to me as if I could never sleep again."

The small gilt clock struck the hour—five! She considered it, turned and went to the window, and, raising the shade, looked out. The shadows of the electric lamps played quivering over the snow; nothing else stirred. She crossed the room and opened her door, listening there in the darkness. Then, treading softly, the tips of her fingers on the mahogany rail to guide her, she felt her way down the stairs, her small bare feet brushing the velvet carpet.

There was an electric jet in the lower hall; she turned it on, groped about on the telephone shelf for the directory, and turned the leaves noiselessly until she came to the letter, L. Very carefully she traced the column of names, eyes following her moving finger, until she found what she wanted. Then she turned, unhooked the receiver, and pressed it to her ear:

"Hello!" she almost whispered. "Please give me nine—O—three—Lenox Hill."

And after a throbbing wait:

"Is this the Lenox Club?"

"Has Mr. Leeds come in yet?"

"Perhaps he isn't asleep. Please find out.... No, I can't give my name."

"Yes; it is of great importance. If he is asleep, please wake him."

"Yes, I'll hold the wire."

The receiver against her ear was trembling, but she could not control her hand.

"Yes! ... Is that you, Mr. Leeds?"

"Can't you guess who it is?"

"You *can't!* Do you mean to intimate that other gir—other people call you up at five o'clock in the morning!"

"Of *course* it is I!"

"Yes, Naida."

"I am at home. I could not sleep, so I thought I would find out whether you could. Besides, I wanted to know whether you stayed for the cotillon."

"But *why* didn't you?"

"Oh! that is very nice of you—to say that I—And haven't you really been asleep?"

"Doing what?"

"Thinking of *me!*"

"All alone in your room at this ghastly hour of the morning, thinking about *me?* Do you expect me to believe—"

"I won't tell you—now."

"Haven't I enough to keep me awake thinking?"

"No, I *don't* mean that. You know perfectly well that *you* gave me sufficient to think about—for the rest of my days."

"Don't say that over the 'phone! Yes, it was the first—the very first time it had ever been—been done to me."

"No, I don't forget *anything*; I never shall. What do you mean by a ghost of a chance?"

"Oh! Do you truly mean that? I am so—so dreadfully happy to hear you say that—"

"Yes."

"Yes."

"Yes."

"Yes-s—"

"Oh-h!"

"What! *Now!!*"

"Do you mean now?—at five o'clock in the—"

"I *do!* I *am* in love with you! But I'm not insane—"

"Oh, this is dreadful!—Yes, I'll hold the wire. Yes, the other name for it is the Church of the Transfiguration, but—"

"*Nobody* will do it for us at *this* hour!"

"Well, I'll wait—"
She leaned against the telephone shelf, the receiver pressed convulsively to her ear, blue eyes closed. Years seemed to drag Time in endless chains across her vision; her knees fell trembling; thought, run riot, raced through her brain, and every little pulse clamored to the heart's hard beating.
"Yes!" she gasped with a start; "I'm still here."

"No, I am not dressed for—for the street—"

"Yes—if you wish it.... It will take only a few minutes. But, oh—do you think—?"

"Truly I will; I *do* love you."

"Yes, I will hurry. Good by—"

"I do! I do! You will see!"
Up the dark stairway once more in velvet-footed haste, giving herself no moment for considering what she was about to do; masses of heavy, glowing hair in a tangle, with comb and brush flying; the soft, intimate perfume of lace and delicate linen, silk, and the flutter of ribbon; then gown and hat and furs—a stare at the unknown face in the mirror—her last adieu to the girl she had known so long. But, in the dark outside her door, she heard the summons—the voiceless call of the Ghost of Chance, waiting attendance; and her heart responded passionately. Down through the darkness again—fumbling at chain and bolt—the keen night air in her throat; and,

through the wintry silence veiled in darkness, the yellow lamps of a brougham gilding her face, dazzling her as she laid her groping hand on the arm of the man who sprang forward to guide her.

"You mustn't shiver so—you must not tremble that way," he whispered. "It is all right, dear; I've got McManus and Kenna for witnesses; they're at the church; I've made arrangements. Naida! Naida! The inevitable was never inevitable while there was the ghost of a chance that you loved me."

She caught his hands in hers, staring into his face, which was as white as her own. "Oh!" she breathed. "I love you so. As maid—as wife, you have taken all there is to me—all of good, of evil—with my first kiss! I am yours—no matter what an outward fate might hold for me.... Listen; look at me! Am I to go with you? Shall you repent it? Wait—hush, dear; it is not too late yet. I am not thinking of myself—for the first time in my life I am not thinking of self; nor of my mother; she is easily reconciled. I am thinking of you—of you and all that splendor your spirit lives in—all the heavenly world into which you set me—into which you painted me, transfigured, with eyes that seemed just opening in paradise!

"Tell me, dear; your life is important; it is really not your own to throw away. Shall I go with you? Shall I stay here, quiet with your memory—my life already fulfilled?"

His answer was so low that she bent her head close to his to listen. And, after a long while, unclosing her eyes, she saw through the carriage window the dim gas lamps shining and the stained light of a church window tracing across the snow a celestial pathway tinted with crimson, azure, and gold. The horses halted with a snowy thud of dancing hoofs; the wintry air rushed into her face as the carriage door was opened by two tall Irishmen wearing very shiny silk hats.

"Naida, Mr. McManus—Mr. Kenna—"

The tall hats of the tall Irishmen swept the snow; to each in turn she offered an unsteady little hand; then leaning on Leeds's arm she entered the iron gateway, the two contractors following.

"The purty lady," purred Kenna; "d'ye mind the little hand of her, McManus?"

"I did so; an' I seen the mitten to fit it. Shquare yer chist, man; we're walkin' on shtocks and bonds; we're walkin' on the red neck o' pride and power, Kenna. Whisht; cock yer hat, an' thread majestic!"

And so through the snowy darkness of dawn they passed across the frozen gardens to that little church around the corner where no sweeter bride shall ever kneel than knelt there then at prayer among the tinted shadows. And behind them knelt the Ghost of Chance.

The sun rose at seven; and a little later the bride left the church, her pale, enraptured face uplifted to the rosy zenith. She returned to earth presently: "Jim, shall we stop and breakfast with—our mother?"

He pressed her hand in agonized acquiescence; he was too scared to speak. At the same time he seemed to be conscious of something at his elbow, laughing in silence. It was the Ghost of Chance bidding them *au revoir*. Then the brougham drove up at a signal from Kenna; the bride entered, and Leeds turned to McManus: "At five o'clock this morning I wired Thorne that the key panel was finished and ready to deliver. We leave for Florida this afternoon. Will you see that the contract is carried out?"

"Arrah, leave it to Kenna, Misther Leeds. Is that all, sorr?"

"All—I think—"

"There is wan little item I'm thinkin' yer sweet lady has forgotten—but mayhap she has no need av it—now—"

"What's that, McManus?"

"The other mitten, sorr," giggled McManus. Leeds looked at him for a full second; they shook hands very seriously.

Then, as the carriage wheeled and drove west, the bride, leaning on her husband's shoulder to look back, caught a last glimpse of a snowy little church, an ice-festooned fountain behind the shrubbery, and, moving majestically in the middle distance, shoulder to shoulder, arm under arm, two dignified Irishmen, their tall hats burnished into splendor by the rising sun.

THE END

ROBERT W. CHAMBERS BIBLIOGRAPHY

In the Quarter (1894)
The King in Yellow (1895; stories)
The Red Republic (1895)
With the Band (1896; poetry)
A King and a Few Dukes (1896)
The Maker of Moons (1896; stories)
The Mystery of Choice (1897; stories)
The Haunts of Men (1898; war stories)
Ashes of Empire (1898)
Lorraine (1898)
Outsiders (1899)
Cambric Mask (1899)
The Conspirators (1900)
Cardigan (1901)
The Maid-at-Arms (1902)
The Maids of Paradise (1903)
In Search of the Unknown (1904)
A Young Man in a Hurry and Other Short Stories (1904)
The Reckoning (1905)
Iole (1905)
The Tracer of Lost Persons (1906)
The Fighting Chance (1906)
The Tree of Heaven (1907; stories)
The Younger Set (1907)
The Firing Line (1908)
Some Ladies in Haste (1908)
Special Messenger (1909)
The Danger Mark (1909)
Ailsa Paige (1910)
The Green Mouse (1910)
Adventures of a Modest Man (1911)
The Common Law (1911)
The Streets of Ascalon (1912)
Japonette (1912)
The Gay Rebellion (1913)
The Business of Life (1913)
Blue-Bird Weather (1913)
Quick Action (1914; stories)
The Hidden Children (1914)
Anne's Bridge (1914)
Between Friends (1914; stories)
Who Goes There! (1915)
Athalie (1915)
Police!!! (1915; stories)
The Better Man (1916; stories)
The Girl Philippa (1916)
Barbarians (1917; interconnected war stories)
The Dark Star (1917)
The Restless Sex (1918)
The Laughing Girl (1918)
In Secret (1919)
The Moonlight Way (1919)
The Crimson Tide (1919)
The Slayer of Souls (1920)
A Story of Primitive Love (1920; story)
The Little Red Foot (1921)
Eris (1922)
The Flaming Jewel (1922)
The Talkers (1923)
The Hi-Jackers (1923)
America, or the Sacrifice (1924)
Marie Halkett (UK: 1925; US: 1937)
The Girl in Golden Rags (UK: 1925; US: 1936)
The Mystery Lady (1925)
The Man They Hanged (1926)
The Way of Dionysia (1926; *Red Book Magazine* serial)
The Drums of Aulone (1927)
The Gold Chase (1927)
The Rogue's Moon (1928)

The Sun Hawk (1928)
The Happy Parrot (1929)
Painted Minx (1930)
The Rake and the Hussy (1930)
Beating Wings (UK: 1930; US: 1936)
War Paint and Rouge (1931)
Gitana (1931)
Silver Knees (1931; *Liberty* magazine serial)
The Whistling Cat (1932)
Whatever Love Is (1933)
The Young Man's Girl (1934)
Secret Service Operator 13 (1934; stories)
Love and the Lieutenant (1935)
The Fifth Horseman (1937)
Smoke of Battle (1938; completed by Rupert Hughes)

PLAYS/MUSICALS

The Witch of Ellangowan (1897; aka Meg Merrilies)
Iole (1913; musical comedy based on the novel)
Sintram and His Companions (opera libretto)

CHILDREN'S BOOKS

Outdoorland (1903)
Orchard-Land (1903)
River-Land (1904)
Forest-Land (1905)
Mountain-Land (1906)
Garden-Land (1907)

ART

Washington: or The Revolution (1895) [text by Ethan Allen]
Halifax in Wartime (1943) [text by Frank W. Doyle]

* 9 7 8 1 9 4 4 5 2 0 3 9 7 *